Praise for The Book of Drachma Series

I0549000

"A novel that is rich and elaborately woven like the most exquisite mantel lambrequin you can set your eyes upon, albeit the story flows so naturally like the river into the sea of fantasy and reality. Each character brought into life by the author, carefully and intricately. It is not an ordinary read; it is extraordinary. My own experience in reading this masterpiece is like staring intently into Van Gogh's *Starry Night*. The whirlpool of colours, the words of the book, and its characters bring me into a dimension of time and place I have not seen but I feel I know well. You find something about yourself in every character. You move from the past to the here and now just as much as each character is faced with the same challenges. The city shapes of Van Gogh below the night stars are like the books' chronicles when it jumps to certainties of the present times.

"The narrative put together as a whole picture melds fantasy into substance so perfectly and snugly. The fact that it is set in a medical frame of reference is so unique and gives this novel its distinctive edge. I did not foresee how this could be done but this book has done the mix of fiction and the medical sciences superbly.

"If you are looking for a novel that will allow you to experience the wonders of times past and largely how characters from the 'then and now' can hold much similarities despite the difference of periods in the millennia, then let this meticulously written novel take you to a journey of friendships, men and women of passion, loyalty, ethics, the medical practice and profession, its dignity, career dedication, human relationships, love, life, and death."

—Petite Paradero
Psychologist
The Philippines

"The Book of Drachma will keep you glued to the pages as you follow the gripping tale of a modern day cardiologist, along with the shattering revelations of a fifteenth-century healer, and behind both lies the hand of the mysterious Drachma.

"Written with an easy flow, this novel will stir your emotions as well as capture your imagination and keep you treading a thin line between reality and fantasy till the line itself is blurred. Intensely potent and written with a combination of wit, humour, and with a philosophic touch, *The Book of Drachma* is immensely enjoyable and a compelling must-read."

—Subha Majumder
IT Recruiter
Mumbai, India

TURBULENCE
AND
RESTORATION

The Book of Drachma

TURBULENCE AND RESTORATION

Second Edition

Timothy H. Cook

Published by Drachma Publishing

Published in the United States of America

ISBN: 978-0-9991403-4-5
1. Fiction / Action & Adventure
2. Fiction / Alternative History
15.07.07

The Book of Drachma

Part Three

Turbulence and Restoration

Dedication

This book is dedicated to Dr. Solomon Stough,
my great great grandfather.

Acknowledgments

First and foremost, I would like to thank my wife, Sara Cook, for her unwavering support. I do know that during the writing of this book, in particular, I was not the easiest person to abide.

And I wish to express again my thanks to a number of persons, who may or may not have known how much they had to do with this book's outcome. These include Michael Thayer, Diego Green and Michelle Ogle.

And to you, my faithful blog readers, it is to you that I wish to express my sincere thanks for being there and inspiring my imagination, and include Angie, Tawna, Alex, Psycho, Just Me 99, Cayman, Legacy, Volataire, and Diane.

Chapter One

Apart from it being the middle of January and cold, even for the month, one would have thought the sight of Craycroft, Melchior, Rust, and Bob walking down the sheltered walkway toward Barncuddy's was just another group of workers getting off at nine bells, heading on down to their favorite watering hole to raise a frothy glass with the common folk. Adding to the jovial atmosphere was the presence of Aaron and Hermes, who skipped along in front of the quartet.

Craycroft's thoughts were on his newly developed plans for the island, and the people that would be helping him. He had thought for some time about just how to assign the tasks of his new government, and to whom they should report. What he wanted was governance by the people of the island, not imposed from outside, or even by those who sought rule as a means of increasing their own wealth and power. But while these thoughts were mulling around in his head, he chatted amiably with Rust and Melchior.

Melchior, who was thrilled that his mentor was back and safe, was too excited over his new responsibilities to think any deep thoughts, so the chatter was just right for him.

Rust, who had been struggling with the council over matters seemingly trivial, was just fine with the nonsensical banter back and forth, and he was eyeing the warmth of the inn.

Bob, though, could not get his mind off Judy. He viscerally remembered how, in that gorgeous wine-colored satin gown, she had hugged him and whispered in his ear. His whole inside ached to feel her presence again, to hear her voice, feel her touch.

My God, he thought, *here I am, a married man, having these adolescent feelings for another woman.*

The idea that this might all be permanent was little comfort, indeed. This was too distressing for him right now. He, too, looked forward to this evening's doings and felt better that his companions were all male.

The group arrived at Barncuddy's, which was bustling at this hour. Seeing the rooms hit Bob like a blow. This was the place, indeed! He could see where he had been seated, and where Craycroft sat and told his tale and where Willie had been seated. He suddenly felt an aching remembrance of the tale told by Craycroft, almost every word.

"Craycroft," Bob said, "the book. You were telling a tale of a book sought after by powerful men and found by a humble friar. You were seated right there." He gestured toward one of the tables. "And a fellow named Willie then played on his harp. My God, it's coming back to me now."

"Indeed, Master Robert. I was, in fact, here, as you remember, telling the tale of a book, one of power and knowledge. But what I did not say was that the book had a name. Would it surprise you to know that it was called *The Book of Drachma*?"

"Oh, my..." Bob stood silent for the moment, letting this revelation sink in.

"My good friend, Master Craycroft, the magical storyteller, indeed." Barncuddy seized the opportunity. "Is this going to be another tale-telling tonight?"

"Nay, I'm afraid not, my good man. What we shall be needing tonight is merely a table where these good friends of mine may sit, and while you serve us some of your famous brew, we may talk not of books of power, but of ways to save the life of one in need."

"Ye know, Master Craycroft, there are some things about ye that will never change. As I recall, the last time ye were not going to talk either. Ah, well, come here, Diane. Could ye please seat these fine men? That table in the back should be fine I should think. But tell me, who be these fine men that ye have with ye this evening? I know this one be a councilor, am I right? But these other two I know not."

"Well, my good man, this is Master Melchior, apprentice to Master Falma, and as good a man with the matters of law as any. And over here is Master Robert, from far away, a healer, who brings with him knowledge the like of which exceeds our ken."

"And a most hearty welcome to ye. Diane shall seat ye. A couple of pitchers, is it?"

"Aye, and keep it flowing, my good man."

The quartet followed Diane toward the back where there was a large table with rough-hewn benches. They all sat down, and soon the ale was flowing and the talk at their table was lost in the noise of the inn.

"So then, Master Robert, what you are telling us is that you believe the earl has something called pneumonia, which may be thought of as a war between these so-called bacteria and the earl's own body."

"That's right, and now it looks as though the bacteria are winning and we have nothing to turn the tide in his favor."

"And in your time, you have such things, is that not right?"

"Yes, we have antibiotics; but we also have oxygen, intravenous fluids, including blood, as well as machines that can do a person's job of breathing if needed. All these things can help patients with pneumonia stem the tide of overwhelming infection. And besides that, we have tests to determine how our patients are doing with their antibiotics, such as x-rays, which can show us pictures of a person's insides; arterial blood gasses to see how well the blood is delivering oxygen; blood counts; chemistries, and so on. All of these things give us road maps we can follow. But I'll tell you

what, we still lose patients. In fact, death is still a universal thing. Everyone still dies. We haven't fixed that problem."

"Well said, Master Robert. What you have told us is that even if we had antibiotics, as you call them, we might still lose the earl. Is the illness too far along for the antibiotic to do any good?"

"Perhaps; I don't really know. What I will tell you is that any antibiotic is likely to be more effective in your time, simply because you don't have any yet. When penicillin first came out, it was like a miracle. It cured almost any infection. Then, after years of use, its effectiveness was much less because the bacteria learned to grow in the presence of antibiotics by developing resistance mechanisms."

"Now wait. These bacteria you likened to tiny maggots, too tiny to see,"—Melchior could not help but interrupt. "Then tell me two things. The first is how can anything so small cause so much damage? And the second is how do the bacteria know what is an antibiotic, and what they must do to avoid its effects? Do they talk?"

"Well, I can see that I've opened a real can of worms," Bob said but realized quickly they would not understand that expression. "What I meant to say is that I've opened up a whole new line of questions by stating a couple of small facts."

"Now, to answer your questions: firstly, bacteria are not even the smallest organisms to cause disease. Their size is actually why they can cause so much damage, for they can insinuate themselves into the tiny spaces of the body, such as the air sacs of the lungs, the organs we breathe with. Within those tiny spaces, then, the bacteria reproduce, and what a few organisms are unable to do, millions can, and eventually destroy the whole organ. Some day, I'm going to have to give you a lesson, with illustrations, eh, Melchior?"

"Now to answer your second line of questioning, well, let me give you an illustration. Suppose there was a war and the king of one side said, 'Kill all those whose hair was shoulder-

length or greater.' After some time, the people would figure out that by cutting their hair, they could stay alive. This is a great oversimplification, of course. We can think of the population of bacteria as the great mass of people, of whom those with short hair survived. So the bacteria would only have short hair, or they wouldn't survive in this environment and this information would be passed on to their offspring.

"And that leads me to the subject of yet another illustrated lecture."

"My good fellows," said Diane, coming back with another pitcher of ale, "who would like another one? Ah, I see we're all up for another. And who, might I ask, are these fine young men that I'd be servin' here tonight?"

"Well, m'lass," said Craycroft, "this is young Melchior, apprentice to Master Falma, and as fine a mind as in all of Shepperton, I should say; a man of letters and real learning. And this serious fellow is none other than our good Councilor Rust, who is actually, I am told, new to your fine establishment. He is on the council, but I must tell you that the council would be a loss without him. He is truly our man on the council. And this fellow is the good Master Robert, healer of extraordinary power and knowledge. He comes to us courtesy of none other than Drachma himself. I must tell you that he is spoken for, and I would not, if I were you, try to get between them, for she is here in the castle as well, and is quite the lady."

Bob just felt his face flush at this. He was still reeling from his encounter with Judy, and now with the ale flowing and tongues loosening, he was not at all sure where to go. Fortunately for him, Councilor Rust was there to deflect some of the attention.

Rust looked about him and realized with a start that he was not a stranger after all to this establishment. He had been here as a child, but it was not Barncuddy's then. Rather, at that time, it was known as the Three Knights Inn and was operated by an

old crony of his father's whose name he could not remember. He then asked Diane if he could speak to the proprietor.

"My heavens, you look like you've seen a ghost, my good councilor," said Craycroft. "What is it? Can you not tell us?"

"Nay, I cannot, but not because I choose not to; but rather, because I only remember this place from my childhood before I moved away and then came back as a young man. I do believe that I have deliberately avoided this place because of this memory. Now let me think. Back then it was known as the Three Knights Inn. I would assume that Master Barncuddy could enlighten us on what transpired and why I feel this odd sensation of someone watching."

"Then, my good man, we should by all means seek out our good Master Barncuddy and inquire of him what did happen. How old were you when all this did happen?"

"I was but a very wee lad, perhaps four years old. Why I remember the name so well, I do not know; but I remember being inside this room. And there be a stairway up the back from in there." He pointed toward the kitchen. "But, I tell you, it was not just an ordinary stairway, but something else. I know not what."

"I have never been back there, in the kitchen…"

"But it was not a kitchen then."

"Here comes Barncuddy. We shall ask him."

"And what, pray tell, would ye like to ask me, my good men?"

Craycroft spoke for them. "Master Barncuddy, our friend here, the councilor, would like to ask you some questions about your establishment."

"Now, mind ye it's all bought and paid for…"

"Nay, that's not what is on his mind, is it?"

"It most assuredly is not. Now, as I was sitting here, I started to remember that I had actually been here before, back when I was a mere lad of about four. Why I remember that, I cannot say, but I do remember that this place was called something else, the

Three Knights Inn. And, for some reason, I remember that there was a stairway back there where your kitchen is now."

"Ah, ye'd be remembering right. This place was called the Three Knights Inn, named fer the three gentlemen who owned it. And ye're absolutely right. There was a stairway in the back, but that was no ordinary stairway. It was a stairway up to the private entrance to one of the rooms, which was the room of a musician named Charlie McFerris. I have been told that this McFerris was a true master of any instrument, and he lived upstairs in that strange room of his, coming down, scarin' the young ones that would, of occasion, be in the inn. Now there were, as I said, three men who did own the place, including the father of Master Genet—who is on the council; a Master Finch, and someone else whose name I did not learn. And it is said of the three men that they were each murdered in the same way by poisoning, and that when suspicion fell upon McFerris, he was found dead upon the stairway, discovered by a young lad who was playin' hide and seek. This was all before my time, but the buildin' was not used until I was able to buy it and turn it into me ale house."

"Now, let me guess," said Craycroft, "that it was thee, was it not Councilor Rust, who was the boy who discovered the body?"

The councilor looked a bit pale and shaken. Then he spoke, "Aye, I do believe that what Master Barncuddy said is the truth. For it fits with what I do know, and also it explains why I have had these reoccurring dreams since I was a boy, and why I have been so afraid of small, dark places like that stairway."

"Ah, well, have no fear then, my good councilor, for that stairway is no more, and I shan't ask ye back to inspect the place. But what I will tell ye is that the old musician did leave his harp, and that is the very harp that Willie'll be a playin' on this evening when he gets here. I do so hope that ye'll make the time to stay and listen to Willie."

As Barncuddy was explaining this, Bob was thinking back to his own dreams of this place, and in his own dreams, there was a stairway.

"Now, you say there is no stairway back there? Would you mind, Mr. Barncuddy, if I took a look back there with you?" asked Bob.

"Naw, I wouldna' mind, me friend. Come on back with me. I'll show ye my kitchen."

So Bob got up, a little bit unsteadily, and went with Barncuddy into his kitchen at the back. As he walked back, things were taking shape in his memory. Right by the back door, where they had placed a cupboard with dishes, there had been a small stairway leading upwards, and he remembered the man, remembered that he was carrying a violin, and saying something...

"Now that is where the stairway was, behind that cupboard. I remember, it went up, and there was a man on the stairway carrying a violin, saying something about...something about water, and something about a book."

"Well, Master Robert, though I know nothing about this man, I would say that ye are right, that there was a stairway right there where ye said, but I canna' say how ye'd of known that, nor can I say how ye'd known that Charlie McFerris was found with a fiddle on that very stairway. Very peculiar, indeed."

"I'd say..."

When Bob regained his seat, he was silent at first; he just sat down and sipped his ale.

Then Melchior said, "Now, Master Robert, I know that something significant happened and that you and Master Craycroft know something, and also that Councilor Rust knows something. Why do you not tell us all about it? It sounds like a great tale in the making."

"Well, since you put it so eloquently, how can I refuse? All right, I'll tell you of the dream I had before this whole thing ever got started.

"Now, you have to realize, this dream occurred in my own place and time, some five hundred years beyond anything happening here. I had just gotten home from a very busy day working at the hospital, caring for the very ill patients who demanded my time. I was exhausted, and I really just wanted to go to bed. I was telling my wife—and, oh yes, I have a wife—just how tired I was, and that we really did not seem to have any time for the things that we both enjoy, even going out and eating a nice meal, without the hospital or my answering service paging me. My wife just sort of agreed with me, but really didn't say anything. Then I fell asleep and had this most peculiar dream; and I say peculiar because it was a dream with features so incredibly real that I knew, even though I was dreaming, that what was happening was significant.

"Well, in my dream, I was right here, and by that, I mean I was sitting exactly where I'm sitting now, and I was enjoying the ale and bread that was on the table. And Craycroft was right there—I mean, he was at the next table—with what looked like a gathering of young men, and he was telling a tale; but let me tell you, it was no ordinary tale. It was the story of a book with men of power seeking it out; but it was eventually found by a young friar who lost everything to obtain this book. And Craycroft told us that there was one on this island who had seen this book, someone called Drachma.

"Then, after he had told this story, Willie Minstrel picked up his harp and played for us, and his playing was so profound that I was moved to tears. But then, I was suddenly in the back of the inn, but it was somewhat different. There was a stairway going up, and on that stairway was a young man, and he was holding a fiddle. He was trying to tell me something. Something about a book and something about water. But then I found myself outside. I could still hear Willie's playing, but this time I felt as though his music was transporting me to someplace deep and green, with running water; and it was late springtime; it was pleasantly warm, and there was the smell of newly turned earth. Then my dream abruptly ended. It was the hospital calling about Josh."

It was Councilor Rust who broke the profound silence.

"Now, Master Robert, that is quite a story. And here we are, right where all this took place, though I would venture that you had not actually set foot in this establishment before today. And I have been avoiding it for so long that I might as well be a stranger."

Bob agreed. "So it would appear. But it seems that there are forces that would like it if we would all be here. You know, you've now got me believing in these wild things."

The door to the inn opened up just then and in walked Willie. He quickly shut the door behind him and then looked around. His eyes caught Craycroft's and then lit up with a smile. He rushed over to the table and eagerly grabbed Craycroft's hand.

"Ah, Master Craycroft, it be so good to see ye here. I know me own misery shall have someone to commiserate with. What be ye doin' out and about on a night such as this?"

"Why, just waiting for you, my good friend. Might I introduce you to my friends here? On my left, here is our good Councilor Rust, whom you have heard about, but I do not believe that you have truly met. On his left is Master Melchior, apprentice to Falma, whom I am certain you have not met. And on my right is the good Master Robert, whom you have never seen, but believe me knows thy music."

There were handshakes all around, but when Willie reached over to take Bob's hand, Willie instantly recognized his features.

"Now, I shouldn't know ye, but I do." Willie thought for a moment. "Nay, I just cannot place ye."

"Oh, Diane," Craycroft said loudly, "could ye bring another flagon for Willie Minstrel? He is here to charm us with his music, so make his good and stout."

Diane appeared moments later from the kitchen with another pitcher and a glass. Then she sidled up to Willie.

"Willie, last time ye played, ye were so smashed that I thought I would have to hold yer harp for ye, so here's hopin' yer better able to hold yer ale for the evening."

"Oh, my, was it that obvious? I was really despondent, for it was just after the funeral of Lady Felicia. I know ye'll never understand…"

"Well then, why don't ye try me? Just hold me like that instrument of thine, an' whisper of the times ye could have had…"

"Ah, Diane, ye don't know half of it. Oh, be botherin' some of the other gentlemen with yer pretty face and figure, and see if they can stand up to ye."

"But Willie, there shall never be another fer me."

"Oh, go on, then."

"I shall, but I'll be around if ye need anythin', love." She poured him a full flagon of ale and then made her rounds to the others' half empty glasses. She was just as flirtatious with Melchior and Bob, but then she stopped herself when she poured Craycroft's glass full. "Oh, m'lord, I should remember that ye'r our liege, now shouldn't I?"

"I shall tell you a secret, m'lass. When I choose to come down here to Barncuddy's, I come as just another man, not as any lord."

"If it be thy bidding, m'lord," she said, then kissed him quickly on the cheek. She was gone before she could see what effect she had on the blushing Craycroft.

The banter turned good-natured again. As the ale flowed, the company became looser, more relaxed. After consuming a couple of flagons of ale, Willie agreed to give a concert. He then took up his clarsach as all became silent in the inn, and attention turned toward the musician.

As usual, he began with gentle strumming. Then he closed his eyes, and from the depths of his harp there arose a melody, at once familiar and forbidding, then embellished, over and over in variations as enthralling as they were mysterious. The harp playing continued as his audience sat spellbound.

To Bob this was more than music. It was the voice from another dimension saying to him that he did belong, and this was right; was good. He began to feel the warmth; not of the inn, but of the outside world, as a gentle breeze stirred the treetops and the stream flowed gently beside him. He could hear her voice saying it would be all right again. He tried to answer, but no words came. Her hand gently stroked his face, the stubble on his cheeks.

"Come, now, Master Robert, it is time we went back. The hour is late."

Bob woke to the sound of Hermes's speech. He roused himself and stood up with some effort. Hermes was there to steady him. Then he turned to Melchior and said, "Tomorrow, I'll come by in the morning."

Melchior—himself half-sleeping—acknowledged this with a mumbled assent. Then they all bundled up and headed back to their respective places of repose.

Councilor Reordan awoke early, as was his custom. After getting up, he sent his servant after some bread and cheese.

"And make certain that the bread is fresh. That last batch was a week old, if it were a day."

"Aye, sir, I shall make sure this time," the servant answered, remembering what happened to the last servant who tried to fool his master. Then he hurried off toward the kitchen.

With his breakfast now before him, and having assured himself that the bread was indeed fresh, he sent for his aide—a mousey sort of a man, whom none seemed to notice in a crowd, just as Reordan liked it. Carruthers stepped quietly into the room and waited for his master to speak.

"Well, Carruthers, what have you heard from the castle and the village?"

"M'lord, from the castle I have learned that a Lady Judy has arrived, accompanied by Master Falma. Both seem unharmed, but there was one of Drachma's guards who appears to have been injured. More than that, I cannot be sure, but I shall find out more. There is also a councilor, methinks it is Councilor Genet, who is also injured, but is yet alive. I know no more than that as of yet."

"Then there is the matter of the man LeGace, who may have stabbed one of the peddlers in the market."

"Ah, that is no matter," said Reordan, "just another peddler. But please keep your eyes and ears open as to the condition of Councilor Genet."

"Of course, m'lord."

"Anything else to report?

"Only that this man, LeGace, seems to have taken residence in the village, though I know not where. But he does seem to be keeping out of sight most of the time."

"That is good. Now you are paying our little urchins their pittance, I assume, and that they are reporting to you as directed?"

"Aye, m'lord."

"Very well then, Carruthers. Be off with you now, and come back on the morrow with more reports."

Carruthers bowed slightly, stepping out of his master's chambers as obsequiously as he came.

Chapter Two

Judy was awake early, but she lay in her bed just looking out at the room, a bit afraid to get out from under the covers. The light was still dim, and it looked too cold; and this was the most comfortable sleep she had in many nights. It was luxurious to feel rested. She just couldn't get over the notion that this was permanent. Now that she was able to admit to herself that part of the reason that she was here had to do with her feelings for Bob, she wondered what his own feelings were.

I guess I'll just have to sort all this out, she thought. *It would seem that I've got time, and I've certainly got opportunity.*

She stretched under the covers and thought about last night. It was sort of fun to dress up in that gown and to make something of a grand entrance, but there they were—Falma, Bob, and the others—who looked weary and who looked so serious. Maybe after resting they would relax just a little.

Now, what was she supposed to do today? *Oh, yes, go to Craycroft's place this morning.*

Well, she wondered, *no telling when that's to occur.* She thought about Cairn and how he did overnight, and whether she needed to check on him.

Then she noticed she was not alone in the room. There was someone tending to her fire. She sat up in bed, and that drew the attention of the other.

"Oh, pardon me, ma'am, but I was just bringing thee somethin' to eat, and I see that yer fire needed some attention. I was hopin' ye wouldn't mind. And me name's Clarice. I've been assigned to yer care, if ye don't mind."

"No, not at all, Clarice. I'm just not used to all this attention. Back where I come from, I live alone and there is no one to do all these little things for me."

"No one? You do not have servants?"

"Ah, no, Clarice. Hardly anyone has servants. They just can't afford them."

"Canna' afford servants? That is most strange. For they tell me ye're a great healer with great powers."

Judy just chuckled at that. The thought of her being a great healer, and with great powers, was ludicrous. She was just a nurse and did not heal patients. She could help them through their misery, and she learned over time that simple touch had an ameliorating effect on those in pain or misery. But then, what difference would it make if she were a 'great healer'? Even those that she considered great in the world of medicine, and that definitely included Bob Gilsen, did not have servants. In fact, the only people she could think of that had servants were so "out of her league" that she just couldn't imagine their existence.

"No, Clarice, I am not a great healer, and I have no special powers. I do, though, deal with persons who are ill and injured, and I try to help them feel better. And I must ask you, do you know the way to get to Sick Bay? There is a person there who is injured, and I do need to check on him."

"Of course, m'lady. But first ye must have something to eat and something to wear, no?"

"Naturally."

So then Judy got up, and with Clarice's help, got ready for the day's events. She was able to find another of Felicia's outfits to wear, much more subdued than the outfit she wore the previous night, and one which gave her a little more freedom to move about.

Then she found Jeanne, who was up and about, and told her of her plans to go to Sick Bay to check on Cairn. She would be back before too long, so that Jeanne could take her to Craycroft's before the day got too far along.

Judy and Clarice arrived at Sick Bay as the guards were changing. She stepped into the closely packed quarters and found Cairn where she had left him the previous evening. She went up to him, smiled, and asked how he was doing.

"Ah, m'lady, it is thee, indeed. I am glad to see thee."

"Oh, Mr. Cairn, I'm just checking on you. You know, you did save my life and all. I guess I owe you that much at least."

Judy went up to him, felt his forehead, checked his pulse, and then checked his flank. He felt somewhat warm, but his fever was not ragingly high at least. His pulse was reassuringly strong and steady, though a little fast. But the look of his flank was worrisome. It was somewhat redder and more tender than it had been.

"Has Dr. Gil…that is, has Master Robert been in to see you yet?"

"Nay, m'lady, not yet. Ye be the first this morn. May I suggest that you look at Leroy over yonder? There is something about him that worries me."

"Only you, Cairn, only you would be concerned enough about others while you lie there with a wounded side. All right, I'll check on him too."

Judy went over to where Old Leroy was lying under some blankets. As she peeled away the blankets, she saw immediately why Cairn was so worried. Leroy looked as pale a ghost, was not responsive, and his breathing, though not labored, was not normal. His belly was even more protuberant than it had been.

"Oh, if only we were back home with our ER staff. Listen, can someone find Dr. Gilsen… I'm sorry, Master Robert. tell him to get here right away. I believe that this man is dying."

One of the pages took off at a run to try to find Master Robert. Judy then took another look at Leroy and felt for his pulse. It was there, but it was rapid and thready. Then she let her nursing instincts take over and tried as well as she could to comfort Old Leroy. She searched and found another blanket. She laid her hand on his head and spoke to him in soothing tones. Cairn could see Leroy visibly relax. There was definitely something to this woman, something ethereal and wise.

After only a few minutes, the page returned with Bob and Hermes. They came over to where Judy was tending the dying man.

"Oh, Bob, I'm so sorry to call you like this, but this man appears to be dying. I realize there is little we can do here in the boonies, away from anything remotely like our ER; but I thought that, if anyone could think of something, it might be you."

"Well, let me have a look. Here we've got this old man who has been stabbed, and is bleeding inside his belly. From the looks of things, I'd say he's got at least four units in his belly already, and who knows if he's perforated a viscus. Let me see."

He pulled out his stethoscope from the little satchel, listened to Leroy's heart and lungs, listened to his abdomen, and pressed gently on his belly. He then turned toward Judy.

"He's apparently in shock from blood loss. If it's any help, I don't think it's a perforated viscus. Probably, though, he's bleeding from his spleen. We've got no blood to give and not even IV fluids. We could try raising his legs up, sort of a poor man's Trendelenberg, and try some water if he'll take any. And let's hope that he will somehow stop bleeding internally."

Dutifully, Judy, with the help of Bob and Hermes, got the old man's legs raised. His color improved some, but he still looked very pale and near death. Judy again comforted the old man. In the meantime, Bob saw to the others in Sick Bay. He checked on Councilor Genet, who seemed to be making good progress and was actually hungry and able to speak coherently. What he told Bob was that he had just left the earl's side with a letter to the

council and was heading back to the council chambers when he felt a blow and then lapsed into unconsciousness. He did notice there was another figure, but he never got a look at him, other than to notice that there was a dog barking, and then the man took off. Where his letter was, he could not say, but he thought it possible that his assailant took it with him.

Bob took note of what the injured councillor told him, and made a mental note to discuss this with Craycroft.

Next Bob turned his attention toward Cairn. He was relieved to find Cairn fully coherent. He, too, noticed that the man was febrile and his pulse was rapid, but that his color was good. He examined his arm wound and noticed that it looked all right, with no purulence. Then he checked his flank and found, like Judy did, that his side was swollen and tender. And right where the arrow had been pulled out there appeared to be some pus coming out.

"What do you think, Bob?"

"Well, I'd say that we need a good surgeon. This wound seems to be festering up. Now, Master Cairn, have you been able to pass urine?

"Oh, aye."

"And have you noticed any blood in the urine?"

"Nay, it was clear."

"And have your bowels moved?"

"Aye, that they have."

"And was there any blood in them, or any blackness?"

"Nay, none."

"Well, that is good, for it appears that your arrow avoided hitting any vital organs."

It was then that Kerlin appeared at the door with Eustace at his side.

"Good morrow, Master Robert, I was told that you were here. I thought I would check on my guard, Cairn, while you were about."

"And good morning to you. What I can tell you is that he is doing remarkably well, but I'm afraid he is going to need surgery. I have absolutely no idea how you would even go about arranging something like surgery around here. Does Craycroft do any? It would be a simple incision and drainage, I believe."

"I know not whether Craycroft does anything like what you are suggesting. Perhaps one of the pages could seek him out."

While the page sought out Craycroft, Bob checked on Old Leroy once more. Kerlin also came over, and Bob explained why he had positioned him the way he had. Judy just kept gently touching his face and talked soothingly to the old peddler.

Kerlin came up to the peddler's face and asked, "Now, Leroy, I must ask: do you remember the man who hurt you? Think back, if you can. Do you remember anything at all? Was he in any way connected to your former occupation? I know that you worked with my brother Sean."

A light shone in his eyes at the mention of that name. Then he spoke in a voice quiet, but firm. "Oh, me friend, Sean, he be one fine gentleman. And if anyone could have saved me from me own doings, it would be Sean. And aye, I did not believe it, but now I do. That man it was who attacked me, it was LeGace. He I did know... and tried to run from..."

Then he let out a sudden, loud moan, clutched his side, and went limp. Bob quickly checked for a carotid pulse, felt nothing, and then he pulled out his stethoscope again and listened for heart sounds; he heard nothing.

Hermes and Eustace just stared, stunned by what had just happened. Eustace was fighting back tears because this was, oddly, the old man who had led him to his own new life, and now it appeared he had just given up his own.

"I'm afraid he's gone." Bob paused, and then looked to Kerlin. "There was really nothing we could have done for him without major surgery."

Judy asked, "Does he have any family? Is there no one we could call upon?"

"No, m'lady, none," answered Kerlin. "We should send for Father Henri. I shall tell you that he is now in peace."

"You know, I get the feeling that there's more to this story. You're going to have to tell me more, Kerlin."

"Ah, I shall, sometime when we are sitting down, for the story is quite a long one."

"Aren't they all?"

Judy turned her attention to the old man on the table. She started to cover his head with the sheet, but noticed something peculiar.

"Bob," she said, "what do you think about this?"

"What?"

"This mark, here on his wrist."

Bob looked at the arm and then signaled for Kerlin to come over. On the left forearm, just above the wrist, there was a tattoo unlike any Judy or Bob had seen; it was a picture of a serpent and skull with some writing in a script neither one of them recognized.

"Kerlin, do you recognize this tattoo? It seems an odd sort of mark for an old street peddler to have on his arm."

"Aye, that I do recognize, but I have not seen that mark for a long time. It is a symbol of the ancient order of Byzantium, and, as I understand, it is only seen on the highest of the magnates of that order. That one would be hard to explain. Maybe we can get an explanation from Master Falma."

"I'll be sure to ask him about that next time I see him."

"Ah, here comes Craycroft, perhaps we could ask him."

"Well, I see my healers have been about early this morn. What now, may I ask?" Craycroft started.

"Why, Mr. Craycroft," said Bob. "We've been rather busy this morning. Attending to the sick, and, I'm afraid, also the dying."

"The dying? Not Cairn, I hope."

"No, not Cairn, but rather our peddler, Leroy, who appears to have some secrets that may have died with him."

"Oh? Could you explain?"

"Well, come take a look."

Bob took him over to the peddler and lifted up his arm. "Here, take a look. Tell us what you make of this."

Craycroft studied the tattoo. A look of something like remorse clouded his features. He paused and then turned to Bob, Kerlin, and Judy.

"In truth, I have not seen this mark since my youth. It does hold some significance for me, which I shall explain later this morning. Have we called Father Henri?"

"Aye, we have."

"Well then, I understand you have some concerns regarding Cairn."

"Oh, yes I do. Come this way."

The two of them, plus Judy, approached Cairn's bedside. Cairn looked up at the group assembled, then he singled out Judy.

"M'lady," he said, "I wanted to let ye know that whatever is decided in my care, and whatever happens to me, that I shall never doubt ye. And if I should recover, I would request that I be assigned to be thy guard."

"Oh, Mr. Cairn, I owe you so much more than you'll ever know. I do feel certain, though, that Craycroft will be happy to honor your request."

"But aye, that would be quite a certainty, I would assure you. Now, tell me, how are you feeling?" Crycroft asked.

"Just now, my side does hurt where the arrow pierced me. But the pain is endurable." He raised his tunic to show his side. Craycroft and Robert looked at his wound. There on his left flank was the point where the arrow had entered. Below this was a large bruise. But just around the wound, there was redness, swelling, and just a small opening, which, when Bob pressed gently beside it, produced a mixture of pus and old, dark blood.

"What think you, Master Robert?"

"Well, I would have to say that if he were in our ER I would be calling a surgeon for an I&D—sorry, that would be incision and drainage—but this would be after getting a CT scan to see if there were any signs of visceral damage. But clinically, I can tell you that he does not have any significant damage because his urine is clear and he's having bowel movements."

"So then, what you are telling me is that this arrow wound has signs of 'infection,' which I would surmise is from bacteria penetrating the barrier of the skin. But that you do not believe that there is anything to suggest that the bacteria have invaded either the bowel or the urinary apparatus; would that seem to be a correct summation?"

Bob was thoroughly impressed. For he realized just what an amazing mind this was to be able to grasp in so short a period of time what it had taken the medical world many centuries to discover. And this included the issues of bacterial infection, the barrier that the skin represented, and the sense that there were, indeed, viscera within the abdomen that had their own protection.

"My God, that is a really remarkably accurate summary. You have an amazing conceptual grasp of both bacteriology and human anatomy. I would assume that this Master Cartho had something to do with this."

"Aye, I owe him a great debt of gratitude, for he was a great inspiration, as well as a master teacher and master physician."

"Well then, you're definitely going to have to show me some of his writing. Anyway, back to our patient. Yes, I do believe that he has an infection and that we would typically prescribe antibiotics; but, in this case, I don't really think they would be necessary because the primary treatment would be surgical. And that brings me to my next question; specifically, do you do any surgery? Or do you know anyone who does?"

"Nay, I would not trust any of the barbers here to do this surgery that you talk of, for it seems to me that their results are

not good. And no, I do no surgical operations. So, that I think, leaves you, my friend. I would be happy to assist you in any way you desire, but if you honestly feel that surgery is what he needs, then I think you should proceed."

"Well, let me think, what I shall be needing are some clean, dry cloths, some sharp instruments that have been boiled in water, some water to wash with, and anything antiseptic, such as alcohol—preferably somewhat distilled—something I can give this gentleman for pain, and a clean basin—oh, about this big." Bob gestured with his hands how big the basin should be.

Craycroft thought for a moment, and then said, "By sharp instruments, do you mean knives or needles?

"One very sharp knife ought to do, and some slender, long metal rods." He gestured again with his hands to describe how long the metal rods should be.

"As to your request for some "antiseptic" as you say, perhaps some brandy."

"Yes, that should do."

"And as for something for the man's pain, I do believe that Falma has something he can provide that should suit your purposes quite well. Very well then, we shall try to get all your things together today. Now, did you want to say anything else to Cairn?"

"Um, yes; listen, Mr. Cairn, what you've got in your wound is the beginning of an abscess, and the best treatment for that is surgical drainage, which should then allow your body to heal. And I believe, as oddly as this may sound, that I am the best person here to perform this minor surgical procedure on you. And yes, I can assure you that Judy here will be by your side."

"I am in your hands, my good Master Robert."

"Well, then it is set. When we get all the stuff prepared, I'll be back, and we'll get your abscess drained."

Craycroft went over to Councilor Genet's bedside and found him, as Bob did, to be making good progress. Then an idea struck

Craycroft as to how he could turn things to his advantage, as he knew that the Sick Bay was being watched. He went over to the window to be sure of it, and there were definitely eyes watching from across the plaza. He motioned Kerlin over and told Bob, Kerlin, and Judy of his plan, which included the councilor.

"Oh, so this is how it's done, is it? I knew you were clever, but I didn't think that you were devious as well. I better watch my step around here," Bob noted, with a bemused look.

That brought a lighthearted chuckle out of Councilor Genet.

"Well, my friends, now we must depart this place, but we shall be back whenever we gather the necessary supplies for the surgery on Master Cairn. Now you two should accompany me back to the earl's place, and we may then decide how further to proceed."

The earl's chambers were dark, a bit close and warm. Craycroft entered with Bob and Judy in tow. Aaron, Hermes, and Clarice stayed outside the inner chambers, but remained ready for anything. Bob had his satchel with him.

Craycroft then spoke with the ailing nobleman. "M'liege, how are you this morning? And how was your night?"

"Oh, Craycroft, it is you. Good of you to come. I see Master Robert is with you, and a new lady. Now would this be the Lady Judy of which I have heard…"

His speech was interrupted by a violent paroxysm of coughing. This left him weaker but still able to talk after a moment to catch his breath.

"Come closer, m'lady, let me look upon you. I have heard about you and your travails in getting here. For that I am truly sorry, but so thankful that you are here among us at last. Now you shall have to tell Master Craycroft that I was not forewarned to expect someone of such rare beauty, and that dress… of silk. One of Felicia's, no?" He paused, and they all expected another fit

of coughing, but then he went on. "M'lady, I shall have to chide Drachma just a little as well, for I was not told of your amazing beauty, though I have been told of your soothing touch."

"Oh, my lord," Judy said, blushing. "I'm afraid that Drachma, dear man that he is, may have exaggerated just a little. You see, I am just a nurse, and though I like to think that I have a natural tendency to reach out to those in pain, or who suffer, I do not believe that I have any special talents. And I do not believe that my touch is anymore soothing than anyone else's."

Bob was instantly reminded of his visit to the ER—in that distant past/future—in which he came down to get a bite to eat with the weight of the day riding on his aching shoulders, and how Judy had touched his shoulder and in that brief instant of time, that touch was the most soothing thing in the world.

"No, Judy, you're wrong. Your touch, when extended to a person in need, is an extraordinary thing indeed—truly remarkable. It is really the most healing thing I have experienced," Bob said.

"You see, m'lady, there is testimony from an unexpected source."

Judy looked at Bob, then at the earl; then at Bob again.

"I am humbled, my lord…"

"Do come here, m'lady, and let this tired, sick, old man feel your touch, for I, though not in severe pain, am seriously ill. This much I know, and further I do know that there is naught we can do to change the course of this illness. It is precisely for this reason I have appointed our good Master Craycroft to rule in my stead."

Judy stepped forward and clasped both of the earl's hands. In that moment, if you had been watching carefully, you could have seen what Carlo Vincente had seen, and which Bob and Cairn had felt. There was no doubt in the earl, and he could feel his illness momentarily recede. Judy could feel something out of the ordinary; she could feel the older, febrile patient's warm, moist skin in her hands; she could sense that he relaxed and his breathing, ever so slightly, eased. She could, however, sense

something no one else was aware of, and that was that there was something right about what she was doing, something right about being here, in this time and place. She could feel the warmth of springtime, with the breeze rustling the high branches; she could almost feel the soft earth beneath her feet and the smell of newly turned earth.

Chapter Three

The guard was riding hard through some truly foul weather. His horse was well suited for such a ride, however, and it seemed to be eagerly running through the muddy paths that his master had chosen. The rain, which seemed to be driven by some evil tunnel of shadows, was icy cold on the rider's exposed face. He came out of the hills to the north, then, before turning east, had to cross yet another stream. This was one of the strangest tasks he had ever been asked to complete in his years of service. The book made some sense, though not in this foul weather, but the jar of water was a bit too strange. But when Angelica tried to explain it to him, he just said, "Enough, I'll just have to take thy word on this matter."

Finding the stream had been a bit of a challenge as well. It was over some rocky terrain, then down a slippery bed to where it meandered down from the high hills, tumbling down over some falls to where he could approach the water. When he got down to the water's edge, he could hear Angelica's warning, "Mind ye, do not, and I repeat, do not get into the water, for it has been known to kill."

So he then took the small jar and held it close with the rag around it; then he got his sample of water, discarded the rag at the side of the stream, put the jar of water inside his satchel, and stood up to leave. Then it hit him; that smell. What was it? Where

was it coming from? He looked around him, saw nothing; but that smell, though not overpowering, was distinctly unpleasant, like the smell of grapes rotting on the vine. Then, as he got ready to leave, he noticed one more thing. That was the vegetation, or, more particularly, the lack of vegetation along the banks. He could see only a few yellowed strands of grass anywhere near the water's edge. He then left with the feeling that he was leaving a place of death.

"Now I've never seen this Master Craycroft," thought Ervin, as he waded the stream, so unlike that stream of strange water back in the hills. "I wonder what sort of a man this be, who, according to Drachma, was chosen by the earl himself as his own successor, even while still alive." He knew his directions. Find Kerlin and ask to be shown to this Master Craycroft, and then to give his message and his parcels to the master.

And then the castle came into view, though only in the distance, visible at intervals through the rain. He then gently urged his horse on, who virtually leapt at the encouragement. He rode at a thundering pace through the villages, then up to the castle gates. Once inside, he made the turn toward the stables and was encouraged to find that his favorite groom, Dunstan, was on hand to receive him.

"And how d'ye do, me good man? Was it rough riding in this weather? I'm sure that ye could use a warming fire and a good cup o' the brown, liquid refreshment, am I right?"

"Of course ye're right. The ride was rough enough and colder'n even this January could boast, but 'twas a strange purpose in me comin' out here today, let me tell ye."

Dunstan knew better than to ask. And then they could see Master Dowdell hurrying from the direction of the keep.

"Well, ye leave yer mount wi' me. I shall make certain he's cared fer, fed, and groomed, and he'll be ready fer thy next adventure."

"As usual, me good man, and thank ye. Now here's some copper fer ye, and some fer the missus."

Dunstan pocketed the tip, thanked him, and then he took the great gray back into the stables. Dowdell arrived, and the two of them hugged like brothers, and then went off toward the constabulary.

"Y'know, I thought that it was ye ridin' this way. There's just somethin' about that great gray horse of thine that sets it apart from all the others. It's a good thing ye weren't leadin' a battle charge, fer the enemy would be too feared to fight, I tell ye."

"And it's good to see thee too, my comrade. Too long it's been since we sat and talked. Maybe tonight, over some flagons of ale, eh?"

"Aye to that."

The two of them entered the constabulary where they were met with the raucous laughter of men-at-arms enjoying the sport of the day.

"What did I tell ye? I knew it was Ervin the Red. I knew that horse from afar. There's none like him anywhere on this isle," Kevin exclaimed.

"Welcome, Ervin. This place has been changin'…"

"But not thee, eh Blodwen?"

"Nay, not me."

"Now can someone find me somethin' to drink, while I make use of yer privy."

"Aye, we'll have ye some by the fireside."

When Ervin returned to the warmth of the fireside, he was met by the same crowd, plus Cayman and Eustace, who had come in from their aborted attempt at horsemanship. The weather had just gotten too bad to do anything but sit inside by the fire. So the two, wet and dripping, joined the throng in the main room by the fire.

"Well, Eustace, it looks like ye'll meet up with the wild rider after all, as he is here now. My good man, Ervin, what brings ye in on a day such as this? We did watch ye ride up to the castle as if to bring us some bad news."

"Ah, so it was ye, was it? Down by the village? I should have known, Cayman. It looked like ye. But what, pray tell, were ye doin' outside on a day like this?"

"Well, when we started out it was a fairer day, then ye brought this winter storm with ye out of the hills."

"Ah, so it was me, was it?"

"Ah, aye, or so it would seem. Let me introduce ye to the newest member of our guard. This is young Eustace, who is the new assistant to me commandant, Kerlin."

"To Kerlin? It is he who I need to seek out. For I need to speak with Master Craycroft, who I hear is now taking charge at the appointment by the earl. And it is Kerlin who has the ear of Craycroft. I bear both a message and some items for Craycroft."

"Well, then, get yerself some ale and some bread, and I'm certain we can find Master Kerlin fer ye."

So Ervin sat down by the fire, rubbed the feeling back into his hands, drank some ale, had some bread and cheese, and talked of old campaigns while a messenger was sent to seek out Kerlin.

When Kerlin walked into the constabulary, it was like drifting back into his old life, however briefly. Here was Ervin, sitting and making merry among his old friends and acquaintances. The atmosphere was thick with camaraderie. He instantly felt at home among the rough and rowdy crowd.

"My good friend, Ervin, how now? And tell me, was it Drachma that sent thee?"

"Aye, it was, but also his age-defying assistant Angelica; and also Tom sends his greetings."

"Tom, indeed. I do hope he is well."

"Oh, he seemed well enough, but I could tell that he was restless, just cooped up like a bird."

"At least he is safe there."

"I should think so."

"Well, my friend, I'm sure that you have heard about my new duties…"

"And that they call thee commandant, oh, aye. The talk here in the barracks confirmed what I had heard from Drachma. It would seem that it is a good thing, no?"

"This week, this month, I do think so, but in another year—we shall see."

"Now that ye've arrived, I think we should find this Master Craycroft. I shall like to meet him. And I have a message to tell him, and some items to deliver to him as well."

"Come then, and might I bring along Cayman and my assistant Eustace?

"Of course, me friend."

Bob was told that everything was now ready for him in Sick Bay, so he and Judy, with Craycroft and their three attendants, left the keep and headed out into the weather outside, which was now a blinding, cold rainstorm. No one talked as they huddled inside their cloaks and made their way across the plaza toward the building with its one window.

He felt certain that no one saw him in this weather, but Antoine LeGace stood across from the Sick Bay and merely watched. He, too, was bundled up against the cold, and where he stood was deeply shadowed and protected from the rain. He watched as Craycroft and the two strangers entered. He had all the time he needed, so he just watched.

Inside Sick Bay, it was the same crowded, little place that Bob remembered. He walked over to Cairn's bed and made certain that all was there as he requested. He found the cloths, the basin, the water, the instruments in their small pot of water, which was still steaming, and, of course, the brandy, as well as a small vial of some liquid that Bob assumed was the analgesic from Falma.

"Well now, Mr. Cairn, you say that you are ready. Here is Judy to assist with your care. And we also have Mr. Craycroft here. Do you have any questions or concerns before we get started?"

"Nay, I am ready, and I know that I am safe in thy hands."

"Thanks for that vote of confidence. Now, before anything else, we should probably give you some of this medicine from Master Falma to ease the pain. I really don't know the correct dosing, so why don't you just take a couple of swallows, then we'll see if you need more? And while his analgesic is working, I think I'll get all this other stuff set up."

Craycroft, in the meantime, asked about Leroy and whether Father Henri had been by. He was told that the Father had, in fact, come by, and he pronounced last rites over poor Leroy. He was also told of Craycroft's plan, which he amazingly endorsed, as it did not involve the telling of lies and would not jeopardize his position in any way.

"And you, my young friend, do you see him still outside the window?"

"Aye, that I do, m'lord," answered the attendant. "He remains across the plaza, watching, even now."

"That is good. Now, is everything in place as I requested?"

"Aye, that it is."

"Then proceed as I instructed. Call Father Henri and tell him that we should proceed as planned."

"Aye, m'lord. I shall summon him anon."

Bob then went about preparing for his surgical procedure, which he really felt was going to be something of a letdown after all the preparation. It was, after all, going to be just a simple incision and drainage of an abscess. As he saw the medication was taking hold of Cairn, he decided to begin. First, he had Cairn turn so that his left side was upright, and he had Cairn take off his top to expose the abscess. Then he washed his hands with some of the boiled water, and he cleaned his hands with some of the brandy, letting them air dry. Next, he had Judy poured some

of the brandy over Cairn's wound. He then took some of the cloths and laid them around his wound to create a surgical field.

"Now," he said, "I don't know how effective that medication is going to be, so I'll have Judy hold your hand, and you can squeeze it if you need to. You may feel some pain, but I'm hoping that it will be brief."

He got no response from Cairn, which he took to be a good sign. He had Judy hold his hand. Then he felt the flank wound, noticing that since earlier this morning it had grown and was redder. He took the knife with one hand, the basin in the other hand. With the knife, he made a quick three-centimeter incision from back to front. Cairn winced involuntarily but did not cry out. What came gushing out was about one hundred milliliters of pus and old blood. Bob then took one of the metal rods, poked down into the hole that he created. Cairn winced again. Using the rod, he then extruded another quantity of old blood with only a minimal amount of pus. He then felt down into the incision and he could feel no foreign objects such as bits of bone or cloth. Next, he took some of the boiled water, poured it into the incision. Finally, he took one of the cloths, tore a long strip from the edge, and poked one end of it into the incision with another of the metal rods. And, using the rod, he packed the wound with most of the strip of cloth, leaving the last ten centimeters outside.

During all of this, Craycroft looked on with great interest and some obvious admiration. Then he asked, "Master Robert, I noticed that you inserted a portion of the cloth into the wound. Why did you do that?"

"This is a so-called dirty operation, and he will have to heal from the inside out, I'm afraid. I left that strip of gauze in there so that we can clean the wound daily with more of the boiled water and place a new drain inside for two purposes. The first is that the drain can let the fluids out, acting like a wick. The second reason is that the gauze will act to debride the wound…"

"Debride? What is that?

"Well, you may think of debridement as daily surgery on the decaying tissue within the wound."

"I see. Very clever. Will there be much pain?"

"Not nearly as much as today. Speaking of pain, how are you feeling, Mr. Cairn?"

From Cairn, there came only a slight grunting.

"Wow, you're going to have to let me know what it was in that concoction that Falma brought over. It seems to have worked wonderfully."

"Unfortunately, with Falma, there is no telling."

Judy extricated herself from Cairn's sleepy grip and placed a hand on his forehead.

"Bob, do you want me to bandage that? I'm quite sure that I can find something to do that with."

"Yeah, we'd better put on some kind of loose dressing on that," he answered, while washing up.

After he had dried his hands, he then went over to Councilor Genet's bed, talked to the man, examined him, finding nothing abnormal at all on the neurological exam. Then he called Craycroft over.

"Master Craycroft, it appears that our patient has made essentially a complete recovery, and I do believe that he may return to his work whenever you say. Now, according to your plan, we should keep him here for now, is that not right?"

"Oh, aye. It would seem fitting. It would be better if, under cover of darkness, the good councilor should come out and stay within the keep for now."

"Now, Mr. Craycroft," Judy spoke, "you said that the councilor..."

There was a sudden sound from the door as Father Henri, along with half a dozen monks, appeared. They were cold, but a hardy bunch, with the exception of brother Gabriel, who wheezed as if he had just run all the way over from the priory.

"Father Henri, it is good of you to come. Might I introduce you to our two guests who do come from far away? This is Master

Robert, a healer, and one skilled as well in the arts of surgery, pharmacy, and medical hermeneutics. And with him is the Lady Judy Morrison, also skilled as a healer, also well-versed in the arts of wound care; and she has the touch of one graced by the presence of Heierocles."

Bob was a bit baffled by all that blather but played along. Judy, who could not make sense of what Craycroft was saying, just looked down at her feet.

"It is indeed my pleasure to meet you both. It is a rare privilege." The Father looked at the two with a sense of awe. "I am certain that Master Craycroft's hospitality has proven acceptable."

"Oh, it has been more than that, Father. We have been treated like royalty."

Judy remained demurely silent.

"Well then, Father," said Craycroft, "do you have the shroud? And did you bring incense?"

In answer, Father Henri reached into his tunic and brought out the old incense holder. Brother Gabriel brought out the linen shroud. Then the monks got busy with Old Leroy, wrapping him carefully with the linen shroud.

"Oh, Father," said one of the monks, "look at this," indicating the tattoo on his forearm.

"Hmm, I've never seen anything like that. I shall have to search the library to see if that represents anything sinister."

"Do not bother," interjected Craycroft. "I can tell you what that mark represents. It is a sign of the secret order of Byzantium, and it represents one who is high up in the ranks. I would surmise that, in a former existence, Leroy was one of the high officials in the order, somewhere in Ireland, and that he did run afoul of his order. I cannot be certain, but I do believe that he resided here in an escape from his former life."

"I see," said Father Henri. "And would his being killed have anything to do with his former profession?"

"Oh, I believe that is very likely, indeed. I have no proof as of yet, but it makes sense of his pitiful, lonely life. Now, Jimmy, can you see? Is the man still out there, across the way?"

"Aye, m'lord, he is still there."

"That is good. Now, can I help you in any way, Father?"

"Nay, Master Craycroft, we shall do what we must." The Father then lit his incense while the monks gathered up Leroy, placed him on a stretcher, and then, with an appropriate show of ostentation, began their journey across the plaza to the priory. Father Henri was leading the way with his incense wafting across the plaza toward the man who watched the procession with avid interest.

"Well, let us hope," said Craycroft, with nods from Judy and Bob.

Falma welcomed Judy and Bob warmly into his alchemist shop.

"Oh, do come in, my good friends. And this weather, it must truly end sometime in our lifetime."

Judy gave the old man a hug while Bob looked around, amazed by all he saw.

"Now the sign on the door says you're an alchemist, but tell me, you do much more than look for ways to produce gold from lead, don't you?"

"Oh, I gave up on that pursuit many years ago, for that produced nothing in the way of results. No, my main purpose has been to discover compounds of much greater use. For example, the medicine for pain that you used on Master Cairn, how did that work?"

"Like magic," said Bob. "It was really effective. I am truly amazed at all of this work in the fifteenth century. You know, I wonder what happened, because I have heard nothing about Shepperton, nothing about Craycroft or Cartho, or anyone here.

It's like you've got this great little medical miracle brewing here, but nothing in the history books."

"Ah, well, if you will let me digress my good friends, I do believe that is part of why you may be here right now."

"What…what can you possibly mean?

"Come in, have a seat by my fireside and we'll chat." He led the way back to his study, down the hallway—with all the strange odors—to his little, but comfortable study. "Melchior is out, seeking some papers at the registrar's office. I believe you know what that is about."

"Yes, that would be in regard to Tom's parentage, I think."

"Precisely. Please come in and sit down. Here, let me clear some of this clutter." He picked up a stack of papers that were lying abandoned on a chair. Then Judy and Bob sat down. Next, he took one of the fireplace instruments, adjusted the logs in his fireplace, and then sat down himself.

"Well now, let me explain a little of our circumstance from a slightly different perspective than either of you have heard so far. You may or may not have heard, but for the earl, I have acted as loremaster for many years. This is a singular position on this isle, and one created many years ago by none other than Drachma."

"Somehow I knew that he was behind this," said Judy. "He always seems to be in the thick of these things."

"Doesn't he now?" Falma just chuckled. "In any event, when we were but youths upon the isle, before the present earl was in power, Drachma was constrained to leave this isle under what were less than ideal circumstances. You might have guessed that they involved the Lady Felicia—then Felicia the daughter of the ambassador, before her 'resurrection' in the eyes of her adoring public. Before he fled the isle, however, Drachma met with the earl and with Ambassador Gianni (Felicia's father), and set up my present office of loremaster, and, as is true of most of Drachma's doings, this was not an official post, but rather, one of true value. He then contacted me as I was a young and, shall we say, a

somewhat gullible alchemist, just starting up in this trade. Why he chose me, I shall never know, but he told me that I should keep up appearances as an alchemist, but that I would become the 'repository of great and fearsome knowledge.' Now, this had tremendous appeal to my youthful imagination."

"So, while Drachma was away from the isle, he told me of his circumstances as to the Lady Felicia, their unborn child, and her needs. He also would send me books and papers that he held in high esteem, and he encouraged me to read them as I was able. It was also around this time that I got to know Master Cartho, of whom you have heard from Craycroft. Under Master Cartho's supervision, I began to experiment with compounding, not seeking the gold of alchemists of yore, but the true gold of medicines that would prove useful for the ill and suffering. Master Cartho died some forty years ago, if I recall correctly, and the old earl shortly thereafter, but my position remained with the new earl, and Master Craycroft has taken up where Master Cartho left off."

"Wow, Mr. Falma, I thought that you were much more than just a fine man with a real way with the ladies," said Judy. "It's good to hear your side of this tale."

"Ah, my dear lady, would that it were so; for you see, I, too, remain unmarried, as does Craycroft, and I believe that we both have one to thank for that. For now, as Lady Felicia returned from her 'exile' in Killiburn, she found that her family were taken away in an accident at sea; all but one elder brother. Now I did help her through this troubled time with the encouragement of Drachma, and I helped in setting her up with a 'new' identity as Felicia Vincente. One of the things that I did, as she was as voracious a reader as I, was to set up in her home the library that now exists with many rare and wonderful volumes. In fact, if I did receive a volume of true merit, it went to her library, rather than my own here, as I would not wish for anything to happen to

those books should we, in the occasional pursuit of chemicals for our own purposes, have an accident, if you know what I mean."

"Ah, yes," said Bob, "I do know exactly what you mean."

"As you may imagine, over the years, we formed a true friendship that included Craycroft, Drachma, the earl, as well as Felicia's adoptive father Carlo Vincente, and Felicia herself. In fact, it has been said that our little group of friends did, in fact, rule this isle for good or ill.

"And now, that brings me around to your own lives and how they have come to interact with ours. Several things have happened within this past year that have led to this point. Let me explain. For one thing, there has been this illness that began killing off our beloved painters and potters, and, as you know by now, that represents the true livelihood of many persons on this island. It is the reason that we have been left alone by the meddlesome forces of the king's men. Then there has been the illness of Lady Felicia (may she rest with the saints), and of the earl. And I, incidentally, do not believe that both illnesses are the same; that is, the illness which affected our painters and potters, I see as different from that which has now afflicted our lady and our earl. Which now brings us to the crux of this matter. For you see, there is a real threat that the king's forces might just seek to take over the island's activities. And what that would mean would be extermination of all that Drachma, Cartho, Craycroft, Felicia, Carlo Vincente, and I have given our lives to develop and to pursue."

"How can you be sure? I mean, here you have real medicine and real treatment and real learning. How do you know that it would be threatened?" Bob asked.

"Ah, Master Robert, I think you have answered that yourself. For did you not say that you had not heard of Shepperton, Cartho, Craycroft, or Drachma?"

"My God, I did… Now this has staggering implications… Just let me think this through." Bob suddenly looked pale, like he had when he heard that Josh had died.

Judy reached out her hand and found Bob's. "You know you're not alone, don't you?"

Bob just sat for a minute, holding Judy's hand, as his thoughts were tumbling about in his mind. Finally, he seemed to relax, and, as he did, he smiled.

"You know how when you're growing up, you keep wanting to do something or to be something significant? Well, Judy, I do believe we've been given our opportunity. I've been sensing that there was something more, something compelling, something driving this whole thing."

Then, with a flash of intuition, Bob remembered something Craycroft had said.

"The book! This has got to involve the book."

"Ah, m'lady, you are not the only one who sees clearly through the haze."

There was a rapping at the door. Falma excused himself and went to the door to see who it was. He came back, and with a twinkle in his eye, said, "It is a messenger from Craycroft. He wants the three of us, as well as Melchior, to come to his abode anon. I am not certain of his reasons, but I suspect that this could be something of significance."

Chapter Four

Antoine LeGace left the plaza after the procession went through the muddy, rain-swept plaza. His interest in the activities in Sick Bay suddenly waned after he could see that the councilor had died and was being taken by the priests back to the sanctuary of the priory. He knew that Councilor Genet lived out of town, and it might be a while before arrangements would be completed for burial. He had work to do, and he knew it. His constituency would be eager to hear of his activities. He then pulled his overcoat around himself, as the rain came down mercilessly. He thought about stopping at Barncuddy's, then thought better of it; after all, he didn't pay the last time he was there. So he went on past the keep and toward the main gates of the castle. There was a small cluster of people at the gate, including several of the usual urchins, who fled the scene as he approached. He paid little attention to them as he went on down the road toward the village. There, he bought some bread at the baker's, along with a pitcher of ale, and took them back to his room up the stairs.

Inside his room, he took out his notebook, found his ink and quill, and then recorded in his notebook:

> January, the sixteenth, year one thousand four hundred ninety-two.

I observed from my spot across the plaza that the Councilman has now apparently died. The priest and his brother monks took him back to the priory. I do not think he will be troubling us anymore.

As to the other man, I would not be too concerned, as he was seen to be no more than a peddler. Whether he lives or dies, it is of little consequence to me now. But that one needed to be exterminated, according to our custom.

A. LeGace, court of Byzantium, third prefect

He then closed the notebook and ate his bread in silence. He then took some ale from the pitcher and drank a glass full, noting that it was not the fresh ale that Barncuddy was serving, but it did relieve his thirst.

Again, he hadn't noticed the two urchins who had observed his steps, and who took careful notice of where he was staying.

Melchior had been at work in the registrar's office, getting little help from the old, shriveled man behind the desk. After a number of fruitless searches, he did find a notation in one ledger that indicated that the Lady Felicia had been taking sums of money from her father's account, to be sent to Killiburn via courier, apparently coinciding with the time Maggie had been under Angelica's care.

So, when the page came to the door and told him that Craycroft wanted to see him, along with Master Falma, Master Robert, and the Lady Judy, it was something of a relief. He hurriedly noted down just where those monies came from, put his papers in the satchel, thanked the registrar (who rather disdainfully took the ledger and put it back), and then bundled up and headed out into the cold, stinging rain toward the keep.

As Russ took him up the stairs to the chambers of the earl, Melchior thought he could hear some of the pages' whispered comments about the man with the cane. They went on down the hallway, then turned into the stairway, ascended the stairs, and came out into another hallway—this time, much more lavishly appointed. Russ led him on down past a couple of rooms, then turned into the same room where they had eaten just last evening.

"Ah, Melchior, welcome," said Craycroft.

Melchior looked about the room and noticed that Craycroft, Judy, Robert, and Falma were there, as well as Kerlin, Eustace, Cayman, and Jeanne. But there was a new person present.

"Now, Melchior, this is Guardsman Ervin of the elite guard, or Drachma's army. He has been riding here to bring us some news, as well as some artifacts, am I not right, Master Ervin?"

"Most assuredly, m'lord," answered Ervin.

"Now, if you could tell us the message from Drachma. Mind you, these are my trusted allies and you may speak freely."

"Firstly, let me tell you how glad Drachma is to know that the Lady Judy and Falma are now safe. And he does wish to extend his personal apologies for their tension-filled journey, and best wishes for their continued welfare."

Falma nodded as Judy smiled. "I am unable to speak for m'lady, but let me tell thee that I am grateful to be back here. It was not a journey that I would care to make again, except as a final one," Falma commented.

"And I, for one, am grateful that he is back," added Melchior.

"M'lord," Ervin went on, "as it was, Master Falma, as well as m'lady, were captured by Master Finch, whom we all know to be a mercenary. Now, we did find out that he was acting on orders from Councilor Reordan. We do not know with certainty just what the councilor was going to do with them, but rest assured that Master Finch has paid for doing what he did, and his band of mercenaries has had to learn a hard lesson."

"I would assume that Master Finch is no longer a threat, then?"

"Nay, he is no longer any threat to anyone."

"I see."

"Now, further, Drachma does wish for ye to proceed with the plans laid out by the Lady Felicia and the earl. Also, he plans to come here sometime next week, though I am unable to say when that should be."

"And I assume it will be in his usual way, with his usual lack of fanfare…"

"But of course."

"Now, m'lady. I do know that you have met Drachma, at least several times. But you, Master Robert, have not. Is that correct?" Craycoft asked.

"You could say that I have come thus far without meeting him in the flesh, but that is not the real story. For I did, in fact, meet him before I ever got here. You see, on the day I came here, I was kind of tired, half-awake, in the hospital back home. The first time was in a state that I think falls somewhere between wakefulness and sleep, and I found myself wandering in some deep woods in springtime. I was walking, but suddenly I heard someone speaking, so I turned and there he was, wearing his gray cloak, with his voice that you could not forget and that look in his eyes that said, 'I am he.' And then, just before I came here, he was there again in the hospital room, telling me that it was time. So, even though I may not have met him in the usual sense, I have seen him, and I would have no trouble recognizing him at all."

"Very well, Master Robert. It would seem that our Drachma had been making himself quite busy with your arrival. Yours and the lady's, eh?"

"Yeah, it seems that way."

Jeanne then added, rather unexpectedly, "It would seem to me that Drachma did know of Master Robert and our lady's presence before any of us here, or even there, knew what was to transpire. It seems a mystery to me. How and why did he seek both of you out, and to what purpose?"

"Well, Jeanne, it seems that there is more to this story every time I turn around, and I'm just learning of some of the purposes that this fellow had in mind. I don't know, though, how he knew us or picked us out of the universe of physicians and nurses, or that this is a permanent thing; but it's looking more and more like it probably is."

"Indeed, Master Robert," said Craycroft, who could not keep the note of resignation out of his voice. "Now, my good Master Ervin, you told me that you also have some artifacts that you brought with you."

"Aye, that I have. Let me get them out of me satchel. Here is the first, and it comes with a letter from Master Tom."

"Tom?"

"Aye."

Craycroft immediately recognized the book from its binding, and he was stunned.

"Is that what I think it is? Here, let me see that. I fear that you have no knowledge of what that book contains. Here, at last, Master Robert, is the volume of Cartho's that he talked of, but it was lost. Lost, until now.

Craycroft then turned to Bob and said, "Come hence, my friend, and you shall see why you have been summoned."

"But there is also this letter." Ervin reached back into his satchel and brought out the folded letter with the red seal.

"Let me see the letter. You say it is from Tom?"

He handed him the letter.

Craycroft looked at the folded paper and the red wax seal. Then a smile appeared on his face.

"Now I have seen this seal before. My good friend, I would ask you if you recognize this seal?" He passed the envelope down to Falma.

Falma picked up the letter, looked at the seal, felt it, and then looked at Craycroft.

"You know, my friend, that this brings back memories too powerful for words."

"Aye, that I know. Now, you may open the letter. I fell certain that it contains something of value."

Falma carefully opened the letter, preserving the wax seal, and then he looked at what was written and handed it back to Craycroft. He also looked down at the neatly written script, and then was silent as Craycroft read the letter aloud.

My Dear Master Craycroft,

As thou knowest, I am at Drachma's place, here in the forest. I have made some unusual discoveries here in Drachma's house, and, most particularly, as to the presence of one whom I, of course, do not remember, but the aura of my own mother, Maggie 'o' Killiburn, is exceedingly strong. In her room there be a most astounding library, with many volumes, only some of which I am able to read.

Of particular interest to thee, I suppose, is one volume by someone named Cartho, about whom I assume thou art more familiar than I. It is a book, mostly of a medical nature. Within the book there be a chapter, which he entitled, "What We Know of the Plague of Shepperton," which I have marked for thee.

I am certain that thou shalt find it of interest, as I did as well. Of particular note is that Angelica, who watches Drachma's house, knows of this stream of which he speaks in his book.

With kindest regards,
Drachma, known to thee as Tom.

Bob, who had been watching all of this, let out a low whistle. He then spoke. "Now you're going to have to tell me about this plague of Shepperton. And I can see that I'm going to have to

study this fellow Cartho's writing, for I think that he may have the potential to turn the world of medicine upside down."

"It is not without hope that we shall be doing, what you say, 'turning the world of medicine upside down.' But I would advise caution, as many of the king's men would be upset mightily by our doing just what you say."

"I see," replied Bob. Then he thought about how the world of medicine had not always thought well of those that wanted to change what was traditional. "I was thinking of Spallanzani and his trials, and how his ideas were regarded as heresy."

"Ah, then you do know, indeed, what challenges we shall face. I welcome you to my world, my fellow heretic. Come, let us look at what our friend Tom has marked, for I feel that if he found it interesting, that you and I might also."

So Bob moved next to Craycroft and the two of them started reading Cartho's description of the illness that was called the plague of Shepperton, and while Bob read on as to how he found a common source for the illness, Craycroft, remembering his loss, buried his face in his hands.

"It's truly amazing. This is an extraordinarily accurate description of what the earl is suffering from. I am really amazed," Bob commented.

"And to think that this is also a description of the Lady Felicia's illness. Oh, I now feel her loss ever more. If only…"

"Pardon my interruption," said Ervin, "but I also have this sample of water from the creek called the Creek of the Dead. I cannot think how that might be of use to ye, but it is certainly of no use to me. In fact, it does make me just a little uncomfortable to be carryin' this around."

He brought out the small jar of water and laid it on the table. Jeanne and Melchior both backed off a little. Falma, though, smiled. As the others stared, he reached across the table, took the lid off, and smelled the water. Then he put the lid back on the jar and handed over to Melchior.

"Now, my friends, you may wonder why I did such a thing. To answer you, I think a little lesson in our history would be appropriate. Now, I am probably the only one here old enough to remember the significance of this creek and this water.

"Back in my youth, which was spent mainly on the interior of this island, we got to know that there were certain creeks, streams, and rivers that we were told by the older ones on the isle that were not to be entered, and certain ones that could only be entered safely at certain times."

He then asked if he could have some paper and writing material. Craycroft found him a sheet of paper, and while his page went in search of a quill and some ink, Bob reached into his satchel and pulled out a pen. He handed it to Falma.

"Here, try this," he said. "I think you might like it."

Falma took the ballpoint pen, studied it, and then asked, "What is this St. Jude thing that is written on your instrument?"

"Oh, that? That's the name of a company that manufactures artificial heart valves…"

"Artificial heart valves? I can see that you are going to have to educate me sometime about this. Now, what do I do with this?"

By now, they were all straining to see this marvelous thing that Master Robert had pulled out of his satchel. He instructed Falma to just pull the cap off and then start writing. Falma did just that, and to the utter amazement of everyone there, there was a line of ink flowing from the tip of this instrument. Bob and Judy just smiled at each other while the others in the room were standing around, agape at this most incredible invention.

"This is most amazing, for you have within your little bag all that you would need to communicate with any and all persons, and not have to carry around ink and quills. Now let me ask you, how long can one write with this instrument?"

"Without refills, you could probably write a hundred pages or more. That's just a guess."

"Oh, my… Here, let me pass this instrument around so all can see its marvelous manufacture."

The pen created quite a sensation, and Bob was reminded of the events with his beeper and penlight on the way here—things that he took for granted, but were truly beyond the imagining of these folks in this time. It also reminded him of something he read some time ago about how, when science reaches beyond people's ability to comprehend it, it becomes indistinguishable from magic.

Eventually, the furor over his ballpoint pen subsided, and the room returned to its state of anticipation. Falma was again able to resume his talk. First, he drew a map of the island.

"And here be Croftus Knob, and Lough Teagle at its base, and from it there come the three main rivers that feed the island. Now here is where our potters get their clay for our pots." He indicated a place between the two arms of the lake. "And it is from here that the streams run that I shall tell you about.

"Now, if you follow this one stream, you shall see that it runs off to the east and then turns back and joins up with two more streams, but before it does, one of its branches just seems to disappear into the ground and comes out here, on the far side of the east ridge of Croftus Knob. Now it has been said that there were times when these waters were harmless, and times when they have been deadly. Now, as to the other streams from this same source, the most that could be said of their waters was that they would cause a rash where the person would bathe in the waters; and, further, that the streams and creeks from the one source were called red creeks while the other were called blue creeks. But the one creek that ran underground has been called the Creek of the Dead, and it has been shunned by most because it contains no life and has a most unpleasant odor. Am I right, Master Ervin?"

"Oh, aye, m'lord. That would be the truth. And it is from that creek that I brought this water."

"Now, why have we not heard of this creek, or these creeks?" asked Jeanne.

"As a youth, I did hear often of theses stories, but as I got older, I rarely heard of them anymore. I think it was because the waters seemed to cause less offense, for reasons that I know not. Or it may be that the people have become less susceptible to the influence of the waters."

All this talk of the waters coming from this mountain lake with its powerful effects got Bob thinking. He got to thinking about what he had read, heard, and seen about water-borne infections. Most, it seems, had to do with sewage and waste in the water, which did not seem to apply here. And what, if anything, did this have to do with the earl's illness? Perhaps nothing, but something kept nagging at him, telling him that he was perhaps onto something.

"Now, Judy," he said, "Why don't you read this thing by Cartho and offer your opinion on it? I would really like to know what you think."

"Okay, but you have to realize that I'm just a nurse, and my opinion is not likely to influence you."

"Oh, come on, that line might have worked six years ago when I was just getting to know you, working in the ICU; but not now. Judy, I highly value your opinion and you know it."

"Well, since you put it that way…" She smiled at Bob. "Okay, let me see what all this fuss is about."

She read Cartho's text with increasing interest, as Craycroft looked on with a bemused expression. Finally, she looked up from the page. Her expression suddenly changed. She looked straight at Craycroft and said, "Now, this Master Cartho was your teacher, right? What did you hear about this? Surely you must recall something."

"Indeed, he was my teacher and mentor. I was his apprentice. Before he died, he told me of another volume that he had written 'for another time,' and said that it would be found when it was

needed. I asked him about it, but that is all he would tell me except the title, which he called, 'Anathema.' He said that I would understand when it was discovered. Now, if you would look at the title page, I think you will find that it is correct that this volume is called Anathema."

Judy then opened the volume to the title page and read:

Anathema

a book by

Cartho

Written upon this season of spring

In the Year of our Lord

One Thousand Four Hundred Forty Three

"Now, you haven't seen this title page before this, have you?"

"Nay, my dear, I have not."

"And yet you knew…"

"Aye, that I did. And let me explain a little about this book and why it is called what it is.

"While Cartho was yet alive, he did investigate many illnesses and deaths, and as he became older, he gradually came to the conclusion that the 'fathers of medicine' from years ago had gotten it all wrong. He could find no evidence of unbalanced humors or bad air, or even bad living, and, further, he noted no efficacy in the recommended therapies tried over time, such as bleeding, purging, and other attempts to reestablish the proper balance of bodily humors. He expressed dismay to me over these greats of medicine and their blind reliance on the word of masters, discounting the simple observations to be made by looking, listening, and good note taking. As always, he thought of his discoveries as likely to be thought of as anathema, and so, fittingly, he would call his last work "Anathema." Then, he

mentioned to me, as he was in his last illness later in the year one thousand, four hundred and forty-three, that he had discovered something about a plague of Shepperton that might shed some light as to the cause of one mysterious illness. Though I begged him to show me what he found out, he simply told me to keep on observing and noting, and that in due time it would be Drachma's own grandson who would provide the key to understanding."

One could have breathed the stillness in that room. No one moved, as all attention was centered on Craycroft.

"And now, with this plague unleashed upon our beloved Lady Felicia, and our earl, and your fortuitous arrival on our isle, m'lady and Master Robert, it would seem that the time is definitely right."

Chapter Five

Kerlin had remained quiet during the whole scene—with the message and the items brought by Ervin—but now he was again feeling the burden of responsibility. For this was sure to be a turbulent time ahead. He turned toward his companions, Eustace, Cayman, and Ervin, and asked if any one of them understood what was happening in that room.

"All I know," said Ervin, "is that I came here to deliver some news and some goods to this fellow Craycroft, and what I'll be takin' back with me is the impression that my delivery is setting off something much bigger. It's kind of like bringin' a small torch and watchin' it set a whole field afire."

"Aye, I was thinking much the same way. And I was also thinking that whatever this new healer uncovers, it'll take all our wit and wiles to keep it from the king's men, for you know that it shall be enormous and we shall be part of it," Kerlin agreed.

"What I would like," said Eustace unexpectedly, "is one of those magic quills with its own ink. That was truly something amazing. Something I'll ne'er forget."

"Truly, it was," agreed Cayman. "And what was it that it said on the quill? Was it St. Jude?"

"Aye, I think it was St. Jude, patron saint of the hopeless; interesting."

"Now how would ye know that?" asked Cayman.

"I learned it from me mum?"

"Your mum; you mean Diane?"

"None other."

"Hmm. There is more to yer mum than meets the eye, m'lad. Next time I see her, I'll have to ask her about what she knows of the saints." Cayman said this, all the time thinking of just how he was going to meet her, perhaps privately, perhaps as a way of communicating with her son.

"Well, m'lads, we are here." Kerlin indicated their arrival at the constabulary. "The weather is still too foul for any riding to be done, so why not come in by the fire and have some bread and cheese, and we'll talk about what's to be done."

When he opened the door and stepped in, he noticed that people inside were all abuzz about something.

"Ah, here be Kerlin. He can answer the question. Can't ye?" asked Blodwen.

"Most assuredly, but can I answer it correctly? That would be the real question, now wouldn't it, Blodwen? And what is this question that is burning in your mind?"

"Well, me mates here want to know, did this Master Robert use his magic to cure Master Cairn and Councilor Genet?"

"And what, may I ask, led to this line of inquiry? Would you be referring to his watchful waiting of Councilor Genet's condition, or to the intervention that he performed on Cairn? For I'll tell you that it was his skill as a healer and not his magic that led to the successful work on both those persons. Now if you want to talk of magic, then you should talk to young Eustace here as to what he observed."

"Er, me, Master? I can only recount what I saw. And what I saw was that Master Robert and Lady Judy performed some rite upon Cairn, during which he produced a whole tub full of vile pus and blood. It was rather astounding, as Cairn seemed to feel none of the pain. And when I was ready to leave the Sick Bay, he was looking and talking as if nothing had happened. Now, as to

the councilor, I should say that he seemed none too bad for one who had been hit upon the head…"

"Now, I should say to all here," Kerlin interrupted, "that none of us are to talk of the councilor outside of these walls. Is that clear? Good…I see that you are in agreement."

"Might I ask why not?"

"Let me just say this one time. I have been told by Craycroft not to speak of this matter to anyone not intimately involved in his care. Now, what his reasons may be are mysterious, but I have given my word, is that not right, Cayman?"

"Aye, that be the truth."

"Good, then, is that understood?"

There were somber faces nodding in agreement.

"Well then, m'lads, let us get out of this drafty hallway and let us sit down and we shall talk some more."

The group then reassembled in the sitting room with the roaring fire in the fireplace and comfortable chairs all around.

"Oh, here ye be, Cayman, ye did receive this message by pigeon post just now." Blodwen handed him the little cylinder.

Cayman opened the small tube and brought out a yellow piece of paper. He looked down at the small paper, and then showed it to Kerlin. On it was written:

> To Cayman, now captain.
>
> Extend to Kerlin and to Proust this message:
>
> Have an estimate of strength and numbers of forces, as well as location of said forces, being subject to Reordan. I shall talk more when I see them.
>
> Drachma

"As usual, Drachma implies more than he states. Now where are Martin and Stoneheft? Somehow I knew they would be most useful to me. Proust, have you any idea where they are?"

"Nay, my friend, I know not where they are, but I do know that they will check with me before they go anywhere outside of the castle area."

"I know that they were planning to see where this Councilor Reordan lived. Perhaps they're visiting with the councilor himself right now," added Dowdell with a chuckle.

"Let us hope not. Now, in light of this, what do you propose we do? And how many men do we have to get the information that Drachma requests?"

"Beside Martin and Stoneheft, I have three that can ride out, talk to the villages, and get what information they can. What of your former allies? Can any of them obtain any useful information?"

"That would be information that Drachma himself would have at his disposal, so I think no. Though I can send him a post to suggest that."

"Very well. Let us do that. Cayman, I shall leave that task to you."

"Aye, that, my commandant, is that yer wish as well?" Cayman replied.

This made Eustace laugh.

"And thee, my assistant, what do you think we should do? Is this the sort of information you think you would be able to obtain? How about the street urchins? What do they do besides lurk about, getting underway and causing trouble?"

"In my experience, they have quite a band whose main purpose would be the gathering of information that may be sold to whomever is paying them, and sometimes that information is useful, much of it is not. But as to the veracity of the information, ye may guess, as it depends on many factors, most especially who is paying."

"Are you saying that you may obtain information, but whether that information is useful depends on how much one is willing to pay?"

"Not entirely. For they do have certain favorites, and certain, shall we say, dislikes. So that if, say, Reordan were to pay three

pennies, and Blodwen here were to pay just two pennies, I should say that they would provide more reliable, less-colored information to Blodwen, as he is definitely the more favored—not that they might not provide information to both."

"Hmm, I see. Blodwen, did you know of this?

"Nay, this is the first that I had heard of this. I must say, this makes the game more interesting. Indeed, it does," Blodwen replied.

"Let me ask you, can you find out any information that this band of street urchins is obtaining and let us know of it?"

"I do suppose I could, but at my own peril," Eustace answered with a note of caution.

"Please explain."

"Well, ye see. Among the fellas, there be a pact, of sorts, that if any one of them were to join up with any of the *outsides* (that'd be what we call ye), then that one is to be shunned, and never to be trusted again."

"And what do you call yourselves, this band of young ones that you refer to?"

"We're called the Druids on this part of the isle."

"And let me ask you, if one of you Druids were to become a page and begin working for the earl or one of the lords, would this be considered joining up with the *outsides*?"

"Aye, with exceptions."

"Oh? And what might they be?"

"Why, Tom and me. We have been able to work as pages and still be Druids, but we be the only ones."

"Very interesting, my young assistant."

Melchior sat down as Bob looked about the place, amazed by all the peculiar shapes of the glassware, all the stoppered vials, and the strange odors. Falma had gone with Craycroft to seek

out Rust to see how the council was doing, and if there were any leaks. Judy had gone with Jeanne to see to the preparations for dinner, as well as to check once more on the folks in Sick Bay.

The time was quiet, with no one talking, telling tales, or expecting anything of him. And Bob found himself enjoying the quiet, exploring the laboratory of this ancient alchemist who seemed to be so much more than that. He was both puzzled and intrigued by what this Master Falma had been able to accomplish, knowing so little of modern chemistry. And now, with this latest round of revelations about what he was doing here, he needed time to think things through. And just how much did Drachma know?

Melchior, too, was enjoying the quiet in which he thrived. He had figured out already what Falma wanted him to do with the water, and he knew that with Robert's assistance, he could succeed; but he was not certain of the next step. So, while Bob was wandering around, looking at all the laboratory glassware and looking like he himself was enjoying the quiet, Melchior was busy looking up things in Falma's journals. He paged through descriptions of condensers and coils used in refining salt from seawater, as well as from human urine. He looked through the passages describing how to purify sheep blood, so as to keep it from rotting. Then he stumbled upon a description of using the purified sheep's blood as an agent to tell if an individual was likely to die of his wounds. This was buried in a chapter that was devoted mainly to the preparation of poultices and salves for soldiers in times of warfare.

Finally, Melchior broke the silence.

"Ah, Master Robert, here I've found something that may be useful."

Bob was startled out of his reverie.

"Oh, I'm sorry. I was just in my own world here. Now, what was it you've got?"

"If you look upon this, what I have may be of some interest to thee."

Bob came over to look over Melchior's shoulder and began reading where he pointed. He read silently, with growing interest about what was on the page. He remembered something from medical school about sheep's blood used in agar for cultures.

"What do you think? And are you thinking what I'm thinking? Could we obtain some sheep blood? And how about something to act as thickener, such as seaweed?" Bob asked, his own mind now racing.

"Ah, I see that you are certainly thinking much the same kind of thoughts as I. Now, I do not know if this shall bring success or not, but do you not think it is worth a try? As to obtaining some sheep's blood, I think that shall be little problem."

"Well, I see nothing to be gained by just waiting around. Let's get us some of the ingredients and get to work. What do you say?"

Now, after dinner, Tom was left alone again. He was in his mother's room with a small, cozy fire in the fireplace. As he sat down, he reached for the little, gray volume that he had been trying not to read. He opened the little book, and again read the title page.

Of Powers and Dangers Learned in Eastern Lands

Notes taken for the benefit of any who may be in great need.

Drachma, the elder.

Then he turned the page and read again that fearsome preface.

Be warned, ye who venture to read these lines, for there is much power of which we have little knowledge and even less control. To summon forth the fearsome powers that exist within the stuff of life, and within the Earth and

heavens, even in the times of direst need, is to put one's very soul at the mercy of powers and principalities beyond reach of human hands and human reason. Nevertheless, I endeavor, as I must, to record for the future generations of the Earth what I have learned of these awful forces, and how they may be sensed and perhaps called upon when the need is truly great.

Be further warned that knowledge contained herein is more precious than purest gold. The powerful of the Earth can and will sense the threat that this knowledge carries. If ye read no further, and replace this whence it came, ye may return to life, as always, free of this danger.

This, then, is the final warning. Turn the page, and all shall be for the reader as never before. Ye can never return!

He then remembered why he had been afraid to read the book, for he was still not certain that he was ready. But now, here in the safety of Drachma's house, in his mother's library, he felt an unreasoning push toward the future of which he now felt a small part. And so, with tremulous fingers, he turned the page.

Part One, Sensing the Great Powers within and around Thee

Now, having read of the warnings in the preface, let me first tell thee, good reader, that thou art embarking upon a journey—one that shall take thee from thy world and its sense of safety and belonging, toward a future that shall have even more promise and danger than thou canst imagine. The first place I would take thee is right where thou art, but to see and to sense everything around thee in a new light.

There are powers at work, even in the common things of thy existence. Consider the common stones that thou hast handled many a time. By themselves, they have no

power, nor the will to change, but they do have within themselves the power to create and to destroy. When power is transferred to the common stones, they can become instruments of power, either as the sustaining power in building or the destroying power when hurled from a catapult. And consider the power of fire, which, when dormant within an unlit torch, assumes the power to heat our homes, cook our meals, or to destroy everything within its reach. We do, you see, have some innate sense that there are things all around us with power to perform both good and evil things. Now where does that power reside? It resides in everything.

To sense the extraordinary powers contained within ordinary things, I would have you do something now. Find something ordinary, such as a quill. Look at it. Think about whence it came, what purpose it served, and what power lay within it. Now look at it again; think about what its purpose has become, but also realize that it, in itself, does not have the power to do anything.

Now, take the quill in thy hand and find a piece of writing paper and some ink.

Tom searched and found the quill and some writing paper and ink. He looked at the quill, which was from a sea eagle. He contemplated where it came from, as well as its purpose, and its present inertia.

Then, taking quill in hand and the sheet of paper, write down upon the paper the name of the person that thou didst last harm.

Tom thought about this. He thought and then wrote down the name:

Eustace

Next to the name of the person, write down your offence, and what thou canst do to make amends.

Eustace. I did keep from thee the penny I promised I would give thee for the information that made me page to Master Craycroft. I now know that I did wrong by thee. Here is thy penny, and with it I give to thee my position as page to Master Craycroft.

I do wish thee the best.

Tom

Now, dear reader, I wish thee to consider what all this represents. I have shown thee that there is more power within the simplest things than within the larger, more typically powerful workings of mankind. And now, I wish to tell thee of further sources of power that are available to thee.

Next, consider the power within common plants. And I point thee toward the commonest of plants, the grasses of the fields. Rarely would one consider such a thing as containing any power at all, but then consider the great coursers and field horses around thee. And where do they get their power, but from the grasses of the field? As anyone who tends horses knows, even the greatest of these is dependent upon a steady supply of grass in order to function.

And even dry, lifeless grass has the power to burn anything in its path. That power resides within the grass itself, and one may not take it away without converting its power into some other power; such as the power of a racing horse or the burning of fields.

Then there is the wind. Normally one would not consider the air around us as having any power at all, but to sailors who depend upon winds for their power do not take the air for granted, nor do those in a gale consider the air to be powerless.

So, ye can see that there is power to be contained within everything, and everything that exists contains much more than would be obvious. Further, I shall show thee how this power may be sought out and used if one is willing to accept the consequences, for there is grave risk in the invoking of these great powers.

Now, consider again the consequences of the first exercise that I had thee perform. I know that thou hast done what I asked of thee. That power to alter the course of human endeavors has always been with thee. It was similar to the powers of stones and grass, but, by doing the thing which I suggested, thou has set into motion a chain of events over which thou hast little control, but which thou knowest was right, was good, and not evil. This is the essence of what I am to teach thee. The need that I shall speak of later in this book is dependent upon a clear understanding of this concept of good and evil.

Tom shuddered ever so slightly as he read these words, written by his grandfather years ago. How did he know that Tom would do the thing that he asked of him? Perhaps the answer lay within the book, and so he turned the page and kept reading.

He read on in the book and he became more and more entranced in his reading. The minutes became hours, as he read

of Drachma's travels to eastern lands and to the Isle of Patmos where Drachma was finally able to distill all the knowledge that he had obtained in order to write all this down.

He failed to notice that he was no longer alone, that there was someone else in the room; someone who was tending to the fire that was dying. As he read on, he was becoming someone else as well. Someone who mattered and made a difference.

Finally, the other person in the room spoke.

"Now, Tom, you're to be more careful of where you put that book in the future."

Tom was startled out of his reverie.

"Oh, Drachma, it is you, indeed! I've just been reading…"

"Ah, I know what you have been reading." Drachma grasped his glass of wine and sat down next to his grandson. "And I think that I know why, though you may only partly understand it now."

"It is good to see you. Now, what can you tell me of doings in the wide world of Shepperton?"

"What I can tell you is that it appears to be time for you to be heading back to the earl's castle tomorrow. This time I shall be accompanying you, along with my guards, and I think that it is time to return the book whence it came, to Felicia's library. And I also think it time that when you do get back to the castle, that you should meet your new adoptive father. And when you do, you should ask him about another book that was the origin of that book that you are reading…"

"Wait, you said my new adoptive father…"

"Aye, that would be Craycroft."

"Craycroft? But then…how…does he even know?"

"Aye, that he does now."

Tom was silent, letting all of this sink in. He simply stared into the fireplace. He just sat there with a blank expression for several minutes as Drachma sipped his wine, saying nothing. Eventually, he turned toward his grandfather and asked him if he was responsible for bringing Master Robert to the island.

Drachma then took a few seconds to answer, as he himself stared into the fireplace, and then he spoke, "It was I, but there were others involved…"

"Let me guess, there were also Master Falma, the Lady Felicia, and Carlo Vincente."

"That was more than a guess, was it not?"

"Oh, aye. That was certainly more than a simple guess."

"Well then, Drachma the younger, you and I shall have much to discuss on the way back to the earl's castle upon the morrow. Why not then finish your reading, for I see that you are nearly done with my book? I shall leave you now and prepare for yet another journey. We shall be leaving early, before sunrise."

Chapter Six

Judy and Jeanne were having a wonderful afternoon. With the men away, they were left to themselves, and they were making the most of their opportunity. Judy took Jeanne over to the Sick Bay to check on Cairn, where she inspected his surgical site and changed his dressing. And next, she found herself getting caught up in conversation with Councilor Genet.

Obviously recovered from his head injury, he regaled the two women with tales of the doings of the council. As a councilor, he had at first been timid, but as he got to know the council, he came to realize that he would never become a friend of either Councilor Reordan or Silvo. Coming as he did from the other side of the island, beyond even the reaches of the marshland, it took him a couple of years to see that those who lived close to the castle were soon subjugated to the will of Reordan; and often by less than scrupulous means.

A notable exception had been Councilor Rust, who seemed aloof and distant, but who could ever be relied upon to act as his own man. Though not always in agreement with the earl's recommendations, he was never one to back down from a disagreement, and he was often alone in his opposition to the majority opinion. A couple of the others on the council seemed reasonable, namely Councilors Donovan and Fitzgibbon; but as often as not, their votes were with the majority.

And now, with this latest wave of bad news about the painters and potters, and still more, the monumental appearance of Craycroft in their midst, he found himself squarely in camp with Rust and against Reordan and his allies. The councilor next told them of his own ordeal, the loss of that very important paper, and how it now seemed as if they were fighting an uphill battle.

"I know," said Judy. "If it's any help, I do know that Rust feels the same way that you do. And I get the impression that Craycroft is not going away. It seems he is already moving to shore up defenses against this fellow Reordan. And besides that, you have Master Robert and me here, and it does not look like we're going anyplace too fast."

"My, how you do make my day brighter! I thank thee, lady."

"Any time, my good man. Now, did they tell you what they'll be doing with you? It seems that you're hardly sick enough to stay here much longer."

"Aye, they shall be taking me to the keep after dark. There I shall meet with Master Craycroft to discuss just what he has in mind. I understand that he has something in mind for me, but I know not what."

"And I don't either, except that it's all secret," said Judy with a smile.

The councilor laughed at this.

"Well, I'll certainly see you later. Now this lady and I are going to see about getting dinner ready for the 'boys.' Isn't that right, Jeanne?"

Jeanne smiled and winked. And then she rather coquettishly touched his cheek and said, "Well now, I do think that we'll make room for one more at the table, shall we not?"

"Oh, I do believe we can accommodate one more. See you tonight, then, eh?"

Genet then blushed, stammered, and mumbled something that sounded like an assent.

Councilor Reordan was in a foul mood as he left the council chambers, and the weather was not helping at all.

This horrid winter! he thought, as he tried vainly to wrap up even tighter in his cloak. *I cannot wait to get back home.*

Then he turned to his page and told him to run ahead, and notify Carruthers to begin to implement the alternate plan.

"The alternate plan? What is that?"

"I do not pay you to ask impertinent questions. Just do as I say," he spat with as much vitriol as the page had ever heard.

"Aye, m'lord," he answered, and he was gone.

The councilor plowed on through the wind and rain, out the main gate, and off toward his mansion, thinking all the while that he should have hired a horse to take him the short way back to his home. As he turned into his lane, he thought he saw movement out toward the left side of his vision, but then he realized it was probably just this terrible rain and thought no more about it until he was inside. Once indoors, he shucked his cloak and left it in the hallway, knowing that one of the servants would pick it up. He headed back toward his study where he knew there would be a roaring fire and some sherry. He was starting to get comfortable, settling into his chair and sipping on his sherry, when Carruthers came to his door.

"You know, Carruthers, that if I did not have so much to do here, and if I had anyone I could to trust to run my businesses properly, I would happily take a holiday someplace warmer, like Italy. This is just woeful... Did that infernal pageboy give you the message?"

"Aye, m'lord. Ye wish to proceed with the alternate plan?"

"Aye, aye, that I do. Have you sent for LeGace?"

"We have sent for him, though I am not certain that we can find him. It will depend on what the urchins have turned up. They

do know where he is staying, though he may be out and about during the day."

"Very well; bring me my ledger and make certain that my accountant, that slimy old fellow Cornelius, is given today's entries."

"As you wish; I shall bring thy ledger."

As Carruthers left, Reordan found himself finally comfortable, but alone in his study. He thought about what Rust had said and also about what he did not say, but implied. Just when he thought that the council was finally his to manipulate, these two things happened. First, there was the illness of the painters and potters, and the earl—the old fool—assigned Rust to investigate. And then this newest thing with the earl's illness. Something that should have gone his way now appeared to be, if anything, turning against him. *Craycroft! Where did this upstart get the authority? He—of no background, no money, no power—now comes on with the authority given him by the earl—the fool!*

What does he have that I could use against him? What indeed! Nothing! Mainly this lack of anything that he could claim as entitlement—just his knowledge, which should not constitute any power. He does not even have a family that could be bothered. Ah, if only that imbecile had not gotten his hands onto the Lady Felicia, as well as the earl. Surely we could have used her against him. And whatever happened to Carlo Vincente? Now his death was as mysterious as any that Reordan could remember. He thought about this and decided that taking on Craycroft on this matter might just be too risky.

And now, who should be making himself an incredible nuisance but Drachma! He thought about just how much of a pain in his side Drachma had become—with his history of disrupting the normal flow of events and his fearlessness. He knew, even without being told, that Finch's attempted capture of Judy had been foiled; and he knew full well that it was Drachma who was behind that.

Oh, why do you not go back to the forest where you belong?

His thoughts were a jumble when Carruthers came back in with his ledger, which he handed to his employer without a word. He could tell when it was time to keep quiet. He looked at the ledger, opened it to the most current page, then entered the date and the entries for the payment of Antoine LeGace, as well as the payment to Councilor Silvo. He then handed the ledger back to Carruthers. Reaching into his tunic, he took out two pennies, and then told Carruthers to make certain the urchins were paid their due.

"Very well, m'lord. By the usual method?"

"Aye, of course. Now be off."

With that, Carruthers turned and left. Reordan was again alone with his thoughts—turbulent and distressing as they were.

Judy and Jeanne moved happily toward the keep. This meal was going to be in the earl's dining room, at Craycroft's request, and Jeanne had asked that she be allowed to help prepare it. Judy then volunteered her services as well to help with the cooking. Jeanne fairly beamed at this opportunity to get more acquainted with her new friend. There was no way, she knew, to replace her recent loss, but the promise of new friendship was like a soothing balm to her tortured soul. And to know that Judy was actually volunteering to help made it so much more special. As they walked into the main hallway, they were met by a page who was running with a message for Master Cayman.

As he almost ran right into the two women, he apologized and said, "Please, madam, I'm so sorry. Do either of ye know this Master Cayman? I've got a message for him, but I don't know what he looks like."

"Well, m'lad, since ye're in such a hurry, let us show ye where he is likely to be. If ye come this way, we're right by the constabulary;

and I do know that if he's not there, then they shall know where he is," Jeanne explained.

"The constab'lry? Is that where he is then? I was told by Herschel up in the bird place to be lookin' fer this important lookin' man…"

"Cayman? Important looking? No, my son, Cayman is rather ordinary in appearance, though I would say that his job is now rather important. This Herschel does not see very well, does he?"

"Nay, M'lady, he canna' see well."

"Very well, come with us, I'll show ye Cayman."

So the two ladies, with their young page, walked down the hallway to the constabulary and turned into the door. There they were met by the sight of utter maleness caught unawares. There were a half dozen, partly-clothed, embarrassed men who scurried to make themselves presentable, or else invisible.

"Now, m'ladies," said Blodwen, acting as spokesman. "What can I do fer ye? Oh, Johnny, ye'll have to cover up. Pardon, m'ladies, fer ye've caught us at our most relaxed."

"Oh, that's all right, never ye mind. It's just that this young lad bears a message for Cayman, and we naturally assumed he would be here." Jeanne and Judy just smiled. Jeanne was thinking that this was quite a sight for Judy to absorb, while Judy was just enjoying the scenery.

"Cayman… Oh, Cayman, there's a couple of ladies fer ye!"

Cayman then appeared from the back. He looked and noticed the two ladies. He became acutely embarrassed, for he had never seen any ladies in the constabulary.

"There, ye see, m'lad. There's Master Cayman fer ye. Now, does he not look the picture of importance? Master Cayman, this young lad has a message fer ye," Jeanne said.

"Oh, for me?"

"Aye, Master Cayman, here ye be. It's from Herschel, up yonder."

The page quickly handed him the little cylinder, and then ran out of the building.

Cayman opened up the cylinder and pulled out the small yellow paper. He scanned it, and then said, "It is from Drachma. He shall be coming here tomorrow; should be here by evening. He said to have everything prepared for him by then."

"Well, we shall tell Master Craycroft, as we are having dinner with him. But it sounds from your tone that you may have more to do, and we shall not tarry. Now, carry on."

As the ladies left the constabulary, the place erupted in laughter.

"Ye'll have to tell us, Cayman, who those most fine and beautiful ladies were. And next time, ye'll have to tell us before they do come down."

"Now, Blodwen, I had no idea that they were coming. The one who did the speaking is Jeanne, who is a special assistant to Craycroft."

This was met with a chorus of gasps and low whistles.

"And the other, more beautiful one, is the Lady Judy, a healer who comes here with Master Robert from far off; and I have been given special permission to turn anyone who tarries with her into a eunuch."

More gasps and groans, as well as general laughter.

When Jeanne and Judy reached the upstairs, they checked in on the earl. He was awake, but sleepy. His color was dusky, and he appeared too weak to even cough. There was that sickly sweet smell in the room, which was warm, and the atmosphere was close. Jeanne came by the bedside and checked to make sure that there was enough aromatic oil for his breathing treatments. Judy came up to the earl, checked his forehead, and checked his pulse, which was rapid and getting threadier. She just smiled down at him.

"Ah, m'lady, it is thee. How nice of you to come by to see me. Come here and let me see thee."

Judy moved just a little so that she was standing halfway down at his bedside, and then she knelt down and held his hands in hers.

"My lord," she said, unconsciously using that title. "I am here in hopes that I can bring you some ease. I'm here with Jeanne, who's checking on your medicine. Is there anything that you need?"

"Nay, nothing but what you are providing. It is a great comfort to me. I thank thee."

Judy stayed, holding his hands in hers as she watched. Then his breathing eased and he drifted off to sleep—a peaceful slumber. A tear escaped her eye as she watched, helpless to do anything more.

Eventually, she got back up, wiped the tears from her eyes, and then she and Jeanne silently left his side and went toward the kitchen.

As they entered the massive kitchen, they were met by the cooks, who were eager to meet the two ladies, though they were somewhat suspicious. The head cook curtsied and introduced herself and her staff.

"Welcome, m'ladies. I am Melinda, chief cook, and these are my helpers—Maria, Constance, and Felicity." Each, in turn, curtsied. "Now, let me show ye around."

They were given the tour of the kitchen, as well as the pantries, larders, wine storage, and cold storage rooms; and then the main kitchen with its massive counters, ovens, and stoves.

Then the ladies decided on the menu for the night's dinner, which included lamb, sausage, soup, yeast rolls, and vegetables. For after dinner they decided on fruit-filled cakes. Jeanne selected the wine for dinner and the brandy for after dinner.

"You know, the only thing missing is coffee," said Judy. "What I wouldn't give for a great cup of coffee."

"Coffee? What is that? Is it some kind of liquor?"

"Oh, no. It's what we drank back home. It's a most amazing drink, made even more so by its absence here. It's made from beans that are dried, roasted, then ground fine; and then hot

water is run over them. I know one person here who really likes his coffee."

"And that person, I assume, is your Master Robert?"

"Yeah, that would be him."

Then the ladies got busy getting all the things they needed. An operation, it seemed, that was smooth and coordinated. Melinda was delighted to discover that Jeanne and Judy were there to help, and they were soon cutting vegetables, stirring flour, and adding ingredients to the soup. They were, in fact, having a great time, with no worries in that huge old kitchen getting flour and cooking grease on their aprons, and talking of things that really didn't seem to matter.

That was until Jeanne brought up the subject of Bob, and Judy's relationship with him.

"Well, let me tell you. I think it's complex. Not for me, of course, for I'm single and unattached. I'm in love with him, head over heels in love; so much so that I know there'll never be another. But for Bob things are quite complicated. You see, back in our time and place, he's married. I assume that it is a good marriage, though I've no way to be sure, and I've never met his wife. Anyway, even though I'm pretty sure that he does love me, he's torn because of his commitment. And let me tell you that it is hard not throwing my arms around him and planting a big one on him whenever I see him."

Jeanne just laughed at that. "Now I thought so when I saw ye, as soon as ye walked into the room and he looked at thee, and he said those nice things about thee, and it made ye blush…I knew there was something there. Now, I must ask, do ye think this is permanent, this coming to Shepperton and all?"

"Oh, I do believe it is, but how can I say? I've never been transported to another time before."

This made Jeanne laugh some more.

"All right then, ladies." It was Melinda. "Now that we've gotten along with preparations for the dinner, it's time to decide about

the dining room, who sits where and all that. So, come with me, you two who are having such a good time, and show me where ye'd like all of the guests to sit."

"Oh, all right. Come on, Judy. Let us go and decide."

Judy was absolutely stunned by the dining room. This was even more elegant and spacious than any place she had ever eaten before. There was a big fireplace and then the huge oval table carved ornately out of oak. Around it were chairs carved of some beautiful wood with elegant cushions. All around were paintings, busts, and magnificent draperies. The floor was carpeted with soft, ornate rugs.

"Are we really going to eat in here?" she asked, somewhat intimidated by her surroundings.

"Oh, aye, m'lady. Master Craycroft himself said so."

"Well then, we'll have to thank him. He's really got superb taste. Okay then, let's get on to the seating arrangements. Now, Craycroft has got to sit at the head of the table, right here with the big chair with arms."

And so they decided where everyone was to sit, which glasses were right, which bowls for the soup, and so on. Then the two ladies bid farewell to Melinda and cheerfully told her that they had to go get ready for the occasion, and that they would return within the hour. Melinda thanked them for their courtesy and kindness, and said she was looking forward to seeing them again. They then found Clarice, and the three of them hurried off to Felicia's house to get ready. Jeanne and Judy were glowing in the warmth of their newfound friendship.

The atmosphere at Reordan's mansion was anything but friendly. Antoine LeGace sensed it the minute he walked into the hallway.

"Come this way, if ye will, sire," said the obsequious servant. "Master Reordan has been expecting thee."

He led LeGace down the hallway as before, to the same grand study. The servant announced his presence, and LeGace was led in.

"Why, come in Master LeGace and have a seat. Here is an advance of payment for thee. Now I have a most dangerous little mission for thee as well. There shall be more money after ye have accomplished your goal."

LeGace took the bag of silver. The weight, he noticed, was considerably more than the last. He cocked his head slightly to the side as if intent on what the councilor was planning.

"This is substantially more than the last payment. I presume that the risk is also substantially greater."

"Ye surmise correctly, my good fellow, and your reward shall be increased even more upon successful completion of thy task."

"And what, pray tell, would that task be?"

"I shall tell thee. But first, what news have ye for me?"

"Well, as to the two strangers, I surmise that they are guests of Craycroft and have been seen often going and coming from Sick Bay with some regularity. So one could suppose that the man might be a physician, or healer of some type. The lady I am not so certain about, for she has been seen in the company of Craycroft, the stranger, and some other woman whom I know not.

"As to our councilor, I would surmise that he is now deceased, for I saw the priest and six monks come and carry the body away."

"Ah, then ye are most certain that it was he?" Reordan inquired.

"Aye."

"That is good, then. And now to the task I have for thee. It is one that carries definite and serious risk, so tell me if ye do not feel that ye be capable of accomplishing it. What I am asking of thee is to kill the one called Drachma. He is now making my life much more difficult, and I see little alternative to killing him. I am sure that ye be aware that he is heavily guarded, is crafty, stealthy, and has survived multiple previous attempts upon his life. Are ye aware of that?"

"Oh, aye. Of that I am fully knowledgeable."

"Good. Then what say ye? Will ye do the deed?"

"I ask only one thing from thee, besides the silver. And that would be my safe removal from this island after it is done."

"Very well, I shall have a boat ready with the remainder of thy payment on board. Just let me know when, and that is all I need to know of thy plan."

"It shall be done."

With that, Antoine LeGace got up, walked out, looked about him, and decided that it might just work out after all. He really did like this mansion.

Chapter Seven

With this last message that Drachma sent, there was much information to be gathered and not much time. This, as Kerlin knew, was typical of Drachma. He expected perfection, and generally obtained it from the people who worked for him, partly because the anxiety it caused seemed to heighten the urge to please. Kerlin sat and waited for Proust to return, drumming his fingers, occasionally getting up and pacing. He was, by nature, in impatient man, but he tried not to let his impatience show. Eustace sat at his side in the little room high up in the watchtower. Then Eustace got up, looked out one of the tiny windows and looked toward the mountains, but he could only see about a mile.

"Can ye see aught?" Kerlin asked. "It would seem to me that this would be a bad day to be on guard duty."

"Nay, I canna' see. Just clouds and this freezin' rain. Oh, wait, there be somethin' down below. I believe it be a pair of riders."

Kerlin came up next to Eustace and peered out over the rampart. "Aye, that is Proust, no doubt, but who that is with him, I cannot tell."

"And I cannot even tell that is Proust, but I'll take ye at yer word."

"Well then, we should go down and meet him at the stables."

The two of them then quickly descended the stairs and came out on the ground floor. They hurried over to the stables and

arrived just as Proust rode in with another man that neither of them knew on sight. As Dunstan held the reins, the two riders alit and then came over to Kerlin and Eustace.

"Kerlin, this is my good friend Raymond. He is from the village of Bierney and brings news of some import. I hope ye don't mind that I brought him. Now Raymond, this is my Commandant Kerlin, and this young lad is Kerlin's assistant, Eustace."

"Glad to make yer acquaintance, I'm sure," said Raymond. "Now I'd heard that there ha' been some changes here."

"And I'm most pleased to meet ye, too. Now let us get thy horses off to the stables, and then come wi' me."

"Ah, don't ye worry about these horses, Master Kerlin, I'll take good care o' them," said Dunstan. "Ye've got the best groomsman in these parts."

"Very well, then let us be off."

Kerlin handed Dunstan a substantial tip.

"Me thanks to ye."

It was back across the cold, muddy plaza toward the constabulary that the quartet went.

"Hey, Jeremy," said Eustace, "I know ye're workin' fer the councilman. I can see ye from here. Now come on out o' there."

The street urchin came out from behind the abandoned cart and he looked like he was going to dash for the gates.

"Now, don't ye run, or one of these men'll catch ye," Eustace warned.

Kerlin picked up right away on Eustace's ploy.

"He's right, ye know. Now come with us, and I'll make it worth yer while."

So, the bedraggled urchin came forth and joined the foursome as they went on to the constabulary. He looked like one who was trying to disappear into the rain and mud.

"Now, Jeremy, let me tell ye that ye've nothing to fear from these men if ye but tell the truth."

"I…I…was just watchin'," he stuttered.

"That's all right, Jeremy," Kerlin told him kindly, "as Eustace said, ye have nothing to fear from us. Just come with us and we'll make it worth your while."

Jeremy followed them as they made their way into the constabulary. When they stepped in, the atmosphere was warm, jovial, and relaxed. The five of them now entered the confines and Kerlin made it a point to offer Proust, Raymond, and Jeremy some warm cider.

"Now, while I'm getting your cider, Jeremy, why don't ye come with us? I'm quite certain that Proust and Raymond can fend for themselves for a few minutes." He said this with a wink that was not lost on Proust.

So Jeremy followed Kerlin and his friend Eustace back into the building. Jeremy was visibly nervous, so Eustace explained to him that his own life had been changed by a chance encounter with the strange man called LeGace, whom Eustace knew was being watched by the Druids. But he also knew that they themselves were being watched, as was evident today. And he knew just who was paying them to watch and just how much the going rate was.

"So, can ye tell me what this Master LeGace has been doing? He seems most interested in our comings and goings from Sick Bay."

"Aye, that he does. Now he's been staying at the widow O'Malley's. Appears to have a room upstairs at her place. As far as I know, he's just been watchin', nothin' more. But he's a strange one, he is. Walkin' around wi' that cane of his, which he doesn't need for walkin', if ye ask me," Jeremy recounted.

"Nay, I would say that he doesn't," Eustace said, careful not to reveal the true use for his walking stick.

"Let me ask ye," put in Kerlin, "who is it that's paying ye to watch us, then? And what does he want to know?"

"That I don't know for certain, but it's a man that works fer the councilman that pays us. What he does with the stuff we tell him, that I can't tell ye, for I don't know."

Kerlin reached into his tunic, took out a couple of copper coins, and handed them to Jeremy.

"Why, thank ye, sir."

And then, he reached back into his tunic, took out a couple more copper coins, and then said, "And for doubling your payment, I would like ye to think about what ye can do for us. For, I tell ye, we're really here for yer protection, as well as the protection of the whole castle, and I think that ye'd like to be a part of that."

"Aye, that I would, but I should speak to me superior."

"Oh, I think that would be a good idea. What say ye to that, Eustace?"

"Oh, aye. That would be a good idea. Why don't ye bring Erik around? We'd like to talk to him as well."

"All right, then. Here's some warm cider fer ye. Why don't the two of ye just talk here. I'll take the two riders some cider as well. Maybe later, then, eh Eustace?"

Eustace nodded and winked at Kerlin.

When Kerlin returned with the drinks, he found that Cayman had joined in with the others. He was in an animated conversation with Proust, Raymond, and Ervin.

"Here's some warm cider for you, my friends."

"What, and none for me?"

"I can only carry so many, Cayman, who d'you think I am? I'm not like that maid of Barncuddy's…"

"Who? Diane? Ah, I see that Captain Cayman's got his eye on her now," Proust chided.

"Aye, and I'll soon have more than my eye upon her, mark my words. I would say that Eustace has been a bit of luck, now, wouldn't ye? Where is that lad?"

Kerlin gestured with his head. "Back by the cider, along with one of his former colleagues."

As Cayman went in search of Eustace and some cider, Kerlin led the others back to the sitting room where they found some comfortable old chairs to sit in.

"I assume that you bring some news. Is that not right?"

"Oh, aye, that we do. Some would say important news, but not what we expected."

"Oh? Please explain."

"Well, as ye know, I was asked to scout out what forces Reordan was amassing and where they are. And as I was contacting my friends among the villages, Raymond here, comes to me with the news that Reordan has apparently been acquiring property along the shoreline by Cromwell's Marsh. Now this, as ye know to be very strange indeed, as the marshland is not where any would want to build or set up any sort of operation."

"But does it not have a cove that is accessible anytime—winter or summer—that is protected from freezing by the two rivers that feed into it? Is that where he is acquiring his land?"

"Aye, it is, and all the land back from that cove to the road to Champour."

"That is most interesting. If I recall, then, he could easily ship things, including men and supplies, without having to dock at our port…"

"And more than that, it would appear that he is acquiring most of the village of Champour. Now he is offering steady work to the villagers who are eager, it seems, for work—besides fishing—at this time of year."

"Any idea as to numbers of forces in the area?"

"I would say about a hundred or so, but not well-trained fighters; with maybe forty horses."

"Well then, Master Proust, I would suggest that we should perhaps gather up our own troops here in the castle, get some back from the woods and villages; what say you? Ah, here comes our own captain, with our young lads."

Cayman was followed by the two youths, who were both drinking their cider. He smiled at the gathering, as he sat down, with the two boys on either side of him.

"It appears to me, Commandant, as if we may have successfully recruited the aid of our good youth corps in our endeavors. It would seem that young Jeremy, here, would be willing to assist Eustace in searching out and reporting from the grounds of our castle and the village. It seems that their present *employer* has been less than honest with them, and I believe that we could use their services."

"Well then, me young lad. I should leave you to work out the arrangement with Eustace, who reports to me. There is no higher calling than to work for thy liege lord in times of peril. Remember that, m'lad."

"Oh, I shall remember."

As Eustace and Jeremy went off in one corner to talk and to drink their cider, Kerlin, Cayman, Proust, and Ervin sat around and made plans; for they all knew that Drachma was coming, and they wanted to be ready for him. Cayman prepared a couple of messages to be sent by the birds, while Kerlin and Proust plotted about how to bring more troops into the castle without causing too much alarm.

Next, Kerlin called the two boys over, and they set about planning something of a diversion, which would involve the Druids.

"That sounds like it should work."

"But, of course it should. We shall make it work," vowed Jeremy.

"Very well then, Jeremy. And remember..."

"Aye, m'lord, I shall. We work fer the earl, our liege."

The butcher shop was an unusual place to be right in the middle of the afternoon in January, and the pair that entered made quite a sight indeed. Tall, lanky, and stooped over, Melchior was unusual enough, but at least he had been here before. The stranger who was with him had never set foot in a fifteenth century butcher

shop, and you could tell. He was used to odors of all kinds, but this was just a bit much—the overpowering stench of the meat and spilled blood that came from the back of the shop was as nauseating as anything Bob had experienced.

"What is the matter?" asked Melchior, who seemed oblivious to the odors.

"Oh, nothing," Bob lied, "I'm all right. It's just the smell seems kind of strong."

"Oh, well, we shall try to keep it brief. Now, here is Master Frankie. Frankie, we're here to see if we might obtain some sheep or lamb blood from ye."

"Well, Master Melchior, I see that ye've come back." The butcher rubbed his blood-covered hands on his filthy apron, which covered his ample midriff. "Now what might I do fer ye this grand afternoon? And who be this stranger that ye have with ye?"

It was obvious that Frankie had heard nothing and was a bit deaf.

"This is the famous healer, Master Robert, who comes from the land of Ewe Ass. He is here to provide teaching to us on the medicinal uses of materials that many would consider common."

"Ah, like your own Master Falma did through the years, then…"

"Precisely. Now can ye furnish us with a supply of sheep's blood?"

"Sheep's blood?" He cocked his head to the side quizzically. "Now, what might you be usin' that fer?"

"I'm afraid that I canna' tell ye right now."

"Ah, well, it's a bit of a secret, is it?"

"Well, aye, it is…"

"Let me see, now, as I've got a lamb that's due for the slaughter this afternoon for Councilor Reordan, I'm sure that she'll bleed enough fer ye. Why don't ye come back in around an hour and I should have some of the blood that ye'll be needin'. Now, how much do ye think ye'll be a needin'?"

"Oh, about a quart should be more than enough, I would think," said Bob, rather unexpectedly.

"Very well then, me good man. I'll have it fer ye in an hour."

Bob was thankful that Frankie had not offered to shake his hand. The twosome left the little butcher shop, and it felt to Bob like he could breathe again, despite the cold.

"You know, it seems ironic that we're going to be taking the blood of the lamb being slaughtered for this Councilor Reordan; as much as I've heard of him, the thought of him just gives me the creeps."

"Aye, it does seem just a bit ironic to me, as well. And I'll tell ye that I've never really met him, but I get the same feeling. Maybe we shall find some good use for this lamb's blood, what think you, Master Robert?"

"I was never a believer in fate, but that appears to be changing. And I just get the feeling that we are somehow obligated; to whom, I can't say, but obligated nonetheless to make the most of this opportunity."

"Well said, Master Robert, well said."

What they did the next hour was to devise what they were going to do with the blood when they got it, and how they were to handle it. Also, they had obtained some seaweed that had been dried to use as a thickening agent. They then ground up the seaweed finely into a powder and put it aside for their later use.

Falma had come in about then and told them that he would be available to help out, as he had done some of the research years ago on sheep blood. And when Bob told him of just what he had in mind with the sheep blood and the water, Falma's eyes lit up with youthful enthusiasm.

When Bob told him of the visit to the butcher's and how the blood was being obtained from a lamb that was being slaughtered

for Councilor Reordan, Falma just thought that it was about the most amusing thing he had heard in some time, and he just couldn't stop chuckling over the whole scenario. He then went about his study trying to find pertinent bits of writing that he had done that might help out.

And when Bob and Melchior went back to the butcher, Frankie was waiting for them with a bucket of lamb's blood. When Melchior offered to pay for it, Frankie refused. For he could tell, by something in their eyes, that it was going to be used for something very important and useful.

Then Bob thought of something. He reached for his wallet and found a dollar bill, which he gave to Frankie. Frankie was amazed at it, for he had never seen anything at all like it.

"Oh, nay, Master Robert, I canna' take that from ye."

"Oh, sure you can, I insist. For I know that you've done something for the sake of humanity that may be very important."

So, Frankie was persuaded to take the dollar bill, and he stared at it, holding it in his grimy hands. Then, as the two of them left, carrying the bucket between them, Frankie carefully took the dollar bill and put it away in a safe place—away from prying eyes. It was a memento of something significant; he just didn't know what.

Craycroft sat in the earl's bedchamber and reflected. He had been the center of so much, so fast, that now he just wanted to take a few minutes in the presence of his beloved earl to talk to someone he knew had to be behind much of all that was happening.

"M'liege, you have been here this whole time, and I thought that I would come by, not as your physician and not as your employee; but as your friend, to try to talk of some of the things that have happened."

"Well, Craycroft, I should tell you that it would now be appropriate for me to address you as m'liege, for that is what you are, is it not so?"

"Ah, nay, m'lord, for you are always and have been my liege. Just because you have given me authority does not change our relationship."

"You know, Craycroft, that is why I chose you. For you do not let these matters of title or birthright, nor even money and power, stand in your way. For you see them for what they are—merely tools in the hands of mortal men."

Craycroft sat silent for a time. The ticking of the clock was the only sound in that room.

"You know, m'lord, that Master Robert and young Melchior are at this very time working to save you?"

"Save me? From what, my friend? You do know, deep down, that I am dying, and there is naught anyone can do to prevent that."

This brought about a spell of violent coughing, with the earl bringing up a clothful of the most vile, blood-stained sputum. Craycroft quickly and expertly assembled his mist apparatus and then lit the little flame underneath. Within minutes, it was steaming, and the earl was breathing in the vapors. His color, at first quite dusky, became pinker. But then he settled back down, exhausted—too exhausted for more talk. He was sweating profusely.

Just as Craycroft was himself settling back down, the earl turned to him and asked, "My friend, if it would be possible… could you have the lady, the Lady Judy, come see me? I would like some of what…she can do for me."

"Of course, m'lord. I shall summon her anon."

Craycroft stepped out to talk to one of the pages, and, after the page was dispatched, he retuned to the earl's side. He just sat by the side of his friend and confidant, and watched as his breathing, though labored, did ease. His color remained dusky, and every now and then the earl would suddenly gasp for breath,

then his respirations would ease again. This went on for perhaps fifteen minutes.

"M'lord," came a voice from the doorway, "m'lord, I bring the Lady Judy."

"Oh, do come in, my lady. The earl requested you in particular to be at his side. And you, my good friend, you have come as well. Do come in."

"Thank you," said Bob. "I was just on my way here when I ran into Judy coming in a hurry."

Judy stepped in first, and then Bob followed. Again, she gently approached the earl and laid her hand on his forehead. She noticed it was very warm and felt his pulse, noting again that it was rapid, with occasional missed beats.

"He's febrile and tachycardic," she told Bob, "but now he's got some irregularity to his rhythm."

While Bob pulled out his stethoscope from his satchel, Judy knelt at the side of the bed and held the earl's hands in hers. That seemed to rouse him, enough that he smiled. Bob listened to his lungs, noticing that the crackles were more and that the character of his breathing had changed. He noticed as well that there was now a friction rub, indicating involvement of the pleura, the lining of the lung. He then moved his stethoscope toward the front of his chest and listened intently to the familiar lub-dub of the heartbeat, but he noticed that every third beat was premature, that his rhythm was rapid, and that he could now hear a clear-cut fourth heart sound that varied with the earl's respirations.

"Well, what now?" asked Judy.

"I'd have to say that I'm worried. He's got a new friction rub and a new, right-sided S4, as well as the arrhythmia that you noticed."

"Not good, huh?"

"No, not at all good, I'm afraid. And me, here, without a chest X-ray, ABGs, CBC, or chemistries. And, also, we've got no O2, no IV fluids, and no antibiotics."

"Any good news?" Judy asked, not really expecting any.

"Well, thanks to your good friend Falma, and his good buddy Melchior, it looks as though we've got some agar available in the lab for cultures. Now, has he produced any sputum?" Craycroft handed him the cloth.

"I would presume that you meant, has he coughed up any phlegm?"

"Yeah, I've got to watch it with my lingo. Yes, that's exactly what I meant, and this is a good specimen. Thank you. And before I run back over to the lab, I would like to note that the earl has a couple of things going for him, and that is you, Master Craycroft, the finest physician I know; and he also has you, Judy. The best thing in the world next to IV morphine."

With that, Bob turned away, took the sputum sample wrapped in its cloth, wrapped another cloth around it, put away his stethoscope, and headed out the door. Then he turned and, before he left, said, "I'll see all of you at supper tonight then."

Judy turned toward Craycroft and said, "You know, he's always been like that."

"Whatever do you mean?"

"She means that," the earl spoke, unexpectedly, "when his attention is devoted to a particular problem, such as a dying patient, that he seems just a bit…a bit…"

"Hard-nosed." Judy finished for him. "Enthusiastic, but hard-nosed."

"That is a good way of putting it," said the earl, smiling graciously on Judy and his friend Craycroft. Then he drifted off to sleep; this time, though, his respirations seemed less labored and the sleep peaceful.

As they were now gathering for dinner, Judy was with Craycroft and Jeanne. The guests were shown into the foyer where they had

drinks of spiced cider waiting for them as they stood around, much as Judy had imagined people do at cocktail parties back home. First came Kerlin, along with Eustace, Cayman, Ervin, and Proust. Then came Rust, as ever, somewhat distracted in appearance; and then Councilor Genet, who looked as out of place as Judy to dine in such a fancy setting. Judy took it upon herself to make him feel warmly welcomed. And then Rust came over and commented on his amazing recovery.

"And worry not, my friend, your presence here shall be our little secret for now. I am sure, though, that Master Craycroft here shall fill you in. And welcome back to the land of the living."

"Why thank you, good councilor. I am certain that whatever you and Craycroft may do, I shall fully be a part of it."

"Here comes Craycroft now. What say you, Master Healer? What do you think of our councilor and his return to us?"

"Ah, well, you speak as if I had something to do with his recovery, but I truly did not. That was Master Robert's doing, and I think that we should thank him when he gets here," Craycroft replied.

"Oh, aye, I do think that he has earned my humble thanks. Now he shall be here tonight, no?" Councilor Genet inquired.

"Aye, he said as much. Now the fact that neither Falma nor Melchior are here yet would, I think, be testimony to their great doings with Master Robert. It would seem that they are up to something in regards to the earl's condition, and I would be most interested to hear what they have been doing."

Kerlin was restless again, looking about the rooms as if seeking something, though he would not say what. At his side, Eustace was beaming, looking about the splendid room himself with the look of youthful enthusiasm that caught Jeanne's eye as she went over to him.

"My, you look like a happy cat this evening."

"Oh my, this is such a splendid place. I have never been inside such a place as this. Me mum would be jealous."

"Ah, aye, your mum, indeed," said Cayman. "Remind me, I shall need to speak to her tonight after dinner."

"As if you needed any reminding," chided Kerlin with a wink.

Meanwhile, Ervin and Proust stood by, stoically drinking their cider.

There was just a glint of sadness in Craycroft's eye, which Judy noticed. She came up beside him and touched his arm. He smiled at her, but his smile belied the underlying sadness.

"It's her, isn't it? There was something someone said or did that reminded you of her. Am I right?"

"Aye, for in truth," he answered her, "it was more than that. For it was the Lady Felicia who was always there at the earl's dinner parties, and for just a brief moment, it was as if she were standing in the middle of the gentle chiding of Cayman and Kerlin. It was truly just as one of her own, as if she were really here, but for only the briefest of moments; and then gone again."

"I really missed out on getting to meet someone amazing there, didn't I?"

"Oh, aye, m'lady, you most certainly did," Jeanne answered for Craycroft. "And let me tell you, Lady Felicia was a woman who could turn the men's heads, but she never did know it; for she was such a person that each individual she would meet, and each day that she was alive, were special. And so I also sense that in you. For you do remind me of her."

"Well, if that weren't the compliment to end all compliments. Thank you, Jeanne, for that. Now, how long are we going to wait for Bob and the boys to finish what they're doing, or are we going to go ahead and eat?"

"Are you getting hungry, m'lady?"

"Hungry? I'm famished. And just wait 'til you see what we've been cooking up." That brought out a chuckle from Craycroft.

Jeanne then announced that they could come to dinner in the great room next door, and that they would be serving a truly fine meal. She said that there were still a few persons not yet here, but that the rest could begin.

They were each shown to their places, with Craycroft seated at the head and the rest at various places around the great table. As the servants began ladling out the soup, Craycroft stood and thanked the ladies who had prepared the fine meal, and he then explained that Masters Robert, Falma, and Melchior would be joining them anon.

He then started off the meal with a toast. "Now, my friends, we are here in this time and among these people. We stand at the threshold of something powerful, something worthwhile; something for which the world may not have any answers—at least not in our time upon this earth. But I know that this is true. This is a certainty. There have been many who have given everything for this opportunity, and here it is for us to experience, to share with our colleagues and with those who shall come after us. It is not without some fear that I took on this role, but it was thrust upon me, and I shall make the most of my own circumstance. And it is also true that Master Robert and the Lady Judy have been placed here, not of their own choosing, but it is becoming clearer just what their roles shall be. And you, Eustace, have also been chosen from among the many young urchins out there to fulfill a particular role—I know not what, but I do know that it shall be great. And last of all, Tom, who, presently, is safe with Drachma—his grandfather—but who shall, I am most certain, be playing a great role in all our futures. So, to you and all here, I raise my glass, and shall sip of this wine of the incandescent future!"

They, then, all stood and drank, and they all sensed that what Craycroft was saying was right and proper. They felt a part of something truly great.

"Here, here!"

They turned to the sound to find that Bob, Falma, and Melchior had joined them. Their faces were glowing with purpose and resolve. Judy and Jeanne quickly went to the three and sat them at the empty seats. The soup and bread were devoured, the wine was poured and consumed, with great enthusiasm. Then

they feasted on the lamb, the sausage, the vegetables, more rolls, and more wine. Finally, as they were each served the brandy and cakes, Craycroft turned to Bob and asked him to tell them all of what they had been doing.

Bob's face, which normally registered his feelings unmistakably, this time seemed unreadable. He closed his eyes, thought for a moment, and then began.

"Well, my friends, I can tell you that we have been doing something in our little laboratory that is commonplace in our world, but has never been done before in this world. And now that I'm apparently stuck here in your world, and in your time, it is something that you will have the opportunity to share with me. In our time, we have found that most cases of pneumonia are due to the presence of bacteria that get down into the lungs. These are the organs in the chest that take in air, which then get this same air into the bloodstream. Anyway, when these bacteria are ingested into the lungs, they can overgrow, causing the body to respond with an intense reaction that includes high fever and the production of thick mucus. Then the person with this pneumonia has to try to get rid of all this thick mucus, and they do so by coughing up this vile material that is a mixture of the overgrown bacteria, along with the mucus overproduced by the body, as well as dead cells from the lungs, and many white blood cells that try to fight the infection.

"Now, I don't expect you to understand what I have been telling you, but know this—that the person with pneumonia coughs up this material that contains many of these bacteria, and these bacteria can be identified by a process called culturing. It is notable that sheep's blood is a common component of culture material we call agar, which also contains a thickening agent from seaweed. Anyway, it turns out that your own Master Falma wrote of this method of producing agar years ago, though he did not really know what to do with the material. He got pretty close by noting that, in war wounds, those that had infected wounds

seemed to produce a certain pattern on the agar, compared to those that did not have infections. This is an incredible leap of insight, especially since he did not know anything about bacteria or how they related to disease.

"Well then, you might ask, what does all this have to do with our earl? And further, what does this have to do with the water that our good friend Ervin brought from the Creek of the Dead? Well, I have a theory that, as ludicrous as this sounds, that the earl is suffering from pneumonia caused by a specific type of bacteria from this creek; and that, somehow, he was made to ingest a sufficient quantity of these bacteria and is now sick as a result.

"What makes me think this? Well, some of you may recall that when Ervin brought out the water, Falma smelled it and noticed that it had a certain sickly sweet odor. It turns out that the odor is caused by certain bacteria in the water, and that smell is the same smell that some of you have noticed is in the room with the earl, and particularly in the material that he coughs up."

By now, all were intent on listening, and the cakes just sat on the plates of the diners.

"As to smells, they are our body's way of identifying many chemicals in our environment and are very specific. For instance, many of you can recall, by smell, your parents' house from childhood, or the smell of a certain person or animal, or the smell of these wonderful rolls as they were baking. Now, what we have done in our laboratory is set up multiple culture tubes with this agar that we have made, using lamb's blood and seaweed. And we have placed a small quantity of the mucus from the earl in a number of these tubes; and in some of the others we have done the same, using the water from the creek. We shall know, probably within one to two days, if my theory is correct."

Falma was, by now, beaming. For it was his work with sheep's blood that led to this wonderful story that Bob was elucidating. He looked over at Bob as a proud parent would look at his child.

Melchior, characteristically, looked embarrassed and sipped at his brandy. Even Proust and Ervin were moved.

But it was Judy who finally asked, "Now, Bob, even if you do find out that it was the creek water that is causing the earl's illness, will that do him any good?"

"That I don't know, Judy. We are trying several things in our laboratory that may or may not provide an answer to what substances might be helpful in the treatment of persons with early forms of his illness; but I, like you, worry that it might be too little, too late for our earl."

It was then Craycroft who spoke.

"May I say, Master Robert, that we who have come to love the earl, and are hopeful beyond all reason that he should recover, do wish you and your esteemed colleagues the best. But I am not one whose world is tied down to that hope. What I do know, and Cartho knew as well, is that the world of medicine as we know it has been given the chance to be altered like never before. For as with Cartho's predictions, and I do not know how he knew, Tom's uncovering of this truth shall be the key."

"Mister Craycroft," said Judy, somewhat unexpectedly. "I, for one, am most appreciative of this chance to eat with good friends and to become part of your world and all of its promise of a most excellent future. But there are many things that I need to discuss with Bob—er, Master Robert—that are playing on my mind. Is it too much to ask that we be allowed some time together to search our own hearts? As you noted earlier, we both came here somewhat without our consent, and though we seem to be part of something much bigger, it is still the two of us, and I think we need to talk."

Bob felt a lump in his throat and looked across the table at Judy, unable to utter a sound.

"Why, of course, m'lady. You most certainly may, and I offer my apologies if you have not had the opportunity to speak with Master Robert before this."

Judy's eyes sparkled just a little as she got up, walked over to his side of the table, and said, "Well, big guy, you gonna take up that offer, or am I gonna have to make you?"

Bob was silent for a moment, then got hold of his own turbulent emotions, and said, "You know, Judy, you've really got a way with words. Okay, let's go. My place or yours?"

Chapter Eight

Marilyn Gilsen woke with a start. Instinctively, she reached over to *his* side of the bed, which was empty. She then panicked and flipped on the light. Then, gradually, it all came back to her. As her breathing slowed down, she recalled in vivid detail the dream that she had.

She had been standing outside in the snow in the middle of winter. Though it was obviously very cold, it did not penetrate her. She stood behind her husband and a youngster as they were walking on a moonlit night. The air was crisp, and it smelt faintly of the sea. The two were having a conversation, but she could not make out the words. She looked around and was surprised to see that she was in the courtyard of some great castle. They stopped walking and were obviously listening to something. There in the stillness they listened, and then she could hear it too. It was the sound of a harp playing, but no ordinary playing. It was mesmerizing. The sound, though quiet, filled that courtyard with beauty. The moonlight glistened off the ice on the ground; the great walls all around her seemed to shimmer in accompaniment to the music. Then the music stopped and she noticed the two people were moving away, but as they were walking away, Bob turned toward her and uttered the word, *Drachma*. Then they were gone. She was alone in the courtyard with the music playing again, the sound of the harp still saying to her, "He is all right."

What an incredibly weird dream that was, thought Marilyn. Then she got up; it was almost light anyway. As she got on her robe and slippers and headed down the stairs, she had a notion to look at the little box left to her by Mr. Vincente. So she turned around on the stairs, headed back into her bedroom, and there on her nightstand was her box, but under it was a sheet of paper. She turned on the overhead light and looked inside the box to reassure herself that her coin was still there. Relieved, she then picked up the paper, noticing that it was a very unusual yellowish color and felt strange in her hand. It was folded in half and she looked inside. She noticed the writing, with an unusual backward slant, and she read the words:

> Janie Crabtree.
> If you but seek her,
> And take to her this coin,
> She shall tell you what you
> Wish to know.
> Know that I wish you peace.
>
> Drachma

Her head was swimming and she suddenly felt very dizzy. She backed into her bed and sat down.

"Oh, wow," she said aloud.

The dream was understandable, as she had every reason to be dreaming about Bob; but she could not shake the feeling of reality about it. It was all too intense, and she remembered it too well, remembering every detail; but then this note. Marilyn had no explanation that made any sense at all for the note. She knew no one was about in her house. The note was signed by someone named Drachma. She recalled how Mr. Vincente had told her of this person named Drachma. She tried to recall what he told her and seemed to remember that this Drachma person was responsible for Mr. Vincente's being here, and that

he had written some book that provided the means for his being here. Looking again at the note, she wondered about this Janie Crabtree. She must be related to Josh Crabtree, one of Bob's longstanding patients. She remembered him mentioning Josh Crabtree any number of times, often with a feeling of fatigue and some frustration in his tone.

Oh, this is all too crazy, she thought to herself. *But it might provide some more of an explanation about Bob.*

His disappearance still made no sense, at least not to her logical mind.

But it's not my logical mind that's being played with.

With a sense of purpose, she heaved herself upright and went downstairs. In the kitchen in a drawer under the phone, she found the phone book. Looking under *C* in the white pages, there it was: Crabtree, Earl and Janie, 4982 Winterstone Drive 406-9873. It was even circled, evidently by Bob. Quickly, she scribbled down the address and phone number, and then she made some coffee.

After that, it was back to something resembling normality, as the coffee worked its magic, leaving her somewhat stronger for the day ahead. Then she went back upstairs and got herself ready to face what was certain to be another crazy, mixed up kind of a day.

It's strange, she thought, *I have never heard from that detective Bryant since that day. I know on the way back here we just sat and said nothing, but then he told me that I'd hear from them "pretty soon." It was like they knew something, but were afraid to tell me. Oh, well, if I don't hear from him, so much the better.*

When Marilyn felt ready, she descended the stairs again and went back into the kitchen. She poured herself another cup and went over to the phone. She was about to dial the number when she was stopped in mid-action by a thought. She put the phone down, found the paper, and looked at it again. She re-read the message, then went back up the stairs, found her little box, and

looked inside once more. Yes, there it was. Then she put the little box inside her purse, along with the small paper.

Sitting now in her kitchen, drinking her coffee, she wondered again about the police and their inquiry. She had already given them permission to search her house, and they had already gotten Bob's car from the hospital parking lot and were searching it; though she could not imagine that they'd find anything useful in his car. But the police had left her alone and not bothered her anymore.

Strange, she thought, *how very odd that they had shown so much interest early on, and then nothing.*

The phone rang and startled her.

"Hello… Yes, this is Mrs. Gilsen. Who did you say you were? No, I'm afraid I don't generally watch Channel 5… And you want to interview me? I'm not really sure… I'll have to check with Detective Bryant. Well, we'll have to see… Today? At three o'clock… I really don't know. Why don't you let me call him and see if that would be okay? Then why not call me back in half an hour? Oh, okay. Good-bye."

Fumbling in her purse, she found the card that had been given to her by Detective Bryant. Then, without thinking about it, she dialed his number. It was answered by an officious person at the other end who said that he'd see if Detective Bryant was around and then put her on hold. After a few minutes, Edgar Bryant was on the line.

"Oh, Detective Bryant, this is Marilyn Gilsen… Oh, thank you, it's good to talk to you too. Well, the reason I'm calling is that I just got a call from someone who works for Channel 5 News… Oh, let me think, he told me his name… Oh, yes, that's it, it's Charlie Stephens… No, I never watch Channel 5… Yes… Well, he said that he wanted to interview me. I told him that I needed to speak to you first… Is that right? Well, he said around three o'clock… No, he didn't say where… I see… Yes. Well, I think that's what I'll tell him. Listen, I haven't heard anything

from you guys about the stuff in my house, or about Bob's car or anything. Is everything all right? I'm not a suspect or anything, right? …Well, at least that's something… No, I haven't come up with any other ideas… If I do, I'll sure call you…"

"No, I haven't heard anything more from Mr. Vincente… You haven't either? Oh, yes, I'll let you know… Okay, I sure will, as soon as I hear from him… All right, good-bye, then."

Marilyn Gilsen's pulse was pounding as she hung up the phone. She took a deep breath and found her piece of paper with Janie's phone number and address on it. Then she took another deep breath and dialed the number. It rang three times and then a male voice answered.

"Hello, may I speak with Janie Crabtree?"

"May I say who's calling?"

"This is Marilyn Gilsen…"

"Mrs. Gilsen?" His voice carried both surprise and relief. "Oh, sure, let me get her on the phone for you. She's right here."

"Mrs. Gilsen?" Janie answered. "Oh, I've been meaning to try to contact you. So much has happened since Josh died, and your husband, uh…disappeared…"

"Josh died? Oh, I'm so sorry, I didn't know… Well, there's a lot that I don't know, which is partly why I'm calling. You see, I got this very strange note from someone named Drachma…"

"Drachma? Did I hear you right? Did you say Drachma? Well, then, Mrs. Gilsen, I think we should get together, and soon."

"Well, how about today?"

They had it all arranged within minutes. Marilyn would go to the Crabtree's place around noon. They would have lunch and a leisurely afternoon, giving them plenty of time to talk.

She sat quietly for a period of time, thinking about all that was going on and how it was all mixed up. Some of what was happening sort of made sense and other things made no sense whatsoever; especially all this stuff about where Bob was, according to Carlo Vincente. *And why Bob, of all people? What did*

anyone expect to accomplish with all of this? There seemed no purpose at all.

Sipping her coffee, she noted that it had cooled off quite a bit, but it still tasted all right; and so she waited for Charlie Stephens to call her back. After another twenty minutes, the phone rang.

"Hello... Yes, this is. And how are you, Mr. Stephens? You want to meet me where? I see...and you want to talk about what, exactly? Well, I'll just tell Detective Bryant... Oh, yes, I think that his presence would be a requirement... Yes, absolutely... May I bring anything with me? Oh, no... No, I don't think so. All right, I'll be there... Bye, now."

As she hung up the phone, she noticed her hand trembling inexplicably. Charlie Stephens had just sounded on the phone like someone trying to sell her something and that made her nervous; very nervous. It had been some time since anyone made her this unsettled. There was something in that tinny little voice that grated on her nerves, and something else that got under her skin. Maybe having a familiar face there would be helpful.

So she picked up the phone and dialed Edgar Bryant's number again.

"Hello, Mr. Bryant. This is Marilyn Gilsen again... Yes, I'm still okay, but I just got off the phone after talking to that little weasel, Charlie Stephens... Yeah, you could definitely say that... Anyway, he wants me to come to the hospital this afternoon... Yeah, around three... Okay, I'll meet you in front of the hospital. Now, you did say I'm not a suspect or anything, and this isn't going to turn into one of those *National Enquirer* kind of things, is it? Oh, good... Well, I'll see you then... Bye."

Feeling already emotionally drained, Marilyn Gilsen let out a big sigh, then got up and went out to the living room, preparing for the day to come.

Oh, Bob, what have you done? This is so unlike you. And now I really feel so lost and alone.

Finally finding Winterstone Drive after taking several wrong turns, Marilyn then saw the number 4982 up on the house and turned into the driveway. After parking, she got out and went to the door. She felt inexplicably nervous, as if this was some sort of job interview. After taking a couple of deep breaths, she pressed the doorbell.

Her fears and anxieties, however, were dispelled when Janie answered the door. Here was a slight, middle-aged woman, who exuded intensity, mixed with a large dose of compassion, and welcomed Marilyn with a warm, sisterly hug.

"Oh, Mrs. Gilsen, you've no idea how I've looked forward to meeting you. Please come in. Make yourself comfortable. Here, let me take your coat. Hey, Earl, it's Mrs. Gilsen. She's here."

Marilyn looked around the small home. It was neatly furnished and smelled faintly of apples and comfort.

"Oh, hi, Mrs. Gilsen. I'm Earl. Do come in and have a seat here in the living room."

"Why, thank you, and please call me Marilyn."

After hanging up Marilyn's coat, Janie joined Earl in welcoming her to their home.

"You know, Marilyn, I've always wondered about you. I got to know your husband quite well, or so I thought until this latest business. And I've always thought that you must be a very special kind of woman. I mean, all the hours and all. I think you might have quite a lonely life. I don't mean that with any disrespect. It's just that you must have some way of dealing with all the separations and all."

"Well, to be perfectly honest, I do have a strong independent streak, but all this has caught me unawares. I guess I just was not ready for any of it." She fumbled in her purse and brought out the little box and the note.

At the sight of the box, Janie gasped.

"Here, this note says I'm to bring you this box, which contains…"

"I know. A drachma."

"You've seen this before? Where?"

"Oh, that's a long story. Are you ready for it? And you have that note, too?"

She handed the box to Janie, who opened it to find the drachma, in a blue velvet bed. Then Janie took the paper.

"Hey, Earl, come over here." She unfolded the paper, and with a look of astonishment, read the writing on the small piece of yellowed parchment.

"Janie, it's the same paper and the same handwriting," said Earl, as amazed as Janie. "Now, how did you come by this paper and this note?"

"Well, now, that is also a long story. And yes, I've got the time, so why don't we start with your story and then I'll tell you mine?"

"Okay," Janie said. "But why don't we sit down and have some lunch? Because I believe that this is going to take some time."

So they gathered at the kitchen table. Janie had made some sandwiches, some soup, and fresh fruit salad. As they sat down to eat, Janie told the tale of Joshua, from her first encounter with Bob, as an overworked young cardiology fellow, through Josh's trials and near misses, with Bob playing an ever more important role in his continuing care, up until his final illness. She told her tale with simplicity that belied her deep caring. Then she began her incredible story of this last illness, with the prelude of weird messages. Then she had Earl tell her of his own strange dream and his message about the "lady healer."

When she returned with coffee and cookies, she resumed her tale, as convoluted as it was, with Bob, Dr. Greshin, Judy, and their interactions with Josh. Then she told the tale of the notes, the coin, and it's mysterious disappearances and reappearances, as if it had a mind of its own; and how Bob was looking more and more worn out, and there seemed a distance between him and the rest of the world around him. She noted that Bob just

seemed to have completely disappeared from the scene. Then she told the heartrending tale of Josh's last day, and how Judy had befriended them and seemed to have gotten mysterious messages of her own; how the coin had been part of Judy's own saga. She told of how Judy had been there at the last and had been a true friend, just when they needed her.

"Wow, this is one special nurse. I'm going to have to seek her out," Marilyn exclaimed.

Janie and Earl looked at one another.

Then Janie told the tale of Josh's funeral, their subsequent visit with Judy, and the note in the mail. Then Janie told of Judy leaving in the snowstorm and of not hearing from her again.

"And have you reported this to anyone?" Marilyn asked.

"Reported what?"

"I get your point. But have you tried contacting her?"

"Never does a day go by without our trying. But so far, nothing," Janie replied.

Silence. For a whole minute, no one spoke.

Marilyn looked into her coffee cup, and then she began her own tale.

"Well, I should tell you," she began, "all this has been a harrowing experience for me, starting with the phone calls from the hospital, and then the visits by Detective Bryant and his little note-taking assistant, Detective Lewinsky. They came to my house and they interviewed me. Then when they were about to leave, I got a phone call from a Carlo Vincente, who said that he knew something of Bob's disappearance. This made their little detective ears perk up. So they came back and took me to the hospital where I met this ancient, but really ageless, fellow named Carlo Vincente. He told me the most incredible tale of how, in this place called Shepperton, there is, or was, this fellow named Drachma who, I guess, kind of runs the place. Anyway, this all involves this ancient guild of potters and painters who produce some amazing pottery, which supposedly protects the health

of those that drink from the pots. And now the health of these painters and potters is in jeopardy, threatening the livelihood of the whole island of Shepperton and the lives of this whole little culture that has developed there.

"And then he goes on to tell me that he has seen Bob and this nurse, who sounds like Judy, and that it was the machinations of this guy named Drachma that allowed him to come to our time and place, and that allowed Bob to go back in time to Shepperton. Now, I know this sounds weird, but he recognized Bob in a way that it could be no other person. And now, through Drachma's doings, Bob is off there in Shepperton. For how long, he wasn't able to say, but I distinctly got the feeling that it was permanent. Then he told me that he had given up his own life for this endeavor. But before he left, he gave me this little box with the drachma inside, and that somehow the presence of the coin indicated that Bob was all right."

"This whole story sounds a bit farfetched," said Earl, "except that now there are people involved who have never met and who tell basically two sides of the same story. The people are basically the same, and the story is consistent. But let me tell you that I don't believe that anyone is going to believe a word of it."

"You're right, Earl. And that brings me to my next dilemma. There's this reporter from Channel 5 who's going to interview me this afternoon…"

"You don't mean Charlie Stephens?"

"Oh, yes I do…"

"Well, I'd beware of that little slime-bag. If he wants to interview you, then he thinks that he's got some kind of angle that he's going to pursue. Oh, I'd beware of that one."

"Well, that's what Detective Bryant told me. So he's going to be there, too."

"If you would like, Earl and I can be there as well," put in Janie. "I know that we've only just met, but maybe you'd like some moral support."

"Did you tell him you would give him the interview?" asked Earl.

"I'm afraid that I did. You see, it's not like me to say no."

"Then I would say, you can count on our support. We'll be there with you."

Charlie Stephens rolled his Nissan wagon into the parking lot, parking rather haphazardly in what he assumed to be a parking space near the main entrance to Memorial Hospital. He had his mind on other things than parking anyway. He got out and quickly noticed that the Channel 5 van had, as usual, beaten him here. He rummaged around in the back of his cluttered wagon for his notepaper, checked his shirt pocket for pens, and then he reached over for his sport coat and hauled it out with him. He almost slipped on the sidewalk as he stepped away from his car. Then he hurried in, looking every bit the distracted reporter that he was.

Inside the main rotunda, he found his cameraman, as well as the newbie driver, setting up their equipment.

"Hey, Ron, how about some shots from outside, and then a few in here? Makes the place look legit, you know," Charlie suggested.

"Okay, Charlie. Why don't you get your act together this time? It's still a quarter 'til. You did say three o'clock, right?"

"Yeah, yeah."

Charlie really thought he smelled a story brewing here, and he was rarely wrong. He was the sort of reporter that left an indelible impression. It was often the wrong impression, but he left one anyway. If you talked with people about him, it was almost unanimously bad, but people watched Channel 5, and Charlie Stephens was one of the reasons. It was not as if he was entertaining, or eloquent. There was just something about that ingratiating, persistent little punk that brought people back.

He read over his notes once more to make sure he had the facts of the case straight.

What he did not notice was an old man, carefully observing from across the rotunda.

As Marilyn walked in with Detective Bryant, Janie, and Earl, Charlie was set up across the rotunda. Edgar Bryant gave her one piece of advice.

"Now, don't you offer anything, let him do the talking. And for heaven's sake, just keep your opinions to yourself."

"Right, Detective."

"Just call me Edgar."

"Okay, Edgar." She flashed him a nervous smile.

"Here," said Janie, "this is yours anyway." She handed Marilyn the little box, which she put into her purse.

Finally, as she was walking over to the cameras, she looked over at the little crowd that had gathered, and in among the people of the crowd, she saw him. The familiar face of Carlo Vincente smiled. He bowed slightly then was gone. That, however, was enough to give her a deep sense of peace.

"Hello, Mr. Stephens. I'm Marilyn Gilsen."

"Charlie Stephens, ma'am. Now let me explain a bit about what we do here. Now, have you ever been on TV before?"

"No, I never have."

"Well, then, I'll tell you. I'm going to be interviewing you about your husband's disappearance…"

Marilyn noticed just how short he was, and just how sure of himself he appeared to be. And she couldn't help noticing just how overpowering his cologne was.

"All right, Mr. Stephens, let's get this thing done."

The interview started off with standard language of TV introductions. With Charlie Stephens beginning by telling of the disappearance of a well-respected cardiologist on staff at Memorial Hospital, and that, to date, there had been no clues as to his disappearance.

"I'm standing here with his wife, Mrs. Marilyn Gilsen."

"Now, can you tell me how many years you've been married to Dr. Gilsen?" he asked Marilyn.

"Yes, we've been married fourteen years."

"And how would you describe your marriage?"

"I would describe it as a solid, comfortable marriage."

"And in the time you've been married, have you had any times when the relationship has felt strained?"

"No, not our relationship. We've been through some rough spots together, but it has been a solid relationship."

"And do you have any children?"

"No, none."

"Has that ever caused tension?"

"Whatever do you mean?"

"I mean, was that ever a sore spot in your marriage?"

"It was heartbreaking, but it never hurt our relationship."

"I see. And as a physician, I imagine your husband works some long hours…"

"Yes, he does."

"Now do you have any idea what may have happened to your husband?"

"No, I really don't."

"I see. And have you gone to the police about this?"

"Well, actually, the police came to me…"

"And what, may I ask, have the police found out?"

"Nothing that I know of."

"Let me ask, how are things financially?"

"They're fine."

"Any hidden assets? Anything that your husband may have been hiding?"

Marilyn's eyes flashed momentarily. Then she took a deep breath and answered, "I handle all our financial stuff. Bob does not have the time or inclination. So I can state, unequivocally, that there have been no financial irregularities."

"And let me ask you, does the name Judy Morrison mean anything to you?"

Marilyn hesitated just an instant, and then answered. "Yes, I understand that she's a nurse at this hospital."

"And did your husband have any dealings with this nurse?"

"I really do not know firsthand."

"But you say that you know she is a nurse at this hospital?"

"Yes, that I found out today."

"And what would you say if I told you that this same nurse, also mysteriously disappeared not three days after your husband disappeared?

"Nothing."

"Nothing at all? Don't you find that the least bit strange?"

"No."

"Well, thank you for your time, Mrs. Gilsen."

"Are we done, then?"

With that, Marilyn Gilsen, turned and walked away toward her friends and the detective.

Charlie Stephens, then, got his things together. He thought about calling Marilyn back for more, but then he thought better about it.

Over the hospital intercom, he heard the announcement. "Would the owner of a blue Nissan wagon parked in the visitor entrance come and move your car immediately? You are blocking the entryway."

Charlie groaned, then got his notebook and told Ron to meet him at the station. Next, he hustled out to the place that he thought was a parking lot, noticing the line of cars backed up. He waved apologetically and quickly got in his car.

He did not notice the man in the back seat, until the man spoke in a foreign accent.

"Master Stephens, my name is Carlo Vincente. I would like to apologize for entering into your transportation, but what I have to tell you may become very important."

Charlie turned around quickly to notice the man sitting in his back seat. A chill ran down his spine as he pulled out of the way of the cars trying to get in behind him.

Chapter Nine

"All right, now, mister. It seems you and I have finally got a chance to talk." Judy was sitting in Felicia's library. There was a warm fire in the fireplace, and the room was impressively cozy. "I tell you, I have been taken on this ride through snow, muck, and rain. I've been captured, I've seen people die, and almost die trying to save me. I've been tended to by a man older and wiser than any I have met, and I've been brought here to this castle where I'm now treated like some princess and given the moniker of "Lady Healer," which I'm not."

Bob was finally sitting down, in a comfortable chair across from Judy.

"And you're here, too. Coming as you did, through this same wicked weather, and I'm sure, having gotten here with some of these same stories to tell your children around the campfire. And here you are, also treated like some sort of nobility, and thought of as a great and powerful healer, which you may be, but now here we are. You and me. The only ones here from *our time*."

Bob had seemed distracted until Judy's little diatribe, which he felt was aimed right at his heart.

"Okay, Judy." Bob seemed to settle down a little and was ready to finally talk. "Now how about if I tell you how I got here? I mean, the whole story, holding nothing back. For I've got no one else I can talk to about how I really feel."

Judy smiled at him, which was a warm, caring gesture that reached him seemingly from across the chasm of time and space. "You go first, and then I'll tell you my tale, also with no pretense, holding back nothing either."

"All right, then. I guess I'll start back in my fellowship when I was doing the *unit*, and you were one of the nurses there, and, I might mention, one of my favorite nurses of all time. I guess I got to know you, or at least I thought I did. I remember how we would sit down at the end of your shift and play a game of who's got the sickest patients and what was the weirdest order of the day; and I found it amazing that you would even sit and talk to me, let alone seem to enjoy it. Anyway, that stuck with me through the years, and even when I got onto the faculty and you had moved on to the ER, the occasions when I would see you and you'd smile in recognition; those moments would lift my spirits in ways that you couldn't even imagine.

"In the meantime, as you know, I became busy with my practice and I got all of the trappings of success—the money and the nice house in a nice neighborhood and all. But with that came something of a burden. It was hard to put into words, but it involved a conflict between my work and my relationship at home. Now don't get me wrong, I love my wife and think the world of her. And if I had the time to devote to being a good husband, I think that I could become one of the best. Well, all of this came to something of a boiling point about the time that Josh became ill. You know, that was the evening when I came down to the ER to get something to eat and you were there, and like some angel of mercy, you touched me. And then, healed, I went home; but that's when things really started unraveling.

"Well, I got home by around 9:30. The house was still and I just sat down in the kitchen and thought about my life; about how it seemed too hectic, that we never had any time to enjoy ourselves. I even thought about the last time Marilyn and I actually sat down to a nice meal, with no interruptions, no phone

calls, no beeper; that had been last year in San Francisco when I was at a conference. We went out to dinner at some restaurant overlooking the bay, and we had an absolutely wonderful meal. It was just amazing, to sit and look out on the beautiful bay, with no worries, no schedule, and no threats of being called away. But then we came back to the grind, and it started all over again. Anyway, I was thinking of all these things as I went upstairs—tired, worn out, and ready to crawl in bed. Actually, I think Marilyn noticed something besides how tired I was, and she asked, but I think I gave her something of an evasion before going to sleep.

"And that's when our friend, Mr. Drachma, stepped into the picture. It began with a strange and memorable dream that night. I know that unusual is becoming commonplace in our lives, but this was one really weird dream. I found myself sitting down in an inn on a rough bench, with a bunch of rough, rugged working folk all around. You could tell it was cold outside, but inside the inn the atmosphere was one of warmth, of camaraderie. We were drinking from these large flagons of ale, and there was bread on the table. And at the table next to me was none other than Craycroft, who was telling a tale of an ancient book that was sought after by powerful men and protected by some humble friar. Now you're going to have to have Craycroft tell you this part of the story, for there is no way that I could do it justice. Anyway, there was a minstrel there who played a harp, as none has ever played in my life, and he played so beautifully that I was transported out of the back of this inn and taken to some deep forest in springtime, where there was the warmth of the sun beating down through the leaves. There was running water, and you could even smell the newly turned earth. It was as if here was what I was looking for; it was right there."

"And then the phone rang. It was Jerry Beasley, telling me that Josh was back in."

"Well, Bob, you said that was when Drachma stepped into the picture. Would you care to elaborate?" Judy remarked.

"Well, as you have come to find out, this guy moves in very mysterious ways. I came to discover that the inn was Barncuddy's, and that Craycroft was really there, Willie Minstrel was there, and that the tale Craycroft was telling, he really told that evening, and that Willie really did play, as fantastically as I remembered. But then I found out that the book that Craycroft was talking about really does exist, and it is called *The Book of Drachma.*"

"Oh, my. You're going to have to give me just a minute to absorb all that you've been telling me. And, pray tell, how did you find out all of this?" Judy inquired.

"Well, you know the night that you came here, you were all decked out and pretty, but you could hardly keep your eyes open? You remember Craycroft inviting us to go with him to Barncuddy's…"

"Yeah, I vaguely remember that." She answered with a smile.

"Anyway, that's when I found out all of this."

"I see. But could you tell me just a bit about how you came to this place, for real? I'm quite certain that you didn't just take a jetliner and land here. That would have been too easy."

Judy winked as she said this.

"Well, when was the last time you saw me, back in our time?"

"You remember the time you came down to the ER and I was in report with Lonnie?"

Bob nodded.

"There you were, sleeping through our report. Then I woke you and told you of my own strange experiences and how I'd gotten this old coin from some old geezer in the ER named Carlo Vincente…"

"Oh, now, there's a name that's hard to forget…"

"Well, that was the last time I saw you before here. I'll tell you more about my frantic search for you, but later. Please, continue your story of how you got here, because I'm really interested."

She touched his hand, but that was not what she really wanted to do.

"Okay. Well, then I got called to the OR and I went up there and "put out some fires" with Josh on the table. Then as I was going about my business on the floors, I got some STAT page from the ER, where they told me some really old man named—get this—Carlo Vincente was claiming to be a patient of mine and was down there in extremis. Well, I rush down there to find your Carlo Vincente about to code, but before he goes out, he tells me that this is the day that I should prepare. But then he coded, and he was gone. I mean, we tried all our tricks, but he was dead."

"After that shaky experience, as I was going back to my business with Josh, I was in some kind of a state—not sleeping exactly, but more like the walking dead. Then I had this little dream where I met this guy Drachma in the forest of my previous dream. He told me to be prepared to make a journey unlike any other I had made. Then, still unable to finish rounds, I got a call from TSurg ICU, where they had Josh, and he had gone into rapid A-fib. Then, as they were getting ready to cardiovert him, there he was, again—this guy, Drachma—with his voice like the whole forest, telling me that now was the time. Only this time, he told me to hang onto what I wanted to take because I was about to depart.

"And that's the last I remember of the *old place*. The next thing I knew, I was waking up on some hillside and there were hunters and their dogs, and then there was the smelly old house with the smelly old man. I was taken prisoner and held in some old barracks. I was sleepy, but I couldn't really sleep, and then there was the page, or actually two pages, from you…"

"Yeah, that was me. If I'd known…"

"Oh, Judy, if you could have seen what those pages did to my guards!" Bob could not help but chuckle. "Anyway, I made it safely, though not comfortably, to the castle. And you know, all the while, I kept thinking of you and hearing your voice and seeing you. And now here we are, the two of us, trying to figure

out day-to-day just how we are expected to behave. Judy, you know I care for you in some way that I've never cared for anyone before. But you've got to give me time, for in my own mind, at least, I'm still a very married man."

"All right, it's a deal, Bob. But I figure, what do they know of us and our lives? And what can they or would they do? Throw us back, try again for something better? Now I've got Jeanne, who is probably just what I need right now. I'm sure that she can keep me in line, if anyone can. And you've got Craycroft—you two wise men of medicine."

"And so, now you'd like to hear what happened while you were away, no doubt. Okay, here goes, and I'm telling you this is the uncensored, unvarnished truth," Judy began.

"Like you, I'll go back a ways, to the days before we got to know each other, and I had just moved to Ohio. I was a bitter, lost, and upset woman who had just gone through a messy breakup in West Virginia. Though I'd been a nurse for a number of years, my self-confidence was lacking. I am, really, a good ER nurse, and I take pride in my work; but the CCU position at Memorial seemed a pretty good fit, so I took it. It was a little rough at first, but I got used to it. The only real difference from ER nursing was the lack of variety. And then you came along. You treated me differently from the other docs who came through. You seemed to care about what I had to say, you actually listened, and, besides, you were kind of cute in your shy, awkward way."

"Oh, I believe that is the first time in many years that I have been called cute," Bob interrupted.

"Well, that was how I saw you. And you know what? You were what I missed most about going to work in the ER. Like you, I enjoyed our little sessions together, and, if I recall, it seems we did more than talk about difficult patients—we seemed to spend quite a bit of time talking about things such as relationships."

At this, Bob looked somewhat chagrined, and said, "I hope I didn't say anything too embarrassing."

"No, nothing like that, but I remember one conversation in particular. Now, you might not remember, but you said that you were thinking that you'd like to have a chance to teach. Not the typical way with med students or residents following you around, but in a classroom with no white coats or any clinical stuff, and you talked about how you'd teach them what it really means to be a doctor. How it was the relationship with the patient that defines who and what a physician is."

"Well, I can imagine me saying something like that, particularly after Grand Rounds, or some other medical fiasco…"

"I was impressed, not so much with your desire to teach, but with what you wanted to teach. And I've had the chance to see, more than once, that you're really very uncompromising in your dedication to your patients."

"That's because this is the only way I know how to practice medicine…"

"And you don't suppose that's why you were chosen, do you?"

"Chosen? What makes you think I was chosen for any of this?"

"Now, think about it. Who do you think came to me with that note about seeking out a doctor of hearts named Gilsen, eh?"

"That was Carlo Vincente, wasn't it?"

"And acting upon whose directions?"

"I imagine Drachma's."

"Right, well, I hear he's coming here this week, so you can ask him yourself. But now, back to my story. As you went about your business and I went about mine, things just seemed to be floating along just fine for me. Then this guy, Carlo Vincente, lands in our ER with his little coin. Then you show up in the ER, Josh comes in, then we're spinning around in circles, it seems. I meet Janie and Earl, and you're wandering about the hospital looking like you're in some kind of a trance.

"Well, bless my maternal instincts, but you really got to me. You, walking around like some lost, lonely, little mutt, with Josh in trouble; and you, as the lone ranger being the only one who could

fix him. But then, Bob, I'll tell you, when you disappeared from our lives with no warning, it was like someone ripped something out of me, and it hurt. It really, really hurt."

Judy's eyes had been bleary with the telling of her tale, but now, she lost it. It was too much for Bob as well, and they embraced— not like lovers, but like long lost friends, finding in each other solace and protection. They remained in that embrace for a long time, feeling the weight of centuries bearing down on them.

Finally, Judy said, "Well, after you disappeared from us, I tried to contact you by phone, by paging you, asking around if anyone had seen you, and I just came up empty. And that's just how I felt. I got closer to Janie and Earl in your absence. And then I was there when Josh died, and you were still nowhere to be found. Then a couple of days later, I went to Josh's funeral and I half-expected to see you there. But in that silence, I met Drachma, and he indicated that you were safe and that you and I would share in this purpose, which he said that I'd discover.

"After the funeral, I went and saw Janie and Earl, and they told me of the strange things that had happened to them. I found out about Earl's dream, and that Drachma was also in his dream. And then one last thing happened. When their mail came, in it was a note from Drachma, but the note was for me, and it told of how I would see an old man on horseback and I was to go with him. Well then, I drove away in a blizzard, lost my way, got into an accident, and, somehow after the accident, I ended up here on this island.

"And you know what, Bob? I am not going to let this separation happen again, even if we get back home sometime in our own future, and you should get back with Marilyn. Even if that were to happen, you're not going to disappear again from my life. It's not that I want you for myself; it's something deeper than that. It's something like a connecting of two souls. Oh, I don't know... Do you understand what I mean?"

"I think so, Judy. Though I must tell you that I'm emotionally confused right now. It seems that there are forces at work in our

lives, all of our lives, which we have no control of—forces both good and evil, constructive and destructive. I can feel them, but I can't identify them. I can sense their presence, but they're gone like smoke about as quickly as they appear; and yet, they seem to be controlling our destiny."

"Well, why don't you take your confused self and take my confused self back to where the people are, Master Robert?" Judy said with a wink. "I do believe that we have achieved some measure of understanding that might hold us for a while, don't you?"

"Well, m'lady, as you wish."

Then Judy hugged him again, thought about kissing him, thought better of it, and settled for holding his hand. Bob could feel the warmth radiating from her contact with his hand and he could feel the peace and acceptance, like a healing balm, spread up his arm and envelop his very soul.

"Oh, you're a most extraordinarily powerful force to deal with, m'lady."

Judy just smiled and held his hand.

When Judy and Bob returned to the dining room, they found it almost deserted, with only Craycroft, Jeanne, and Falma there.

"Well, it would appear that you two are still friends from the looks upon your faces. Did you settle what you needed to settle for the present?" Craycroft's eyes sparkled as he looked upon their faces.

"Oh, yes, I think that we did, but it was something that, I agree, we needed to do now before we went much further. At least I think we did, didn't we?" Bob turned to Judy, a bit of sparkle in his eye.

"Oh, Bob, let's keep 'em guessing," Judy chided. "Now where did everyone go?"

"It seems, m'lady, that they have gone off to Barncuddy's where they await our arrival."

"Well then, why don't we go there as well? It's a place I keep hearing about, but I've never seen. It's not a gentlemen only kind of place, is it?"

"If it were, then it shall no longer be," said Jeanne. "Come, m'lady, let us—you and I—take these gentlemen as our escorts and go." Then Jeanne grabbed the arm of Falma and let Judy do the same to Craycroft.

By the time they got to Barncuddy's, the place was reverberating with activity. There was the usual evening crowd, plus the crowd from Craycroft's place.

"Ah, Master Craycroft, and with Master Falma, these two young and lovely ladies, and the esteemed Master Robert. I welcome ye back. Now yer others are in the large room up the stairs. I'm sure ye can find them. I'll send Diane up to see that ye get yer drinks." Barncuddy's welcome was hearty and sincere.

"My thanks, good man. Yes, I am sure that we can find our way up. Now, might I ask you, are you expecting Willie Minstrel here this evening? This comely young lady, who goes by the name of Judy, has never heard him, though she has heard of his playing."

"You never know about Willie, but I expect that he may be persuaded to come here tonight—after all, you are enticement enough, and with these lovely ladies with thee…"

"Very well, see what you can do."

"Of course, my friend."

As they ascended the stairs, they could hear the revelry in the upstairs room. There were shouts of great laughter, and then, suddenly, Diane came out blushing, almost running into the group coming up the stairs.

"Oh, pardon me, m'lord," she said before realizing who it was. Then she blushed even more, curtseyed, and then stepped back to let the group pass by.

Craycroft couldn't understand what had come over the young lady. This was the same young woman who was so cloying and flirtatious the other night.

"Now, my dear, it is just my companions and I. Why this sudden change? I have surely not changed that much."

"Oh, m'lord Craycroft. It is not thee who has changed, but rather we who have changed in relation to thee. For now thou art our sovereign lord."

"But is it not simply that you are perceiving me as something different? Have I changed?"

"Oh, m'lord, I am not the one to ask that."

"Very well, then, I shall ask you more when you bring our drinks."

"As you wish, m'lord." And then she scuttled off toward the kitchen.

Craycroft's puzzled expression caught the attention of Kerlin as they came in and sat down.

"What is it, m'lord? You look as though you are uncertain."

"Ah, Kerlin, would that some things in this world were immune to change."

"Do you mean things like the inside of Barncuddy's?"

"Aye, that I do."

Kerlin nodded.

"Well, then, why do you not tell us all of what changes you have wrought here tonight? As we were walking up here, it most certainly sounded as if you had made some impact upon the armor of stasis. Am I right?"

"As you thought. Now, why do you not tell what you have done, eh, Cayman?"

"Well, m'lord," answered Cayman, "it would appear that I have succeeded in explaining to our good maid here that you are now lord of us here upon this isle and that she would be better off with someone like me, than thee."

"Oh, then that explains her actions more than mere words could." He let out a hearty laugh. "And let me ask you, were you at all successful?"

"Oh, aye, I was, of sorts. At least, she has agreed to come with me after she gets off here."

"But with me, to keep them company," added Eustace.

"Ah, I see... Well, that is some success."

A somewhat demure Diane then came up with flagons and a pitcher of ale. As she was serving the ale, though, she did ask who the two women were.

"My dear, this fine young lady is Jeanne, my new assistant. And this young lady is the Lady Judy, who came to us from the same place as Master Robert, which is to say she came from a long way away."

"Oh, so you're the lady I was warned about..."

"Warned?" Judy said with surprise.

"Oh, aye, m'lady. I was told that you belong to Master Robert, and I was to stay away from him for that reason." A slight, impish smile returned to her face as she said this.

"Bob, you didn't tell me that you were doing any flirting with the waitresses," Judy teased.

Bob just blushed and shook his head. Then, all eyes were on him.

"Okay, Judy, I don't really remember what happened here, because I think I was just a bit inebriated, but I certainly do not remember any flirting; though if you had been here then maybe there would have been some..."

"Indeed, to flirting!" said Falma, unexpectedly. "Here, here. Let us raise our glasses to one and all, in salute!"

With a feeling of hearty warmth, they all raised their glasses and drank. While they were drinking and the talk was loose and free, no one noticed Aaron coming in. He whispered something in the ear of Craycroft.

Craycroft then got up and went over to Bob and Judy, told them, and then the three of them prepared to go back out. Their expressions were taut and intense.

"It is our earl. He has taken a turn for the worse," said Craycroft. "We may or may not be back. If Willie does come by, have him play something particularly for the earl, our true liege. Now we must be off."

Chapter Ten

The wind bit and it was cold, but there was no rain or snow, so Tom and Drachma, along with three of his retinue, made good progress as they thundered down the mountain pass toward the valley floor. Tom was feeling more alive than he could ever remember feeling, and it felt good to be moving. Now, he didn't mind the stay at Drachma's house, but being a youth and full of verve, he was anxious for this new adventure. This was more the life that he imagined. Then there was the invigoration of having read Drachma's book and the insights that were now flowing through him that made this new venture seem very special, indeed.

As the team came down, they turned leftward, and then went along the river for several miles before sharply turning again to the east. Here they crossed the river where it was safe to ford. On the other side were the forest and the fields that now lay fallow, awaiting the warmth of spring and the plowing. Drachma's men chose to travel along the tree-lined edge of the fields, preferring the safety of some protection rather than the swifter, more direct route.

Ahead were lines of cedars, planted over the years by farmers as windbreaks, and between the lines was a path down which the riders continued their purposeful run from the mountains behind them toward the southeast, toward Shepperton Castle.

Their way took them through villages, but the men stayed off the main roads and only managed to attract the attention of a few youths who were intrigued by the sound of horses pounding by. Tom found himself listening to the voices within him, awakened by his reading. He checked and the book was still safe within his tunic.

As they galloped along a fairly straight segment, he turned his attention to a rather insistent voice within himself. The voice was one of quiet urgency—compelling, subliminal, just beyond reach. The voice seemed to say, "Beware, do not go there!" He tried listening more intently, and again it said, "Beware, do not go there!"

Then he caught up with his grandfather and said, "Drachma, I do not think we should go this way. I can hear a voice now that is telling me we should not go there."

Drachma signaled to his men and then stopped.

"Is it a voice that you recognize?"

"Aye, it sounds like the voice of Felicia, only younger."

"Well, then, I think that you are right. We should choose a different route." Then he said to his men, "I have never been one to back down from a fight, but then I have never been one to take foolish chances either. Now, this up yonder is the road to Champour, is it not?"

"Aye, that be it," one of the men replied.

"And if we but cut that way"—he indicated with his arm—"we may be only an hour or less slower, so let us go that way, m'lads. What say ye to that?"

So the five of them galloped off in a slightly more westerly direction, avoiding the road to Champour entirely. They went around a great rise in the earth and then over several rough hills and back into the forest, where they joined up with a path that was well-worn and turned southeast again. There, Drachma signaled again and they turned abruptly and rode up a steep incline. They climbed for perhaps ten minutes and came out in a clearing at the

top of the hill. From here they could see for miles around them. Then Drachma gestured and Tom came closer.

"There, you see, down there is the road we would be riding upon."

Tom peered down and could see in the distance below them the thin line of the road to Champour. And as he looked, he could see upon the road what looked like a company of riders.

"Riders," he said, "though I cannot tell how many."

"I should say they are about twenty in that group, but look farther down the road. There." Drachma gestured toward another group of riders. "That'd be a company of at least fifty or more. Well, we might be able to handle those twenty, but that larger company, I think not. Well, young Drachma, I should say that we've been given a very special warning from a most unlikely source. Have you heard anything more from Felicia?"

"Nay, nothing."

"Well then, your task shall be to keep listening. Now, Master Armaugh, have you the bird? I believe that the time has come to send it flying."

Drachma then alit, pulled from his saddlebag a small piece of paper, a quill, and some ink in a tiny container. He wrote hastily on the paper, rolled it into a small cylindrical shape, and placed it in a tiny tube, which he then attached to the underside of the pigeon that Armaugh produced. Then, with a word of encouragement, he let fly the bird, who took off over the hills toward Shepperton Castle.

"All right, m'lads. Now that we know what there is upon the road, let us go by way of the forest." With that, he was back in the saddle and they were off again. Though he could not understand it, Tom felt as if he owed a burden of debt to his grandmother.

Eustace woke to find he was not where he thought. His head throbbed and he felt stiff and achy. The feeling was a familiar

one. Where was he? He looked around at the dim surroundings, and then he began to put things back together. He remembered that he had been accompanying Cayman and his mother, and they had talked on into the night. As he became tired of their talk, he went to bed, but he seemed to recall that it had been a different place altogether. He got up and found, in the dimness, the door to the bedroom. He opened it, and with the orange light of morning, he was able to determine that this was not the place he had lain down last night. He went out into the hallway and looked up and down, noticing this place did not look at all familiar. He thought about it and tried to remember if he had done anything unusual that night. He could think of nothing that would explain this. He looked about, wondering where he was, and noticed that this place was one of incredible beauty. It was richly furnished. He looked inside one of the rooms and saw that there was a fire inside, so he stepped into the room. It was obviously a library with the many shelves full of books. There were large, comfortable-looking chairs, and a large, ornate table in the center of the room, with several volumes on it. He could read a little, but not like his friend Tom, who could read like an educated adult.

Funny that he thought of him now, and of how both their lives had recently been taken from the grim, commonplace of the streets and turned into something else. Now Tom, as it turns out, was the grandson of Drachma—that man of legend and mystery. And he himself was the son of an earl, albeit unknown, and now given this new task by Craycroft of assimilating information from the *little people* of the streets. He thought about that for just a minute and about how he had conscripted the aide of the Druids. How fortuitous it had been that Jeremy had been spying on them. And it should be no problem to get Erik to agree to their plan, as he was known to dislike the councilor as much as anyone. He thought about their plan and its permutations, and he wondered if he would ever see his friend Tom again.

He went over to the wall and looked at the astonishing collection of books, shelves upon shelves, with an incredible array of sizes and shapes He took down one volume that looked particularly appealing in its gray binding. He opened it and noticed the writing and the color pictures in the margins. Then he looked up at the wall, and then back to the book and was astounded. There on the wall was a tapestry in vivid color of a knight on horseback, with a tree and flowers and a bright, yellow sun that could have been taken right from the book.

"Oh, hello, Eustace. I see that you're also up."

He whirled at the voice, and, in a pique of embarrassment, dropped the book. Judy tried to reassure the youth who was left stammering as he stooped to pick up what he had dropped.

"I didn't mean to startle you. I'm so sorry. Can you show me what you were looking at with such interest?"

"Oh, m'lady...I...I was looking at this book, and...and this tapestry here upon the wall."

"Ah, I see, and it's a beautiful tapestry, isn't it?"

"Aye, m'lady, it is, but see, in this book, here is the same picture as that upon the wall."

As Judy came over, Eustace reopened the book and showed her the engraving. She looked at the book and then the tapestry; then back to the book.

"You know, we're going to have to ask someone who knows about this tapestry and this book. Now, how did you find this book?"

"It was but an accident. I was just in here looking at this collection of books when I picked up this one from the shelf—I know not why—opened it up, and there it was."

"Ah, I see. Now, let me ask you, do you know where you are or how you got here?"

"No, I fear that I know not how I came to be here, and I know not with certainty where I am, though I think, being that you are here, m'lady, that this must be the Vincente residence. Am I right?"

"Remarkable, young man. That is correct. Now, how you got here is a tale unto itself. Your mother is Diane, the maid at Barncuddy's, isn't that right?"

"Aye, m'lady."

"And you and Cayman were with her last night, isn't that right?"

Eustace nodded.

"Now, I don't mean to pry, but don't you have a condition that causes you to *black out* on occasion? And has that been causing you more trouble lately?"

"Well, that's what me mum says, though I only know that I do wake on occasion and not know where I am. But it would be me mum that seems more distressed about it than I."

"Let me ask you, how do you feel this morning?"

"Why, I feel fine. A bit hungry and thirsty, and me head hurts a bit, right here."

He felt with his hand and found the lump on the back of his head, which was sore. Then Judy felt gently with her hand and she could feel the knot on his occiput. She could tell that it was tender to touch. But then she noticed a smile appear on his face, as well as a look of amazement.

"M'lady," he said, "your touch. It is truly remarkable. I feel much better than I have in many months. It is as if you heal with your very touch. I have been having a hurting in me head for some time, right where you touched me, but now…now, I am healed of the pain. It is like magic. You are not an enchantress, are you?"

"No, young man, I am no enchantress, just a nurse. Now, come with me. I am quite sure that Frieda can find you something to eat and drink."

So they left the library, with the book lying open on the table. The mystery of the tapestry and the engraving, for now, was still up in the air.

When they entered the dining room, Frieda, who had been up prattling about, was there, and she smiled at the two of them.

"Now, here be an endearing pair, the two of ye; and, I expect, ready to eat and drink this day. Well, have a seat here, and I shall bring ye some food for the day's work."

While Frieda went off to get their breakfast, Judy took the opportunity to ask Eustace if he remembered anything from last night.

"I only remember going to bed—it was at the constabulary—then waking this morn with me head hurting, and I was hurting in me arms and legs. I woke up, but I was not certain where I was. Then, as I got up, I began to feel better. I began to wander about and I noticed the library with its fireplace. So I came in to get some of the warmth and I found the book, and then you found me. I hope I've done nothing to offend ye."

"Oh, no, nothing of the sort, for you see, I'm also a stranger to these surroundings. I just got up to check on you, as you had been brought here for safekeeping after you had a seizure…"

"A seizure? What is that?"

"Well, young man, it's hard to explain, and I'm sure that Master Robert can do a much better job than I can; but let's just say that it is a circumstance in which a person's brain misfires and makes you lose consciousness. But all anyone around you sees is that you're thrashing about uncontrollably and there seems to be nothing that they can do for you."

"And… is that what happened to me? If so, I'm most sorry…"

"Oh, Eustace, that is what happened, but there's nothing to be sorry about, for you really have no control over your seizures. But last night, you apparently had a seizure while getting ready for bed. Your mother and Cayman brought you here, thinking that we'd be able to help. Unfortunately, here in this time and place, we have no effective treatment for seizures. But we can give you good information about them, and, more importantly, let you and your mother know what they are not. Have you and your mother talked about them?"

"Nay, m'lady, we have not. But I suspect that she knows more than she tells. I have thought for some time that she has been holding something back, for fear of telling me, and I think that has made it harder for her, especially in light of recent events."

Frieda then came in noisily from the kitchen.

"Now, here ye be, me good people. Eat up, for ye, at least, me young man, look like ye could use some victuals."

She laid down some plates with bread that was still warm from baking, some cheese, and some dried fruits. And she poured vessels full with a brown liquid that smelled of apples, cinnamon, and nutmeg.

"Thank ye, dear Frieda. For I am famished and this is very good."

"And polite, too. I must say that Diane has brought ye up rightly, young man. Now, let me ask ye, d'ye know Tom? I think he's about yer age."

"Oh, aye. Tom and I are good friends. I understand that he's with his grandfather Drachma—his namesake."

"Well, aye. I believe that he is, or so Jeanne has told me. Now that, too, is one fine lad. And me hopes for the future of this isle are now stronger than ever."

"Whatever do ye mean?"

"If ye but think about it. Now who is the person who is now taking the earl's place? None other than Craycroft himself. If ye ask me, and I know that really ye canna', but if ye were to ask me, that is the earl's most important decision ever. And with the Lady Felicia deciding Craycroft should adopt that Tom. Now I find that ye and Master Tom be friends—there ye have it. The future of our island is in yer hands."

Eustace just sat and ate some of his bread, then said, finally, "M'lady, I am afraid that you but give me more credit than I deserve. For I am but a child of the streets."

"Ah, but nay, ye're much more than that, m'lad. For ye see, I've been talking with Master Craycroft. It would appear that

ye're of noble blood, though this has not been public knowledge. And besides that, Craycroft has seen in ye the promise of so much more."

Eustace did not know what to say. He could feel the tremors of fate shaking him to the core.

"And what of the earl, m'lady? I understand that Master Robert and ye were called away to see him last evening?" Eustace turned to Judy.

"That's right, Eustace, we were, and it's looking bad for the earl. He was having some difficulty with his breathing last night, and it looks like he is close to dying. I imagine that Bob is probably with him right now. I told him that I'd stay here and check on you while he saw to the earl this morning. Later, we'll meet up again and go check on our patients in Sick Bay and elsewhere. This is getting to be a lot like the hospital back *home*. Now that you've eaten, we should probably get you back to Kerlin, as I'm quite certain that he'll have something important for you to do."

"Let me ask ye something, if I may. You and Master Robert knew each other back where you came from, is that not right?"

"Yes, it is."

"And Master Robert says that he has a wife back in the place that ye come from."

"That's also right."

"Then how do ye know each other? For it seems to me that ye and he truly do know each other, in ways like a husband and wife would know, without talking."

"Well, here is one perceptive young man, eh, Frieda? Now, I'm going to tell you something that comes from my heart, and so it stays between us, all right?"

Eustace nodded.

"I've known Bob for a number of years. He was in training when I first met him, learning to become one of the best doctors I've ever had the pleasure of knowing. And, yes, he has been married to a woman whom I've never met, but my guess is that

she's one very special person. Though I've almost never heard him talk of her, what he has said and how he behaves does suggest that this is true. In any event, I work as a nurse in the hospital where he admits his very ill patients. Now, my job is to do the work that doctors want done for their patients, and also to be the patient's help and advocate. I work in what is called the Emergency Department of the hospital, where most of the really sick patients come first, get whatever treatment they need, and then they either get admitted to the hospital or they go home.

"Now, there are doctors I work with in the Emergency Room, who directly oversee what I do, and I take orders from them. I do what they say, and, generally, the patients get the care that they need. But then there are a few of the really special doctors, like Dr. Gilsen, whose patients get extra special care. It is always a privilege to care for them because we know that they are being treated by one of the best. I know Dr. Gilsen does not know this, but it is true.

"Anyway, I have come to really respect, and, you could also say, love Bob Gilsen over the years. I thought that this was just because he took such excellent care of his patients. But now I know it's more than that. For he is a human being with needs that go beyond any that normally we would see, and I think that is why he was chosen by Drachma to be brought here. You see, here is an opportunity to provide care for patients in ways that go beyond any normal means. And I think that this is really where he needs to be.

"So, what am I doing here? Well, I think that your Drachma found in me someone who also saw in Bob Gilsen this special need and would be there for him as no one else could be."

"I see, m'lady. So ye can see things in him (and us) that the common person cannot, and so ye're here as his helpmate."

"Yes, Eustace, I think that is correct. I would like to ask Drachma himself if that is the case, but I think that you have got it right. Now, you know that this is just between you and me, and Frieda."

Antoine LeGace was out and about early. He had heard through his sources that Drachma might be coming this way, and he needed to get himself ready. His usual preparations included a rather set ritual, which involved reading and writing in his diary and then a moment of meditation. This morning, in addition to his usual cleaning of his blade within his walking stick, he put another blade within his tunic. Something told him that he might need it.

He passed by way of the creek that ran down from the castle heights—its usual odor of offal and rotting vegetation seemed tame this morning. Then he spied, up by the castle gate, a small gathering of young boys who scattered as he came closer. As he came up the hill, he could just make out the form of the little fellow known as Wheezer. As he came up closer, he called Wheezer over.

"Now, my little man of shadows, how are things as you've had a chance to observe them?"

"Well, sir, there's been summat up, that's fer certain. I spied Jeremy just yesterday. He was checkin' the folks as was comin' in to the constab'lry. Well, then old Eustace picks him out and takes him with him into the constab'lry with him. Then out comes Jeremy after about an hour, and he sees me and then he disappears. Now I don't know what they were doin' in there, but I do know summat's up. That I know fer certain."

"Very interesting, my young man; very interesting, indeed."

He handed the eager youth a copper coin. Wheezer then quickly departed, and LeGace made his way inside the castle again. It was still very early, and there were few people milling about. He decided to go over to his usual place close to the entryway to the keep, but he kept out of sight as he surveyed the traffic going in and out of the large building. Then he saw the stranger, along with one of the earl's pages, come across the

plaza from the keep and head toward the Sick Bay. He then saw a couple of the forest guards come from the direction of the stables and head into the keep. Their conversation was animated and they had the serious look of business about them as they went by his hiding place.

Hermes had noticed his master had the look of worry and fatigue upon him as he got ready for bed. But later he noticed from his own bed in the hallway that Bob was snoring loudly, and so he, too, fell asleep. But his sleep was interrupted by a vision. While it was still very dark and he could barely see, he noticed her with her own subtle glow—a mere child of nine or ten years, but with a look upon her face that was ageless. There she stood silently at his feet. What actually woke him, he couldn't say; it wasn't any sound or touch, but she was there. She was just staring at him, looking at and through him. He felt he should be afraid, but he was not. He tried to talk to her, but no words came. And so he just stared back at her, transfixed. He watched as she came to him and laid her hand on his chest. He could feel his heart pounding in response.

Then she did a most unusual thing. She took his hand and led him into the room where Bob was sleeping. There she stood by his side with Bob sleeping soundly, touched her own chest, took Hermes hand, and laid it on Bob's chest. He could feel his chest move as he was breathing, and he could feel his heartbeat, slow and steady. Then the girl said, in a voice resonant with age, "His heart beats for all of you. Your task shall be that of his guardian." Then she took her other hand from her chest, touched Hermes's lips, pointed upward toward heaven, and then was gone with the breeze that blew silently through the room.

Now Hermes just stood there at his master's side. All was quiet in the room, but he thought that he could hear from a distance

the music of a harp, like the night when he and Master Robert were out walking. He was confused about what to do, but he let Bob rest. Then, reluctantly, he went back to his own bed and pondered what had just happened.

What could she have meant? And who was that girl?

She was certainly not anyone that he knew, and yet, she seemed familiar. He thought about the whole thing and found it peculiar that he was not afraid at all, though he should have been. For here he had just been visited by an angel—he was sure of that much. And to be told that he was to be his master's guardian; he, a mere youth! He was trying to decide whether to tell his master about his vision, but then sleep overcame him—peaceful and deep.

When the orange light of morning broke through the window overhead, Hermes awoke to find that his master was already up, had tended the fire, and was sitting quietly, looking at something on a piece of paper.

"Oh, hello, Hermes. You were sleeping so soundly, I hated to wake you, so I've been tending the fire. Come here and look at this, will you? It is something Judy loaned me. Can you tell who's pictured here?"

Hermes came over to him and looked at the cream-colored paper Bob was holding. He gave a sudden gasp as the image became apparent.

"Why, that is Drachma himself, none other."

"So, you do recognize him, then?"

"Oh, aye."

"And can you tell me how you recognize him? For there seem to be many on this island that have never seen him, or, at least, do not recognize him. And what can you tell of this engraving? Who made it, and why?"

"Well, Master, ye ask many questions, some of which I am able to answer, but some I can only answer in part, for ye have opened up a mystery."

"Oh?"

"But, aye, there be a mystery right there in yer hands. Now, I have met Drachma. It was when I was but a child. I was still living in the village of Cargill at the time, but we would come up to the castle on certain days of the week to try to sell wares in the market. Me father was a potter, y'know—one of the best of the native potters, or so I've been told. Anyway, one day we were in the castle in the market. The day was warm, and I was sent to get something to drink, so I went to Barncuddy's, and when I walked in, I was met by none other than Master Barncuddy himself. He happily took my coins, went into the kitchen, and came back with a large pitcher of ale. Then, as I was about to leave, a man signaled me to come over to his table. I, not wishing to seem rude, obliged him."

"Now, there at the table was an older man with white hair and a beard, and eyes that seemed to pierce you. He seemed kind, though, and I came over to his table. He told me that he had seen me, and I looked to be the image of Erich, me Pa. He asked me if I was his son and I told him I was. And then he took me aside and said that Erich had made a very special pot that he owned and that I should thank him especially for that pot. *How odd*, I thought, as I had seen many of the pots made by me Pa, and noticed none of them seemed especially fine. But then, he reached into his tunic and pulled out a paper that looked just like that which ye have in yer hand, and on it was the same picture.

"Now, he gave me that paper and said that someday, when I did not expect it, that image would become significant in my life, and important to what I was doing and what I should do. I looked at the paper in my hands, saw that it was signed, "Drachma, the Elder of the Forest." I looked back up at the man, who smiled at me and told me to hurry on then because there were people waiting for their ale."

Then Hermes rummaged in the pocket of his cloak and brought out an old piece of paper, smudged and stained, and

folded in half. He opened it up and handed it to Bob. The orange light of morning fell on the paper, and you could see that it was the same image on both papers, and it was the same person who had signed both. The two of them looked at each other.

"Come on, Hermes," said Bob. "I know that you've got something that you've been burning to tell me about. Why don't we seek out something to eat and drink and you can tell me about it. And then I'll tell you about the earl and what has been happening."

Chapter Eleven

Craycroft was now visibly worried. He sat and looked at his old friend, his liege lord. The earl did not look the same. His respirations were now even, but he spent effort with every breath that he took, and he seemed unaware much of the time. The physician had seen many a person through this transition. But when it was this close, this personal, it seemed as if this was one burden he was unable or unwilling to bear alone.

Aaron was in the room with him and spoke.

"Now, Master Craycroft, would you like me to summon the healers?"

"Aye, Aaron. I should like that. I know they were here last night, and I think that they may not have slept well, but, aye, I do think I would like to have them here. And if you could summon Master Falma as well. We may need his experience, too. Then for this afternoon, I should like to gather our little *congress,* for I do think that we should meet, as there is much that we need to discuss. We should try to meet as close to two bells as possible. And if you could also ask Councilor Genet to be there."

"Certainly, m'lord. As you wish." And then he was gone.

As Aaron left, Craycroft looked at the bed where the earl lay still, and for just an instant thought that he saw the form of a young girl at the foot of the bed. Then he shook his head, looked again, and she was not there. But it was enough that he was shaken

to the core, not by fear, but by a numinous sensation, which still hung about the room. He reached for his tumbler and drank, as much to calm his anxiety as to assuage any thirst. He could feel the pressures of time bearing down on him and realized that even with the efforts of Master Robert, Falma, and Melchior, the earl was rapidly running out of time.

Bob and Judy, led by Eustace and Hermes, came up to the earl's chambers breathlessly. Judy and Bob came to the inner room and were greeted by Craycroft, but this hardly seemed the man they had come to know. In place of the confident leader, they saw only their grieving friend. After quickly surveying his surroundings, Bob looked at Judy, who looked back with understanding. This was familiar territory for both of them. Judy immediately went to the earl's bedside, felt his pulse, which was very rapid and now somewhat weak. She felt his skin and noted that he was no longer febrile. His skin was dry, parched, and had lost its turgor. His respirations were slowed down and even, but with a distinct effort, as though breathing could cease at any time. It was obvious that this was a patient who was dying. She then grasped the earl's hands in hers and spoke softly, evenly to him.

"My lord, is there anything that you need? Is there anything I can do to comfort you?"

He turned toward her and said, "Nay, m'lady, your presence alone is sufficient. I thank thee for coming to my side."

Then, he said, almost as an aside, "Did you know she is waiting for me?"

"Who is?"

"The girl, it is she who waits."

"The girl? Where is she?"

"There at the foot of my bed; there she is…"

Bob and Judy both looked, and though they could see no one, the candle at the foot of his bed flickered and went out. Judy thought she could just see the outline of someone, but then that vision was gone. They looked at each other, and Bob mouthed, "*Later.*"

Then Bob pulled out his stethoscope, went over to the earl's side, and listened intently to his chest. His lungs sounded horrible, full of rattling and sonorous rhonchi. His heart rhythm was now irregularly irregular and rapid. His lips and nail beds were deeply cyanotic, almost purple in color. Bob next felt his forehead, touched his skin, and noticed, too, the decreased turgor. Then turning to Craycroft, he spoke gently to the man that he already considered the greatest physician that he had ever known.

"I'm sorry, Craycroft, but it really does appear as though we are losing this war. You know as well as I that even if we were to get the cultures done, and that they do prove, as I suspect, that the earl has a water-borne infection from which he now has gotten pneumonia, it would take us time to develop an antibiotic, and then the manufacturing of the antibiotic… It all seems impossible to me now. I'm terribly sorry. I just don't know what to say."

Then the earl spoke unexpectedly.

"My friends, listen to me… It was…perhaps…four or five weeks ago…I was at Councilor Reordan's house, when this man named…LeGace…offered me a…beautiful pot, then said that I should drink…daily from it, for with it…came the essence of… Shepperton."

"My God," whispered Craycroft, "that may be just the thing we need to convict that fiend!"

What? thought Bob, *does he think that someone deliberately tried to kill the earl?* Then Bob turned again to the earl and asked, "My lord, if you can remember where that pot is."

They waited for the earl's reply. Then he answered in a careful, measured tone, "The flask you seek…it is with my steward…in the

room with the wines. If you but ask, it is there upon the second shelf…where I have sealed it…so none can become so afflicted."

So, the earl knew, all along, thought Bob. *I wonder what else he knows.* Then he looked down at the earl again, but what he saw was merely a shell of the formerly vigorous man.

As the friends sat around, looking and acting helpless, Falma walked in, with Melchior close behind. What Falma saw stopped him right there in his tread. Here was his long-time friend, the earl, surrounded by people who cared for him separately, each in his own way, who seemed powerless to help, other than Judy, who was at least holding his hands.

"Now, my good friends," he said, "have we come now to this? Are we but powerless to help the earl?"

"I fear," said Craycroft, "that you are right, my friend. What you see are persons held ineffably in the grip of something we now see and can name, but for which we have no answers."

"Well, let me have some time alone with my liege. Then we shall decide."

They all stood about, puzzled, and looked at Falma, not comprehending. He then said, "Listen, my friends, there are powers which we can only partly understand, but are nonetheless at hand. I need to speak with the earl and ask his wishes, for there are also consequences that may affect more than the active participant. Now I will ask Master Robert to remain, as he does need to be a part of the earl's decision."

They all stepped out, somewhat reluctantly, into the anteroom. Then Falma got down upon his knee with his face close to the earl's. He said to his old friend, "M'lord, it comes now to this, I fear. Do you wish for me to call upon the powers that you know are around you? Would you have me perform the *lux de mortuis concentis?*"

At first, the earl did not respond. Falma looked at his friend intently. Bob looked on, not thinking any coherent thoughts, but then he noticed the girl at the foot of the bed. Though he

should have felt some fear, the look on her face cast reassurance about the room. There was a light shining from her face, and she was smiling at Bob, as if to say, "all is well." The room darkened, and she shone more brightly. Then the Earl's eyes opened and he said, "My dear friend, Falma, it is not for me to decide. It is for the traveler who comes here from afar, and it is his life that really matters, both to us and to the people he left behind. He must choose."

"I must choose?" Bob asked. "Choose what?"

Then the girl spoke, but it was not the voice of a young girl, but rather a voice that resonated across time itself. "He speaks the truth. You alone must choose, for the gates of time shall be closing and you shall have no other opportunity, and your time to choose is for all time. Be aware that what you choose shall affect not only you, but those of this time and place, as well as your own time and place."

The girl's pronouncement shook them both to the core. After a moment's reflection, Falma spoke, choosing his words with care.

"So, you see, Master Robert. You hold the key to the door opened briefly in this window of time. You may choose to return now to your own time and place, or you may choose to send the earl in your place. Beyond that, you shall have no power beyond which you possess ordinarily."

Bob's mind was racing with thoughts that were tearing him apart. He was able to ask, eventually, "And what about Judy? What will happen with her?"

"I know not," answered Falma.

Then the girl spoke again, "You have asked, but since she came of her own volition, I cannot answer for her, nor am I able to tell you what she wills. Suffice it to say that your decision shall affect her too, as surely as it does those you have left behind."

Bob's head was now virtually swimming with all of the consequences he thought about, and all of the people that were likely to be affected by his actions and inactions. He thought of

Marilyn and Janie. Then he thought about Hermes, and Tom. And he thought of Craycroft and about his new relationship with the old healer. And finally, he thought about Judy and about the earl, and it was his concern about the earl and Judy that decided it for Bob.

He then reached into his pocket, pulled out the old, smudged paper that Hermes had given him. He then took out the ballpoint pen from his shirt pocket and began writing on the paper below Drachma's signature. When he was done, he put the paper in the earl's hands and told the earl, "My lord, when you are there, give this paper to whoever is caring for you. I think it'll help them figure out just what to do with you."

The earl smiled, gripping the paper in his hands, and then, as he lapsed into unconsciousness, Falma began chanting and humming. Bob found himself caught up in the actions of Falma, and soon he became dizzy and sat down in one of the chairs. Falma did not notice and kept up the chanting.

The room began to get hot, the air changed, and Bob began to notice the smell of hospital disinfectants. He found himself there again in the ER with the clamor, the smells, the sounds of the machines, and the people bustling about. They were bringing in someone on a stretcher. The paramedics had found him outside in the snow and mud. He was having trouble breathing and they had oxygen going. They whisked him into the cardiac room, and the nurses were busy starting an IV line, hooking him up to telemetry, drawing blood. Then he saw Jerry Beasley come into the room, looking his usual disheveled, but efficient self. He began his examination. He seemed puzzled by his dress and began asking questions about the circumstances. It seemed unusual, to say the least, for someone to be out in the parking lot in obvious respiratory distress, dressed the way he was. He quickly gave orders for an EKG, some blood gasses, and a chest x-ray, and he ordered a respiratory treatment, STAT.

He was shaking his head in puzzlement when Alonza Chaves handed him a paper that the man had been clutching in his right hand. The man was now not able to provide any history at all, and when Dr. Beasley saw the note, it was as if he had been hit with a fist in the chest. He actually had to sit down.

"My God, Lonie, do you recognize this handwriting?"

He handed the note to Lonie, who stared, disbelieving, at the small, cream- colored paper.

"Oh, Bob! This is from Dr. Gilsen."

But Bob was already fading from the scene, unseen and unrecognized. He was on his way back where he came from, back to the earl's bedroom, centuries away.

"Bob, oh Bob. Please wake up."

She was shaking him and he heard her, but it was as if she were at a distance. His head was buzzing again and there were those repeating shapes, as if he had been falling through a strange geometric tunnel. Then his vision began clearing and he could see that he was back in the chair, in a dark room, with Judy and Craycroft hovering over him.

"Oh, I think he's coming around. Oh, thank God. Oh, Bob, you had me scared…"

As his eyes regained their focus, he found that he was still in the chair, though only partly. His legs were sticking out and his right arm was draped strangely over the arm of the chair. He looked about and noticed that he had attracted a crowd. Hermes, Eustace, and Aaron had also joined in.

"What a way to travel. I think I'll take the bus next time," Bob said, somewhat laconically, as he shook his head in bewilderment. "Man, I'm sore."

As he looked about him, he noticed that the place the earl had been on the bed was now vacant, with just the indentations on the bed sheets where he had been lying. Then it hit Bob just what he had done, what decision he had made.

"I guess that we owe you some kind of an explanation…" he started.

"Master Robert," Craycroft interrupted, "if I may be so bold as to suggest that perhaps you and Master Falma together might come down the hall where we might all sit down, and then perhaps tell us what you have wrought."

"Okay, but I think that I'm going to need someone to steady me, as I'm just a little shaky right now."

"Oh, Bob, I didn't realize. Here, let me help you…now, just lean on me. Yes, sir, I think you've got some explaining to do about what happened in here."

Bob stood up, unsteadily, and then went over to the earl's bed, looked down on it, felt it, and noticed it was still warm where he had been lying, but there was a distinct chill to the air above the indentation. He looked at Falma who seemed to be in another world yet. Judy then took hold of both men, escorted them down the hall as Craycroft suggested and to the sitting room.

When he had everyone inside who had any notion of what went on, he closed the door. Then he turned to his friend and colleague.

"Now, Master Falma," he began, "I would ask that you explain to us what went on in the earl's bedroom. For what we heard, there was a great sound, as if a rushing wind, then there was a light that came from within the room and then a crashing sound…"

"I believe that crashing sound was me, on re-entry. If my aching body is any indication."

"As Master Robert says, the sound was, in fact, his return to us." Falma had regained his strength. "Now, I shall explain, as well as I am able, just what happened in that room. As you all are aware, the earl has been ill for some weeks, and today, it appeared as though he was dying, as I'm certain Master Robert and Craycroft would concur."

There were nods of assent from both.

"Then, when I saw the little girl in the room at the foot of his bed…"

"The little girl?" asked Hermes unexpectedly. "What was she like?"

"Well, interesting that you should ask, because she was not one I could easily forget. She appeared to be about nine or ten years of age, but yet she seemed ancient as the forest. Now, why do you ask?

"Well, if you must know, I saw her myself, last night, while sleeping. She took me in to see Master Robert."

"Oh, and what came of this encounter?"

"Well, she told me that Master Robert's heart beats for all of us here, and that I should become his guardian."

"Oh, well, that's interesting…very interesting, considering what has transpired. So, let me continue. In any event, this little girl, it seems, does visit when the time is right for the calling from other times and places, but only at the beginning or the end of that time.

"And so she was here, though not all of you saw her. As I suspected, she made it clear that Master Robert could return to his time and place, or that he could stay here, and we could send the earl in his place."

There was general intake of breath as Falma let them in on this little secret.

"Is that not right, Master Robert?"

"That's about right, though she made it clear that I must be the one who decides, and that my decision would be permanent, and whatever I chose would have significant consequences for everyone, both where I came from, as well as the persons here."

Judy sighed. Then she spoke, "So, I take it that you chose to stay here? And what led you to decide that?"

"Well, to put it into context, my decision was not an easy one. I was reminded of what I had left behind. I thought about my wife, about Janie, about my patients. Then I thought about all of you

here. I thought of Hermes, of Falma, of Tom, of Drachma, and of you, Craycroft, and Melchior. But then I thought of two things. The first was the earl, and how he was dying here, and his only chance was to get him where and when he could get antibiotics, oxygen, the IV fluids, the blood that he needed. And then I thought about you, Judy, and she couldn't answer me about what would happen to you, so that made my decision relatively easy.

"But then, you know, before I was ready to send the earl off into the future, I got this idea that, even if he made it to the future, they could use some help, so I took the little note that I got from you Hermes and added my own thoughts for the doctors in the future, in hopes that they give him the right antibiotics and all. Then I gave the note to the earl and had him hold onto it, and then give it to the person who was taking care of him.

"And then Falma started chanting and humming, the room got hot, and I got dizzy. The next thing I remember, I'm in the ER at Memorial, and they're wheeling in the earl and the nurses are running around, getting blood, and putting on telemetry patches. And then, who walks in, but Jerry Beasley, who starts ordering a bunch of stuff to be done to take care of him. then Lonie Chaves finds the note, shows it to Jerry, and they both have a flash of recognition, but then I get whisked back out of the picture and land somewhat unceremoniously in the chair I was in to begin with."

Craycroft had been silent through all of this, but then he felt compelled to speak.

"Now, Master Robert, you say that you did see the earl arrive safely in your time and place, and that he was getting the care that he needed?"

"If there is anyone anywhere more capable of treating our earl than Jerry Beasley, then I don't know who it would be. I would say that he is getting the very best possible care that he can."

"Well, that is some comfort, at least. I feel responsible, as you know. And now my heart is heavily burdened with this new weight

that I must carry. There has to be an announcement. And I must tell the council. It is good, I believe, that we shall have a gathering of our own congress this afternoon at two bells. But, let me tell all of you that what Master Robert has done, he has done with the utmost sincerity and humility. It has not been an easy decision for him, and yet, he has made that decision with the grace befitting a man of true stature. And for that, I must thank him. For without his courageous help, we would still be in the throes of superstition, and I would be at a loss to explain anything to the council.

Now everyone in the room looked at Bob, who just looked down at the floor. He put his head in his hands, overcome with the emotions of the moment. Every one of the people gathered there felt it. For a while, they were silent, and then Hermes spoke up.

"Master Robert, ye said that ye wrote upon the note that I gave thee, is that not right?"

Bob nodded.

"Well, then, at least Drachma's prophecy came true. But not in the way that I would have thought, for he told me that, in time, when I did not expect it, that his image on the paper would become significant to me and important in what I was doing. And now, in some mysterious way, that prophecy is fulfilled."

"Also, it would appear, my young man," continued Craycroft, "that your duty has just begun, that of Master Roberts's protector and companion."

It was then that Judy spoke, and she spoke as one for whom duty, responsibility, love, and companionship had all collided in one great visible act.

"You know," she said, "I have had the opportunity to see just how Bob's heart 'beats for those in need,' and how he is never satisfied unless he has given everything he's got. But this is just almost too much for me right now. I do know that our journeys have been arduous, and this is far from what either Bob or I had expected. But I really did not expect that Bob would give up all for the earl, and for all of you, and, most especially, for me.

Although I have no intention of trying to go back without Bob, the fact that he could have gone back and did not should tell you just what he is made of."

A tear escaped her eye as she reached over and took Bob's hand.

Then he spoke. "It's not such a great a thing that I did. In fact, it is what any good physician would have also done, as far as the earl is concerned. But I'll tell you what, just being back, even for but a few minutes, was one of the most difficult experiences of my life. Just to be there and not be able to talk to anyone, or to have anyone see me. That was really devastating. So, actually, now I'm sort of glad to be back here, if you can believe it."

That's my man, Judy thought, as she gripped his hand more firmly.

Outside, the weather had begun to turn ugly again, with an easterly wind and blowing snow. The howling of the wind in the rooftops, and along the battlements, left no doubt that it was still winter with a while to go before springtime. Antoine LeGace, low in his shelter, had seen the stranger come out of the Sick Bay and was hurriedly escorted toward the keep. He then saw that Master Falma had himself been ushered toward the keep. Then, after about two hours, he saw them leave the keep. Along with them was the lady, another woman, and several youths. They were headed back toward the alchemist's shop, huddled against the wind and snow. As he peered out of his shelter, he noticed that one of the youths saw him and seemed to be alarmed. He saw the youngster stop momentarily and stare in his direction, then hurry and catch up with the others.

LeGace wondered what was happening, and if he should investigate, when there came a thundering sound of hoof beats, as a swarm of men galloped in across the main gate into the courtyard. With the wind and snow, he was not able to determine

the nature of the riders, but it seemed that there were at least fifty of them.

He was torn, but decided that he would see what he could find out about the riders to see if he might catch drift of any of their orders. So he got out of his shelter and made his way across the plaza. There, he found a spot on the other side of an upturned cart and waited.

He was rewarded for his patience a few minutes later when the first group of riders came walking by, talking among themselves. It was a bit hard to make out because of the weather, but it seemed like they were discussing how they were just a bit disgruntled about having been called back to the castle in this weather, in the middle of winter. And who was this Commandant Kerlin anyway? What was there that he was afraid would happen? Was there another king's inquest?

Hmm, thought LeGace, *an inquest? What would that be for?*

Then some more of the riders came by, but they weren't saying much, except that they were hungry and thirsty. He waited some more and then a third group walked by quickly. He heard the name of Drachma mentioned, and then as this last group was about to make the turn into the constabulary, one of the men spotted him and called him out.

"You, there. Yes, you! Come out here."

He looked around him, saw no way out to the right, but there was a small escape route on the left. He lurched to the left, but as he was making his getaway, he slipped on the snowy, muddy walkway. Suddenly, there were two burly men in green uniform blocking his way.

"Hey, now," one of them said, "what have we got 'ere? You, me man, just come with us now. We've got nothin' agin' thee…"

As he spoke these words, LeGace suddenly thrust his walking stick into the man's midsection. The other man made a grab for the stick, and, as he did, he suddenly felt a searing pain in his flank as LeGace buried his knife into his side. By now, the others

hurried over to their fallen comrades as LeGace made good his escape, running quickly along the wall of the castle and out the gate. He clutched his knife, but his walking stick was lost back where the men clustered around their injured comrades. A crowd gathered quickly where the two injured men lay in the snow.

The crowd was still abuzz when Cayman, Martin, and Stoneheft came out from the constabulary and made their way quickly over to the men in green uniforms.

"What happened?" asked Cayman. Then he saw the walking stick with its blade out and he knew. This was no ordinary, petty crime, but it was Antoine LeGace at work again. "Did you happen to see where the man went? Is he still within the castle walls?"

"Nay, he ran away toward the gate. I'm afraid that he is gone."

"Well, then let us get our wounded comrades to Sick Bay. I know very well who that man was, and his crimes are increasing, me friends. Now, if someone will let Master Kerlin know what happened. And here, take this stick with you so that Kerlin may know who did this. I'll go with these men to Sick Bay."

From just inside the gate, Antoine LeGace peered across the plaza to note that they were taking away the wounded. He was satisfied with his information, but, he realized, he was going to have to watch his step more closely, especially since he had just injured two of the guardsmen and they would be watching ever more closely. He then wiped off his knife, put it back into his tunic, and went off in search of his belongings, as well as a new place of residence.

Now, from his perch near the castle gates, Jeremy had been watching as the drama unfolded. He then got down, and, in this weather, knew that he had not been seen as he traced the steps of the man who just stabbed two guards and was walking toward the village.

Chapter Twelve

Sipping on some wine, Craycroft sat alone in what was now his study. He was thinking over all that had happened and what was about to happen. He thought about Robert and Judy. But mostly he thought about the earl, Felicia, and Carlo Vincente, and he thought about Falma. They had been there all along, and together they had, it seemed, weathered many a storm along the way, and now there was only Falma and himself. It was some kind of sadness that only Falma could understand. He thought about his dear old friend and about what he must be going through.

There was a knock on his door, and it was none other than Falma himself.

"Oh, my friend, please come in and sit down. I have been missing you so much of late."

"Oh, I know. I did sense that, which is why I came, and also to tell you of my own sorrows and joys, which I am sure that you share."

"Ah, well said. Here, let me pour you some wine, then let us talk."

Craycroft got up and got a tumbler down from the cupboard; then he poured some of the wine from the wineskin. Falma accepted it with his usual grace. "Now, first of all, my friend. You must tell me of what you have done, and why you did choose today to do it."

"Well, Craycroft, several things did come together today. Firstly, in answer to your summons, I happened upon our earl's room to find him obviously dying. Now I say this with some authority, not as a practitioner of the medical arts, but as the earl's loremaster. You see, at the foot of the earl's bed, she was there. I did not see her at first, but I knew she was there from the light and the smell in the room—it was a subtle, but unmistakable smell, not unlike the smell of newly plowed earth in the springtime. Well, I knew that she could not be there for anyone else but the earl, but then I thought about our Master Robert, and just then I realized something—Robert was probably involved somehow in all of the decisions that led to his coming here, and so he would have the chance to return whence he came, and this would be his only chance."

"Now, let me ask you, as did Hermes, about this girl. You see, I do remember a certain story, which I am certain that you have also heard, about a certain book, as well as a certain friar, and his encounters with what sounds like this same girl."

"Ah, you do remember correctly. For it was certainly this same girl who did appear to brother Philip, lo these many years ago."

"And what Robert said was true. He was given the chance to go back, and he did not take that chance. He gave his reasons, but he did not tell of the internal struggle within him that this decision made him face. I truly believe that it was love, of all of us, of Judy, of the earl, and of his search for peace that finally led him to make his decision. And it is also true what he said, of seeing the earl being brought in upon some cart into a room with people all around him, with bright lights, and all the wonders of that new age being brought to bear upon his struggles. Now I know not what shall become of the earl, but what I can tell you is that the persons there knew of Master Robert, loved him, and respected his opinions, and they knew it was he who sent the earl to them. As he explained, he wrote some note upon a piece of

paper that went with the earl, which explained what the earl had been afflicted with."

Falma took a drink of wine from his glass, set it down again, his eyes moist with the telling of his story.

"Ah, I knew it, too, my friend," said Craycroft, "the earl would be better off where Robert's antibiotics and other methods of cure could reach him and give him a fighting chance in this war. And I knew as well that we could never produce any antibiotics here quickly enough to do any good. And so, I believe that Robert did a just and amazing thing, and we shall have to keep him guarded as if he were our own son, to be protected at all cost."

"Aye, that is true, but I'll tell you, it does not make the loss of our earl any easier for me to bear."

"Nor me."

"Well, let me ask you, my friend, what do we do now? What do we tell the people? What do we tell Father Henri, and what do we tell the council?"

"Now, I should think that we are obligated to tell the people just what we told them of what happened with Carlo Vincente. That the earl has gone on to a better place. Do not worry about Father Henri, for I shall tell him, as I told of Carlo Vincente, and that he shall be the keeper of our secret as he was before."

"And how, pray tell, can you be certain of this?"

"Well, my friend, you do remember the appearance of the girl? It would appear that Father Henri has also seen this girl, and it was Drachma who told of this, and it was because of her that the good Father got where he did." Falma took another drink of his wine. "A tale for another time, with proper accompaniment, ale and music from Willie Minstrel."

"Very well, but then you shall take it upon yourself to tell the good Father of this?"

"But, of course. And you must tell the council. For they should all want to be seen at the service. For, like it or not, the earl has

been their liege lord these many years, and it would be fitting for them to be at his funeral service."

"And that, my dear friend, brings me around to our meeting to be held this afternoon. It shall be the first real meeting of our 'congress.' Now, I deliberately did not ask you to serve on this group that we have named our congress, not because I did not value your aid and expertise, but rather the opposite—you see, I value your opinion perhaps too much."

"Too much? Whatever do you mean?"

"Well, I envisioned a group of individuals who could talk of matters that affect us all, from differing perspectives, with different biases, yet all speaking the truth as they saw it. And for me to be partial, as I would be toward you, would be to take away from the others."

"Yes, I see that. You have made the right choice. But listen, I want to be informed of what happens in these congress meetings."

"My dear Falma, why do you think I come to you now?"

"Ah, well, I see. Now you leave the telling of Father Henri to me. I shall do so as discreetly as possible. You shall need to prepare what you are going to tell the council, and just when."

"I shall, indeed, after our little meeting this afternoon. You see, Councilor Rust is on our congress, and I am certain that he shall have some interesting things to say."

"And, pray tell, who all is in this congress of yours?"

"Well, there is my assistant, Jeanne. And there is Kerlin, Proust, and Cayman from my security contingent. And Melchior, of course, for legal matters. Then there is Rust, of the council, and Eustace, who represents the future as none other can. And finally Robert and Judy."

"My, you have assembled a remarkably able group, my friend. I am certain that they shall provide you with a most reasonable and rational forum."

"Aye, that is my hope, indeed."

Falma sipped his wine and studied his friend. And then, as he was about to leave, he noticed that Craycroft seemed to have something else on his mind.

"What is it? I know you, and there is something else that you need to discuss, is there not?"

"Well, aye, there is. Tell me, if you can, is Drachma really coming here? And if so, when shall it be?"

"You know as well as I that our mysterious Drachma keeps his own council, but I think that it is very likely indeed that he shall be here, from what your men are saying. But tell me, why are you really asking?"

"It would seem that Drachma might be bringing Tom with him, and, as you know, he has now become more than a slight interest to me."

"Ah, aye. It would seem that you are going to adopt young Tom as one of your own, is that not so?"

"Aye, it is. And I am not familiar with being a parent, especially to one as strong and capable as young Tom."

"Oh, I must disagree just a little with you there, my friend. While it is true that you have not been a real father to any children that you may call your own, you have been more than an adequate father to the many small and weak of this island. This I know for a fact, for I have had the opportunity to observe you and your interaction with the many in need. And it is to you that they look up, much as if you were their father. So, no, I would not worry. If I were Tom, I should think that you would be the one that I would pick. Believe me in this, I speak the truth."

"I do thank you for that, and I would guess that any questions that I would have, I can seek Jeanne's advice, eh?"

He noticed Jeanne had arrived at their door and was smiling at the two men sitting down in the sitting room.

"Mercy, gentlemen. You two seem to be having a most serious conversation. May I interrupt your conversation to suggest that your presence is requested at Falma's laboratory?"

"At my laboratory? That must mean that Master Robert has something for us to see. Would that be correct, my good lady?"

"Of course, m'lord Falma." Jeanne couldn't keep from smiling. "It would seem, perhaps, that Master Robert and Master Melchior have something that they wish to show you."

"Well, it would be fitting, indeed, if what they have confirms what Master Robert has been suspecting, this day when the earl is now getting the benefit from Master Robert's knowledge. And nay, Falma, I do not regret what you and Master Robert have done. But come, let us go and see this thing that our friends have for us."

"Hear that? The call of the wolf, at this time of day? That is most unusual."

Martin was explaining this to a young man who had joined them on their search through the forest. The search had been rewarding, though it had been slow. They had spied a contingent that was moving along the road to Champour. It was obvious who had paid them and where they were going, but it was not obvious what their purpose was, so Martin and Stoneheft followed, keeping them just a bit ahead, and so, staying out of earshot and eyesight. Then a youth, of about fourteen years, happened upon the pair as they were following the men on the road. He asked whom they were following, and they told him that they were seeking out the horsemen to find out what they were intent on doing.

"Then let me find out," said the youth, "I shall walk along with them and learn of their tasks. And don't ye worry, I'll not give ye away, nor shall I tell why I'd want to know. Just askin', I'll say."

"And how do we know we can trust ye?" asked Stoneheft.

"Because me mum's one o' yer own," replied the young man. "She works fer the lady what died recently, the lady Felicia."

That took the two by surprise. It had to be Frieda, or one of Felicia's other servants.

Martin asked, "Then tell me, ye must be the son of Frieda, or one of the maids?"

"Aye, Frieda's me mum. I'm called Rowan, and I'm most pleased to meet ye."

So, after introducing themselves, they sent the youth on his way and noticed that he had joined up with the men a quarter of a mile down the road. He stayed with the men for a mile or so, and then left them, going off toward the opposite direction. What they did not see was that the youth circled back around and then came to the north side of the road again and caught up with Martin and Stoneheft.

"Most well done, me lad. And what is it that ye found out?"

"Well, sires, it would appear that this group of horsemen are being paid by Councilor Reordan and are to guard his newly-built boating dock down at the end of the quay. And further, they're on patrol, to look out for Drachma or his men, for they've heard that he might be comin' around these parts."

"Drachma, eh? Why would Reordan care about Drachma?"

"Well, it seems that he has killed one of Reordan's men, and he'd love to catch hold of him."

"Ah, I'd heard that meself. But, out here? It would seem that he'd stay in the forest. What have ye heard, Stoneheft?"

"Ah, I'd heard that he might be payin' a little visit out these parts. Seems that the earl has been ill, and he might want to be payin' his respects."

The youth thought this through for a minute and then said, "I'd be obliged if ye'd let me accompany ye. I know a shorter way to the quay and the boat dock, if ye wanted to see it, to see what's been doin' down there."

"Why certainly, son, show us the way, then we'll be headin' back to the castle. I know where we've got mounts back at the village

up yonder, and I think we'll be needin' them, as there's certain to be weather a'comin' this way. What d'ye say, Master Stoneheft?"

"Oh, aye, that would be well worth it, now wouldn't it?"

"All right, then, come wi' me. Now, earlier ye'd mentioned about the wolf call at this time o' day, and that bein' unusual. What did ye mean by that?"

"Well, young Rowan, what I've heard is that, if you hear a wolf call in the morning, you had best watch your loved ones, for one of them will surely be missing. Now I hope that it is just an old wives' tale, but it's been true for as long as I've been around."

And so Rowan showed the two his short-cut through the forest, and they came out ahead of the contingent of horsemen to the quay, where they saw the newly constructed dock for boats, as well as the shelters for some dozen soldiers or dockworkers. As they heard the horsemen coming, they slipped back into the forest and headed back to the village. All the way back, Martin was wondering what Reordan could be planning, and why he should need all those men to guard his enterprise.

The room was one that the earl had used for conferring with nobles and lords of realms vast and varied. It was now being used for the first meeting of the congress. And Craycroft was obviously very serious about this business. As the participants came in, he offered each a flask of some cider and asked them to sit down, anywhere. When Bob and Judy came in, they noticed that the expressions on the faces of all the members were the same. They looked somewhat nervous, very austere and guarded.

When they had all arrived, Craycroft began by thanking them all for coming, then telling all present that the earl was no longer present and that he had been sent the same way that Robert and Judy were made present in their midst.

"Now, I do not pretend to understand it," he went on, "but it would seem proper to talk of the earl as being gone, or to be in a better place, for that is what I do believe. I think that it would be right for Master Robert to talk to us of his experience, for he was there. Am I right?"

"Oh, yes, I was there all right," said Bob, "though I don't understand it any better than Craycroft."

All eyes were on Bob as he began his narrative, telling again of how Falma had invited him to be a part of the process. How he had to make his decision, right then and there, that would have consequences, not only for the earl, but also for everyone, both here and in the world of the future which he had left behind. He told of seeing the little girl, and how she said to him that his decision would be permanent. He then spoke of seeing the earl being brought in out of the snow, how he was being attended by his former friends and associates, how he sent the note with the earl that was now in the hands of his healers, and how he then came back to them, here and now.

"Might I say something at this point?" asked Judy.

"Of course, m'lady," answered Craycroft, "please do."

"Well, just so you all know, Bob's decision does affect us all, and it is one for the ages. Now I know that he seemed to make a decision right then and there, and I cannot say whether he made the right one, but I tell you, that whatever else he may tell you, that it was something that he made out of love. A deep, heartfelt, and abiding love; not for himself nor even for the earl. It was a decision that he made actually a long time ago when he first laid eyes on a silver coin, back in our old time and place. I know, because it was from me that he got that silver coin. And it was then given away to his patient's family. That coin was an ancient coin, a drachma."

There was a collective intake of breath as she said this.

"Yes, you heard me right, a drachma. Now it is too bad that Mr. Falma is not here, for he knows something of all this. Isn't that right, Mr. Craycroft?"

"Oh, aye, m'lady, you are absolutely right. Now it is for Falma to know, and I think it prudent for us to hear it from him directly, which we shall at dinner tonight, here in our dining room this very evening."

Bob, for his part, was stunned by Judy's revelations. He had never thought that his decision had already been made, but it fit, as he thought about it. When he first laid eyes on that coin, and how it seemed to have a life of its own. And how, when he felt that tug of fate, it pulled him along. And the feel, the smell of newly turned earth, which he again noticed in the presence of that little girl, whose voice was that of the ancient forest itself. This had the feeling of both unreality and inevitability to it.

"Well, Master Craycroft," Bob continued, "now that the decision has been made, through whatever powers it has come to pass, it would appear that you are now stuck with me, and you, too, Judy. Though I will learn, in due time, the real consequences of my action, for now I do not have any real regrets about making the choice that I have made."

There was a pause, as if everyone's emotions were suspended.

"Well, then." Craycroft went on, "Master Robert, if you would be so kind as to tell us of what you and Melchior have discovered, for I am amazed by it all. It is something of which we would have never discovered on our own, and here, you have brought some of your own insights and science to our lives, and we are privileged to witness."

"Well, all right, a little show and tell, eh? Now, Melchior, you have, in your satchel, something that I'll have you show in just a moment. But, first, a little bit of background would be in order. Now you may have heard me talk of many diseases being caused by tiny—what we call microscopic—organisms. Think of maggots, only many times smaller. Now you have microorganisms all around you, through you, and in and around and on your skin. We are covered with these tiny creatures, and most of them are not only harmless, but actually helpful. But every now and then

we get inside us some truly bad microorganisms, which can cause disease, such as what the earl had, and when the bad organisms take over, they may, in fact, kill us.

"Now, how would one prove that it was the microorganisms causing a particular disease? And especially since we do not yet have the capability to see the individual organisms? Well, there are ways, and to let you see, we've brought something for you to look at. Now, Melchior, if you will show them a plain agar plate."

Melchior brought out of his sack a small glass jar, filled at the bottom with a brown substance.

"Now, if you'll look at this plain glass jar and see at the bottom, there is something brown. That is what we call agar, and it is made from sheep blood and ground-up seaweed, which helps it keep its shape. Here, see, it looks like a liquid, but it does not run."

He passed the small jar around and let everyone take a look, and they all did, and they noticed that the agar in the bottom stayed put.

"Now, what you have seen represents agar that has no bacteria (that's what we call the microorganisms). If you'll bring out the next jar, you'll notice that it is quite different. This is a jar in which we have put a few drops of Melchior's spit, and you will notice that this looks quite different from the one you've seen. You'll notice that there are blotches of varying color and type. Now what these represent are the bacteria from the mouth and windpipe of Melchior. The reason that you can see them is that they have reproduced, and each of those spots is made by many millions of the bacteria."

Again, the jar was passed around, amid much *ooing* and *aahing*.

"And now, this brings us to the earl's situation. If you will look at what Melchior has brought out, what you see in the jar looks very different, and if you recall, what I did was to take some of what the earl was coughing up with me and plating out a small amount onto this jar of agar. You will notice that there is much

less variety, and that these colonies look very different from the one that you just saw."

This time, there was intense concentration as the jar was passed around.

"Now, it is my contention that our earl was suffering from pneumonia caused by these organisms that you see before you. You might ask where these organisms came from, and I believe that I've also got answers for that question, as well. Melchior, if you will show the last two jars. This first one was made from the water brought to us by Ervin the other day, from far on the other side of the island, and you'll notice again the same pattern, same color of the colonies."

Realization was hitting them hard by now as they surveyed this most recent jar. There was a quiet, but intense buzzing that accompanied the passing around of the jar.

"And now, what I would like you to consider is that the earl himself told us of his nemesis and potential killer. You might recall that the earl named a certain Antoine LeGace, whom he had met some weeks before—apparently at some function put on by Councilor Reordan—and that, this Mr. LeGace had given him a certain pot and told the earl to drink regularly from it, as it contained the essence of the isle. And you may recall that I was told where this pot was being kept. And so, I went with Mr. Melchior here and we obtained that pot, and from that pot, we were able to plate some of the material on yet another jar of agar, and here is that jar. Now, see for yourselves, and I'll let you decide. What this represents is a line of incriminating evidence that the earl was deliberately made ill, gravely ill, by this Mr. LeGace. I leave it you, my good friends, to do with this information what you may. For it seems that we have on the loose one clever, cunning, and powerful enemy."

The room was hushed in astonishment. This was a *tour de force* unlike any of them had seen. Finally, Kerlin, who had been quietly absorbing all that Bob had been telling them, broke the silence.

"Now, Master Robert, it is truly amazing to me that you were able to deduce all of this from so little. And yet, it would seem to be irrefutable, as your ways have brought us all to an awareness of what has transpired. I know this Antoine LeGace, and I know full well that he is capable of this heinous crime. We now have what proof we need, but we do not yet have him apprehended. I do swear to you all that we shall catch this vile criminal and shall see justice served. This, also, I should note. We now have a new contingent of fighting men here, and they shall serve to protect all of you from dangers, both seen and unseen."

Then Cayman spoke up.

"M'lord, if I may be so bold…"

"My good man," answered Craycroft, "you are, within these walls, as important as anyone here. So, be bold, and let us hear what you have to say."

"Very well. It would seem to me that there is more than this LeGace fellow involved. It would appear that Councilor Reordan is as much a part of this, but he might be harder to eliminate as a threat."

"Aye, that he would," said Proust, "and he, too, is exceedingly cunning, and protected by his wealth and power. And now, it appears from my sources that he has built a dock down at the quay by the road to Champour. I know not for whom and for what he has been building, but I do have men dispatched there who are gaining what knowledge they can."

"And to this, what can you add, my good councilor? For it would seem that you are in a most unique position."

"That is true, Master Craycroft. But alas, I am not in such a privileged position that I can address with any certainty what Councilor Reordan has in mind. But this much I do know, for I have heard it myself. Reordan believes that Councilor Genet is now dead, and so he feels empowered to do what he thinks shall be of benefit to his cause. I believe that his cause would be to oust you and to seize power himself. And with Councilor Genet being

one of the main obstacles to his ascendancy, he does think that he has the necessary tools to do that."

"But you do have plans to deal with that, do you not?" Kerlin asked.

"Oh, aye, that I do indeed," answered Craycroft. "It would appear that our Councilor Reordan may very well get caught in a tangled web of his own making, if all the parts of this fit together. Here's to hope." He raised his cup of cider, as did the others in the room.

"To hope!"

"And now, my assistant, Jeanne, I believe, has something to tell us of the doings of our potters and painters, is that not right?"

"Oh, aye. When you asked me to see how the painters and potters were doing, m'lord, I did go down to shops within the village. There I sat down with a number of the artists, who seemed most pleased that someone had come by asking about them. For they were fearing that they would be beset with another plague, and were only cautiously starting back to work. They showed me some of their wares, which were small, exquisite, little pots, quite unlike any that I've seen so far, and they tell me they are using a new glazing process and they hope that the new pots will sell as well as any."

"Now you did not see the pot that Master Robert mentioned, as had been given him by LeGace?"

"Nay, I did not."

"And did they mention that any of their number had been ill recently?"

"Nay. In fact, they specifically told me that they had been quite healthy of late, with none in their ranks having been ill since the last lad of theirs fell ill and died."

"Not one has been ill of late?"

"Nay, not one."

"Well, Master Robert, what do you think?"

"From what I've been told of these potters and painters, I would surmise that their illness was one of toxic exposure, rather than infection."

There were puzzled looks all around.

"Let me explain," Bob went on. "There are many causes of disease, including infections, such as the earl had. But there are many diseases that are caused by toxins, or poisons, that have nothing to do with any living agents. Now these diseases may mimic infectious illnesses, but the distinguishing features are usually the lack of fever, as well as the prominent effects on one or the other organ system…"

"Bob, I think you lost them with the mention of organ systems."

"Yeah, I expect you're right there, Judy. Anyway, I think that your painters and potters were poisoned, either deliberately or by something that some of them were exposed to. And I do believe that Craycroft would like me to investigate this. Am I right?"

"Most assuredly, Master Robert."

"Well, then, I will try. Again, with the help of Melchior."

"It would appear, then, that everyone—with the exception of Eustace—has had something to say. Now let me ask you, Eustace, and I know that you have been very much involved with the young people of the castle. What have you found that is new or worthy of our attention among the young urchins out there?"

"Well, Cayman and I have gotten some of the Druids to agree to work for ye. You see, Jeremy and I…

"Tom! You're here!"

Everyone looked back to the door where it had just been opened by Tom, and behind him was Drachma—the both of them were still dripping with the rain, looking cold, but happy. Judy was absolutely astonished at the youth, the very image of Josh, but younger, in excellent health, who had all the vitality of the island in its prime.

But then, as everyone's attention was directed toward the front of the room, Bob's attention was diverted, away from the

activities, toward the back of the room, where there was a slight, gentle breeze that carried with it the unmistakable feel and smell of springtime—warm, fragrant, with the smell of newly turned earth. There she was, the young waif. She smiled at him as he came toward her. She reached out her hand, touched his chest, and said that her name was Maggie. Next, she withdrew her hand and she kissed it, looking up, and was gone with the breeze.

Chapter Thirteen

John Doe was now at least more stable. He had been struggling just to breathe, and his oxygen level was too low, so they had to intubate him, and start him on 100 percent oxygen, along with some positive end expiratory pressure (PEEP), to maintain anything near normal blood gases. After the nurses had gotten in a couple of IV lines, it was apparent that he still needed more, so Jerry Beasley put in a central line, but his venous pressure was still zero even after a couple of liters of saline. His labs looked just about as horrible as any in recent memory, and the only good things you could say about his chest x-ray were that the endotracheal tube was in good position, and he hadn't developed a pneumothorax after miraculously getting the central line in. His EKG showed atrial fibrillation with a very rapid ventricular response. But he was now, after being intubated, doing better, and there was little more that could be done in the ER, besides starting antibiotics.

So now, it had become a waiting game. Just waiting for the medicine resident, as well as the pulmonary and cardiac fellows to come take him up to the ICU. Jerry had loaded him up with ceftriaxone and erythromycin, on the advice given in that little note that accompanied him, which struck Jerry as more than a little odd, made even stranger by the signature—R. Gilsen, MD.

"Come in here for a minute, Lonie," he said, trying not to sound too authoritative.

She smiled, catching his drift.

"Okay, Jerry, I know. This whole thing's got me spooked."

"Let's shut the door, okay? Here's that note that came with him. Look at it for a minute. Tell me what you see, and then I'll tell you what spooks me about this whole thing."

He handed the paper to her. She carefully unfolded it, noticing the odd feel of it, and the unusual cream color. She noticed that on the top of the page was a most extraordinary engraving of a man with a flowing beard, whose eyes were, even in that engraving, piercing, as they appeared to look at or through you.

And below the engraving was a handwritten note, which stated simply:

> This shall be to let these persons present
> Know that whosoever bears this
> Does so with my blessing and
> Approval, and is under my protection.
> Drachma, the Elder, of the Forest

And then, under that was a note, written in ballpoint pen, in distinctively different handwriting:

> To whoever is taking care of this man, let it be known that he is the Earl of Shepperton, who is gravely ill with pneumonia, which may be from water-borne bacteria, I would strongly recommend initial therapy be started with ceftriaxone and erythromycin.
>
> And please call in the best pulmonologist you can to take care of my friend.
>
> R. Gilsen MD
>
> P.S. Please tell Marilyn that I love her.

"Well, I don't know anyone but Dr. Bob who could have written that. And I say that as one who has looked at a lot of

doctor's handwriting over the years. Yes, sir, that's Bob Gilsen's note without a doubt."

"Yeah, I would agree with you there. But there are a few things that bother me besides the obvious. First, this was not a note originally intended for us to receive. It was obviously for someone else, and not, I suspect, the Earl of Shepperton—possibly for someone who works under him. Second, look at the paper. It is not normal paper. I've never seen anything quite like it. I don't know, perhaps linen, or papyrus, or something. And lastly, look at the smudges and stains—they're not normal either. This paper has been in someone's possession for some length of time, and, I suspect, one of his prized possessions, so that giving it up really meant something."

"And you know something else?" Lonie added. "This Drachma fellow is someone that I heard Judy talking to Bob about—and now they're both mysteriously gone—and yet we get this, this note. Now I don't mean to tell you what to do, but this note is obviously important, really important. And I don't even know what we should do with it, or if we should turn the note over to anyone."

"You make a good point there, Lonie. And this is obviously way too important to ignore. Why don't we make a couple of copies of the note, at least, and then decide. We can send one up with his chart and keep the other one on his ER record. I've certainly never been in this situation before, and I'm not at all sure what the right thing to do would be."

So they went over to the copy machine, made a couple of copies of the note. They kept one copy with the ER record, sent one up with the patient, and put the original in a drawer and decided that they would reconsider later what to do with it.

With other patients in need, other duties to perform, and their shift really just beginning, there was much that needed to be done. And so, with some reluctance, they went back to it and soon were in full swing. So there it sat, like an echo from some ancient

cave, nagging at their consciousness. Finally, at about three in the morning, when things in the ER seemed to have calmed down considerably, Jerry Beasley and Lonie Chaves revisited their new and thoroughly unexpected finding.

"You know, Lonie. This has been a bit too much for me to keep ignoring."

They walked over to the little office where Jerry had put the note in a manila folder. It was in an area where doctors could sit down with their paperwork, or just a cup of coffee, when time allowed. There they found Dr. Anil Ramchandran waiting.

"Well, Anil, it looks as though you've got one sick fellow up there."

"Yes, he certainly is that. But who is this fellow? Where did he come from?"

"Didn't you see the note?"

"Yes, but it was signed by Dr. Gilsen, the cardiologist who is missing, was it not?"

"Yes, that was his note. Lonie can attest to its authenticity, right?"

"Yep, it's his note all right, but only the bottom of it. I can't answer for what it's written on or where it came from," Lonie answered.

"Yes. And that's what I wanted to talk to you about. Now, for the moment, he is just a John Doe, and is on the ventilator. But, if he recovers, then we may know something. And, to tell you the truth, that's what scares me just a bit. We're likely to become something of a media circus around here, whether he recovers or not. Now, I've instructed my residents that they are not to talk about this case with anyone not directly involved in his care. And I'd like to ask you to do the same."

"You know me. I'll be the picture of discretion."

Lonie chuckled at this.

"Oh, Lonie, you know very well that when it comes to patients, I'm about as tight-lipped as they come. I can't make the same

statement about my coworkers. Why don't you look over here, and we'll show you what the fuss is all about?"

He led the two of them back into the little storage area where he opened one of the filing cabinets and pulled out a folder.

"Here, in this folder is the original note." A look of consternation came over his face, which was replaced by pallor. "Lonie, you saw me put it in here, right?"

"Of course I did. Don't tell me it's gone."

"It was in this folder, right?" Jerry Beasley could not keep the anxiety out of his voice.

"Yep, it was."

"Now, no one's been through here but us… No, this is too weird and too important."

"Come on, we'd better check the ER chart and make sure the copy's still there."

So Lonie went over to where the records from the day's ER visits were stacked. She found the file paper clipped with all the papers together. She looked through the papers and found it, looked at it again, flipped it over, and then handed it to Jerry. He took it, stared at the paper, turned it over, and then, nonplussed, he handed it over to Anil.

They all looked at the paper and found only the fading image of the man with the flowing beard, but whose eyes seemed to look through you, not in scorn, but in sympathy.

Charlie Stephens found it hard to sleep, but he couldn't exactly pinpoint anything that should be keeping him awake. The events of the last week had been nagging at the back of his consciousness like a piece of food stuck in his back teeth. It was something that he couldn't quite get out of his mind long enough to fall asleep. Now that encounter with Carlo Vincente had been odd enough, as the old man had gone on about Master Robert and the Lady

Judy. He acted as if he had some firsthand knowledge, but it could just as easily have been his fevered imagination, or that's what he told himself. And then, what the old man had said as he got out of the car, "Be careful, young man, I shall see you again, soon." His thoughts just kept tumbling about in his brain, one after the other, rattling around, as if looking for a place to land.

Then, suddenly, in the dead of night, as he was finally asleep, there was the sound of his front door opening. Nervously, he got up, put on his slippers and robe, and quietly crept out of the bedroom and down the stairs. There was someone down there. He could hear someone rustling around in the kitchen. He then quietly crept back up the stairs, went to the closet, got out his baseball bat, and crept back down the stairs.

"Good evening, Master Charles…"

He whirled at the voice. And there was Carlo Vincente, sitting calmly on his kitchen chair, and not the least upset or threatened by the little man with the bat.

"May I ask how you got in here? The front door was locked!"

"Oh, aye, it might have been locked, but it opened for me quite easily. Now, I would suggest that you put down your stick and come, sit down, and listen to what I have to tell you. I do think that you shall find it of significance."

The absolutely calm demeanor of the old man caught Charlie off guard. He thought about calling the police but then thought better of it. After all, there might even be a story here. So he put down the bat and came over and sat across from the old man with the white hair and strange clothes.

"Okay. Now you've gotten in here and are sitting at my kitchen table. Apparently, you've got something to say to me. And it sounds like it may be something important, so, go ahead…"

"Let me start by telling you that I have been to see Madame Gilsen, and I gave her a note, written by her husband, but not just any note. It was a note from my time and place, from Shepperton. It was she who suggested that I find you and tell you that, if

you would like the story of your career (I believe that is how she phrased it), that you should listen to what I have to tell you."

"All right, you've got my attention. Tell me about this note."

"Oh, I shall do more than that, for, if you will but come with me, I shall take you to my own liege lord, the earl of Shepperton. Though you may find it hard to believe, he is here, in our time and place."

"Your…liege lord…the earl of Shepperton? Now, wait just a minute. How is it that he's here?"

"He is very ill and is in your hospital. He is being attended by many physicians and other persons."

"Here? In the hospital? You mean Memorial Hospital."

"Oh, aye, the same."

"He's here? And may I ask how you know about this?'

"Well, let us just say, for now, that I was alerted to his coming here by means heretofore unknown. Let us say that one of my friends did let me know of his arriving."

"Okay, okay. Just let me get dressed. Then you can take me to see him. Mind you, this is the middle of the night, in winter."

"Precisely, Master Charles. That is why I came after you at this hour. For I have come to learn that, if you wish to find out what happens in your hospitals without attracting undue attention, it is better to do that in the middle of the night."

"I guess you're right. Well, then, I'll quickly get something on and then we can go."

So Charlie Stephens went back upstairs, quickly got dressed, and came back down to a waiting Carlo.

"Now, are we taking my car, or did you bring some other form of transportation?" asked Charlie, with a touch of sarcasm. Either Carlo Vincente chose to ignore his tone, or else he simply didn't understand.

"Why do we not take your transportation?"

Charlie checked the front door and noticed that it was locked, with the deadbolt in place, with no sign of damage or forced

entry. He looked over at Carlo, whose attention was diverted toward a framed photograph on the wall.

"Is this you?"

"Yes, that's me shaking the hand of the governor of our state. That was taken some years ago when I got a citation for some story I did on people abusing children."

"It is good to know that your heart does beat for the small people of the world."

Charlie was taken aback, just a little.

"Why, thank you," was all he could say.

Then he led Carlo through the back door to the garage.

"Okay, hop in, and while we're going to Memorial Hospital, why don't you tell me a little about this note?"

As they were driving the deserted streets, Charlie Stephens listened with ever increasing interest to the story being told him by the old man, about how he had been wandering in the hospital and wondering why he was still here, when he heard what sounded to him like a piercing shriek coming from the direction of the Emergency Room. Now it was no ordinary sound, and, evidently, the others around had not heard it, or it did not affect them in any way, but he followed the scream and found that it was now dying down, as they were bringing in the earl on a stretcher. He was briefly able to attract the earl's attention, who looked at him, but was barely able to mouth the word *Drachma* before he succumbed to the ministrations of the doctors, nurses, and others.

Now, it appears that the old man was able to observe all of this as he stood in a corner of the Emergency Room, unseen, or at the very least unnoticed. He watched, as they attended to the earl, who looked as if he were dying. He observed them place a tube into his mouth, draw some of his blood, and give him fluids into his arms and into his chest. He became frightened for his earl and was about to enter into the room itself when the little girl held his hand and stayed him.

"Be not afraid," she said. "His time is not yet at hand, and they are doing what they can to save him."

As he turned toward the girl, she smiled at him, took his hand, placed it on her little chest and let him feel the beating of her heart. Then she said something very unusual.

"Go, get that note that was in his hand and take it to Madame Gilsen. Do as she tells you, come back to this hospital, where I shall meet thee, then come with me. Your service then shall have been complete."

"And you did that?" asked Charlie. "This note was in his hand, am I right?"

"Aye, it was, but then one of the women took it out of his clenched hand and showed it to one of the men. They looked at the note, discussed it, and then put it away in a drawer."

"And what did you do? Just go and take it out."

"Not then, but later, after I determined where they had moved the earl—apparently to a place called an ICU on the fifth storey. After I determined that the earl was yet alive, but was not able to recognize me, I then returned to the Emergency Room where I found the note. I took the note with me to Madame Gilsen, as instructed by the little girl."

"This little girl—any idea who she was?"

"I know not her name, and I had not seen her before. But I shall tell you, she was no ordinary little girl. She does reside, though, where I am going."

Charlie thought about asking where that was, but then thought better of it.

"And where is this note?"

"In Madame Gilsen's possession. As I said, I gave it to her, to do with as she pleased. I am quite certain that she means to share it with you."

The night was cold, crisp, and clear, as they brought the little blue wagon into the parking lot, which was considerably emptier than the last time they were here. They stepped out into the

night, but as they headed toward Memorial Hospital, Carlo took Charlie around to the side of the building where there was an old door that he knew was unlatched and unguarded. They came into a long, forgotten hallway; from there, they went back toward the service elevators and then up to the fifth floor.

Charlie Stephens, for all the stories he uncovered and all of the gritty crime that he reported on, was scared of hospitals, especially big ones. It was a nameless fear that went as far back as he could remember. And now here he was, wandering these halls in the middle of the night, in this big, and very old hospital, with some old man from a fairytale; and they were doing what exactly? Looking for his lord, the earl of Shepperton. He could just imagine explaining that to the authorities, or to his boss.

They walked down one long hall after another, and the only person they saw was a janitor mopping the floor. Then, rather abruptly, they turned left, and they were in a more well-lit hallway, which led to a set of double doors marked as Medical ICU. Carlo just walked into the ICU, as if he belonged there, and led Charlie past the nurses' station, with no one looking the least bit interested.

He then went to one of the beds, where he just pulled the curtain slightly around them, so that they were cut off from view of the nurses, who remained amazingly oblivious to their presence.

"You seem to know your way around here remarkably well, Mr. Vincente. Now this, I take it, is your earl."

"Oh, aye, it is he, none other."

What the two men saw almost looked like the other patients around the ICU, all on ventilators, with the machines providing breathing for them. But yet there was something different about him; really different. Despite his being on the ventilator, with all the tubes and wires connecting him to his machine world, here was a man of stature. This was obvious, though Charlie could not exactly say why. There was just an aura about him, and his own

persona shined through, even though it was clear that he was desperately ill.

"Does he know you're here?" Charlie couldn't help asking.

"I know not. But I do know that he is alive, so I believe that the part of him that does understand, does know that we are here."

They looked down at the still form of the earl, and Carlo Vincente got down close to his face and said softly in his ear, "My dear Earl, you are not alone, though you are far from home, both in time and place. I have here with me Master Charles Stephens, and he shall be in contact with a Madame Gilsen, the wife of Master Robert, and they shall care for thee."

Suddenly, the room began to feel warm. Charlie became lightheaded, found that he had to straighten back up, but still he felt ill at ease. He looked with incredulity at Carlo Vincente, who then turned and walked away toward the double doors of the Medical ICU. As he disappeared from view, Charlie thought that he saw a young girl in a gray outfit take his hand.

"Sir, are you lost?"

He turned toward the voice of the nurse.

Caught off guard, Charlie thought of a convenient excuse. "Oh, no, ma'am. It's just that my uncle was up here, and…"

"Oh, but visiting hours were over hours ago… Now, don't I know you from somewhere?"

"No. I just got in from Texas. When are visiting hours?"

"The next one starts at eight in the morning."

"Oh, well, thank you, ma'am…much obliged. I'll just come back then, in the morning."

With that, Charlie made his hasty retreat from the ICU, walking out the double doors into the hallway. But as he came out the door, he noticed the warm feel of the gentle breeze, and the lingering aroma of newly turned earth. It was strange, he thought, that sense of peace, the feeling of longing.

He looked around for Carlo Vincente, but he was nowhere to be found. So he wandered the halls for a spell, and then he

came out in something that looked like a main corridor. There, he recognized the main entryway to the hospital, and the way out to the parking lot. He was suddenly very lonely, as he walked out into the cold night. But he knew what he had to do the next morning.

The doorbell rang, but this time Marilyn Gilsen was actually looking forward to her visitor. She stood up quickly from her seat at the kitchen table and went to answer the door.

"Oh, do come in, Mr. Stephens. You know, it's really something of a pleasure to see you."

"Well, thank you, Mrs. Gilsen. Now I know that you're in a definite minority with that opinion."

Marilyn laughed, and this was the first time that she had laughed in ages. It tickled Charlie's senses in a way that he could do nothing but laugh as well. So he entered, and Marilyn had him sit down at the kitchen table.

"Would you like some coffee? I've just made a pot."

"Oh, thank you…no, I'll take it black," he said as Marilyn offered cream.

Then she sat down next to him, reached into her purse which was on the table, and pulled out a piece of smudged, cream-colored paper.

"We might as well get right down to it, wouldn't you say? Here, have a look at this little note. Then we'll talk."

He took the piece of paper and unfolded it. Wordlessly, he looked at the drawing at the top of the man with the flowing beard and incredibly piercing eyes and he noticed the writing beneath the etching, in that unmistakable hand, with the backward slant. He noticed, below this, in another handwriting, the note from Marilyn's husband. And then that little P.S.

"My goodness, Mrs. Gilsen," he said after absorbing the details of the note. "This does open up a whole new twist to the story, doesn't it? Have you thought about what all this means?"

"Well, I've had quite a night to think about it, I'd say."

"And I understand that you've had a visitor…"

"Yes, and let me tell you about him. But you'd better take notes, because what I'm going to tell you will be the story of your career. And, whether you tell the story as an active participant, which I assume that you now are, or whether you tell the story as a detached and independent observer, doesn't mean that much to me."

Chapter Fourteen

Reordan was a bit uneasy. There was something in the air. He summoned his chief of security, who came promptly. He found his master in his study, as usual.

"Now, tell me, what have you heard?"

"M'lord, I have heard through our channels, but not from any reliable sources, that the earl is dead."

"Have they placed the flag at half-mast."

"Nay, not yet."

"Well now, this then is the hour that we need to get our plan readied. How are our troops, and are they ready?"

"I must be perfectly honest, m'lord. The troops are there, in number and strength. But as to their readiness, I am doubtful. For they see, as I do, that Kerlin has seen fit to bring in troops of his own, back to the castle, as if in anticipation."

"But none know of our plan, is that right?"

"Nay, none."

"Then, I think that we shall be right in what we are doing. Do you not agree?"

Years of training and experience had taught Gilbert when not to say what was on his mind. He simply said, "Oh, m'lord, it is not for me to question you."

Reordan's eyes were fixed on his security chief, to see if he could determine whether he had any misgivings, but Gilbert's

face was a mask. He pondered this for a moment. Then, rather dismissively, he said, "Well, Gilbert, then I should suggest that you get the men ready at the docks, for they shall be busy soon enough."

"Aye, m'lord. That I shall. Will that be all?"

"Aye, for now."

With that, Gilbert was dismissed.

Reordan impatiently drummed his fingers on his chair and sat, looking into his fireplace. He realized that a meeting of the council would certainly be called, and he knew that his card would have to be played. He just hoped that the seas would be quiet enough that the party could land, without too much of an uproar. He had certainly paid enough for their services.

He hoped that LeGace would do his part, and promptly get gone. That man did make him nervous, but he could not say why. There was just something in his eyes that told him to be careful and to not let him too close. It was a hunger, something that he himself knew all too well.

And what of the strangers? They had arrived in the middle of all this turmoil. Their own role had thus far been shrouded, and his chance of finding out more had been foiled by none other than Drachma. What a vermin that man had become. It was apparent that Drachma himself had something to do with the strangers' presence on this isle, and surely he had something to do with the earl's decision to pick Craycroft as successor.

"Carruthers! Come here!"

The old servant had been just out in the hallway, waiting for his summons.

"Aye, m'lord?"

"Carruthers, what have you heard? Is there something happening out there?"

"Oh, m'lord," answered Carruthers, "what I have heard is but rumors, but some are saying that the earl has died. Though no word has come from the castle, I am inclined to believe them. You

know as well as I that he has been gravely ill of late, so it should come as no great surprise."

"And what, pray tell, do you think this all means?"

"Well, m'lord, it would seem to me, then, that we should prepare our plan for the meeting of the council. You know as well as I that a meeting of the council shall have to be called, and you must be prepared."

"Precisely. So, are you then ready? Let us plan what strategy I may use."

And so they began planning. They laid out their responses for all the foreseeable threats and parries that they could anticipate being used by Rust and Craycroft at the meeting, and, in the end, Reordan felt quite confident in what he thought might be coming their way. And he felt even more confident, knowing what his contacts in Ireland had told him. He just hoped that they were now on their way.

"Well, Carruthers, you had best go now and see to it that our informants are paid and that the information is good."

"Oh, aye, m'lord. I shall go anon."

"Well, hello there, laddie. What be ye lookin' at?"

Jeremy turned with a start at the voice.

"Why, Uncle Maxim," the boy responded, "I've been keepin' me eye on those two, what walked into the miller's place, just now."

"Up to no good are they, then?"

"Nay, I think not, uncle. It be that man as works fer the councilor, what lives up on the hill, and the little snitch called Wheezer. I know they're not up to no good, no good at all."

"And who might ye be workin' fer yerself now, laddie?"

"Oh, I'm workin' fer the earl himself, I tell ye." Jeremy reached into his pants and pulled out the two copper coins. "See, uncle, that's me first day's wages."

"Ah, aye. It's good to see ye employed by such as the earl. Now I have some news fer the earl meself…"

"What news? I might be able to get the message to the earl."

"Hmm, I hadn't thought about it, but maybe ye could. Now, why then don't ye come on back wi' me and I'll pour ye some cider and ye can also have some of Martha's bread. And then while we be eatin', I'll tell ye what I know."

That was too much for Jeremy to refuse, so he left his perch by the window and followed his uncle to the inside of the hut. They sat down, ate their bread, drank their cider, and talked.

By the time his uncle had filled him in on what he'd heard, Jeremy knew just what he needed to do with the information, and where to go with it. So he thanked his Uncle Maxim, promised to stop by again, and was gone. As he went back to the castle, he glanced again in the direction of the miller's, and, seeing nothing, hurried on toward the castle and the constabulary.

In the castle, the scene had become intense, both from the emotional tumult created by the presence of Drachma and Tom in the charged environment of the earl's meeting room, and, also, from the distinct absence of the earl and Felicia. Both Judy and Jeanne had sensed it, the atmosphere was thick with it, and even Eustace sensed it. What was not said became almost as important as what was.

What Craycroft did first, upon their arrival, was to send for dry, warm garments for the weary travelers, and hot drinks. And while the servants were obtaining these items, Craycroft made certain that all present knew each other, but, most particularly, he wanted Judy to meet Tom and to have Bob and Drachma finally meet, face to face.

Judy was so taken by young Tom that she found it difficult to control her maternal instincts. But she reined them in, and she

gestured toward Eustace, who came over to meet his well-traveled comrade. And Tom, then, pulled out a copper coin, as well as a note from his tunic and handed them to Eustace. Humbly, he asked for his pardon.

"For what, might I ask?"

"The note explains all, but it would seem that you have achieved more than I could have imagined."

Eustace read the note with eyes that turned bleary, and said, "Now, Tom, you do know that I have achieved much of late, and of that we must speak, but, nay, what led to your being Craycroft's page was beyond my reckoning or control."

"One of many things, my friend, that I have learned of late. Welcome to my world."

"Indeed."

Judy couldn't help but remember what Frieda had foretold, that here was the future of the island, in these two young men. And she was realizing just how wise that observation had been.

Meanwhile, at the back of the room, Bob had come out of his reverie and was now facing Drachma in the flesh. Here, at long last, was the man who, it seems, engineered all of this, including Bob's most unlikely presence in this time and place.

"Well, Mr. Drachma, it's really good to see you at long last. I know we've met before, but this is different."

"And it is with some awe and reverence that I do come upon you as well. We shall have much to talk about, but I am truly honored that you are here, and I extend my hand in friendship."

The servants entered with warm clothing and warm drinks. So after Drachma and Tom were allowed to change and come back, they were asked to sit by the fireplace, relax, enjoy their drinks, and then they would have a chance to talk at leisure.

As the assembled group sat, it was obvious they had all eagerly awaited Drachma's presence. This was the man who had answers to many of their questions, from their various points of concern. So, the first thing Drachma did was to have them tell him of their

individual responsibilities, as he had not gotten the full report yet from Craycroft.

"Now, I know," he said, "that Craycroft has become our new liege lord. And I do understand your most peculiar circumstances. I do know of our earl's leaving and of the circumstances behind that which happened. But what I would like to find out from each of you is what your own individual gifts have produced, as well as what you think you might be able to bring yet to us. For I tell you all, there are forces out there that would have what the earl has wrought come to naught. And you probably know of some of the people involved. But let me hear from you. Now, Councilor Rust, why do you not tell us what you know of the council's doings? I know of some of Craycroft's plans in regard to the council, and I shall tell you that he is more than capable of handling that group of persons."

"I would have to agree with your assessment, my dear Drachma. I do feel confident in Craycroft's abilities. Now, I should tell all of you that there shall be a meeting of the council shortly, for we shall have to announce that the earl's apparent disappearance was his final one, and I think that I should like to put it almost that way to the council.

"And there are those, namely Councilmen Reordan and Silvo, who should like nothing better than to get their hands upon this palace and its powers. And there are those upon the council who, for the sake of expediency, not to mention that they have been bought, would as well see Reordan upon the high seat."

"But, Councilor," asked Judy unexpectedly. "Can they do that?"

"I fear that they can," answered Rust. "And that they intend to do just that. You see, here upon this isle, we are governed not by persons imposed upon us by the crown, but by our own form of royalty. But only one family is truly royal, that being the earl's, who, unfortunately, has no descendants, nor any in-laws, nor even any bastard children. I would be a fool to think that no one has been seeking to usurp the earl's position, as it has been obvious

that Reordan and Silvo have been in pursuit of that position for some years. Reordan now sees this as an opportune time to make his move, but, as you know, the earl had already made other plans."

"So," said Drachma, "I am quite certain that the earl's plans did take shape to deal with this threat, among others, less fully realized."

"Ah, it would appear so," answered Rust, "But it seems to me that there is yet a threat to our peace that the good Master Proust has recently been made aware. Is that not so, Proust?"

"Oh, aye, there is. I have been attempting to find the nature of this most recent threat, but alas, I have only been able to determine that our good Councilor Reordan seems to be behind it. It would appear that Reordan has purchased some land by the old quay, near Champour, and has built a large pier there. Now, as to who or what he intends for that pier is shrouded in mystery. But I can tell you that whatever he does plan for that, we shall be prepared for it. We have assembled more troops in and around the castle, and along the road to Champour. And, furthermore, we have persons stationed along the route who have access to some carrier pigeons who shall report if anything happens."

"Well, thank you very much, Master Proust. We shall speak more later. I should like to hear from Mistress Jeanne, as I do believe that she has found out something, in conjunction with Master Craycroft, as to the matter of the painters and potters. Is that not right, m'lady?"

"Oh, aye, m'lord, that I have, indeed. You see, I have sought out the potters within the castle walls and did meet with several of them, and they wanted to get on with the manufacture and the sale of their pots. Of late, that has not been easy, with all this talk of witchcraft and poisonous spells. As I understand it, Master Robert has concluded that the painters and potters had been poisoned, and he intends to investigate this. Am I right?"

"Oh, quite right, Jeanne. I'll begin my investigation soon, and with help from Melchior, I think we stand a fair chance of proving

that the painters and potters were the subject of some sort of toxic exposure, quite different, I must say, from what affected the earl, and apparently also the lady, Felicia."

"Indeed, Master Robert, and, as I understand, you did a truly masterful job of finding out what did happen to our beloved earl, and even who was responsible. I shall make it my personal goal to avenge the earl of Shepperton," Drachma promised.

"And now, Captain Cayman, what is it that you have learned as the newly appointed liaison between the castle and outside forces?"

"Well, sir, it has come to my attention that, in fact, there has been a pier built by the quay, as Proust did say, but the most significant piece of news from the birds is that you are now a marked man, m'lord. There is a price upon your head to be paid by none other than a Master Balthusar, who is a servant of our Councilor Reordan."

"That is very interesting, Master Cayman. Now, what is the bounty on this dread criminal?"

"It seems to me to be twenty gold pieces. Wait, I have the note here in my possession." Cayman reached into his tunic and produced a small paper, which he then handed to Drachma.

Drachma studied the paper and then handed it back to Cayman. "It seems to me that Councilor Reordan must have another plan for my disposal, for such a paltry sum is just for the masses. What do you think?"

Craycroft chuckled at this, adding, "Oh, I agree with you, my good sir, and I suspect that whatever plan he has, it must involve Master LeGace, at the least, and I know for a fact that his price is much higher."

"That is a certainty," added Kerlin. "But let me be the first to say that it does my heart good to see both you and Tom here, safe and sound. For it is not without incident and trial that you are here, at long last. And let me say that Tom is a changed person since I last saw him, but a week or so ago."

"Oh, that he is, my friend. And why don't you ask him about the change? And what has he to say about his circumstances?" Drachma added, with a subtle twinkle in his eye.

"Well, Tom, what have you to say to that?"

"My good masters and ladies," he began, "as some of you may know, I was but a lowly urchin of the village, who just happened to stumble upon good fortune here in the last few weeks. Now I had been a page to the house of the earl, and, as such, became privy to some knowledge of the doings in the council, and as to the nature of the earl's and m'lady Felicia's troubles, and I thought that, being a curious sort, I could get myself in a better position to learn more about them. And I knew that m'lady was quite ill. As I found that Eustace was assigned to be the page to Master Craycroft, I gave Eustace a penny to trade assignments and he agreed. Now, as it happened, I was sent to call on the master in the middle of the night—seemingly many weeks ago, but, in truth, perhaps three weeks ago. And so began my changing. It turns out that the lady, though very ill, did see right through my ruse, and yet she could sense some greater purpose at work and said nothing, but made certain that I had access to her truly magical library, and one volume in particular, which I took, though I know not why." Tom did not notice, but Craycroft was suddenly smiling. "Also, she made certain that I was introduced to none other than Falma, who is a most amazing man. And, somehow, he knew that I'd taken this volume, though how he knew is beyond my ken.

"Now, Master Falma, as it turns out, knew me better than I knew myself. He did know of my true parentage and my background. And he told me a tale that changed my life completely. Now what he told me was that my given name, Drachma, was no accident, and that my namesake and the Lady Felicia did have a daughter, who was my true mother. And later I found, while staying at Drachma's house in the deep wood, a most incredible woman, named Angelica, who told me more of the sad story of my own

mother. And who this young lady was became the stuff of what I assumed to be fairytales, but actually was the truth. I also learned how this young woman died giving birth to me. Angelica then told of how Drachma rode off with me to find a wet nurse in the village of Killiburn, and then how I was raised by another couple in the castle village before becoming a page."

"Now, Master Tom…" Craycroft spoke up and asked with something of a mischievous twinkle in his eye. "Or should I call you Drachma, the younger? Could you tell us who your mother was?"

"Why her name was Maggie. It was Maggie o' Killiburn."

At the mention of her name, Bob suddenly turned pale. Then, after a moment, asked, "Did you say her name was Maggie?" It seemed suddenly that the mention of Maggie, and now her appearance in their midst, meant more than he was ready for.

"Oh, aye, that was her name."

Drachma then asked, "Master Robert, it would appear that name does carry some significance for you, as well. Does it not?"

"Well, you could say that." And so, Bob then told them of the earl's translation, and how there was this young girl who told him of his choice, and she seemed so young, and yet as old as the forest, and with more knowledge, power, and yet gentleness than anyone he had ever met. And then how, as they were all greeting their returning comrades, he had been distracted by something in the back of the room. It was the girl again, as gentle and as powerful as ever, who laid a hand on his heart, then kissed her hand, and disappeared with the breeze, but before she left, she told him that her name was Maggie.

All in the room were stunned to silence. Finally, Drachma asked, in a voice hoarse with emotion. "Tell me, Master Robert, can you tell me what she looked like?"

"What I can tell you is that she radiated beauty, as no other person I've ever seen. She had large, luminous green eyes, and hair that shone red, as if always caught in evening light."

"My God…" Drachma spoke, almost whispered, "It is she, indeed."

Craycroft nodded. Tom's face gave way to tears, as if Bob had just given him a glimpse of his own mother, and Drachma, his beloved daughter.

After that, the meeting broke up, with Craycroft nearly stunned into silence. He did make certain that they knew there would be yet another dinner that evening and that they were invited.

Bob and Judy, though, had many things to discuss with Drachma and Tom. So they prepared to gather in the library with Eustace, while Craycroft decided that he had much to discuss with Falma and so he sent Melchior off in search of his master.

Before departing, Tom came up to Craycroft, took out the book from his tunic, and handed it to Craycroft, along with a note. Craycroft smiled down at Tom and said, "Before your grandmother passed on to her better life, she told me that I should seek out this little volume. Now, I know just what she meant. I assume that you have read it, for that I could tell from your story."

"Oh, aye, and I think that you should also read it as well."

"Thank you, Drachma, the younger. Maybe I shall one day."

Chapter Fifteen

Despite years of experience on the seas, this particular stretch of water made him cringe. The rocky islands to the west and the treacherous reefs to the east just added to the miseries for his pilot and the crew, trying to wind their way up the channel. The weather was all right for sailing, and the men below were faring well. But the earl of Derrymoor knew that these waters were treacherous. He remembered years before, when, sailing as a young man, these same waters turned forbidding and capsized his ship, the Tremaine. He did not remember doing so, but apparently he was able to swim ashore, and was saved by the residents of that island called Shepperton, which was now his destination yet again.

What an experience that had been. His first real love affair had taken place upon that isle. And what a lass she had been. Her hair black and curly, her smile, the memory of which could still make him ache, and her touch, so gentle and so warm. Ah, the memory of that last night with her still burned in his consciousness. Her name was Diane. He had given her his family broach as a memento, having nothing else to give her at the time. He did wonder what happened to her, and he wondered, too, if it was that memory that drove him back to the island.

"What say ye, m'liege? We could go a wee bit more nor' easterly here. That'd make the islands yonder less of a threat."

Derrymoor was startled out of his reverie by the words of his pilot.

"Oh, aye, but then watch that ye not get too close either to the reefs, which I know to be over there." He pointed over the starboard side.

"Aye, me captain. Me mate shall keep a close eye to the east."

"Very well, then. I shall check on the men below. For I do believe it should be no more than a day before we shall see the island." He said this as much to get away from the waters as anything. Then he went below decks to the main room where there were a number of the men, seasoned warriors all, sitting about as if this were just any ordinary voyage, playing cards, drinking ale, talking of women.

"What's the matter, m'liege? Ye have the look like we're adrift in some storm, but me mates on deck tell me that we're just getting' into the channel, and that they expect smooth sailin'."

"Ah, Bedford, it's just these old memories, is all. You do know that these are the waters I was shipwrecked in, 'twas in my youth."

"These waters, was it?"

"Aye, these very waters, but up the channel a ways, toward where we're going."

"Shepperton, is it not?"

"Aye, that'd be right. Now, if ye would, what I'd like to do is to tell the men a bit about this island, and why we are to be going there."

"All right, me Captain, let me assemble the men that ye need, and ye can tell us all about Shepperton Island and what our business is there."

And so the earl took up a flagon of ale, while Bedford went about the ship, gathering up the expeditionary forces, and brought them all to the main room. And when they were all there, he announced, "Now, me men, your earl has some things to tell ye all about yer expedition on the morrow."

"Well, me mates, let me tell ye a bit of the history of Shepperton Island and why we are going there. Now Shepperton Island was, for its many years, a small, inconsequential island in the channel, 'tween Scotland and Ireland, a place of natural mountainous beauty, but unassuming significance, filled with persons who just filled their days with the pursuits of fishing, farming, hunting, and trapping, and just did not care for the intrusion of strangers. That all changed with the discovery of their magical pots, which were said to protect the health of those who drank regularly from them. They were sold to all the great houses throughout Europe, and, as such, the island took on a whole new significance and became a protectorate of the English king and ruled by a line of earls. And it was this that I saw when I was here in me youth. Now, I must say that the earl was but a young man himself, and I did not see much of him then. But in the intervening years I have kept in some touch with the doings on the island, and it is because of these changes that we go there now.

"For, you see, their present earl is ill and has no rightful heir. There is one man on the island who has been watching this little drama play out. He is on the ruling council there, and I have heard from him that we are just about at the right time to come aboard and storm the castle. But if we were to try to land at the usual location, we would have a harder time than usual to even land. So this man, Lord Reordan, has built a whole pier for our landing, a little northeast of the main port village and up around a well-sheltered bay. He says that there is already a road from the new port to the castle, and he assured us that he shall have horses for us as we make land, and shall have men and warriors to show us the way. He further said that he expects no opposition until we get close to the castle."

"Now, me lord, this sounds all too easy. Let me ask ye a pair of questions, then, if I may."

"Of course, Nigel, please ask now, as we may be busy this time tomorrow."

"It seems to me, mind ye, that this Lord Reordan is not just doing this out of charity, for it would seem to me that he'd like something from ye, m'lord. And that would bring me to my second question, which is that, if this is, indeed, a protectorate of the crown of England, would not the king be interested in the outcome?"

"Ah, those are both good questions. Let me answer both questions with one answer. It would appear that Lord Reordan seems to gain from our incursion and the taking of the castle, for we would need someone we could trust in position to handle things in our absence. And, he assures me that the king cares not who is actually in power, as long as he gets his steady supply of Shepperton pots. And Lord Reordan further assures me that he can take care of that issue, as he is a lifelong resident of Shepperton.

"So, as ye can see, it should be quite an easy mission for us to just come ashore quietly, unannounced, proceed to the castle, and establish our dominance. Then set up Lord Reordan in our stead and leave again with our claim to the island of Shepperton."

"Ye make it sound so much like a mere hunting trip, m'lord. I only hope that it does happen as ye say. But for me, I'm a bit more cautious in my judgment."

"And that is why I brought ye, my dear friend, for we need some of your caution."

"Quite right…quite right."

Cayman couldn't wait to talk to Diane. He found her, as expected, at Barncuddy's. She was in the kitchen, kneading dough for the day's wheat rolls, when he walked in. She looked up, flicked a loose strand of her hair out of her eyes, and smiled.

"Why, Master Cayman, how good of ye to stop by. Now, I'm sorry, but I've got to get this dough kneaded and put up to rise, so ye'll have to talk to me as I work."

"Of course, I understand. Now, yer son, Eustace, seems to be doing well, though I have not heard what the healers have told him, nor what they have recommended for treatment. But I was able to speak to him, and he seemed to be in good spirits, and seemed, in every way, to be in good health."

"Well, that is some relief, at the very least. Can ye tell me what he is doing now?"

"When I left, he was going to talk with Drachma and Tom, along with the two healers, so don't you worry. He is in excellent hands."

She expertly divided up her dough and put the small lumps up on the rack for raising. Then she washed her hands, drying them on her apron. Next, she turned toward Cayman and she asked, "Now, Master Cayman, ye did na' come all the way down to Barncuddy's, when ye've got more important things to do, just to tell me that my son is in good hands, now did ye?"

Cayman blushed suddenly.

"Nay, m'lass, I did not. It was thee I wanted to see, as ye may have guessed."

She smiled at this, and Cayman smiled foolishly back at her. His hands were sweating, his throat parched, and his legs felt like straw. Diane, then, took his sweaty hands in hers.

"Now, I mean to tell ye, that yer attention has not gone without notice. And when a lass gets this kind of attention from a gentleman, she naturally assumes the worst…"

"But, but, Diane…"

"Don't ye fret, fer I can see that ye're a man of honor." She winked at her man, who was like wet clay in her hands. "Now, come wi' me. Fer I know that Barncuddy can do without my services for the next few minutes."

She led him back through the kitchen to one of the storage rooms in the back of the inn. His heart was racing and he could barely see two feet in front of him. There she turned and rather suddenly kissed him, full on the mouth. Cayman could not think.

His mind was a blank, his body a sea of rampaging hormones. He just held her body close, and he smelled and tasted what to him was heaven. After several minutes, Diane broke it off. Panting, she looked at him straight in the face. Then she took his face in her hands, and, with tears in her eyes, said, "Now, me man, you've seen me at me most vulnerable. And I'm askin', is this what ye want? Is this what ye're willing to give it all to get? For let me tell ye that, unless ye're willing to do that, then ye'd be better off leaving me alone, as I have been that since Eustace was born."

Cayman thought about that for a moment, then spoke words that came to him from somewhere deep within the consciousness of the act just completed.

"My dear, Diane, all I can say is that as a man, I do find ye hard to resist, but if that were all, then ye'd be right to turn me away. But there is more to me than that. For I am, if nothing, extremely faithful and loyal. And this much I promise thee, that ye shall have all of me that my work will allow, and ye shall not have want again for Eustace."

Diane then reached around him and hugged him fiercely, as she wept. It seemed as if all the years of bitterness and betrayal, as well as her intense mistrust of men came down to this moment, washed down with her tears.

When she had wept herself dry, she became weak in the knees and just collapsed into his arms.

"Not feeling too strong right now? Well then, come on out with me, and I'll help ye get some air."

"Thank ye, me good man. And, Cayman, please tell Eustace none of this until I can see him."

"Nay, m'lady, I shan't tell him anything. But, I will tell ye that he is one very observant young man."

"Oh, that he is."

"I shall be back then at closing time."

"Very well, I shall see thee then."

Finding some comfortable chairs in a comfortable study, Judy, Tom, Drachma, Eustace, and Bob at first just sat, and for several minutes, no one spoke. Hermes just stayed standing by the door. Both Tom and Drachma were trying to absorb what Bob had told them of Maggie. For Drachma, the thought of his own daughter, whom he loved as he loved no other, so near, yet so far from him, was almost too much. For Tom, the thought of his mother, whom he had just gotten to know through her books, writings, and the stories that Angelica told him, but whom he had never gotten to know in the flesh, was a bit more than he was ready to bear; and yet here were people who had actually seen her! It did not seem fair at all. Why was he not allowed just a brief glimpse of her? He would give anything at all for that rarest of treasured memories.

"Well, Tom," put in Bob, as he noticed the youth's demeanor. "It would appear that I've upset you with my mentioning the name Maggie, and, quite honestly, I did not realize that her name would be of such significance to you or to Drachma."

"Nay, how could you have known that," answered Drachma. "It would appear to have been told you by Maggie herself for a reason, and that, I believe, is part of what brought you to our little island, here in the channel, in our time and place."

"I hadn't thought of it quite that way, but you're right. It would make some sense." Bob thought about it for just a moment, and then spoke again. "And now, Mr. Drachma, it would appear to be time for some explanations, for both Judy and I have so many questions that only you, it would appear, can answer."

"That would seem fair enough," Drachma answered, "so, in that sense of fairness to both you and our lady healer, let me begin by saying just how much I have looked forward to this meeting. For, you see, your arrival in this time and place is no mistake, and no random act. There is a great need here, in this time and in this

place—a greater need than anyone can have foreseen—and you are our chosen ones to answer that need.

"Now, let me begin by telling everyone here the story of Master Robert, the Lady Judy, their travails, and their purpose."

"Well, Mr. Drachma," said Judy, "I would like that very much. And to hear my own story, entwined with Bob's, from your perspective, no less. That is a tale to tell our grandchildren."

Then Judy did something unexpected. She started singing, an old Irish song that was new to all present, but its words and meaning were understood very clearly. Her soft contralto voice was enthralling. All in the room were enchanted, both by her voice and by the lyrics.

> Come, by the hills to the land, where fancy is free,
> And stand where the peaks meet the sky,
> And the loughs meet the sea,
> Where the rivers run clear,
> And the bracken is gold in the sun,
> And the cares of tomorrow can wait, 'til this day is done.
> Come, by the hills to the land, where life is a song,
> And stand where the birds fill the air with their joy all day long,
> Where the trees sway in time,
> And even the wind sings in tune,
> And the cares of tomorrow can wait, 'til this day is done.
> Come, by the hills, to the land where legend remains,
> The stories of old fill our hearts,
> And may yet come again,
> Where the past has been lost, and the future is still to be won,
> And the cares of tomorrow can wait, 'til this day is done.

"Now, Judy, you never told me that you were a singer," said Bob, with moisture in his eye and a lump in his throat. "And that song…it was beautiful, beyond belief. Wherever did you learn it?"

"It was an old Irish song that my mother used to sing to me when I was a little girl, and the melody and the words just came back to me as I was trying to make sense of all of this."

"Ah, m'lady, you are too kind, and your voice too angelic for this place."

They all turned around toward the voice at the door. There was Falma, along with Craycroft and Melchior. Judy stood up quickly and went over and hugged Falma.

"Oh, Mr. Falma, you're just in time. Drachma, here, was just about to tell us of our own story, of Bob and me, and what we're all doing here."

"Well, splendid. I believe that we should love to hear this tale as well. Oh, Drachma, my old friend, it is truly you. Here, at this time and in this place, with all these people, our friends. Come, now, regale us with this story. Tell us of Master Robert, the Lady Judy, of Carlo Vincente, and of powers and plans more ancient and awful."

"It is not some coincidence that brings you forth, my friend; for you and Craycroft, also Melchior, Eustace, and you as well, Hermes. You do all need to hear this tale. And let me tell you that you may as well get comfortable, for 'tis a tale of some length, as well as power. And of that power that did form the world and keeps its heartbeat, I shall but say a few words, as you may experience some of it."

Judy could feel the tingling in her spine as he began. She reached over and grasped Bob's hand, which he gave her as a gift.

"Now, this story does actually begin years before, at a time when Craycroft was but a young man and still working as apprentice to a man named Cartho. As you know, Cartho was a magnificent healer, who did espouse ideas considered dangerous by many. And, it would appear that, if his discoveries were to fall into the hands of the king's advisors, they would be forever crushed. And so, he asked that he be allowed to send a volume of his writing to me, and it would then stay in my library until such time as my own grandson would find it and make use of it.

"Now, as I understand it, you have seen some of the power of this book play out in your own midst. Is that not right, Master Craycroft?" Drachma inquired.

"Oh, aye. I have always known that Cartho was a man most wise, as well as a great healer. But I was not aware of his powers that lay hidden within the pages that he wrote."

"As some would say," Drachma continued, "he knew more than anyone, but felt the powers behind his observations as signs for the future. In any event, these powers were entrusted to me and also to my daughter, Maggie. But they lay in a state of dormancy until last year, when it appeared that our potters were becoming ill. And, as you know by now, that was a mighty blow to our fragile little island."

"So I thought on this matter and I decided to confer with my friends here in the castle. I met with the earl, Falma, Carlo, and Felicia Vincente. And it was decided to watch for further signs. Now, at that time, Carlo Vincente was remarkably silent, and I thought, somewhat uncharacteristically. And we had developed a special language to use should any signs appear. So I returned to the forest and began watching for signs. At first, the signs themselves were quite subtle, and it was actually Angelica who first pointed them out to me. It was she who noticed that the book by Cartho would be down from the shelf each morning for three mornings, and there would be no one about to read, and so she moved it to Maggie's library where it stayed in place until discovered by our Tom.

"And, too, she noticed the flowers that would bloom each day. When she would pick them, they had a certain smell that would linger, but it was not the smell of the flowers themselves; it was the smell of the earth from which they were plucked that she said reminded her of Maggie.

"But, in truth, I did not really notice until one day, when I came back into the house in the evening, the faint sound of music— the music of intense longing, as only music may get through the senses. It was quiet, almost too quiet to hear, but it was there, nonetheless, as if carried upon the breeze. So, I stood there in my doorway, transfixed by the magic of the notes, when Angelica

came to me, and, seeing that I was listening, finally said to me, 'Now, you do know that these are signs, do you not?'"

"And so, I sent a message to Falma that it appeared the time was to be soon. Also, I began my voyages, in order to find just the right people and the right time. What I am able to tell you is that, in all the ages I was able to visit, there were none that struck quite the right note with me, save your time and place. There were not the opportunity, nor the combination of skill and temperament that I did find with you in your time," he said to Judy and Bob. "And none who did complete our own prophecy as you did."

As Bob listened to Drachma talking, he again felt a tugging sensation at the back of his awareness and found himself drifting back to the time several months ago while he was in the hospital up in the CCU at night with one of his sick patients—one of those times when he felt the burden of his profession most acutely weighing him down. When he looked up for a moment from the chart, he felt an overwhelming sense of longing that was hard to describe, but so intensely real that time itself seemed to stop. He could feel himself drift off to another realm, with the sensation of weightlessness. Though he could not recall seeing anything unusual, he remembered that it felt like he was deep in the woods, with the forest creatures around, the sound of the brook, and the smell of the old oak forest.

Drachma had been silent for a moment. Then he looked at Bob and said, "If I could tell you what you were wearing, would it help?"

Bob snapped out of his reverie at these words.

"Were you not wearing, at the time, a shirt of green, and a gray outer cloak, with a dark red stain over the pocket?"

Bob recalled suddenly, and indelibly, how, just moments before his encounter with the numinous, he had been overseeing the resuscitation of that poor, sick soul, when a vial of blood that was supposed to be sent to the lab had broken, and he had the contents spill over his gray coat, right over the jacket pocket. He

recalled how it was that very small encounter that had made him realize just what a burden his life had become. He washed his hands and did the best he could with the jacket before turning to the chart to write, and to get himself back into the real world.

"It was you, wasn't it?"

"Aye, it was."

"Then, may I say, Mr. Drachma, somehow you knew, even before all this happened, how I felt, and how ready I really was for this other life, its opportunities, and challenges."

"It is you who have spoken thus, not I," Drachma said with a smile.

"Okay, Bob. Sounds like you've got some explaining to do."

"Yes, Judy, but later. For now I'd like to hear more of this man's story."

"All right, but remember, you promised."

So, Drachma resumed his narrative. The others in the room did not notice that Drachma had shifted his focus just slightly; from that of purely narrating the events of his tale to actively drawing the others in, so that all became one with the tale being told.

"Now, let me tell you about Carlo Vincente, and I do know that you, m'lady Judy, as well as you, Master Robert, are familiar with that name. But did you also know of his background, and how he came to be someone of importance on this isle?

"Well, my good friend Falma would know of this, and you as well, Master Craycroft. But let me tell you all of this man and what he has wrought. He came from somewhat modest beginnings in Italy, where he was the master craftsman of a guild of potters who did produce some of the finest glazed porcelain in Europe. But their guild came under the servitude of a wealthy nobleman by the name of Count Gregorio, who did, in essence, imprison the guild within one of his castles. It was about this time that I had become aware of Shepperton pots and their boon to the health of those that owned them; but there being no guild to produce these pieces, it would appear that there was a great opportunity

for Shepperton. So I did, with the aid of my own father, arrange for the importation of this entire guild of painters and potters to Shepperton. And so began our association with the great guild of the island, and you do know of its import.

"And, as some of you know, our island's nobility is not one of birth, but of opportunity, and it became apparent that Carlo Vincente, as the leader of the guild, was its own nobleman, so he rose in the ranks and did become Lord Vincente. He was given a place of his own within the castle and was also given power over his painters, potters, and their coming and going, and he soon gained wealth beyond all measure.

"Carlo Vincente and I remained friends, despite our occasional differences. It was he, after all, who did adopt Felicia as his daughter, thereby enabling her rise in the minds and hearts of our island's people. It was she, as well, whom I did adore but could never marry, something that I have come to regret on more than one occasion through the years.

"It seems that sometime last spring, Carlo had heard that the guild was threatened again by this Count Gregorio. He found out that it was some of his own guild that did tell of our location and that the count was planning to attack our island, with the aim of revenge and to get back the guild, which he felt was his by rights. And so, he took matters into his own hands and began eliminating those of his guild that he thought were causing such a stir."

"Now, that is interesting," Craycroft spoke. "For I do know that this is true and I have proof of his doings in this matter. And it was with some astonishment that I did realize this."

"You speak of the note?"

"My God, do you know of this note?"

"Ah, there are many things that I have learned of these last six months, Master Craycroft, of which you shall hear."

"The note?" asked Bob.

"Oh, aye, Master Robert, a note written by Lord Vincente himself, telling a Master Garza that he was next, and to not destroy the note. I have it among my things."

"How odd… Well, continue."

Bob thought about this, and what he knew of the painters and potters, and how his investigation of this might prove fruitful after all.

"As you might surmise, rumors of witchcraft, sorcery, and such soon were about, and it seemed to Carlo that his methods of dealing with this threat to his own place and guild might produce anything but the desired effects.

"And so Carlo Vincente then began the process of calling on the powers that control our own sense of time and place, even as I was searching myself for the same, but for somewhat different reasons."

"Now, wait just a minute, Mr. Drachma." It was Judy who spoke. "There is something that you're not telling us. Something involving time and place and being able to call upon these powers that control them."

"Ah, as usual, m'lady, you have touched upon this mystery, which is at the heart of what has happened." Craycroft reached into his cloak and pulled out the book that he had been given by Tom. It was a fairly small volume, gray in color, unassuming to look upon. "Now, this little book, which looks so ordinary, is none other than the treatise, which was written by Drachma many years ago, and which I have not read; and yet has been read by Master Falma, by Carlo Vincente, as well as by Felicia, and now also by Tom. It tells of mysteries deep and forbidding, which I fear to touch, but they, brave souls that they are, have now awakened, and it is my understanding that it was they that brought you and Master Robert here."

"And what a journey it has been," added Bob, as he gently squeezed Judy's hand. "And, as you were saying, Mr. Drachma, this man, Carlo Vincente, whom I remember dying in our Emergency Room, was guilty of killing off several of his fellow workers, and yet was a friend of yours, and, it seems, was playing with the fire of the ages right under your nose."

"My, what a way you have with words, Master Robert. Well, let me explain, if I may, just what Carlo Vincente had done, and what he had not done. And, aye, he was a dear friend to me, to Falma, and to Craycroft as well."

"Oh, aye, 'tis true," added Falma. "Though he was a difficult man much of the time to read, he was a true friend. And I share with you that knowing the circumstances of this recent behavior would seem to be advantageous. And so I, too, would be most interested in Drachma's story."

"Very well, my friends, I shall tell you what I know of Carlo Vincente's dilemma, his decisions, and his departure. For there never was a man more torn than he. As I told you, the decision that he made, as to his coworkers, he made on his own. He did not consult me, nor anyone, before undertaking what he felt he had to do in order to protect the island. This I found after he came to me, a crushed and ill man. He told me what he himself had discovered of his own men, conspiring not only with forces that had formerly put his own men in drudgery, but were now intent on crushing their own most magnificent life on this island. He felt that he had no choice but to act, and swiftly, but in a way that would eliminate those who had conspired with Count Gregorio. It shook him to the core to do this thing, which he felt he had to do, but, for the last of the conspirators, he gave a note, warning him that he would be the next one, and he told him not to destroy the note. His hope was that this note would be found and traced back to himself.

"That note did, indeed, find its way to Craycroft, who surmised rightly that it came from the hand of Carlo Vincente. But, by the time that Carlo came to me, he was now experiencing even greater anxieties that the king himself would find out about our little island doings, and he was afraid that his actions had made that even more likely. And he seemed a most penitent man, and ready to do what he could to protect the safety of the island and its wonderful secrets. He was also, by this time, quite ill himself.

"And, with the great secrets that were still to be revealed as to the nature of medicine, and with these secrets now in jeopardy, I found that I could be of some assistance to this poor man, who was now in the throes of his own, and, in part, self-inflicted illness. What I offered him was the chance to redeem himself and our island. For this, though, he would have to forfeit his own life in search for his salvation. I would have no say in what went on in the remainder of his life, but I would be able to send Carlo as an ambassador to your world, to do what he was able for those affected by the absence of both the Lady Judy and yourself, Master Robert."

"But I saw him die in our ER," said Bob. "How was he to be an ambassador if he were dead?"

"In answer to your query, my dear Robert, I would note that you, yourself, have seen Maggie, my dear daughter, though I myself did see her die."

Bob was speechless, Drachma became tearful, and all in the room were momentarily breathless. It was eventually Falma who broke the silence.

"My good friends," he said, "I should like to thank Drachma for his efforts, for getting these two fine healers from another time to come and be of assistance to us, and, I believe, to all humanity. But, in truth, I would like very much to hear of the fate of Carlo Vincente, since I was here when he was sent away."

"Indeed, you were, Master Falma. I did send him off to this other time and place. I did give him some instruction, based upon what I knew would be concerns as to our theft of these two individuals. In particular, there was Janie, the mother of Joshua, and her husband, Earl. And there was your wife, Master Robert, whom you did leave, and with whom you have been unable to speak. What I can tell you both is that I did give Lord Vincente a token, an ancient coin of Greece, called a drachma, to take with him."

"That coin, I know it. It was in my possession, though briefly." Tom spoke up for the first time.

"And also, I believe, that it was in the possession of Lady Judy, Master Robert, and also Janie," Drachma added.

"It seems that coin had a will of its own," said Judy. "It had some magic about it. I would be curious to know who has it now."

"And that person, I believe, is Master Robert's wife, and for her, it is a token that tells of Robert's health and well-being."

"Well, I'll be," said Bob. "Are you telling me that Marilyn knows that I'm here and that I'm safe?"

"Well, Master Robert, I do not know with certainty, but what I can tell you is that I did send Carlo Vincente on his way, carrying the token with him, and he did know of all its potential and its mysterious powers and its message. And I would say that Lord Vincente has the guidance of all the ages with him."

"So, you're saying that you've lost contact with Carlo Vincente, but that you sent him to our time and place, carrying this coin, which has a mind of its own, in hopes that he would do with it as you wished. Is that about right?"

"Ah, m'lady, sometime I shall have to tell you the story of that coin—how I acquired it and what it has meant to me..."

"I'm sorry, Mr. Drachma. I didn't mean to sound so crass. But you did say that you sent this Carlo Vincente into the blue, a man who killed his coworkers, as some kind of ambassador of goodwill to an alien people, yet you say that you trusted him to do the right thing?"

"Oh, my Lady Judy, how you do make all our efforts seem so simple and foolish. I have never met anyone with such a clearly discerning eye."

"Ah, my dear friend," added Falma, "if I could have warned you myself of this lady's discernment. But truly, she has been a discovery for me also, for I think that all the forces of evil shall stand no chance against her. I have seen her unflinching

gaze through trials that would have made many a lesser person crumble. And yet, here she is, taking even you to task."

"Oh, I'm so sorry, but I'm no great discerning lady. I'm just a woman, taken out of her comfortable, though somewhat boring life, now given a chance at this most extraordinary journey with the man whom I adore—that's you, Robert, and don't you forget it— who's trying to make sense of all of this. And even though I know it sounds like a lot of mumbo-jumbo, I get the feeling that it is real; so real, in fact, that my old life is starting to feel like a dream."

"And to address your concerns, m'lady, I do not know what happened, nor whether Carlo did, in fact, do all that he could. But, I shall tell you that I do know for certain that Madame Gilsen has the drachma in her possession, and I do know this because I have been allowed one final chance to visit your world, and I was able to see that she has the coin in its small case on a stand by her bed. I was given the opportunity to direct her toward Janie Crabtree in a note that I left her under the coin."

"Well, from what I have seen of this coin, that would most certainly be consistent with its prior behavior, for I don't know how it got to where it was going in the first place."

"Nor I," said Tom. "It was in my possession for a while, but it disappeared as mysteriously as it came to me, and I was given the coin by Master Falma, who obtained it, he said, from Drachma."

"Aye that would be right, young Tom. But I also recall how I came upon that magical coin. But I believe that would be a topic of later discussion.

"Now, Master Craycroft," Drachma asked, "would you be so kind as to provide this old man with some liquid refreshment? And, while we are waiting for that, might I suggest that Eustace tell us of his morning adventures, as I believe they might be pertinent. Oh, aye, I did hear of them, my young man."

"My morning adventures?" He looked toward Judy, who simply shrugged. "Well, if it would be all right, as I might need some help from the Lady Judy…"

Judy smiled her assent.

And so he told of waking up, wandering into the library, and noticing the tapestry on the wall—a beautiful, colorful tapestry of a knight on horseback, with a tree that appeared to be a tree of fire with flowers on it, with a mountain in the background, and a bright yellow sun. And he told of taking down a book from the shelves and opening it to find an engraving of the same scene. And he told of Judy walking in on him, noticing the same things, but not chastising him for either being in the library or taking down the book.

He then told of having breakfast with Judy, and Frieda commenting that the future of the island was in the hands of Tom and himself, what he considered a most strange thing to say.

"Well," continued Falma, "it would seem most strange, indeed, but for the fact that Eustace is of noble birth and Tom is the grandson of Drachma and bears his name. No, it is not really strange at all, especially when you consider the book and the tapestry."

Next, he asked Drachma to fill them in just a little on the significance of the tapestry and the book. And he told of a tale that no one but Falma was familiar with—not even Craycroft knew it fully.

"My good people," he began, "Master Falma is right about many things, and this is no exception. The book, which Eustace and the Lady Judy found, tells the tale of a humble friar and his own pusuit of yet another book. And tells also of the trials and lives lost in its search. And both the book and the tapestry tell the tale of a great knight, whose name was also Drachma. But this was Drachma of the Highlands, whose service in the protection of that book is a tale for yet another day.

"Now, when I was little more than a mere lad, I was sent to one of the Greek isles to study under an old man, who lived an austere life in one of the remote hills. He was a truly remarkable man, who taught me the ancient tongues of Latin, Greek, Aramaic,

and Persian. He also taught me mathematics and the physical sciences, and it was with this background that I was sought after to be a teacher myself to the daughter of the Ambassador Gianni, who would be none other than the Lady Felicia. But before I left him, he turned to me and said that he had something for me. He told me that his name was Drachma of the Desert. He had a copy of a book that he wanted me to read, but that I might not take the book with me, only its message and its power. This was The Book of Drachma, and it was written in ancient Greek. So I read and I studied this text, and I felt its power. It was like nothing else that I had read, before or since.

"So, after this, he took me back into his private room and he christened me with the name I now bear, and he told me that I was to carry on the tradition, to find my own sanctuary, and that my own name would be ever known by my sanctuary. And it was then that he gave me that ancient coin within its small box, and that I would use it as I saw fit, but that it had powers of its own and would be given to whomever I felt needed it the most. It could never be owned by anyone, but would forever be theirs for the time that they needed it.

"And now, what I would ask of you good people, is that when next you see that tapestry, that you look again at the figure of the sun in the sky and see that there are markings on the face of that sun, which match the markings on the coin."

There was a hush in the room ; it was a stillness that went deeply into everyone in that sanctuary.

"And now, let me tell you all of this lady, Judy, whom I also did bring to our island, and with this I should complete my tale. Now, Judy, I did find that you did have a connection with Master Robert. It was something that I only sensed as if something ethereal, something intangible, but it was there. Now, I do not know if you remember, but you were at your work and you were discussing matters with your colleague, and one of Master Gilsen's patients did come in to where you were working, and

this was an elderly woman who was laboring to breathe. And as you were discussing her care with this other woman, you told her that this was 'one of Dr. Bob's patients,' which meant something to you and this other woman. And that look that she gave you, and what she said to you, I do not know if you even remember."

The memory came flooding back to Judy.

"Oh, yes, Mr. Drachma, I do recall. It was Alonza Chaves, my old friend in the ER, who turned to me and said, 'It's only because I know what he means to you that I'll take extra special care of her.' She said it half-joking, but I knew that she sensed something… And you were there?"

"Aye, I was there. And so it was that I did seek out the two of you. And you because of this deeply spiritual connection, which defied all logic, but was, nevertheless, present. Also, I must tell you that your own seeking out of Joshua's parents, as a help when they did need it most, only confirmed for me what I was already learning of you. And I did know that you would be there when the note arrived for Earl Crabtree.

"So, it was you, Lady Healer, who did complete the connection of all these persons, from different times and places, and did allow, as well, the connections to be made with the wife of Master Robert and with our own earl."

"The more you talk of all of this, the more connectedness I sense," said Bob, who had been sitting quietly next to Judy.

"Ah, then you shall see this evening at Craycroft's dinner that there are more connections yet to be uncovered."

"Oh, I can't wait," said Judy, and she quickly kissed Bob on the cheek.

Chapter Sixteen

Jeremy entered the constabulary, breathless, to find that it was full of guardsmen. The guardsmen, however, paid him no mind, as he quickly went up to the man behind the desk.

"Oh hello, Jeremy. Pray tell, what brings ye here in such a state?"

Jeremy recognized him as one of the guards who had been in here before.

"Well, sire, I have some news that Master Kerlin needs to hear."

"Master Kerlin, ye say? Now, let me see. I believe that Master Kerlin is now meeting with Master Craycroft and the others in charge. What is it that ye've got to say, and I'll see if we can get a message to Kerlin."

"Well, meanin' no disrespect, good sire, but I do believe that Kerlin himself needs to be hearin' this."

Martin and Stoneheft were listening to the exchange and were most intrigued.

"May I say, laddie, that I am friends with Kerlin, and I shall take what you say directly to him, if ye'll but tell me. Now come sit down here. I'm called Martin, and this is Master Stoneheft. Both of us have to report to Kerlin, as we have just been checking out doings down the road to Champour. And with us is Rowan, a lad whom we met as we were makin' our investigation."

Jeremy then recognized Rowan, and they smiled.

"Aye, it's ye, indeed, Rowan. Yer mum works fer the lady in the castle, doesn't she?"

"Aye, Frieda's me mum."

That was all Jeremy needed, and he sat down with the two men and the youth.

"Well, let me tell ye what I've just heard from me uncle, as he knows some of the men who've been hired by this Councilor Reordan."

That immediately perked up his listeners.

"Well, what can ye tell us, then, about this Councilor Reordan's plans?"

"Aye, sire, it seems that this councilor has hired many men, mostly villagers, but some farmers as well. It seems that he was needin' a pier built out by the quay. Whatever for, I do not definitely know, but this much I do know—he has brought up fifty or more sturdy horses from the surrounding villages, and he has outfitted the horses for stout riders. And what is more, those same horses are now down at the quay, apparently awaiting riders."

"Just how certain of this are ye, m'lad?"

"About as sure I can be, sire. For it was told me by me uncle who has never lied. And he was going to try to get the message to the guards up here in the castle, with hopes of reaching Kerlin with the news. But I told him that I was now paid by the earl for obtaining information such as this, and so I told him that I would do so."

"Well, Stoneheft, does this not fit with what we saw?"

"Oh, aye, it does, and we thank ye fer that information. And it does seem fortuitous that it came to us today. Now, can ye tell me, lad, how ye came by that information this day?"

"Aye, sire, ye see, I was just keepin' me eyes open, as I was told to do, when I saw this little snitch, called Wheezer, go down by the main gate o' the castle, and I saw him conferin' wi' some man—a man who works fer Councilor Reordan. I saw them walk off together down toward the village. Anyway, I followed them

down a piece, and then I saw them turn into the miller's place. Then I went across the road to me uncle's place, so as to watch them. Well, me uncle finds me and we get to talkin', and that's how we got onto this business goin' on."

"And might I ask your uncle's name, lad? For we might just be able to use some of what he told ye."

"Aye, his name's Maxim, and he's the one sells leather goods, so he'd know if there were more than the usual market in boots, jerkins, saddles, and such."

"Ah, so he would… I believe that I know him—a tall, sturdy fellow, with a scar on his forehead, isn't he?"

"Aye, that'd be he. Walks with a bit of a limp, he does."

"And a fine man, he is, too."

Something told Martin that this bit of information was important, so he suggested to Stoneheft that they go right away and try to find Kerlin. Then Stoneheft suggested that they bring Jeremy along, as it was he who brought them word. He also suggested that someone seek out Maxim in the village and have a talk with him. To their surprise, Rowan volunteered to go talk with Maxim, and so Rowan left with another guard, as the other three went out, going toward the keep.

The three of them did not have far to walk, when they saw Kerlin and Proust walking toward them. They were walking at leisure, talking and gesturing, and almost bumped into the trio.

"Ah, my friends, Martin and Stoneheft, and Jeremy also. This bodes of something important. And, aye, I did receive your bird message, and I would guess that this has something to do with your being about this afternoon."

"As usual, Kerlin, ye've proven to be a right good judge of men and their actions."

"Well, come along with me and I shall take you to a quiet corner of the constabulary, where we may discuss this all, and what it means.

"And here comes Cayman. Come along, my friend, these folks have some important news for us. And what, might I ask, causes that glow in your cheeks and that glitter in your eye? Last that I heard, you were going to see our fine serving wench at Barncuddy's."

"Indeed, I was, and I would guess my efforts were something of a success, if I do say so."

"Ah, well, a story for another time, then, eh?"

"Aye, another time."

Councilor Rust was sitting in his study but was restless. He could not get over the fact that Drachma had seemed to have a chink in his emotional armor. He observed that Drachma and Tom had both reacted as if this ethereal creature named Maggie was somehow an answer kept out of their grasps. It was as if she were what they had been searching for—yet was never attainable. And he thought about his own life and how the revelations at Barncuddy's had left him with the same feeling; a longing so powerful—so near, and yet not quite within reach. And what of Diane? The more he thought about it, the more he became convinced that it was she.

He began searching through his files, which were under his bed, hidden by age, but never fully forgotten. He looked through boxes of documents, and there he found the slip of paper, and looked at the date and also the name. *Aye, there it is! It was she... who and when I thought, and it appears to fit! Here is yet another piece to this puzzle.* He thought about it more and decided that he should investigate.

But first there was the matter of the meeting of the Council of Lords, which Craycroft had asked him to be certain was set up right and proper for the next day. So, he got up, got his cloak, scarf and hat, and headed out the door.

It is a good thing that I do not have to do this sort of thing more frequently, thought Rust, as he wandered over toward the council chambers, *for I've found that I have no stomach for such things.*

Ever since Craycroft conscripted his efforts, Rust had felt ever more alone, and then this business with Councilor Genet was weighing him down as well. He was used to being the minority on the council, and the other councilors were also used to his unnerving ways. They expected that, if there were two sides to any issue, that they would hear it from the good councilor. But most of the disputations had been good hearted, and Rust did take some delight in that many of the decisions that he had most adamantly opposed, he had seen turn against the council in time. But that was then, and this was now. His determined opposition to Reordan was beginning to take its toll on him. He was more careful than ever with his walking about, having seen what happened to Genet, and he kept wondering what Reordan's plans were.

And now, this whole business with the earl. He wasn't certain how he felt about this at all. How could he tell them all that the earl was dead, when he really wasn't, at least not according to Craycroft and Falma; he was sent away, apparently whence Master Robert came, but how was he even to try to explain that? It was too nebulous and a bit too much like magic.

Rust arrived at the council chambers, which were presently deserted, other than a couple of pages.

Good, he thought, *I can just tell the pages, then, to get the message out and not have to answer any questions.*

He found Felix and Ambrose milling about, and he called them over.

"Now, m'lads, we have to call a very important meeting of the council for tomorrow. This is upon the orders of our liege lord, and must be attended by all within the council. Do you understand?" They nodded in agreement. "Now the meeting shall commence tomorrow, at two bells, precisely, and it shall be a closed meeting.

So any who shall attend need to be there, in place, by the time the meeting starts."

"Aye, Councilor, we shall do as ye order," said Ambrose, the older of the two. "Now ye say that it's to be at two bells, sharp, and it is to be a closed meeting?"

"Aye, that's right, m'lad." And then he sighed with relief. He had done his part, now it was up to the others to come through.

And the boys were off, with the enthusiasm of youth and inexperience. Rust looked after the pages, disappearing into the mists of the afternoon. He looked about him, and, seeing no one, decided to venture forth and pay a visit to old Barncuddy, for, he realized, he had scores to settle that were seemingly ancient, and yet newly unearthed that were vexing him.

The way to Barncuddy's was straight across the courtyard, then down the walkway, and he found that he became chilled as he walked down the long corridor and realized that his chilling had more to do with what he anticipated seeing there than with the weather. By the time he got to his destination, he was dreading it so much that he almost turned aside, but then he saw Cayman leaving, his face flushed, and the look in his eyes suggesting confidence, more true than his own dread.

"Good afternoon, Captain Cayman."

"And good afternoon to you, sire. Going to get yer own sorrows drowned?"

"You just might say that, Cayman. Aye, I think I shall do that."

"Well, there's no place better, I'd say. And, if ye were to ask me, I should say that Master Barncuddy himself would dearly love to see thee for a bit."

"All right, and thank you, my friend."

"Well, g'day, then."

And so Rust stepped into the warm ambience, the clamor and clutter of Barncuddy's Ale House.

"Ah, Councilor. I thought that ye'd be back," said Barncuddy from across the room. "Now, come in here wi' me and we'll talk.

Oh, Diane, would ye bring some o' the Carlisle's brew for our good councilor here? Now, sire, just this way back to our little private dining area back here."

"Gracious me, my good man, I did not expect such a warm welcome, but I thank thee."

"It is but a rare treat that we find someone of yer stature visiting our establishment. But I know that is not really why ye came back, now, is it?"

"Nay, my good man, it is not."

"Well, let me just pull up a chair here, and ye sit down, and we'll talk."

Diane arrived with a tall flagon of the rich, brown, fragrant drink. She smiled as she set it down in front of the councilor, but said nothing. Rust, though, could sense something about the barmaid had changed.

Before she could turn and walk away, he turned toward her, held her arm gently, and said, "If you please, my good lassie, do not run off so soon, but rather, sit down for but a few minutes and join in our talk."

Diane looked questioningly at Barncuddy, who simply smiled and gestured toward the chair.

"I thank thee, m'lass. Now, can you tell us but a little of yourself? You see, I have had a chance to speak with Craycroft, and he has indicated that your own background has been a well-kept secret, especially as to being the mother of our own Eustace, who, it seems, is becoming quite an important young man in our island's future."

"Eustace? Important? Oh, Councilor, to me he is the world, but to thee.... Is he doing well, and is he behavin' all right?"

"Exemplary, m'lass, a truly remarkable lad, indeed, and as capable a young man as I've come to know, and a friend to Tom. Ah, I see greatness in there, my lady."

"Lady? Nay, sire, I am no lady. I am but a serving maid here in this establishment..."

"Well then, why not tell us of your most interesting background? I am quite certain that our esteemed Master Barncuddy would like to hear of it. Is that not right?"

The innkeeper's eyes sparkled as he said, "It would seem, Diane, that yer background has been hidden from me, that is, until recently, and that Craycroft himself has made a point of speaking on yer behalf. So, aye, I would love to hear of it."

Diane blushed and sat demurely for a moment. Rust began drinking of that spiced and fragrant beverage.

Then she began telling her tale. She started with how, as a little girl, she had come to the island with her mother, how the women of the island had shunned them, and how her own mother had taken what work she could so that they could eat and have clothing, but that the work itself was menial. She recalled how her mother would spend the hours weeping, as she grew up thinking there was something wrong in all of this. And she also told of how her mother had spent countless hours teaching her to read and do simple calculations in her attempt to try to provide for some education. She told how she thought of her mother as a saint, even though she kept the company of men who seemed to always be drunk and often would have to be thrown out into the street.

Next, she told them of how her mother had died, how she had been sick with fever and boils for months before she finally breathed her last. And how, on the day that her mother died, she had given Diane a book, which she looked upon with awe, as it was a book with the most marvelous illustrations. She remembered one in particular. It was a most colorful illustration with a knight on a horse, riding down a golden path with a tree of flame, a mountain, and a golden sun in the sky. And she remembered her mother telling her that within that book she would find answers as to whence she came and what she must do, but as a small girl with only a limited ability to read, she was not able to gain much from the book; nevertheless, it was precious to her.

"And what became of that book, may I ask?" There was a subtle gleam in Rust's eye as he asked this, knowing where that book probably resided.

"I know not, precisely. But I shall tell thee I was lost for a period of time after me mother died. I was wandering about with no one to look after me. And then, after lonely and hungry weeks went by, a kindly couple took me in unexpectedly, and to them I shall be always grateful. I had nothing with me except the clothes I wore and that selfsame book. My mother's few belongings were taken by the village vultures and by the time those good folk were able to show me to her place, there was nothing left at all, and, I was told, the house belonged to one of the councilors.

"As it happened, then they took me in as their own, and for the next few years I became like a daughter to them. I learned how to cook and clean, to sew and mend, and I learned as well that there were people in this world who were good hearted, without gainin' anything from bein' good. Then, in that time when the king's inquest occurred, I was home and one of the king's men just came in and took them away. I hid in me own room and did not come out until I knew it was safe.

"But when I did come out and looked around for me adoptive parents, they were nowhere to be seen—no trace, nothing. I just sat down and cried. Just as it seemed as if something good had happened in me life, someone snatched it away. So it was back to bein' an orphan, and this time, too, the house became the property of Councilor Reordan. And I found that the skills I had learned were sufficient to keep me fed and clothed, but the book seemed to have no more appeal for me, so one day I sold it in the market and I bought me a warm coat."

"Now, if you'll let me, m'lady, I would like to ask you a pair of pertinent questions. The first is what was the name of your adoptive parents? And the second one is do you know the person to whom you sold your book?"

"Of course, you have the right to ask. Now me adoptive parents were named Emile and Sondra, and they lived in the village of Champour most all their lives. Emile was in the employ of the magistrate of the village, but what he did, I never did find out. Now, as to the identity of the person to whom I sold the book, that I never did know, though I admit I have been curious to learn."

"Well, my lass, I shall attempt to answer both queries, but first, let us hear then of your further history, as to how you became the mother of Eustace. Then I shall attempt to shed some light on your past."

"As you may have heard, sire, there was a shipwreck off this island with the loss of most on board, but one who somehow swam to shore safely…now he was the earl of Derrymoor, though I did not learn of that 'til much later. All that I knew was there was this one who survived and needed the care that I could provide, which was cookin', cleanin', mendin', and such, and the house of our own earl was willin' to pay a small wage for the privilege of caring for him. As it was, this most charming and handsome young man came to live in our village, and I was his caretaker. And then he seemed most taken with me also. Well, I was also a young thing, and here was this fine young man who paid attention to me, and I did come to be with child. Now, mind you, I know I have no one to blame for this but meself.

"But then, his family had heard of his survivin' and sent for him in a ship. And he and I spent one last night together. He gave me his broach, which I have since given to me son, Eustace, as a keepsake. Now, he said that he didna' have anything else, and that I should keep the broach as a memento of our love, and that someday it may become valuable. I have raised me son meself, as a good, God-fearin', strong young man. And I have not sought the company of any man since that time. And me only remembrances of that time have been the broach and me own son."

Rust, then, took a long swallow of Carlisle's brew and set it down on the table.

"And I do thank you, m'lady. And let me tell you that I believe I know where that book you talked of resides, how it got there, who your adoptive parents were, and why they are no longer here. I might also tell you who your true mother was and why she sought safety upon this isle.

"I have been a resident of this island most of my life, and, though I have ventured off the island a few times, I have always come back, as this is my true home. Now, let me deal with your adoptive parents first. I do recall the last time there was a royal inquest—it was one that we all remember with apprehension and considerable regret. In fact, if anyone mentions a royal inquiry to any member of the council, it is met with stern avoidance, for all know that such an inquest invites disaster. During this last inquest, the king's men simply gathered up any whom they saw as any kind of threat and took them back to England with them on their ships, and it is said that only a few of those so deported have survived. As to Emile and Sondra, I cannot say with certainty, but it would seem fair to assume that their fate was no different from the many others. As to their supposed crimes, it may be nothing more than working for someone deemed to be disloyal to the crown, and I do know that Master Torpin was himself put to death for behavior against the crown.

"As to the real question, though, of your own ancestry, I would refer to a tale, no doubt told you by your own mother, of a man from the South, who would ride down the pathways…"

"…of the magnificent mountains, upon his steed of gray, a man alone, who stood against the winds of evil." She finished his sentence for him. "Aye, I remember that line that she would recite!"

Then the truth dawned on her.

"Ye…ye're the man! The man who brought all the books for me to learn to read and write."

"Aye, I am he. And unfortunately, I had gone off the island when your mother died, and when I came back, no one knew of you or your mother, so all these years, until recently, I knew nothing of your life and how intertwined it was to mine.

"Now, then, let me tell you a little about your own mother; where she came from, and of your own origins. Did you ever notice that your mother had an accent?"

"Well, if ye mean, did she talk like everyone else? I didna' think too much about that. I just assumed that it was because we came from off this island."

"Let me tell you that your mother was Greek. She came from the same land as Drachma. And it was from there that she was fleeing. Though I never did find out precisely why, I did find out that she was a lady of some importance, and in some definite danger."

Rust took another large swallow of his drink while Barncuddy had been listening intently. He sighed heavily as he looked upon Diane with new eyes.

"Methinks that this ale house has lately become a place of great revelations."

"And, speaking of great revelations, my good man, I should like very much to revisit something from my youth. If you recall, when I was last in your establishment, you had talked of the changes that had occurred, partly, in some way, as a result of my youthful tomfoolery."

"Ye'd be talkin' about the business with old Charlie McFerris, I presume?"

"Aye, that is precisely what I'm talking about. Now, when Master Robert was here and he was talking of his dream, he mentioned seeing someone upon the stairway, who I presume was Charlie McFerris…"

"Aye, that I do remember, said he was standin' on the stairway, talkin' about some book and some water, if I recall what Master Robert was saying."

"I believe that is right," said Rust, "and I do believe that Master Robert answered the question of the water through his extraordinary display to us just yesterday. But I wonder about the book—whether he was referring to the book by Cartho, or

another. Do you know of any books that Master McFerris might have had in his possession when he died?"

"Well, there be several books that were among his possessions, which are now in a trunk up in a room upstairs. I believe that most of them are books of musical notation, but there may be others. You would be most welcome to peruse them if you would like. Diane, here, could help you. I shall have to find the key to open the trunk."

As Barncuddy left, Diane turned toward Rust and said, "Now, ye don't suppose…"

"Nay, m'lass, it is not the book that you spoke of, for this occurred many years before. And besides, I do know what happened to your book, and I know to whom you sold that book."

"Ye know?"

"Oh, aye, for I purchased it from him. He was but a merchant in the market, looking for a quick profit, not knowing anything about the value of the book that he was selling me. Now, as to where it is, it is probably in Lady Felicia's library with many other valuable books. And believe me, we shall go there and you shall have your book returned to you. That is my promise to you."

Diane could not speak. The tears were overflowing from her eyes for the second time that day.

Barncuddy then came bustling back into the room.

"Now, here ye be. The key… What is the matter, Diane? Are your tears of sadness? What did the councilor say to ye?"

Diane waved him off and then wiped her tears on her apron. "Aye, but my tears are for all the years of sadness, which Master Rust has just mercifully brought to a close."

"Why, then, m'lassie, I shall manage down here for now. Why do ye not take the good councilor up to the room, ye know which one, and find the trunk. Here's the key."

The upper floors of the inn were almost never used, except for storage. Diane knew the way—up the stairs, down a long hall, then back up the stairs at the other end. Up at the top of the

stairway was a single room. The door was a heavy one and creaked on its hinges. Inside was a cold, dusty room with little light. As their eyes adjusted to the dimness, Rust could see, very suddenly, what had been his frequent hiding place as a child.

"If there be any ghosts of memory, then they are here for certain," he said almost wistfully. "For I do remember this room from oh so many years ago."

"Ye do remember, from yer childhood, no?"

"Aye, that I do. Now, where is that trunk of which Master Barncuddy spoke?"

"Methinks it be around to the left, here…ah, here it is."

Before them was a fairly large trunk with a lock. Diane stooped down, tried the key, and sighed with relief that it worked. She then opened it up. Out of the trunk came the odors of must, seafaring voyages, many musical concerts, and old leather. For a while, in the dimness, they had to search by feel, but then, Diane pulled out a small, thick, leather-bound volume and handed it to Rust. He then took the book over to the light and brushed the dust off the cover. There was something written upon it, but it was not in a language that Rust knew well, but he was able to read one of the words; it said "Drachma."

"My God, dost thou know what we have here?" Rust had lapsed into formal speech.

"Nay, m'lord, I know not."

"This appears to be The Book of Drachma, the original, or at the very least a good copy! This volume is truly priceless!"

"Well, I should say that our search has come to an end. And, I should say, that my own search has been fulfilled."

Then she did something totally unexpected. She reached around Rust's thin frame and held him close. Then she reached up on tiptoes, kissed the old man, and said, "Today, my life has begun to matter, and it is to thee that I owe it."

All Rust could think of was what a lucky man Cayman must be.

Chapter Seventeen

The sounds and smells of the Medical ICU were now so familiar to Carol that she no longer seemed to react viscerally to them. Even the alarms were just something that seemed to move her automatically through the motions. Fix this. Put more IV fluid in that one. This other one needed some suctioning. So that when the patient in Bed 5 needed his IV fluids changed again, she did that, almost without consciously thinking about what she was doing. But, as she went about the task of changing out his IV bag, she looked down at his still form and realized that there was really something different about this patient. Looking at him again, so quiet on the bed, amid the tubes and wires, with the ventilator doing his work of breathing, there it was. As if he were trying to communicate something so much deeper, she looked yet again. Yes, there was that spark of greatness, of otherworldly power.

She took a couple of minutes more than necessary with him, laying her hand on his distressed forehead, wiping the stray hair from his face, suctioning his mouth with tender care. She spoke very gently to him, saying that it was going to be all right and explaining what she was about to do. She sensed him physically relax in her care.

Carol was a foreigner herself, having come over from Scotland five years earlier, and somehow she knew there was a kinship, even without the strange note, which had mysteriously vanished

the night he came into the hospital. In her own mind, this was a most special charge, and now she knew it.

So, when she got the visit from the two women, it was not a surprise. It was as though here, at long last, was someone who cared, and in such a way that Carol could finally relax herself.

Marilyn had introduced herself, said that she was the wife of Dr. Robert Gilsen and that she was coming to check on this patient, having heard that he had some connection with her husband.

"And this is Janie Crabtree, the mother of…"

"…Josh! Oh, Mrs. Crabtree, I'm so sorry about Josh. He was such a fighter. I just don't know what to say. And Josh was such a special patient, of such an incredible doctor…"

There were tears in Carol's eyes. This was really the first time that she had put it all together, and here were women who mattered, coming to see her patient.

"Pardon me, I'm just taken aback is all. It's not your everyday patient, I know, and you're not just ordinary visitors, either."

"We're not?" Marilyn seemed genuinely surprised.

"Hardly. You two are like messengers from heaven."

Janie and Marilyn looked at each other and then at Carol to see if she was kidding. It was obvious that she was not.

"Listen, I know who he is," said Marilyn quietly. "I know it sounds so strange, but here is the earl of Shepperton, who comes here from some age in the past, and a whole ocean away."

Then she took out of her purse a folded, cream-colored paper, and showed it to Janie and to Carol. They were both awed by its presence and by what was written upon it. Then Carol looked at it again, shook her head, and for a moment was silent. After absorbing its meaning, she turned to Marilyn and said in a most quiet and humble way, "Now, don't you ever lose this piece of paper, for it is something that appears to be a gift from history itself. I do not know the circumstances, but I know truth when I

see it. And this speaks of truth, so much more than anything that I have ever seen."

"Well, I have no intention of ever losing this paper, for it may be the last thing that I ever get from Bob. And that really hurts. It hurts too deeply to talk about."

Carol gave her a moment to compose herself and asked, "I suppose you'd like to visit with your man of mystery, wouldn't you?"

"Yeah, if we could just see your patient, we'd be eternally grateful," Janie answered for them both, as Marilyn was still composing herself.

So Carol led them into the cubicle of Bed 5, with its own beepings and whooshes, indicating that the ventilator was working, breathing for the earl, and there was the usual tangle of plastic tubes, going both in and out of the Earl. And here, in the midst of all the trappings of modern medicine, lay a man of indeterminate age. He had longish hair, which was graying about the temples, and a full beard of black hair. And there was the endotracheal tube projecting from his mouth and taped in place to one side. He was gurgling, and there was foamy spittle coming out of his mouth.

But he was definitely alive. Janie could feel it, and she told Marilyn. But Marilyn was too absorbed in his aura to notice, as if he were royalty and not allowed to die. *Not here, not now.* She reached for his hand and found his skin to be cool, but dry. She just held his hand gently, as she watched his mechanical breathing, and listened to the *beep-beep-beep* of his heart.

"Master Earl," said Marilyn, "I am Robert Gilsen's wife, and I have come to tell you that we know of your coming here. I do not know how or why you are here, but believe me, you are cared for. I have at my side Janie Crabtree, a very good friend of mine, and who is also a friend of both my husband and of Judy Morrison. Now I do not know if you have any reason to believe us, or whether the names mean anything to you, but I wanted to tell you this. And if it is all right, I will return as you get better,

and I will be here for you, that is my promise, as it is also my promise to my husband."

As she said this, she could feel his hand grasping hers and noticed his heart rate pick up. With her other hand, she reached up to his face and gently stroked his beard. His breathing continued mechanically as the oxygen flowed in and out.

She heard the sound of an electrical motor coming closer and turned to notice that there were two persons in scrubs pushing a portable x-ray machine, and were headed toward her. She gripped his hand a bit more tightly.

"Listen, I've got to go now, but I will be back. That is my promise. Remember."

In answer, he squeezed her hand still more firmly.

As the two women left the hospital, neither one spoke. The experience had been just a bit more difficult than either of them wanted to admit. And each was wrapped up in her own thoughts. When they arrived at Marilyn's car and got in, Janie finally spoke, but it was as if she had just been through another replay of Josh's recent death.

"Oh, Marilyn, that was more of an experience than I was really ready for. And how you kept your composure and said those things to the Earl was beyond anything that I could have done."

At that, Marilyn began weeping, and for several minutes she just shook with grief. It had all been too soon, too much, and too unbelievable. Eventually, she was able to regain some sense of herself and found some of the strength that she had displayed in the ICU. Janie had relegated herself to handing her friend some tissues as needed. Then, Marilyn spoke again, finding, after all, that she had some reserve left.

"You know, Janie, I had all kinds of things that I planned to do and to say, but when I saw him there, taped down within our

modern medical entrapments, with his dignity all but taken from him, I just forgot what I was going to do or to say, and what I did say came from some place inside me that I didn't know was even there. Now I hate to ask you, but could you help me?"

"Help you, of course. What is it you need help with?"

"Well, I've got to have lunch with Charlie Stephens, you remember him? Anyway, I agreed to help him with his story, our story. I just thought that…"

"Of course, I'll help you. Just tell me what you want me to do."

"Could you have lunch with us? And then to go see Detective Bryant after lunch? It's these two whom we've got to convince of our story. Charlie Stephens thinks that it's the story of his lifetime in the making. And Detective Bryant is quite confused. It seems that the facts don't add up in his mind."

"Nor mine. But, of course, I'll have lunch with the two of you, and then we'll see about convincing Mr. Bryant as well. Sister, it's a deal."

"Well, let's get going then."

The place that Charlie Stephens had picked to have lunch was actually a diner off 42nd Street, and it was not what Marilyn would have picked. It was a throwback to some earlier age, but without charm or anything to recommend it, as if it were something stale, out of date, but refusing to die. Perhaps that was why he chose the place, for it certainly looked the part of run-down and anonymous.

Janie and Marilyn arrived at the front door and had to step up to the main floor. They looked around and spotted a booth in the back with Charlie sitting down, reading a paper. When they came back to him, he looked up and beamed that slightly smarmy smile that his viewers had come to know well, and which caused heartburn in so many.

"Well, Marilyn, I see you've brought some reinforcements with you. It's Janie Crabtree, right?"

"Why, yes it is, I'm surprised that you remembered."

"With something this big, I rarely forget anything, especially a voice and name. Now, please excuse the décor, but this is a place I've found where we can have a real conversation, without having to think about the food or the wine list."

"You've got a point, there."

So the two women sat down across from Charlie and the conversation started up in neutral. A middle-aged waitress with a shapeless, formerly pink dress, and a voice coarsened by too many cigarettes, appeared at their table and asked if they wanted coffee or just water. Then she handed the two women menus. "So, Charlie, what do you recommend?" asked Marilyn.

"In this high class establishment, I just stick with the usual—burger and fries. You notice that Bev didn't even hand me a menu?"

"Uh-huh. So you come here a lot?"

"This is where I get most of my background information. It's a place that serves a definite purpose."

"I see. Well, I'll have the burger and fries, too. How about you, Janie?"

"Oh, I'm not really too hungry; maybe just some toast," Janie replied.

"Okay, Charlie, you've picked the place and you've got the floor. So tell us, what do you want from us?"

"Well, all right then, why don't we start at the beginning. And that, I assume, is where you come in. Isn't that right, Mrs. Crabtree?"

"I guess so. And, please, call me Janie."

So Janie reiterated her tale of Josh and his woes, and she told of how Dr. Gilsen had wandered into their lives and had been a pillar of strength and reliability. And she told of Josh's last illness, and how Judy Morrison had befriended her, and was there until the end. Next she told of all the weird stuff, with the drachma, the

notes, and the dreams. And then she began telling Charlie how, after Josh's funeral, a letter appeared with the mail, addressed to her husband, but with a message for the Lady Healer.

"Now, wait just a minute, you said that you got this letter in the mail, with no actual mailing address, and yet you tell me that it was addressed to your husband. What exactly do you mean?"

"Well, Mr. Stephens, I'm so glad that you were paying close attention. Now I have the envelope that the note came in here in my purse. And don't ask me why I brought it with me, because I don't know. But I think that the envelope might just be able to shed some light on this whole thing. I don't have the note that was in the envelope, we sent that with Judy."

She pulled out of her purse a small, plastic sandwich bag, and within that was a cream-colored envelope. She handed it to Charlie who looked with some awe upon the envelope.

"You may open the bag, Mr. Stephens. I just have it in there, so as not to smudge it."

Charlie opened the bag, somewhat ceremoniously, and placed the envelope on the table. They all looked at it, noticing the unusual feel of the paper, the big, red seal with what looked like a wolf on it, and then the writing upon the front of the envelope with the words: Master Earl, esq.

Marilyn pulled out of her purse her own letter, written on the same very unusual cream-colored paper with the etching of the man, and the two different samples of handwriting. Now Charlie, who had, until this time, been rather skeptical, just sat and stared at the two pieces of paper. He compared the two; he looked at the seal and looked at the paper with the engraving, then back to the envelope. It was as if he had just figured out that what they were telling him might just be the truth, and the truth was something that he rarely dealt with in his profession.

The waitress in pink arrived with their drinks. She left a decanter with more coffee in it.

"So, let me get this straight," said Charlie, "your son, Josh—a longtime patient of Dr. Gilsen—gets admitted to the hospital for the last time. And Dr. Gilsen comes out to the hospital in one of our horrible snowstorms. He takes care of Josh, but you say he doesn't look too good. Dr Gilsen, though, sees him through surgery. But before Josh dies, Dr. Gilsen is gone. Just gone, with no trace of him to be found. Have I got this right so far?"

Janie nodded.

"And in the meantime, this nurse, Judy Morrison, appears in your life. She is some kind of a Florence Nightingale, who helps you through all this. At this same time there is this old coin, apparently a drachma, which makes the rounds of all involved and ends up where? With you, am I right?"

Marilyn nodded.

"And next, this same Judy Morrison appears at Josh's funeral, goes home with you, and you get this most peculiar letter from someone named Drachma. Then she goes and disappears herself, with no trace, no evidence of any foul play. Have I got it right so far?"

"Yes, you have the facts right, Mr. Stephens, but, when you say it, it sounds like something from some National Enquirer story. The facts may be right, but the feeling is wrong."

Charlie Stephens's eyebrows arched, as if in question.

"What I'm trying to tell you is that, despite the facts being right, you have not gotten to the truth of the matter."

"And that would be…"

"Let me put it this way, Charlie," said Marilyn, "if I may use a musical analogy. It is as if you have described a symphony of Beethoven accurately, with all the notes right, and the dynamics, and the pace of the symphony; but without hearing it, you miss the truth of it. For with music, as with life, the truth is not found in the describing, but in the actual participating."

They were all silent for a moment.

"Touché, madame," was all Charlie could say to that.

Charlie Stephens drank his coffee, while thinking about his next line of questioning.

"Let me make this a little easier for you, Charlie," Marilyn said, a note of real empathy in her voice. "As I tell you of my involvement in this tale, let's just suspend all our preconceived notions of reality and just concentrate on the story. Just forget for a moment that you have a boss and that I have a police inspector waiting in the wings, both of whom are expecting a cut and dried tale to wrap up. Okay?"

"Very well, my lady, it shall be as you wish."

It was as if it weren't Charlie speaking at all, as though someone else's thoughts were being expressed. Marilyn just smiled, for she knew whence came that voice.

So, Marilyn began her tale again, starting with that fateful night, seemingly ages ago, in which Bob came home late, and for the very last time.

Marilyn went on to talk about the next few tension-filled days—of the phone calls and the visit from the police, of Edgar Bryant and his note-taking assistant, and the phone call from Carlo Vincente. This really grabbed Charlie's attention.

"Could you tell me more about this phone call?"

"Well, as I'm sure that you are now aware, this man, Carlo Vincente, whom you have now had the occasion to meet as well, is someone so extraordinary, so different, that I don't really have words to describe him."

"Yes, I know what you mean."

"Now, this fellow, Carlo Vincente," Janie interrupted, "is this the same fellow that you were telling Earl and me about, the other day?"

"Oh, yes, the same one. And let me tell you, he has been quite an amazement, and quite a source of information to me."

"And me." Charlie, then, rather unexpectedly, started telling of his own encounters with this man, which was something of a revelation to Marilyn. "Now, mind you, I'm a pragmatic man

and not given to talking about my own experiences, so what I am about to tell you is from the heart, and know that whatever I do or say on TV has nothing to do with my own sense of what has happened here."

Marilyn and Janie both stared wide-eyed at this reporter who was spilling his guts to them.

Charlie began telling them of how he first encountered Carlo Vincente as the uninvited passenger in his car and how this strange old man then told him about Master Robert and Lady Judy. How the old guy then disappeared and then reappeared in his kitchen in the middle of the night. And Carlo spoke of how he had just been to see Marilyn. Next, he was prepared to accompany Charlie to visit the earl of Shepperton, his liege lord, a fifteenth century nobleman, now a patient in our modern day ICU on the respirator, with IVs, tubes, and wires coming out of him.

"Now, what am I supposed to make of all this? Marilyn, you speak of this being the story of my lifetime, and even though I do believe you, I find it hard to put into words that make any sense to anyone who has not experienced any of this weird stuff."

"Do you see what I mean by the truth? The truth cannot really be told to those not ready to listen, but, rather, it is there for those willing to experience life in all its quirky, strange, and mysterious ways. There is no way that I can tell you how to do your job, but what I can do is to tell you that whatever tactics you use to tell your story, you'll do so having seen and felt the truth of this most amazing tale."

The waitress returned, this time with two orders of burger and fries and with one order of toast, buttered. She put down their orders and noticed the thoughtful expressions on their faces.

"My goodness, Charlie, I've never seen you produce such serious expressions on any women before. You know, usually by now your people are ready to strangle you. Isn't that why you like this spot, because there are so few witnesses?"

"Hush, you'll give away all my secrets, Bev. These ladies were under the misguided notion that I'm some kind of human being, while all the world knows otherwise."

"Y'all heard that from him, not me. Remember that."

"All right, Bev…"

"Now, don't say I didn't warn you."

As she left, Marilyn reached over and touched Charlie's hand. She said, "Now, Charlie, you've been recently initiated into the world of human beings, and I suspect that you might be surprised by the people in this world. While you're eating, is there anything that you would like to know, that you haven't already been told about?"

"Actually, I was invited some years ago to join the human race when I did a series of pieces about child molesters, and, for a while…"

"Was that you, Charlie? I remember that as being a particularly effective, lucid, and touching series."

"Yeah, that was me. And afterward, the governor even gave me a plaque and a handshake and said that it was the best local thing that he'd seen on TV in some time. But then, later, that scumbag got himself in trouble—you know that business of paying his wife under the table and all. Anyway, it was then that I'd decided to take a step outside the human race and just do the reporting from my safe vantage place. But that was before Carlo Vincente came into my car, my house, and my life, and, while looking at that framed picture of the governor shaking my hand, he turned to me and said that it was good to know that my heart beats for the small people of the world."

"Well, I'd like to offer you this opportunity to rejoin, if you'd like."

Charlie looked down at his hamburger and fries and realized that he wasn't hungry. He sipped some more of his coffee and then refilled his and Marilyn's cups. He picked up a French fry,

and, while munching it, said, "How can I turn down such an invitation from you, m'lady?"

"Now that sounds," said Janie, "like something from this other world. The one with Dr. Bob and Judy Morrison in it."

"And that brings me around to my next question. What do you think really happened to those two?"

"You want my real, honest opinion? Or do you want what I'd tell Edgar Bryant?"

"If I'm going to rejoin the human race, then I want your honest opinion. But I would be curious to know what you'll tell Mr. Bryant."

Marilyn sipped her coffee and then put it down. She looked right at Charlie and said, "Okay, here is what I intend to tell Edgar Bryant. I'll tell him that, considering all the fuzzy facts of the case, I have no idea what happened to Bob or to Judy Morrison. And further, I'll tell him that it seems to me that it is his job to come up with the right conclusions."

"And don't you suppose that he'll push you for more than that?"

"Of course, if he's any sort of a detective, he'll try to back me into a corner, to make me commit to some sort of statement that he could use against me, if needed. And that is precisely why I'm bringing Janie with me, who, as you know, was just about the last person to have seen either of them here."

"Do you think Mr. Bryant knows that?"

"No, I don't think he does."

"Well, then, that brings us around to the real question. What do you honestly, without any pretense or any cover, think happened to your husband, and to Judy?"

"Until today, my opinion would have been the same, that I honestly did not know. But today we have met the earl of Shepperton, who is a real person, and a really sick patient in the intensive care unit of Memorial Hospital, and I know that he has seen my husband, who sent this note with him, and to whom I have promised to care for when he gets out. How can

even you, Charlie Stephens, ace reporter, who has also met this earl and seen the note sent with him…how can you even doubt what Carlo Vincente told us—that he is now in Shepperton, in another time and place? That is what I do believe, for it is the only thing that makes sense to me right now."

"I must say, that is the best, most succinct statement of the improbable, made possible, my lady. And you should know that I, in my ever-improbable way, have found myself believing the same, despite years of being a professional skeptic. Mind you, though, that this is just between us here at this table. For you'll have to watch my segment on Channel 5 and tell me what you think of it."

"Okay, Charlie, even though I rarely watch TV, I'll look for your segment. When will it be on the news?"

"The news? No, my friend, it's going to be a whole hour segment, next Monday."

"Does this mean that you're going to make TV stars of us all?"

"Yep, you got that right. Both you and Janie are going to be stars, just you wait."

"Well, I don't know about you, but that's not anything I want to be," said Janie. "I would just like some peace, you know, just to fade away, back into my own family, just my own Earl and me."

When they got to the police station, Janie and Marilyn sensed something was not quite right. There was an odd feel to the place, more than just because it was a police station. They went up to the main desk and told them that they had an appointment with Edgar Bryant. The man behind the desk suddenly got pale and excused himself. After a minute or so, Detective Lewinsky came down the hallway and asked them to follow her. Marilyn looked at Judy with a most questioning expression.

When they came down the hallway, they turned to the left, where Detective Lewinsky had them sit down across the desk from herself.

Then Chris spoke, saying, "I don't really know how to tell you this, but Edgar Bryant was taken to the hospital this morning."

Marilyn's hand went to her mouth. "Oh my. What happened?"

"Well, from what I could get out of the hospital people, he's in Memorial Hospital, in the Intensive Care Unit. Something about an aneurysm, and they rushed him to surgery."

"Do they know whether he is going to make it?"

"That I don't know, but what I do know is that his words to me, as he was being wheeled out of here, were to tell you, Mrs. Gilsen, not to worry about him. To tell you that we have your whole conversation with Mr. Vincente on tape and that everything will be all right."

"My conversation? You were recording that?"

"Oh, yes, with that little lapel pin."

"My, oh my. And can you tell me what this all means? What more do you need from me?"

"Not a thing, Mrs. Gilsen. For we know, off the record, of course, that your husband is not here, nor is he anywhere to be found. And what Edgar was going to tell you…"

Here she paused, took out a tissue, and blew her nose on it. Then, regaining her composure, she said, "He was going to tell you that we are closing up your case. That unless something new turns up, you are most free to go about your business."

"Well, thank him for me, and I'm so sorry to hear about his taking ill. If you see him, send him my prayers and best thoughts."

"Oh, I'll do that."

By the time Marilyn made it back to her house, she was exhausted. She parked the car in the garage, got out, and went

into her cluttered kitchen. She just sat down at the kitchen table and cried solidly for a half hour. She then managed to get back up and make herself some tea. Taking her tea with her, she went upstairs to the bedroom. She looked and saw that the box was still there on her dresser. She opened it and saw that the coin was still there. She kissed the coin before closing the lid. She very reverently placed it back on the dresser.

"Oh, Bob, I hope that you're happy and that your new life is fulfilling in ways that it never was before. Take care, and know that I'll always love you."

Chapter Eighteen

The wind had been but a mild breeze until they started out in the evening. Now it was picking up in a big way, blowing the light snow sideways. Kerlin had amassed his army in little over two hours from the time he got the news. He quickly conferred with Craycroft and Drachma, and then he set upon getting his troops of guardsmen ready for the hard ride down the road to Champour. He assigned roles, both in and out of the castle.

He put Proust in charge of seeing to it that the castle remained well fortified, with sentries alerted and placed strategically about the wings of the castle. He put Cayman in charge of communication and asked him to be certain that the pigeons were ready and that messages were sent to the sentries on the outside. And he made sure that Eustace was looked after by Cayman—something that Eustace himself saw as yet another adventure in the making. He had Martin and Stoneheft ride to the fore, one on each flank, while he himself rode with the main force down the middle. He did all this with as little noise and fanfare as possible, so that the spies of Reordan were not alerted to anything more than the forces leaving the castle, in three large groups of riders of fifty-to-sixty heavily armed men.

As they pulled out of the castle gates, he had the castle guards pull up the drawbridge, something that had not been done in years, with the instructions not to open the gates without the password.

As he rode out, he thought about what had changed, who had changed, and what all this meant. His own role had certainly been altered by recent trials and events and had made him more perceptive and also a true leader. And, he wondered too, how had all the recent events affected the others? Craycroft was now, in the minds of all his own men, their new liege lord, and it was really remarkable how Craycroft himself had been changed. Cayman had seemed to come out of the blue and had become a most trusted colleague in a very valuable position. And Tom—he had probably been the most affected by everything that he had seen, done, and been part of—how he had grown. He wondered if Drachma had seen the need for all this.

"Sire, if I may ask?" It was Blackfist, one of Drachma's own men. "What do ye know of this party trying to land? Be they mercenaries or are they fighting men of one o' the lords?"

"I know not, but I do know why you're asking. For if they be mercenaries, then they have little to lose if our plan should succeed, but if they are trusted fighters and guardsmen of a lord, they shall likely be stubborn and zealous fighters to a man. Let me tell you, though I do not know this with certainty, but it would seem most foolish to be sending a party to another island if they were anything but loyal men-at-arms. So, what I'm saying is, be prepared for a real skirmish."

"Aye, m'lord. Me men and I shall be most ready."

"That is good."

They thundered through the hamlets, an armed and dangerous lot, with the people of the villages looking out with awe at the force headed toward the coastline.

As the troops headed ever closer to their appointed destination, Kerlin had them separated again—one directly down the road and the other two toward each flank—and each captain knew what was expected of him and his men.

"Now," said Antoine LeGace, "I would rather like it now."

"I shall see what I can do."

The blacksmith took his work to the back of the shop where he started working on his project for the strange man in the front of the shop. He had paid well enough for what? A new blade. But he had wanted it tempered just so, and sharpened just so, and to be the length of his outstretched hand, and thin, like a fisherman's knife. And he had asked for it to be made in a hurry. But with what the stranger was paying, how could he refuse?

So, he fired up the furnace some more, and then he began the tedious process of repetitive hammering, cooling, and hammering again. After a period of a couple of hours, he had his raw material, which he then worked over on another anvil. When he had shaped it carefully, he took it over to the grinder, where he worked it to a fine, sharp-edged blade, in the precise dimensions that his customer had given him.

When he walked back out to the front room, LeGace was there, waiting impatiently. The blacksmith handed him the blade and said, "Now ye're free to inspect it and let me know if ye're satisfied."

LeGace looked it over with a well-trained eye. He tested the blade's tone by rapping it on the edge of the doorframe. He felt the weight and balance of it, and then he tested its edge with a couple of strands of his own hair. He was quite impressed, but stated only that, "This will do," and then he walked out of the shop and back to the room where he was now staying in the village just to the east of his former habitation.

While in the room, he took his new walking stick with the hollowed out end, and his newly forged blade, which he fitted into the end of the stick. He worked for the next hour, perfecting the triggering mechanism. He tried it out over and over again, readjusting the mechanism, and when he was satisfied that everything was working just right, he checked his traveling sack and made certain that everything was in place.

Next, before he left the premises, he took the lamp with its oil, tipped it over on its side, and watched as the cloth and straw caught fire. Then he walked out of the room, closing the door behind him. He left the village, walking along the road toward Champour. He walked along at an unhurried pace, and as he heard the sound of numerous horses' hooves behind him, he looked quickly for some place to hide. There was a sheltering copse of trees just ahead. He quickly went up to the trees and hid within them as the troop of horses and armed men thundered down the road. He waited, noticed a second and yet a third group of armed men of around fifty in each group go by, down the road toward the village, and down toward the new docks built by Reordan.

He wondered for a moment. He listened and then headed back toward the castle, the way he had come. The wind blew, and it was cold, but his way was now clear. He smiled to himself as he passed by the house with the flames now just reaching the roofline.

Well, he thought to himself, *it would appear that you have played your hand, and this might just be easy pickings after all.*

"Now, what do you think?" asked Bob, as he cautiously examined the guardsman who had been injured in the belly by the blade of LeGace. "Do you think he'll make it? I sure wish we really had something to offer him, more than just our concern and diagnostic acumen."

"Bob, I don't know. He's got a fever, and he's tachycardic…"

"And his belly's hard as a board. I just wish I had some more surgical training, as it seems that it's really surgical skills that are needed. My training and experience in cardiology seem to be wasted here. At least if I were a trained surgeon, I might stand a chance with these cases."

"I don't believe that your training is wasted, in any way. While it is true that I also miss having a surgeon handy, your own expertise and your special way with difficult patients and difficult circumstances, I think more than makes up for any lack of surgical skills. And besides that, your surgical skills are better than anything they've seen around these parts."

"Oh, aye, Master Robert," added Cairn from the corner. "I would agree with the lady, and I do think that I have some experience in that regard."

"Well, my thanks to you, Mr. Cairn. It's just that our friend here has had a penetrating injury to his belly, and it would appear that, unlike your situation, peritonitis is setting in, which is a circumstance in which the bowel was certainly penetrated by his assailant's knife, and the usual treatment of that would be immediate surgery, along with antibiotics. And, unfortunately, I'm not adequately trained to do this kind of surgery, nor do we have adequate anesthesia, not even IV fluids, let alone antibiotics. I'm afraid that immediate surgical intervention would be out of the question. I'm really afraid that today, at least, I seem to be out of miracles."

"Master Robert"—it was Melchior—"what is this ivy that you refer to? For I do know of the various ivies that grow around here, and obtaining their fluids should not be too difficult."

Bob thought for a moment and realized that what he said was heard as "ivy fluids" by Melchior, so he just chuckled at that.

"My good man, when we're done here, it looks like I'm going to have to give you yet another lecture on modern medicine. You, Craycroft, and Tom.

"And now, let's check on you, Mr. Cairn. I must say that you are looking much better today."

He walked over to where Cairn was sitting, and he had Judy carefully expose his flank where the incision was. He then pulled out the packing. Bob examined the area and found, to his satisfaction, that the wound was looking as good as could

be expected. There was little tenderness left in the area and the redness was receding.

"Very good, very, very good. You seem to be healing remarkably well, my friend. You haven't developed any new problems, such as with your bowels, or any change in the appearance of or difficulty passing urine?"

"Nay, m'lord, I have no problem with either. And may I ask, if it would be permitted for me to resume my duties, as guardian to m'lady?"

"Permitted? Well I can only answer as your physician. From my own perspective, I would say that, as long as you get your dressing changed daily and that you remain free of any new worrisome symptoms and you understand the risks, I see no reason that you may not resume your duties. But I am not really in charge, am I? I would suggest that you speak with Kerlin or one of his designees to be sure."

"Let me say," said Judy, "that I'd be happy to act in my practiced capacity of nurse. I do feel that Cairn is tired of just doing nothing but recovering. And I know that he'll be happier if he feels that he's doing something productive. Isn't that right, Cairn?"

"Oh, aye, m'lady."

Bob just smiled and shook his head. "You know, Judy, I still can't argue with you. I've never been able to argue with you."

"Yeah, I know that, Bob." She laughed.

"Well, Judy, it looks like you've got yourself a bodyguard. You want to take care of his dressing change?"

"You got it, Dr. Bob." She couldn't quite wipe the smirk off her face. "You know, you're even starting to sound like a surgeon."

Bob thought back to his own experience with Dr. Greshin, then said, rather sheepishly, "Well, if that's all it takes…"

"Oh, Bob, you know I'm kidding. You could never be one of them—you've got too much humility. And yes, of course, I'll see to getting this dressing changed. And then, I think I'll go see

Jeanne—you know, I've got to get ready for dinner this evening, as any lady of stature in this realm can tell you."

She winked at Bob, who caught the drift, and he suddenly became acutely embarrassed. He remembered her entrance at dinner the other evening and the effect that had on him.

"Well, then, it sounds like something of a date. And be sure to keep your bodyguard with you. I am quite certain that Craycroft would like to see how our Master Cairn is doing. And, in the meantime, I'll try to get together with Craycroft, Tom, and Melchior, as it seems that they are in need of some twentieth century training."

"Yeah, I'll know where to find you. You go on and get 'em educated."

Bob and Melchior found Craycroft and Tom deep in conversation. Drachma had gone out to check on Kerlin's doings and to check any messages that might be coming back from out in the realm. They were announced by the page and let inside.

"Well, my good Master Robert, and Melchior as well," Craycroft said.

"I hope that we're not interrupting anything too important. I'm glad that Tom is here with you."

"Nay, my good man, nothing but a bit of family business, eh, Tom? But do come in and sit down. Here, let us send for some liquid refreshment." He turned to his page and asked that he bring around some brandy. "Now tell us, what is it that brings you to our house this afternoon?"

"Education," answered Bob.

"Ah, education is it? Splendid! Tell me, Master Robert, what led to your determining that we needed education? Not that we do not, but there must have been something that set you upon this path."

"Very perceptive, as usual, Master Craycroft. Well, there was something. I was examining the unfortunate guard who got a penetrating injury to his abdomen from some sort of a knife. Now, his situation is very desperate and I am ill equipped to deal with it, I'm afraid. Besides the fact that I am not surgically trained, even if I were the best surgeon in the world…"

"But are you not, at this point in time?"

"Hmm, I guess you've got a point there." This was one aspect of his new reality that Bob had not considered. There was, in fact, probably no one better trained as physician and surgeon anywhere in the world as they knew it.

"No, Master Robert," Craycroft continued, "I would venture to state that there is none more highly educated, nor anyone more experienced than you, anywhere in this whole world."

The effect of that dawning realization was enough to make Bob sit back and think about what he was doing.

"All right. Point made and accepted."

And so they sat, in a small semicircle, eagerness on their faces. This was obviously going to be an experience for all. Bob began by explaining how he had come to his conclusion after Melchior had misheard what Bob was trying to tell him.

His lesson began with simple anatomy. He used Tom as an example, demonstrating his venous anatomy and then tying it in with arterial anatomy. He explained how the heart did pump the blood throughout the body, and you could feel the pulsating rhythm of the heart, again demonstrating on Tom where his pulses were. He next took his stethoscope from his satchel and had them listen to Tom's heart beating, and how the *lub-dub, lub-dub* represented the valves opening and closing. He then explained to his rapt audience how the heart had four chambers and four valves and the function of each.

"Now," he said, "this is in the normal state of the body. In the body with disease or injury, there can be effects on this system of circulation that may be sensed by others. For example, in the

injured person who has lost much blood, the pulse may become weak, and the rate of beating of the heart becomes more rapid, as the heart senses that there is loss of blood volume and tries to compensate; first, by beating faster and harder, then also by clamping down some of the arteries so that this blood circulation is maintained to the vital organs, such as the brain, the kidneys, and the lungs. This is what happened to poor old Leroy, who died because of loss of blood into the abdomen.

"Now, there is a separate thing happening in our injured guard. His body is now trying to fight off an infection, caused by perforation of his bowel. Some of the same signs are there, namely the rise in heart rate, and the fall in blood pressure, but from a different cause. In any event, what we really need, especially in the absence of any antibiotics, is some means of getting more volume of blood, or at the very least, fluid, into the circulation. So, I would propose that we should begin working on this. What it will entail will be that we are going to need to develop a way to produce fluid that can be safely given into the veins of persons for whom these conditions develop.

"And besides that, we are going to need to develop a means of getting this same fluid from the container into the veins. This will require development of thin, flexible tubes and hollow needles."

"Well, Master Melchior," said Craycroft, "it would appear to be your task, then, to develop, with the guidance of Master Robert, such a system of fluids, tubes, and needles. This, along with your own pursuit of antibiotics, shall be your task. Let me assure you, gentlemen, that your searches will mean not wealth, but renown, in that Shepperton shall be remembered down the ages."

Melchior was silent for a time, but then spoke, and what he said seemed to resonate with truth.

"M'lord, it is with some humility that I accept this challenge, and it shall be as you say, for out of this humble island there shall come a center of learning, and we shall surely be remembered. For to us there is now given this one time opportunity. Nowhere

has there been anything akin to this, and there probably never shall be again."

"Indeed, Master Melchior," Craycroft added, "and it would seem fortuitous that you were brought to this island by Drachma himself and put in a position this momentous. We shall have to speak to him, this man of shadows. I would dearly love to learn what he himself knew of all this. It could be a most interesting dinner tonight."

"Master Melchior, if I may be so bold"—Tom spoke for the first time—"it would seem that you have the makings of greatness in this. But I would be wondering if you might need some assistance? And I myself would like to offer my services, and would like to suggest that Eustace, Hermes, and Aaron might offer theirs as well. We would be ever loyal and true, and we would be at your disposal."

"But, of course, Tom. And I do think that your choices would be most excellent."

Bob thought about the implications of all this, and as he thought, he began to realize that it was this that had been tugging at his consciousness. He could feel the path open up before him; he could feel the warmth of the earth and the smell of the springtime breezes.

A servant then brought them brandy, and those in the room each took a small amount in his snifter. Craycroft rose up and offered a toast to them all.

"Now, here, here. This is to the future of the island, to the founding of its center of teaching, to its founders and benefactors. May you be forever blessed among men, and may your future shine with the light of the Almighty, to whom we are truly indebted."

The clink of glasses seemed to resonate throughout the castle that afternoon.

The ship pulled alongside and set anchor. The boats then set out to bring the men onto the pier. Meanwhile, onboard the ship, the earl of Derrymoor and his men looked out with the evening light fading rapidly.

"This looks like the right place, and there would be the boats coming for us anon. Now, me lads, you know what to do and where to be. I shall go aboard the last boat, and we'll meet upon the dock."

The unloading of the men went smoothly. What they did not notice was that the boatmen signaled to the men up higher on land and rowed away. It was now nightfall and the visibility was very poor, so the earl lit his own torch from the one handed him by the boatmen. He held it aloft and he addressed his men.

"Me lads, it would appear that we were expected, and I was told that there would be horses for us all to ride and someone to show us the way to the castle. I shall go up to the buildings here with a few of me men, and I'll be back with news."

There was a restless stirring among the men. It was Bedford who spoke.

"M'lord, I feel that it would be better if thou were to send a small search party, rather than go yerself. I know that I'd feel safer with ye here upon the dock, among yer men."

Derrymoor thought about it for a moment and answered, "If ye'd feel better, then, I shall stay here and send but a few of ye up yonder. Ye know the signal, if there be any trouble at all."

"Oh, aye, m'lord."

So Bedford and three others went on ahead, while the others stayed behind. They lit the rest of the torches from the earl's. The men on the dock looked on, as their fellows went up the hill toward the buildings. They watched the torch as it ascended, then disappeared around the building. They were gone for perhaps a quarter hour, and then the silence was broken by the sound of horses.

"Ah, good, here be our mounts, now," said the earl. He could just make out the form of many horses and riders.

"Derrymoor!" came the voice from the pack of horses. "Will ye not step forth? We have yer horses here."

That voice! It was familiar, but he couldn't place it.

"Aye! That be me. Now are ye the party to show us the way to the castle?"

"The castle, aye."

The earl of Derrymoor walked up the path toward the horses. He walked right into the trap being sprung by Kerlin and his men. When he realized what was happening, it was too late, and he turned to his men and shouted, "We're trapped, m'lads! Run for your lives!"

The men on the dock looked about themselves and saw nowhere to run, and now they were being approached from both sides by the sound of many horses. They drew their swords, but the ruin was mercifully swift. The few that were able to flee the dock were not able to flee the terrible horses, nor the swords of Kerlin's men. Those left upon the dock who did not resist were quickly disarmed, then corralled to the side. Of the sixty men who came ashore that evening, there were but twenty standing. The whole rout took less than two hours, and the dock was littered with the bodies of the slain fighters. The wounded were brought to the shore, and they were placed upon horses and taken back toward the castle. The captured fighters were led away toward one of the buildings to await further instructions from Kerlin.

Meanwhile, Bedford and his men were quickly brought to join their liege lord, who stood shackled and quietly defiant beside Kerlin, who had gotten off his great horse and was looking at his captive somewhat quizzically.

"Now, my lord Derrymoor, you do realize what you have done, do you not? I would advise you that truth shall serve you best, for we have heard from the men who were supposed to provide you with horses, as well as show you the way back to the Castle

of Shepperton. And let me say that those men are being dealt a harsher punishment than your own men shall have suffered."

"Kerlin, is it not? For I do remember you from before, when I was but a youth upon this island."

There was no fear in his voice as he spoke.

"Aye, it is I, the same, yet now we meet under different circumstances."

"Aye, these circumstances are different, yet not so much to my way of thinking. The treacherous sea did once try to claim me, and now it is men."

Kerlin found himself admiring this young nobleman. Though not expecting this trap and this rout, he was still philosophical about his circumstances. He wondered what really went on in that regal head and that heart, and he wondered if he even knew of his child here on the island. Kerlin had suspected that it might just be the earl of Derrymoor that was on that ship. Finding out from his captured party that it was in fact he that landed, provided Kerlin with just the right information to spring his little trap.

Yes, the interrogation should prove most interesting. Kerlin had his men take the four of them on to the castle and have them locked in the constabulary until he himself had the chance to talk some more with the men on the morrow. He could tell that this was going to be another sleepless night.

The sun had set. It was dark and quiet in the castle. Craycroft was sitting quietly in his room, thinking back on his meeting with Bob, Melchior, and Tom. He recalled the look on their faces as they all realized what they had here on the island, and what this could mean to the island, to the realm, and to the world. How he longed to tell Falma of this, and to talk with Drachma about what he had foreseen in all of this.

And when the Lady Judy had come by with Cairn, her "bodyguard" she called him, they joined in with the others in their festivity. And to see Cairn looking so eager and appreciative warmed Craycroft to the core. *Yes, it had been a most extraordinary afternoon.*

So now, he was thoroughly enjoying the quiet time, the let down. He sank back into his chair and enjoyed some more of the brandy.

Then there came the page with news. He said that Cayman was outside and would like to speak with the lord. Craycroft was not yet used to being called that, and the title stuck in his craw.

"By all means, let him in." It would be news from outside, and he was eager to hear it.

Cayman was let in, and there was a look of both excitement and some apprehension in his eyes.

"What is the news, my good man, that has you in such a state?"

"Here it is, m'lord." *Again, that title.* "I shall let ye read it, and ye can see fer yerself."

He handed Craycroft a small, folded paper, certainly a message from the outside, delivered by the pigeons. Craycroft took the paper, read the terse message, and then he smiled, for it suddenly became clear what had gotten Cayman in such a state. The message stated:

> Mission successful. Landing party killed or captured, with prisoners on their way to castle.
>
> Earl of Derrymoor was the one.
>
> Kerlin

"Well, well, Master Cayman. This is both good news, and important news, but it does carry implications for us all, does it not? Here, sit down, have a glass of brandy, my friend. Now, would you care to tell me where things be with your Diane?"

"Ah, that's the heart of it, is it not? Now I must tell her meself of this news, and it would be for her to decide—and Eustace as well." He drank some of the brandy and felt its warming, soothing influence. "And to think that I did just see her, and, until this note, she was mine."

They both were silent, each thinking about the implications of that small note, which lay on the table at Craycroft's side.

"Well, then," began Craycroft, "let me make this whole business just a little bit easier for you, or so I would hope. Why don't you go to Barncuddy's and invite your Diane to come to our dinner tonight, which should begin within the hour here at my dining room? And take this with you and give it to Barncuddy—it should compensate him for the loss of his maid and his minstrel for the night—and tell him that Craycroft has need of his minstrel and his maid."

He handed Cayman a sack with silver coins—enough, he figured, for more than the loss of his minstrel and maid for a month.

"I shall do just that, and might I say that ye do see things that mere mortals do not, and that, I believe, is why ye be our lord."

Cayman then left with a new purpose in his stride toward the inn, having picked up Eustace at Craycroft's doorway. Craycroft just sat and mused over the implications, and he thought about the meeting of the council to be held the next day. And he thought about Reordan, what he was planning to do, and whether Reordan knew of the capture of his war party.

Chapter Nineteen

The thought of having yet another dinner party seemed strange to Bob. In his brief stay at the castle, he could not complain about the food or the drink, except for the lack of coffee. And even the hospital stuff that he lived on would seem to be the elixir of love right now.

"What is it, Master Robert? Ye have that faraway look yet again."

"Well, if you must know, Hermes, I was thinking about coffee. Now, I do know that you haven't got any here, but where I come from, coffee is often what we drink each morning, and almost as often throughout the day. It's a very special drink made from pouring very hot water over the roasted and ground up beans from the coffee plant. It's a drink that picks you up in the morning and gives you that extra little stimulus to keep going, and, let me tell you, that if I miss anything at all about my old life, it's coffee and a toothbrush that I miss the most."

"Well, master, if there is one thing that I have learned about ye, we shall have coffee upon this island ere long, eh? And toothbrush? That I canna' say, but it would seem to me to be something quite within our capabilities to produce."

"All right, Hermes, I'll give you the task of inventing the toothbrush, and we'll call it the…the… Let me think. Okay, we'll call it the Hermetic brush, in your honor."

Hermes thought that was just about the funniest thing that he had heard. And as the two of them began their task of reinventing the commonplace with pictures and diagrams, courtesy of Bob and his magical pen, they passed the time away quickly and were blissfully unaware of the intrusion by Falma and Rust into their little lair, until Falma spoke.

"Master Robert, if I may be so bold…"

"Oh, my goodness, Mr. Falma, and Mr. Rust as well. You surprised us. Come on in and have a seat."

"Thank you, but nay. It is your presence that we are seeking, but not here. We should like you to come with us to see the library of Lady Felicia Vincente. We have sent Master Melchior on ahead, and he shall meet us there."

"My, this is getting to be quite something. Now, if I recall correctly, this library has inside it a book with some sort of etching, and it also contains a tapestry depicting the same scene. And further, if I recall, this volume tells of the exploits of another person named Drachma. Have I got it right so far?"

"Aye, you do remember, and very well, I might add. And that is precisely what we have come to see you about, for it seems that you have a connection, as well, with this book."

"Oh? And how is that?"

"Well, come along with us, then, and we shall tell you of it." Rust's answer, as incomplete as it was, got Bob's attention.

"All right, then, and can Hermes come along? He's becoming quite a sidekick for me."

"Of course, Master Robert. Now, what is this term 'sidekick'?"

"Come along then, Hermes, it seems that you and I have some explaining to do, eh? And some listening, too, I'd say."

So, as the four of them headed over to Lady Felicia's house, Bob explained the notion of a sidekick, much to Hermes's amusement, and to the delight of Rust and Falma. And Bob got to hear again of that strange encounter, which he had almost forgotten, with the man on the stairway in the inn of his dream.

He listened as Rust told again of Charlie McFerris, his strange and private ways, and of his most peculiar end.

As Rust was speaking, Bob found himself back in his dream, having just been listening to the magical strains of Willie's harp, and he could see the stairway, going up into the darkness, and there he was, a man of middle age on the stairway, holding an instrument that looked like a violin, and suddenly he remembered his words.

Now, Master Robert, you shall come back to this place and to these people. You shall tell them of the waters, and by this you shall earn your own place in history. And there is also a book, one of power and of purpose. It shall be for the later ages, but not for thee.

"How odd," thought Bob aloud.

"What, Master Robert? For I saw that faraway look in your visage yet again, just now," Hermes said, bringing Bob back to reality.

So Bob told them and quoted, word-for-word, what the man on the stairway had said. The astonishment was evident on the faces of Rust and Hermes, but not Falma, who nodded, and then said, "Now, I believe that we are upon the cusp of history. And you, Master Robert, whether you are ready or not for this, are going to play a role bigger than you ever dreamed."

They had arrived at Lady Felicia's and were quickly shown into the library. All the time, Bob was pondering what Falma had just said. In the library sat Melchior, who was poring over some great tome. He looked up and smiled.

"Ah, Master Robert, I am glad to see you again. And you, as well, Hermes."

But Bob's attention was taken by the tapestry on the wall. He looked at the magnificent piece hanging near the fireplace, with its beauty accentuated by the light of multiple torches. The cloth was of rough linen, but the embroidery was done with brilliant silk. He looked at it closely and saw the image of a knight, traveling on the back of a great, gray horse down a mountain

road with a huge, flaming tree shading his path. Behind the rider was a majestic range of mountains, and in the sky, there was a huge, golden sun. And, just as Drachma had said, within that sun there were markings, which Bob now recognized to be those on the silver coin that had passed through his fingers seemingly ages ago.

"You do recognize the markings, do you not, Master Robert?"

Even in the confines of the library, it was not possible to contain the voice of the ancient forest.

"Ah, Drachma," Bob said, not turning around, but studying the magical stitchery, "if I had known what I know now, I'm not at all certain that I would have chosen to come. Though I am not really certain that I did choose."

He did turn around, then, and acknowledged Drachma's presence.

"You see, I'm not really cut out to be a historical figure. And here I'm being told that it has become my destiny."

"Indeed, Master Robert, welcome to the makings of history."

"Well enough, Drachma," answered Bob, "and I believe that I may refer to you as my friend. Please come on in and let us all sit down. It would seem that there are forces at work in this world that would have me here and have foreseen my own arrival, at such a time that critically fits in with the knowledge that I have, and with the raw materials that you possess. And now, if you have not spoken with Craycroft, we are going to establish a center of learning on your island, which will tear apart the world of medicine and the world of science, and that will be something to behold—truly something for the ages."

"You do amaze me, my friend, and aye, I know that what you speak is the truth."

"If I might, Master Robert," said Falma, "I would like to show you this book, and I understand that Rust has found the rightful owner of this volume, right here, upon this isle…"

"You do not mean the granddaughter of Archipedes? Here, upon this island?"

"I do, indeed, Drachma," added Rust. "It is quite a tale, but one that I think we had best save for all at dinner this evening."

So Falma showed Bob the book, which Bob took with the utmost care. He immediately opened it to the page with the etching, identical to the tapestry on the wall. Below the etching were words in ancient Greek, which they had Drachma translate.

"This be the tale of a man from the South, who would ride down the pathways of the magnificent mountains upon his steed of gray; a man alone, who stood against the winds of evil. He would do battle with the great ones on the plains of Aramis and would be killed in battle. For years the tales told would lie quietly within the books of wonder. And he would rise yet again, in time still to be. But not as one who would be noticed as a warrior. Rather, he would be a scholar and a healer, a doctor of hearts, named Gilsen. He would be the one to turn the tides of ignorance and usher in the new age of learning. These, then, are the words of Drachma of the Highlands."

Bob's head was reeling at these words, at his position, in this time and place, foretold many centuries ago. He felt his own reluctance to accept, let alone embrace this incredible opportunity, begin to dissipate within the walls of this library.

"Now tell me, is there a doctor of hearts named Gilsen in here somewhere?"

"Judy! My God, just look at you." Seeing her in the light of the library torches in her gown of dark green velvet was all it took to knock the wind from his sails. "My lady," was all he could utter.

"Oh, Robert, just come here and give me a hug. Then let us all go to the dinner that our most gracious host has prepared. And let me tell you that anyone, ever, who comes between us will have me, as well as Drachma, to answer to. Isn't that right?"

Drachma smiled his assent, as Bob did get up and gave Judy the hug that both of them had been missing. It was one that seemed to come down the centuries to this moment, to this place.

What they walked into was no ordinary feast. Around the huge table, set with the seats for all the guests, there were servants holding goblets of rich, brown ale. And as the guests came in and sat down, there was bread, still warm and fragrant from the ovens, at each place. After they were all seated, Craycroft rose, took his glass of ale, raised it, and offered a toast to everyone there.

"To my friends, all of you, I wish to offer my thanks for being present this evening. Now, I know some of you are wondering just where Kerlin is tonight. Let me say that Kerlin is now occupied with the service of keeping us safe, and for that we thank him. I did receive notification that he was successful in his endeavors, and we should be hearing from him on the morrow.

"It has also come to my attention that there are books about that have only just begun to reveal their truths, and it is my hope that this forum shall be where we may hear of their all-important, and, heretofore, closely guarded, secrets.

"But my friends, that shall be after we have partaken of this wondrous meal that has been prepared with love and true affection by the servants of the earl of Shepperton, as a gift to all of you. For you have truly opened up the gates to a new and powerful future. From this day forth, I tell you, Shepperton has changed, and it has changed irrevocably, and for the better. So here is my toast, and my thanks to all of you!"

"Here, Here!"

With that, the feast began. For the first course, there was a rich and hearty soup of beans and sausage, with a seasoning of subtle herbs. Following this, there came the next course of root vegetables, simmered in a brown sauce. Next, the servants brought in roast venison, fish, and savory meat pies, along with a very special wine from the private cellar of the earl, to be served only upon high occasions. And with all this, there came more fragrant yeast rolls.

Then, as the servants were clearing away the dishes and the guests were deciding whether to have yet another piece of mince meat pie, Drachma stood up and addressed the company. His presence still carried an aura—one of ancient and honorable heritage—and it became apparent that this was to be a most auspicious and unforgettable occasion.

"My dear friends," he began, "though you have all, by now, learned the names of everyone present, let me begin by sharing with you each one's history, for there is none among you who does not have such a rich heritage, and that it should not be known among your own friends here."

The assembled looked at each other and wondered just how much this man knew, how much he would tell, and what secrets he might reveal.

"Now, let me begin with our own liege lord, Master Craycroft. He among us is truly of this island, for he did grow up in the village of Ashon, the son of a kitchen maid and a metal smith, but he did forge his own history by following within his own heart that guiding light of learning and lore. He did become one of the old earl's pages, and, as such, did meet with the powerful and the noble upon this isle. It was said that none knew more of the castle and its doings than Craycroft. And as you know, he then became a pupil of the most advanced and profound teacher of the medical arts, Master Cartho. But did you know how that came about? Now it was Felicia who saw in this gangly youth, with the deep-set eyes, his true potential and persuaded the old earl that he would be a most fitting one to apprentice with Master Cartho. Now I would wager that even you, Craycroft, never knew how that happened. Am I correct?"

"Nay, I never did know. But that, my friend, is completely plausible, as I do know how taken our old earl was with this raven-haired lass, and he would do anything that she told him."

"Indeed. But then, anyone who knows anything at all about this island in later years knows that Craycroft is a man of true

honor and learning, and he has now risen, with the assent of the people of the isle, to become its new liege lord. Now I raise my glass to you, Master Craycroft."

"To Craycroft!" came the chorus, with a clinking of glasses.

"Now, Rust, who does sit upon the ruling council of lords, is also a man whose life is worth noting. He is also of this isle. But did you know that Rust is the only one present to have studied at Cambridge University in England? Aye, that he did, and graduated with honors, too. It was only after his studies that he came back to Shepperton to begin serving in his present capacity. He is one fountain of true learning and true honor as well."

Rust actually blushed at this accolade, stammered slightly, and then said, "Might I add, my dear Master Drachma, that I really had little choice in the matter, as my father was dying and I did need to come back to manage the family business. And while it is true what you have said, it is also my love of this isle that kept me here."

"And for that we are grateful. Now, here's to you, Master Rust!"

"To Rust!" And another round of clinking and drinking.

And then Drachma told them the history of Jeanne, who came to the island from Ireland, worked as a maid, but who caught the eye, first, of the Lady Felicia, then of Craycroft, and was also a wonderful asset, but who, it turns out, was the grandchild of the famous Charlie McFerris—little known, underappreciated loner that he seemed to be, but who had fathered a child while in Ireland. A son, whose life had been a waste, but who then had a daughter—a restless young thing—who ran away at age thirteen, and ran away where? Right back to the land of her own grandfather.

"Oh, Master Drachma, it is with some shame that I admit that you have accurately told of my troubled past. I am but grateful that Master Craycroft has chosen to overlook my past, for the present is what concerns me."

"Ah, but, as you shall see, my dear woman, your past is but interlinked and interwoven with our story here tonight. And it

is with great affection and also with admiration that I raise my glass to you as well."

"To Jeanne!" The ale was flowing and the servants were keeping up with the unfilled flagons.

"And so, to you, Master Falma, I must next turn. Now, there are none here that know of your history, I would wager, but I. And to think that you, of all people, have kept it hidden, lo these many years."

"And, may I ask, dear Drachma, where have you found anything of substance in regard to my own history?"

"Well, my dear loremaster, does the name Eowen mean anything to you?"

Falma's eyes darkened at the mention of that name. "So, you have unearthed a name that I thought was buried in the past. What, then, have you been able to find, my friend?"

"What I have found, Master Falma, is that you do have a history, and it is also intimately linked with ours. It would appear that your own parents did die, and you were left to the care of one woman named…"

"…Carmella. She was my true mother, if indeed I had one. She resided in a tiny village, way back on the northwest part of the island, where she taught me the rudiments of behavior, but I was still a fairly wild, undisciplined youth. So, when I reached the age of thirteen summers, Carmella had me shipped across the sea to Ireland where I attended a boarding school, and it was at this boarding school that I learned what I could of languages, mathematics, and the physical sciences. It was obvious early on that I had an aptitude for alchemy, so that was when they had me apprenticed to a woman named Eowen. Now Eowen was a truly different kind of alchemist, for she was alchemist in name only, and, at that, she was never allowed to ply her trade openly, being a woman. So she would use her apprentices to make her alchemy work for her, but every evening she would take us back inside her shop and teach us of the things we could really do with her

knowledge—to make medicinal powders that really worked upon the ailments and the pains of the human body. And it was she who did teach me of the lore within the human heart. It was she, more than the historical teachings of alchemy, who did influence me in my pursuits upon the isle."

"And, if I may be so bold as to ask, what of Eowen's daughter? Did she not have influence upon you and your decisions in life?" Drachma asked, his eyes twinkling.

Falma's voice changed timber as he replied. "My good friend, it is apparent that you do know how it was and who it was that made me come to this isle. For it was Megan who persuaded me to come back to Shepperton, or, should I say, in fact, that it was her circumstances that made my decision. Now, I should tell the persons here that Megan, Eowen's daughter, was a most intelligent and charming young lass when I knew her, but she was betrothed at the time to eldest of the sons of the earl of Derrymoor. And though I felt at the time that she did love me, and she said as much, it became increasingly difficult for me to be within her household. I was, after all, a young man, and was afflicted with a youth's carefree love of life. So, sadly, I did leave her to go back to Shepperton to begin my employment with the earl of Shepperton, as both alchemist and loremaster. It should be noted that this earl of Derrymoor's son and my Megan did, in fact, marry, and after several daughters, did have a son, who lived, and who is now the present earl of Derrymoor. And I suspect that you shall be hearing more of this earl, yet this evening."

"Indeed, we shall. And I thank you, my good friend, for that most precious information. For it does come from the heart of one most close to us. I now raise my own glass to this most wonderful of loremasters. To Falma!"

"To Falma! Here, here!"

Then the servants began to serve some of the sweet rolls that were rightly famous throughout the island, with bits of dried apple and currants baked within a light, fluffy roll.

"Oh, my," said Judy, after tasting one. "These are really so good, and after such an incredible meal, too. Oh, Bob wait 'til you bite into one—you'll never think about dessert the same way again."

"Now, let me ask," continued Judy, "Drachma, you have managed to dig up some ancient dirt on these folks, and I'm beginning to sense a common thread in all their stories, and it's as if you yourself are telling a story through the lives of these wonderful people. Have I got that right?"

"My, how observant you are, indeed, Lady Judy. For I do have a story to tell, but these people's lives do make up the story in ways that would make it impossible to tell otherwise. And now then, Cayman, I do know something of your background as well. And could you enlighten us on just where you fit in with all this?"

"Oh, m'lord, it is with some humility that I do even come to this table, for I am but a humble guardsman of the castle."

"But was your mother not one of the most well-read women of her time? And was she not someone referred to as Cecilia the Wise?"

"Aye, m'lord, she was. And what a great woman she was. She raised me and my brother Gilman with the notion that an education was our best chance to find success in this world. Now Gilman studied and became a prior, and he lives in England, in Gloucester, and he does continue to teach. He is a very wise and devout man, though I have not seen him in perhaps ten or twelve years. And I was also educated, though not as well as my older brother. You see, I was abroad and in school when me mum took ill, and it was me who was more free to come home and care for me mum.

"And so, I left St. Adolphus School for Young Men, and came back to Shepperton, and I've stayed here ever since. It was the earl himself who arranged for me to become trained as a guardsman, something that I have never regretted, I might add."

"Now, your story is all well and good as it gets, my dear Cayman, but tell us just a couple of further points, if you will. The

first is in regard to your own mother, what her role was, and what she told you upon her deathbed. And the second is to tell us just what it was that you were studying to become. Somehow, I think that would be pertinent."

"Well, I never did consider it important, but what I was studying was the ancient tongues, namely, Greek, Hebrew, and, naturally, Latin. I did so with the idea of becoming, like my own mother, a librarian. And the love of great and ancient texts is still my own personal weakness."

"You see, Master Cayman, it would be a serious mistake to assume that you are but a simple guardsman. And, now, what did your own mother tell you before she died?"

"My mother did work for the earl as his own librarian, and so she was ever watching out for the old texts that might become available. And she would always talk with the ships' captains as they came ashore. Over the years, she amassed quite a collection of ancient books, which she kept faithfully at the earl's library, but on her deathbed, she informed me that she had tried for years to obtain a certain volume, which she knew had somehow gotten onto the island, but that she had never been able to find out where it was. She said it was a book unlike any other. That it was an authoritative translation of an ancient Greek text, which told of powers and principles of what might even be considered magic. She was not sure of its name, but said that it was here upon the island somewhere, and that if I should ever find it, to never let it go, but to donate it to the library of the earl."

"Ah, Cayman," said Diane, "we may have a surprise for you, and for Drachma."

There was a smile on Drachma's face, etched deeply into the lines on his face.

"Diane," he said, "I believe I know of your surprise, and we shall hear of that shortly. But for now, before you tell us of yours and Rust's adventures today, I would like to hear some of what brings our guests from afar to Shepperton, now that they have

had the chance to think on just what it was that truly brought them here. So what say you, Master Robert? Are you ready to tell your own tale?"

Bob, who had been silent for some time, took a deep, sighing breath, then he began to tell his own story, as it was now becoming obvious to him that his own saga had as much to do with Shepperton as with his old life back in the States, and how Judy's own tale intertwined with his.

"All right, I'll try to tell you a bit about myself, my life back in the States, and what I believe drove me to come on this journey. For I now do believe that it was my own actions and motivations that impelled me to make this leap of faith. As you know, I was trained as a physician, and our training period was a long one—so long, in fact, that I was in my thirties when I got out of training. After university, which was a four-year period, I enrolled in medical school, which was another four years, and after that I did my internal medicine training for three years, then finally my cardiology fellowship for another four years, so by the time I got out of that training and was ready to start my own practice of cardiology, which is dealing with disorders of the heart. I was very tired of being a student, and I thought that I knew far more than I really did about being a human being.

"Fortunately for me, I had a patient who taught me more about being a doctor and a human being than anything in my training ever could. His name was Joshua, or Josh as we called him. He was a simple sort, whose trust in me was absolute and unshakable. And through the years, I treated him for a number of things, including multiple episodes of pneumonia. But what Josh had was a condition that began at birth and got steadily worse with age, and it was this that actually was going to limit his lifespan. And it was his last illness that led to my coming here. Oddly enough, I was primed for my own trip to Shepperton very carefully and thoroughly by Drachma. And I do believe that it was Drachma who did oversee, through his care and planning,

that I was brought to this castle. Anyway, here I am, and I guess you're probably stuck with me.

Drachma smiled his own secret smile at these words. He then he tuned toward Judy and said, "Now, m'lady, we would certainly await your own perspective on this matter."

So she began telling of her own life, how she was so admired Dr. Gilsen and how during Josh's final illness, she had befriended Josh's parents. It was they who facilitated her coming to Shepperton.

"Now, as most of you probably know, my trek across your little island was a little bit more adventurous than I was ready for. And, fortunately, I had two extraordinary companions on my route here—Falma, and Cairn—who provided considerable stability and also sanity to my trip here. And I can never thank them enough, though Cairn seems to feel obligated to be my bodyguard, for what that's worth."

"Worth the whole world to him, no doubt, m'lady," added Falma. "For to him, you were everything that he ever dreamed of protecting, and that is his life, m'lady, protecting the valuable of this earth."

"And I would agree with that," said Drachma. "Now, let us hear from Rust, as to what happened this day, and what he and Diane did find."

"Well, my good gentlemen and ladies, what I have to tell you is that I went down to Barncuddy's with the notion of clarifying some old issues as to Master Charlie McFerris. And, most particularly, what he had within his belongings, for I did have reason to believe that he had some important books among things that he had left behind. While I was there, I had the good fortune to talk with Diane, who, it turns out, has the distinction of being both the mother of, as well as the daughter of, nobility. Her mother was Greek and came to this isle as a woman tortured to leave her own homeland, but who had no choice as the wife of a noble tyrant who was caught by a rival ruler and put to death,

though more of this tale, I know not. Suffice it to say, that she, who would not even give to us her true name, brought with her Diane and raised her to be the charming woman that you see before you this day. Now, it appears that she brought from the old country a book, as her only tie with her past. And, while here, she felt the obligation to educate her daughter. So she was my own pupil for a time and did learn to read, write, and do simple arithmetic as a young girl. But then tragedy struck and she was left to drift, as it were, alone. Then, after some years, as it happened, there came a shipwreck victim who happened to be the very earl of Derrymoor. And it was she who was given the task of nursing this young man back to health, and who also cooked, cleaned, and cared for him. Now, I must ask your indulgence, as this becomes a tale told best by the person involved. So, Diane…"

"I thank ye, friends, for invitin' me to come to this table, for I am not used to dinin' among the gracious, and my inclination is that I should be serving ye. And so, I would also ask yer pardon, for my own story is not one that I would consider worthy. While it is true, what the good councilor told ye, that I was but a lass, eager to work, when I found out about this nobleman who did wash up on our shore and was in need of help with the cleanin', cookin', and such, and our own earl was willin' to pay a small living wage for the privilege, well, I just took that job in a heartbeat. Now I must tell ye that the earl of Derrymoor at that time was a most striking young man, and he did fancy the attention, which I lavished upon him, and, well, I did become pregnant, about the time that his parents did send for him.

"If it were just anyone whose child I carried, perhaps I would not be here. But now, ye've discovered my own son, Eustace, as one of yer own, and a young man of true virtue, who does carry the seal of Derrymoor with him. Now, just what is to happen to him and where he will go with his life, I shall have to leave to the hands of God, as I have no more that I shall likely be able to direct him."

"Ah, my lady," said Drachma, "you do not know what you are truly saying, for you are none other than the granddaughter of the mighty Archipedes, whose power did keep peace within the region of Aramis, but whose son became a cruel despot and was overthrown, and it was that which made your mother an exile and did make of you a woman of enduring strength. Is that not right, councilor?"

Rust spoke up and addressed Drachma's question. "My friends, what Drachma said is true. Diane is but a very strong woman who has learned the secret of survival, both from her mother and from life itself. She is indeed the granddaughter of a great man and the daughter of a lesser tyrant, but, in truth, she is now the mother of someone with potential far beyond even her own noble lineage.

"I must tell of what did happen this day. As I said, I was at Barncuddy's talking with the good Brewster and with m'lady, and I said that I had reason to believe that old Charlie McFerris had books within his personal possession that might be of significant value. Then Barncuddy did let us into Master McFerris's rooms, where Diane opened his old trunk, and there, among his papers, binders, and books of all type, was a single volume, which I have here. It is not much to look at, but this little leather-bound book does contain writings which only one person alive upon this isle has ever read. So, here it is, my friend, as the one whose name it does carry—here is The Book of Drachma, and may you be blessed by its return."

He handed the small, leather-bound volume over to Drachma, who accepted the book with a bow of his head.

"Now, it is with some wonder that I accept this book, my friend. And could you tell me what did make you look where you did for it?"

"It was, in reality, something that Master Robert said, in which he told of a dream that he had before he ever came here, which clarified for me my search."

Drachma's eyebrows arched, and he then said, "Someday, Master Robert, when all is quiet and you are with me in my own home in the forest and we are seated comfortably in chairs about the fire, then shall I ask of you your dream. But for now, I only ask that you remember that you have wrought great comfort by your works, and they shall be remembered for generations.

"For now, our tale is nearly complete, but for the telling of what Master Kerlin has been doing, and, also, the presentation of this other book to its rightful owner. M'lady Diane, here is thy book, which does establish that thy own bloodline, and Master Robert's, do come together. As is evident from the foreword, which is prophecy, your path and the path of the healer are to be connected by history. I do not know how, nor in what way, but they are connected."

The silence in the room was thick—almost too thick to breathe. Bob looked at Diane, and she, in turn, looked at Bob. Neither one of them looked too eager to enter into this new world opened up by Drachma in their midst. It was finally Judy who broke the stillness.

"See, Bob, this is what happens to doctors who get out of their warm, comfortable beds in the middle of the night, in winter, to help out someone in distress. No good deed goes unpunished, so they say. And look around you now, at this collection of formerly unrelated persons, who now will share your new adventures, each of whom, it seems, has their own part to play, their own little piece of the action. If you had only known…"

"As you say, Judy, if I'd only known. But then, Josh's own distress that night was more than this doctor could turn down, and so, I think the die was cast before I ever got that phone call. And, I guess that it's all of you that I've got to thank for this opportunity to be part of something bigger and more amazing than I ever thought possible. And finally, I'd like to say that dreams can really get you into a whole heap of trouble.

"And speaking of trouble, I am somehow certain that Craycroft is just itching to tell us all of the trouble that Mr. Kerlin has been keeping from our doors today. Am I right?"

"Quite right, Master Robert. Now as some of you might have heard, thanks to our youthful crew, including Eustace, Jeremy, and, of course, our own birdman, Cayman, we had heard that there was a ship headed our way and that Councilor Reordan had built a special pier for them to use to land upon. This was presumably to take over our own castle and the running of this island. Master Kerlin was able to put together an armed force to deal with this threat, and he was successful in routing our potential adversaries, and he is bringing back to the castle prisoners, of whom the earl of Derrymoor is the main one."

At the mention of his name, Diane immediately turned pale. Suddenly it all seemed too much, too sudden, and too dangerous. With a word of apology, she left hurriedly, with Cayman close behind. As the rest of the assembled guests began talking among themselves, one of the servants announced that a most special guest was here for their entertainment.

Willie Minstrel came in, bowed to the assembled throng, and sat down. He had with him his harp, which he sat between his legs. After downing most of a pint of ale, he turned toward Bob and said, "Now, Master Robert, tell me if ye recognize this one."

Again, he began with gentle strumming in the lower strings, and then, slowly, out of the middle strings, there rose a new melody, which froze Bob in his seat. It was a melody that he had not heard since childhood, which he associated with his grandparents' home in rural Illinois. He remembered his grandfather would put on the record and would hum along. And he remembered the photograph on the jacket, one of a bucolic scene from Ireland, with a fiddler, a piper, and someone playing something that looked like a guitar. He could not remember the name of it. But then he heard Judy begin to hum the tune—one

of longing and promise. He just closed his eyes in thankfulness for the music.

After the piece was finished, there were tears in Bob's eyes—tears of gratitude, of yearning, and of loss.

"Oh, Willie, how would you have known? How in the world?"

"Ah, Master Robert, that is my own secret."

Willie played on for the next hour, a concert not like any that Bob, or Judy, or any one of them had heard, with the exception of Falma, who had heard the likes of Charlie McFerris years ago in another time and place.

Chapter Twenty

Something had happened last evening, but Reordan was unable to figure out what it was, though there were some disturbing bits of information from his sources. He did find out about some of the men leaving the castle, but the number was not reliable. The reports said they were heavily armed, but that could mean anything. He did not have any reliable sentries that had reported back yet. He wondered if Derrymoor and his men had landed, and, if so, were the horses delivered as promised?

And so he fretted.

And then there was this council meeting called for today. He noticed that the flag was at half-mast, so he figured that the earl had died, and they would hear about it this afternoon. So he at least had that much to look forward to. And if Councilor Silvo would but hold steady, he figured that he stood a better than even chance of being able to turn things his way with the council.

He summoned his faithful servant, Carruthers.

"Carruthers, have you heard any more news? There is stillness in the air that speaks to me of trouble. I now know that the earl is dead, and we have the meeting of the council this afternoon, so I am certain that it shall be announced. Tell me, have you heard anything from LeGace, or have you seen anything of him?"

"Nay, master, I have not seen him nor have I heard anything of his whereabouts. It seems he has vanished from our view. And

as to any news, I would only note that which you already know—that there were riders, heavily armed, who rode out of the castle, but of them I have heard nothing more.

"Oh, but there is one other thing. The drawbridge—it was pulled up."

"The drawbridge pulled up, I wonder... Ah, no matter. If things do go as planned with the council, then we shan't worry about the drawbridge. And, Carruthers..."

"Aye, m'lord?"

"What do our contacts tell us is happening?"

"Nothing, m'lord."

"Nothing? What do you mean, nothing?"

"What I mean is that our formerly reliable urchins are nowhere to be found, with the exception of Wheezer, and I do not know how much to believe him."

"Are we not paying them?"

"Oh, I would be paying them, if they would but bring me information, but for the past week or so they have not been coming about."

"Well, that is disturbing, I would say. And what does this Wheezer say about this?"

"Only that his former friends are not talking to him."

"Hmm, I see. Well, if I am right, we may not need the help of the urchins much longer. Anyway, why do you not try again to gain some information before the council meeting today? Anything at all that you believe that might be of use."

"Very well, m'lord. I shall bring you what I am able."

Carruthers left his master and went out to the cloakroom and retrieved his cloak, and, before he went out, he checked his inside pockets and found that he had enough money, at least for the transaction that he had in mind. He left by the back door and headed out toward the road by the side of the old servants' quarters. Then, coming around the back, he saw him by the side

of the road just looking about. He went out to the other side of the muddy road and came up next to the man in the dark shawl.

"And you have the money that we agreed to?"

"Aye, it is here in my bag, I shall get it for you. He…"

He did not even see the man's weapon come toward his belly, and, suddenly, he was lying slumped over, blood pouring from his abdominal wound into the mud. He tried to utter a call for help, but his cries were stifled by the cawing of crows overhead. Then he just lay there, as he watched the man walking away, calmly, as if on his morning stroll.

Kerlin's night had been as full as he expected, and by the time he got around to his famous prisoner, it was late morning. He had already been to see Craycroft and Drachma by then and had gotten instructions from them in regard to his prisoner, so he was prepared. As he descended the stairway in the back of the constabulary with Proust at his side, he remembered the earl of Derrymoor from prior years as an engaging and affable sort, and he didn't see him as anyone to take off and try to conquer a peaceful land belonging to the king. He wondered just how much the earl knew of the history of this island.

They came down and found where the floor leveled off and the hallways of the prison began. There was the ever-present, musty stench of underground corridors with inadequate ventilation, along with the smells of human excrement, sweat, and blood. They turned toward the first chamber and opened the door. The light was provided by torches on the wall and was inadequate to see very well, but what they could see surprised them. There was not the expected prisoner angry at his present circumstances, ready to try breaking his shackles, or even the depressed son of privilege, moping in his present circumstance. Rather, they were

greeted by the same engaging, youthful, and optimistic man who had left the island those many years ago.

"Ah, Kerlin, it is really good to see you again. Tell me, how have you been these years I was away? I am able to see that you have advanced in standing within the guard. What is your position now?"

Proust answered for Kerlin. "M'lord, you are looking at the new commandant of the security forces of this island. And as such, he is not one to be trifled with."

"Ah, my good man, I had no intention of doing that. It is just that Kerlin and I have some, shall we say, shared history, and I am most gratified that he has risen in stature to such a position. And may I also say that it is truly an honor to be interrogated by the chief of the security forces—that is what you came down here to do, is it not?"

"It is, indeed," answered Kerlin, "and might I say that this is not what we expected from a prisoner taken roughly in the night to the castle's keep in shackles. Tell me, have they fed you?"

"If that be what you call it, aye, I have been offered food—it is over there, if you'd care to partake. I should be more than happy to share what remains of my excellent repast."

At this bit of sarcasm, Kerlin did smile and go over to his prisoner and unclasp his shackles, and then he took the earl by the arm and led him out of the prison, up the stairway, and into the constabulary. He took him to one of the back rooms where he offered him a seat. And he spoke to one of his men and suggested that they bring his prisoner some bread, cheese, and ale.

"Well, then, m'lord, Earl, why do we not begin by having you tell us just what it was you were doing, landing on a pier especially constructed for you in secret by our Councilor Reordan? Mind you that we have also had occasion to talk with Reordan's men, who seemed only too eager to talk when they were threatened with having to explain things to the king's men."

"That is quite an elaborate way of telling me to speak the truth, is it not? Well, then, I should back up a few months when we received an envoy from Master Reordan, who told us that things were not looking too favorable in Shepperton. There was the illness of your potters and painters and talk of witchcraft and poisonings. And he also indicated that the earl of Shepperton's rule was becoming ineffectual and that your commerce was becoming threatened. Now, as you know, I have always loved this island and its people, and would do almost anything to salvage what is great about it. So, I asked this envoy to find out what I could do to help. Then came the message from Reordan himself that what I needed to do was to get together an expeditionary force and to send it to the island—and he did say that he would build a new pier for that purpose, and, further, that he would provide horses and guides, and that we were to march on up to the castle. He would make certain that the earl was rendered ineffective (I believe that is the way he phrased it).

"Further, he noted that the earl had no legitimate heir to his rule, and he felt quite certain, with his own position on the ruling Council of Lords, that he could have me installed as the newly ruling earl, and that would be all right with the king."

"Hmm, that is quite clever of Lord Reordan," Kerlin mused. "And I assume, knowing what I do about Reordan and the council, that, in turn for all your favors, he would like himself to become the *de facto* ruler and answering only to you. Have I got that about right?"

"Oh, aye. I myself could not have put it better. And I might add, he did sweeten the deal with gold, as a 'gesture of good will.'"

"I see. Well here comes some real food for you. And while you partake of it, I shall proceed to tell you the real truth of the matter, and then we shall take you to see a couple of persons who do, in fact, rule here upon the Isle of Shepperton. And furthermore, I shall tell you the truth about our good Councilor Reordan."

"Ah, my thanks to you. This looks like a real meal, as I have not had one in days." He bit into a roll and paused, with a faraway look in his eyes. "My God, this roll reminds me of years ago, here on Shepperton, with a certain lass... It was not she who made these rolls, was it?"

"Almost certainly, it was Diane who made those rolls, and that's another tale which you must surely hear."

The room was cozy, with a fire burning in the fireplace, and the people in the room sitting quite comfortably about, enjoying the ambience and the chance to just relax for a spell. Jeanne was there, as well as Judy, along with Tom and Eustace, and sitting next to him was his mother. Next to her was Cayman, who looked the part of the faithful household pet, but who told himself that he was really there because of his promise to Kerlin not to leave Eaustace alone.

"All right," chided Judy, "now that you've got your man, can you go back to being the flirtatious barmaid at Barncuddy's that you always were?"

"Well, m'lady, I know not. It has been such a part of my nature for lo these many years—it would be such a hard thing to give up."

"And Barncuddy—would his business not suffer the loss of such as ye, m'lady?" It was Frieda, who popped in to clear away the dishes—yet another thing that Diane's newfound status made it hard to avoid doing. "And what say ye, Master Cayman? What of yer mistress flirting with other men? Would it not bother ye?"

Cayman's tone was remarkably matter-of-fact as he answered. "Now you must realize that it was just such a woman whom I loved all this time. And just because she said that she would be mine, do not think that she is any different because of that. Who she is and how she behaves I cannot control. That is up to her. All I know is that I shall be faithful to her, no matter the cost. I

am not her master, no matter what others may think. I am truly beholden to her for letting me into her life—that is all."

Diane just sat with tears in her eyes. She looked at Cayman and said, "Ye know what I did say to thee—and I am beholden to thee as well, and though ye might not know it, I do consider ye my master, none other."

It was then, perhaps by coincidence, perhaps not, that Kerlin brought his captive by, asking the whereabouts of Tom and Eustace. But what Kerlin and the earl of Derrymoor were not expecting was the profound, wrenching effect that the meeting of Eustace with his own father, and of Diane, again coming face to face with her former love, would have upon all their hearts.

Chapter Twenty-One

As the two o'clock hour drew near, Craycroft was alone and thought through his plans once more. This was no ordinary meeting of the council—he knew that, and yet he did not know at all how things would go with the councilors. He knew that Rust was with him, and he had Genet primed and ready. And Councilor Fitzgibbon was probably going to be supportive. However, there was the elusive Councilor Donovan, who was felt by Rust to be with them, but Craycroft was not so sure, and, also, he wondered whether Reordan had done anything to change that councilor's mind. And, of course, Reordan and his puppet, Councilor Silvo—he knew where they stood.

But Craycroft now had more allies, thanks to Kerlin and the combined efforts of Councilor Genet and Derrymoor. He thought wistfully of what a cataclysmic event it must have been to both Derrymoor and Diane to face each other after so many years and so many miles.

Besides that, Craycroft had one more surprise—Master Robert. What an incredible force he had turned out to be.

As he was alone and there were so many people depending on him, Craycroft knelt down to pray. He prayed for the well being of all, for forgiveness, for he was not able to fully tell the truth of what happened to the earl of Shepperton, and for protection and guidance for the precious youth of the island, upon whom

the great responsibility of leadership was now being laid down before them all. And lastly, he prayed that he be given a portion of strength to do what he had to do. For a while he just stayed upon his knees, thinking no thoughts, just letting the winds of time seep through him and to heal him.

When he got up, he felt renewed. Ready to do battle with Reordan, and ready for that most uncertain of things—the future. He called for Aaron and told him that he was now at peace and to summon Drachma. But Drachma had been waiting outside and came in.

"Well, my friend, are you ready?"

"Aye. And are our forces ready to do battle, as I am most certain that it shall be a battle this day?"

"Fear not, for we have the foes surrounded, emotionally, if not physically."

"Oh, I fear not for my sake, as I did not ask for this position, and it comes with no provisions for my safety. Rather, it is all the others for whom I feel responsible. For Rust, and Councilor Genet, for Diane and Cayman, for Eustace and Tom, for Melchior, for Kerlin, and most especially for the Lady Judy and Master Robert, whom we have torn from their lives and brought so many miles and years hence."

"Indeed, my friend, this has been an amazing journey for many persons who mean so much to us. And let me tell you, that never have I felt so certain that we now have the right persons in place to achieve so much. So saying, then, let us gather our forces and go into battle."

Reordan kept pacing back and forth in his rooms. Where was Carruthers? Why had he not returned? This was an ill omen, for certain. It was now close to two o'clock, and Councilor Silvo was

to be here by now. This was tearing at his insides. He was unable to eat any of his midday meal, and he just kept fuming.

He heard someone at the front door, and when the servant let Silvo in, he breathed a quick sigh of relief.

"Ah, good, you are here. Now, Councilor, we must be off. You did not happen to see Carruthers outside, did you?"

"Nay, I did not, good sir. Were you expecting him?"

"Well, he has not returned since this morning. I was hoping that he had found something useful. It appears that our sources of information may be drying up. I am thinking that it should be no matter after the meeting today, but I am worried. He has never gone out on an assignment and not come back."

"Why, I think it unlikely that any major trouble has befallen him. As you say, though, we should be going. This would not be any meeting that we should be late in attending."

"Nay, indeed. I shall explain what I have planned as we go to the meeting."

He left word with his servants to be on the lookout for Carruthers. He got his cloak and the two of them set out for the castle. As they went along, Reordan explained to Silvo the details of his plan.

The man in the shroud followed at a safe distance, keeping to the shadows, unnoticed and unrecognized.

As they entered the castle, Reordan noticed the drawbridge was back down, and he wondered just what that meant, but said nothing, as Silvo did not comment on it. They entered the gates, and they both noticed just how quiet it was at this time of day, as if even the common people of the castle knew that something was brewing.

And so they walked on, hardly even daring to make a sound; they went along the familiar walkways toward the council chambers. As they got to the door, Silvo looked about them. He saw, out of the corner of his vision, a fleeting glimpse of the man as he ducked back into the shadows.

"Good afternoon, Councilor Reordan and Councilor Silvo."

Silvo acknowledged the welcome from the page, but Reordan just quietly entered and sat down in his place.

Before taking his own seat, Silvo surveyed the room, noticing that Rust and Fitzgibbon were seated and talking quietly to each other; and he saw that Councilor Donovan was just walking in, not looking at anyone. He sat down quietly in his seat, his face registering nothing. Then he himself sat down and waited for it all to begin.

As the bell in the clock tower chimed twice, Craycroft walked in and looked every bit the part of leader. The councilors all stood up as he came forth, though none dared to look directly at him. When he reached the front, he turned and addressed them.

"Good councilors, all. It is with deepest sadness that I must tell you of the departure of our great friend, the earl of Shepperton. As you know, he had been quite gravely ill, and he passed on this week. I know you shall join me in remembrance of this sad time, mourning our loss, which is yet too great for words. Now, I was with him as was Master Falma, and I should tell you that his parting was at least peaceful.

"His memorial mass shall be held tomorrow at ten o'clock in the morning, and the entire public shall be there, and there shall be places reserved for all of you at the front of the chancel. I have spoken with Father Henri, and he expects all of you there by nine-thirty, so that things might proceed in an orderly manner. There shall also be a burial service at four o' clock tomorrow in the afternoon, which you may also attend."

Craycroft waited a minute to see if there were any questions. The councilors were all looking down, avoiding his eyes.

"Well, seeing that none have questions, I believe we should move on to the business of this council meeting, and I yield the floor to Master Reordan, who, I feel certain, has some important matters to discuss with all of you."

Reordan was a bit surprised that Craycroft would yield the floor so easily. For just a second, he thought to himself, "Caution, he has something planned," but then he tossed aside caution and rose to address the council.

"My thanks to you, Master Craycroft," he said, as he began his statement to the council. "It is with a definite note of sadness that I address you today. As you know, the earl has left no heir to his estate. It would be normal to have this issue decided by the king, but as this has caused us such turmoil in the past, it would seem reasonable, I would think, for us to decide our own fate as to the rule of our own island. I am sure that you would agree with me on this."

He looked around and saw that Councilor Silvo was looking eagerly at him, but the others were avoiding his eyes. That is, everyone except Craycroft, who looked benevolently at the councilor, but his true feelings were not readable.

"As to the matters at hand, I should note the absence of our esteemed colleague, Councilor Genet. And I should like to ask if anyone knows anything of his absence."

Craycroft answered, with a question, "And what do you know of this? I was under the assumption that our good councilor was detained and would be joining us in short order."

Reordan was a little taken back by Craycoft's ploy. He thought about calling him out on this, but quickly realized that any attempt at this would only bring suspicion upon himself. So he let the matter drop for the moment.

"Ah, well, I know nothing definite, but I was led to believe that some harm may have come to him.

"Now, I understand"—he quickly changed the subject—"that the earl, himself wished Master Craycroft to act as his voice while he was still alive, and this is most understandable, as Craycroft has been his trusted advisor. But consider for a moment that Craycroft, though obviously skilled as a healer and advisor, is not of noble birth or ancestry. And consider how this would set with

the king, in our report to His Majesty, which we must make. How we, out here upon this isle, just elected a person of common parentage to be our ruler. I do not think that the king would look favorably upon that notice, and he might even send one of his own to rule—one who would have no experience with our commerce, and who might just destroy our trade and our guilds."

Now he had the attention of Councilor Donovan, who seemed to be considering what Reordan was saying as somehow valid.

"Next, I would have you consider who among you has been the one champion of the guild of painters and potters, and who has been at once seen as favorable in the eyes of the council, as well as a representative to the king's court. That I would humbly submit to you is I, myself. I have been to the king's court and have represented our guilds to the king's men on more than one occasion. And I myself do come from parents of noble birth."

It was Councilor Fitzgibbon who spoke next. And it was obvious that he spoke from a deep rage that he had heretofore kept hidden.

"Now hear me, all of you. I have had the occasion to see and to speak with the earl before he died. And let me tell you that this man"—he pointed to Reordan—"does not speak the truth. He tells you that he is a man of honor. I, for one, do not believe him. He tells you that he has been a champion of our guilds before the king, yet I do know that he had been conspiring to wrest control of the guilds away from Lord Vincente (may he rest in peace), and that it was the members of the guild who had been taken in by this man, who seemed to suffer from these most fearsome afflictions, which I can only assume was divine retribution. Further, I would note that it was Councilor Genet and I that met with the earl before he was taken from us, and it was apparent that the earl had stated his wishes, and did, in fact, record them on paper, with his seal. And it was Councilor Genet who had, upon his person, that selfsame paper. And he has not been heard from since then. Now what do you say to that?"

"Master Fitzgibbon, I fear you are mistaken. I am but a man of true honor, and these accusations are unfounded."

"Are they? Now if I were to bring up Master Fabbiano of the guild of painters and have him tell us of Master Guarneri and what you intended for all of the guild—what would you say to that?"

Rust stood up and raised his arm to restore order.

"If it is of any consequence, Master Fitzgibbon, I, along with two of my colleagues, did have occasion to talk with this fellow Fabbiano earlier today, and I should like to bring that up, but a little later. In any event, I should think it appropriate to let our Councilor Reordan speak his mind, and then we may decide the worth of what he has to say and to determine its validity. What say you to that?"

"Very well, Master Rust—I may have misspoken. You are absolutely right." He sat back down, but did so with a subtle smile on his lips.

"And now, you were saying, Master Reordan, how you were of noble birth, and how that puts you in position to seek control of our island. I would be curious to hear your justification for that."

Reordan was obviously shaken, for this was not the way that he thought that things would go. He took a deep breath and continued with his voice quavering ever so slightly.

"Ah, aye, for you see," he went on. "When it comes to dealing with the king and his men, one's nobility is paramount. For the king's control over his realm is due, in large part, to his ability to control his own noblemen, or at least that is the way it is seen in London."

"Oh, is it now?" It was Councilor Donovan who spoke up, unexpectedly. "Now, could you please explain your own parentage, and also explain just how their nobility would in any way assist in our cause?"

It was apparent that Councilor Donovan might have had his own agenda in asking that question.

"Gladly. Now my own father was a knight, of the order of Edward the Green. He married my mother, who was the daughter of Lord and Lady Cavendish. It was my father's holdings in Ireland that led him to come to Shepperton and establish further lands and holdings, which I manage to this day."

"Ah, so you have lands and holdings. Do go on, as I am most curious to see how that does, indeed, have influence." This was again Councilor Donovan speaking, whose family held the most land upon Shepperton. The bite in his words was obvious to Reordan.

"Good councilor, although just having land is important, how one does acquire it is also of note. Now my parents did have their land bequeathed to them by the king's own men, in return for favors to the king two generations ago. And when asked, the king did know of my parents and did look upon me with favor."

"Point well made," said Silvo, ever the one to defend his comrade. "Now I, for one, do feel that Councilor Reordan, of all of the council, does carry with him the social graces and the backing to be our future leader, and I should cast my vote for him."

Rust spoke again. "Duly noted, Councilor Silvo, but remember that there is much to disclose before we are to the point of deciding anything like that. And keep in mind that you are free to change your vote after we present all the factors to consider."

Silvo sat back down, a somewhat puzzled look upon his face.

"Now, I should like to ask Councilor Reordan a few questions," continued Rust, his manner cool and calm. "First, as to the question of Councilor Genet. I would be most interested as to your knowledge of his doings, and your suspicions of what may have happened to him. Most notably, from whom had you heard any rumors of anything untoward happening to him."

"Well, now, I do not recall precisely who told me, it might have been that I heard it from one of the street urchins?"

"Tell us, then, are you in the habit of getting your information from these 'street urchins,' as you call them?"

"Not all of them…"

"Not all. Just the ones that you pay for certain kinds of information?"

"Ah, no, but there are some more worthy than others."

"And, tell me, how is it that you determine the worth of any of these informers?"

"Well, it seems that many of the ones that are worthy are deemed so by my staff."

"Well, then let me rephrase my original question. Do you know from whom you had heard of Councilor Genet's circumstances? Do you remember, and, if not, why not? For it would seem extraordinary to me that you would not remember from whom you heard that some harm had come to Councilor Genet, an important member of this council."

Reordan's face now became red. He began to perspire.

"Ah, it is…not so likely that…it would seem… Now let me think."

"How would it be if I refreshed your memory and brought in Councilor Genet? Now, here he is, and, I believe, quite well…"

The door to the council room had opened and in walked Genet, who went right up to Reordan. Reordan looked at Genet with sudden pallor.

"My good councilor. It is I, and I am both hale and hearty"—then he turned toward Reordan—"no thanks to you and your hired henchman, and I have in my possession a certain letter…"

"No! That is not possible, I burned…"

"You did what?" It was Councilor Rust again. "Did I hear you say that you burned the letter, which Councilor Fitzgibbon has already said that Councilor Genet carried upon his person? And this, a letter, signed and sealed by the earl, which was addressed to this Council of Lords. Are you telling me that you, yourself burned this letter? And from whom, may I ask, did you get this letter?"

"I…that is…it was something similar…"

The room was so quiet that breathing almost came to a stop.

"Now, Councilor Reordan, I would advise you to think before you answer any more questions. For the truth shall prevail."

"I think that I had better take a few minutes."

"To do what? Think up some better lies?" It was Fitzgibbon. "Now, my fellow councilors, it is apparent that Councilor Reordan has been caught in some serious misconduct, and I, for one, would not think it at all wise that we appoint him to our position of leadership. Let us rather turn to the earl's own choice to succeed him, namely Master Craycroft, and hear from him, for I do suspect that Master Craycroft has some surprises in store for us. Is that not right, master?"

"Indeed, that I do. I have three such surprises." He turned to one of the pages, whispered in his ear. "Now, then, Master Reordan, I am certain that you are wondering what did happen yesterday, and, in particular, to the troops and horses that you sent down to the pier that you had built. And to tell of what did happen, I have asked Master Kerlin to address this body with the details."

The door opened again and in walked Kerlin. Tall and sturdy, in his uniform, he looked for all the world like the commander that he had become. Yet he addressed this company with humility that they did not expect.

"I am honored," he said, "to speak to this august body, and I do so at the request of Master Craycroft, our liege lord. Now, as it happened, we had gotten messages that a large pier had been built not far from Champour. And we had also gotten word that a ship, with a possible war party, was on its way toward this island. Further, that there were about fifty heavy warhorses down by the pier, evidently ready to meet this expeditionary force. So, I got our own troops ready, and we headed out to this pier and found that there were, in fact, around fifty horses—all stallions and geldings—and obviously prepared for war. We then captured the persons holding these horses and found that our own Councilor

Reordan, in fact, purchased them, and that there was, at this time, a ship about to land with a party to whom these horses were to be delivered. And further, there were some among those holding the horses who were prepared to show this party toward the castle.

"As it turned out, then, we were able to rout this expeditionary force, and to capture its leader, who was none other than the earl of Derrymoor. After his capture, he told us of the deal that he had agreed to with Councilor Reordan to storm the castle and to take it over, as our own earl had been 'rendered ineffective' by Reordan."

There were murmurings of astonishment within the room. Reordan was still looking pale as he sat slumped down in his chair. Silvo was looking helpless at his own place.

"Now, before I bring in the earl of Derrymoor, for all of you to see and to meet, Master Craycroft asked that I bring one more person before you, namely, Master Robert Gilsen, who comes from many miles away, across a very large ocean. Now Master Robert is one whom you shall be hearing from much, I suspect, in the days to come, and he brings with him a craft and skill in the form of healing, which you shall no doubt find astonishing."

Bob, meanwhile, had been in the anteroom, waiting his turn. He was nervous. Never had he faced an audience like this one before. He tended to shy away from confrontation, and this was clearly going to be an afternoon of confrontation. Drachma had been most encouraging, but this was his own domain, and Bob felt like a foreigner, more even than when he first appeared on the island and had been confronted by the hunters, near Killiburn. He was pale, nauseated, and shaky when the page opened the door and called his name.

He picked up his sack, with its mysterious bottles, and headed into the main chamber. He was now dressed as one of them— gone were the scrubs and white coat, and in their place were the leggings, the undergarments, and outer garments of the well-dressed, late fifteenth-century gentleman. He was still wearing

his own brown loafers, though, because they were comfortable. Looking around the room he could see familiar and some unfamiliar faces. The one who caught his attention, though, was Councilor Genet, who was beaming at him. With a nod and a smile toward his patient, Bob began.

"Gentlemen, I come before you as one taken from his own environment, many miles away from here. I came, not really against my will, but without any of the things that I was familiar with, and to a time and place in which my arrival was alternately seen as something threatening and something wonderful. And sometime, when it would be more appropriate, I can sit down with you and discuss all that.

"Anyway, I did arrive on this island and was brought here to your earl's castle to find the earl quite ill with a condition that we call pneumonia, and which is usually caused by tiny organisms called bacteria. Now I don't have the time right now to discuss this with you in detail, but, in this case, I was able to discover the cause of your earl's illness.

"Now, if you'll allow me, I can show you how I came to this conclusion." Then he reached into his sack and pulled out the vial of agar, which had remained sterile. As he explained to them how they had been able to obtain the sheep's blood and the seaweed thickener, he passed the flask around. They all looked at this demonstration, even Reordan and Silvo. Next he brought out the flask with Melchoir's spit and demonstrated all the various mouth flora within the vial. His audience was now beginning to murmur in astonishment as this new vial was passed around.

Next, he told them of the copious, foul material that the earl was coughing up, and how, upon the agar of this next flask, one could obviously see a totally different pattern. Then he explained how a small flask of water had been brought to them, from one of the creeks, called the Creek of the Dead, and he showed them this next flask, which contained the same pattern as that taken from the earl.

Then he explained to them how, before the earl became too ill to talk, he had told them of how he himself had been given a gift of pottery, while at Councilor Reordan's house, by someone named LeGace, and he was told to drink daily from this vessel, as it contained the essence of Shepperton.

"And now, if you look at this last vial, with samples taken from this pot in question, you'll notice that it contains the same bacterial strains as the previous two. And so, I was able to conclude that the earl had been given a continuing source of very lethal, water-borne bacteria from one of his own councilors, and that this sequence of events had occurred before, with the Lady Felicia Vincente, whom I had not met because she died before I ever got here."

Again, there were murmurings among the people in the room.

"Let me ask you, if I may"—it was Reordan who spoke, but Bob did not recognize him, as he had not been introduced—"did you conclude that this was done with any intention to harm the earl?"

"No, sir, I did not. For the earl gave no indication of the intent of the gift, except that it was given him, apparently, by this fellow LeGace."

"My thanks to you, Master Robert," Reordan continued, "for that very illuminating discourse, and your obviously excellent knowledge of matters far beyond anyone's experience."

"But now, Master Reordan," Kerlin spoke up, "I should like to know what you were doing in the company of this known killer by the name of Antoine LeGace?"

"I was not aware, Master Kerlin, of this man's reputation as a killer, for he seemed quite a fine gentleman."

"Oh, did you not know of his reputation?" It was Rust again taking the offensive. "Then tell us, Master Reordan, of the nature of your relationship with this man."

"It is just that I had him do some private things for me."

"Private things, eh? Such as killing our Lady Felicia, and our beloved earl, and beating poor Councilor Genet senseless, leaving

him for dead, and taking that which was given him by the earl to be given to the council and destroying it. Is that what you consider 'some private things?'

"No, Councilor Reordan, you have come into this hall, have spread lies upon lies, have tried even to forcibly take over the castle, and then you would ask that we make you our leader. Nay, Master Reordan, you are not worthy even to sit upon this council!"

"I would agree with you, Master Rust, but it is not for me to say who is worthy to sit upon this council." Craycroft's voice was firm, but soothing. "Were it not for our next person to come before this assembly, I would say, be done with you, and go ye hence. But now, I should like to bring the earl of Derrymoor forward for you to see. And be prepared, Councilor Reordan, for what he says and what he brings to this hall is nothing but the truth, and you must face this truth, sooner or later."

And so the earl of Derrymoor strode into the chamber. He appeared composed, and, amazingly, not the least bit nervous.

"It is with some awe that I approach this ruling body. For I recall, years ago, that I was rescued from a shipwreck, which claimed the lives of all but me here upon your isle. I was brought back to health by none other than an angel of mercy, and to her and to your own island's hospitality, I owe an unpayable debt.

"So, imagine my distress, when I heard, from your own Councilor Reordan's envoy of the illness affecting your potters and painters, with talk of witchcraft and murder. And the envoy also indicated that the earl of Shepperton's rule had become ineffectual, and that the island's commerce was threatened. I was curious and sent the envoy on to ask Councilor Reordan what I could do that might be helpful. What I then got back from the councilor was a proposal, sweetened with gold, in which, for our sending an expeditionary force to the island, he would then provide a place to land, enough horses, adequately equipped, and guides to the castle. He further went on to tell me that he would see to it that the earl was rendered ineffective. Now, this

should have told me that things were not quite as straightforward as presented.

"And what he was asking in return was that I would take over as ruling earl, but that he be allowed to rule in my absence, as his surrogate, here upon the isle. Now, as you know, this was at best a sham, and one that cost the lives of many of my good men.

"I find no fault at all with Kerlin's raid—he was doing the right thing. Nor do I find any fault at all with Master Craycroft's plans, as he was protecting his province from outward attack. In point of fact, the use of carrier pigeons that led to quick and logical actions is something that I think I must copy. But I do find fault with you, Councilor Reordan, for you betrayed your earl, your liege lord, probably even murdered him—for what? For the chance to sit upon his throne and to take over the running of his castle when there was no need. Indeed, there shall be a report to the king, and I shall spare no details of your treachery. Do you hear me, councilor?"

Reordan sat, pale and mute.

"And as to the gold with which you thought that you would be buying my services, that shall be returned to the isle and be used to start what may become the greatest center of learning on the British Isles. So, all within these walls, you have heard it from me, the earl of Derrymoor, that there shall be established upon the Island of Shepperton a center of education, unlike anything that has ever been, and with the assistance of Drachma and Master Robert Gilsen, you shall heal the wounds of the past and become what you may, a shining star within this sea."

Craycroft bowed his head for a moment, then, looking back up at his colleagues, stated, "I do not know if the earl of Derrymoor should be willing, but I myself would like it very much if he would consider being the ruling earl here, upon this island. Now I do know that this is what Councilor Reordan, though misguided in his approach, was, in effect, setting out to achieve..."

"My friends, this is really too great an honor to consider, and I would consider it only if the ruling council were to decide. And

further, it could be in name only, as you have your true liege lord here, at my right hand—Master Craycroft."

"Craycroft! Craycroft!" The cries rose and filled the hall, as if reverberating from the hearts of all Shepperton.

Having been told that he was no longer welcome on the Council of Lords, but was otherwise absolved from any legal action, Reordan quietly slipped out the door of the council chambers. He noticed that it had become dark and that there was still celebrating being done within the chamber. He left alone, Councilor Silvo finding himself caught up in the doings of the council and its joviality.

His own mood was black, and his thoughts were turned toward what he was going to do. This whole thing with the council was eating at him, nagging him. He thought about what he could have done differently.

That wretch, Derrymoor, I should never have asked for his aid, he thought as he plodded along.

He turned the corner and there he was, grinning at him.

"LeGace, whatever do you want?"

"What I want, I have already gotten—your lands, your house, your servants—they are now mine."

The blade flashed from his cane, as it ripped effortlessly through the councilor's garments. This time he made sure, and he stabbed him several more times. As the councilor lay on the ground, in a spreading pool of blood, his assailant walked quietly off toward the outside of the castle, where a waiting horse was ready to take him down to the pier and the boat. He knew that it would be some time before he came back to Shepperton, but the house was there and would be waiting. He smiled again, pleased with himself.

Chapter Twenty-Two

"Hello, and welcome to an hour with some seemingly ordinary persons, who just happen to have one of the most unusual stories that you will ever see on television. My name is Charlie Stephens, and I am an investigative reporter for WIOX, Channel Five. Now, I would ask that you do a couple of things for the next hour. The first would be to get yourselves comfortable, and preferably sitting down, with your favorite beverage at your side. The second would be to turn off any distractions, for this promises to be an hour that will grab you unlike anything on the tube.

"Oh, and one more thing—I would ask that you hold both your judgment and your disbelief to the very end, for this story will stretch both.

"I'll begin by telling you how this whole story got started. I got a call a few weeks ago to look into the mysterious disappearance of one of our cardiologists from Memorial Hospital. This turned out to be Dr. Robert Gilsen, a well-respected and busy cardiologist. He's a person of some renown in his field, and universally loved by his many patients. He is a person who puts in incredibly long hours, and whom you could find at the hospital at all hours of the day and night. His reputation is impeccable, and he is in solo private practice, which many consider to be a dying entity.

"Now, one day, Dr. Gilsen just disappeared. I mean that one minute he was in the hospital, caring for the severely ill, and the next

minute he was gone—just like that—gone! And he left no note, no mysterious phone calls, and no arguments with coworkers—not even a phone call to his lovely wife. He just plain disappeared.

"And you can believe that the hospital staff, as well as their security, searched high and low for him. And they found absolutely nothing. His switch, indicating his presence in the hospital was turned on all this time.

"Anyway, by the time I got this call, I found out about yet another mysterious disappearance from the staff of Memorial Hospital. This was a nurse who worked in the ER named Judy Morrison. Now it turns out that these two knew each other, and so my own investigative hairs were tingling, and I set off to "find the truth" of the matter, and let me tell you that this truth is far stranger and more powerful than any fiction.

"The first person I interviewed was Mrs. Marilyn Gilsen, who is here at my right. And as you will discover, she is quite an amazing woman. Now, Mrs. Gilsen, or should I call you Marilyn? I imagine that you thought hard about granting me that initial interview."

"Oh, you bet I did," answered Marilyn, who sat demurely at her place on the couch next to Charlie, "and please, do call me Marilyn. I thought about it very hard, and I even called one of the detectives, a Mr. Edgar Bryant—whom I had spoken to about Bob's disappearance—before I agreed to speak with you. And let me tell you that your own reputation made my decision even harder."

"Oh, and what kind of reputation do I have?"

"Let's just say that between you and a pit bull, most people would choose the pit bull."

"Marilyn, I'm afraid that many would agree with you about that. Anyway, do you remember that interview and where it took place?"

"Of course I do. It took place at Memorial Hospital in the rotunda."

"And were you alone?"

"Well, no. I had called Edgar Bryant, who was there, as well as Janie and Earl Crabtree…"

"…who are sitting on my left. And we'll get to them in a minute. But can you recall anything about the interview, and how you felt?"

"I can recall very well how I felt. I felt like I was on trial, and you were the prosecuting attorney. Now I'm sure that you didn't mean to intimidate me, knowing you as I do now, but still, you did intimidate me."

"And was there anyone else that you remember being there?"

"Oh, yes. There was a Mr. Vincente. He was not there long, but he smiled at me, and that smile seemed to say to me that everything would be all right."

"So, now, Marilyn, it seems that there are now a number of people involved with your story. And I would ask that you tell us just what happened, keeping nothing back, no matter how incredible or fanciful it seems."

"Okay. But remember, you asked for it."

Charlie nodded and said, "That's right, I did."

"All right, then, I'll start at the beginning. The night that Bob disappeared from my life was really no different from so many other nights. He got a call from the ER, which obviously upset him, I could tell, but he just got dressed, kissed me, and then he left. There was really nothing to say this night was special.

"But all the next day, he didn't call, which was a bit unusual, not unheard of, just a little out of the ordinary. But then he didn't come home that night, which was starting to get really weird. I had tried calling the hospital operator, who told me that, yes, he was still in the building, and I didn't want to disturb him, so I just fretted, tried to sleep, but wasn't very successful. Then, the next day I got a call from hospital security, and, let me tell you, that at this point I began to get scared, really scared. And later that day one of the hospital administrative people called me in. He told

me that Bob had just simply disappeared. And then he started asking nosy questions that were none of his business, and I guess I just clammed up. Anyway, he suggested that I make a missing persons report, which I did. And that's when Edgar Bryant, as well as Chris Lewinsky, stepped into the picture. They came over to my house and interviewed me."

"Wait just a minute. On a missing persons report, they actually came to your house and interviewed you? Did that seem at all strange to you?"

"Well, to be perfectly honest, I wasn't thinking too clearly at this point. But I guess that's a bit different, isn't it?"

"Oh, yes, that's different, all right. It would seem that they had been tipped by the hospital that this was no ordinary missing person story. But do go on..."

"Anyway, Mr. Bryant and Ms. Lewinsky came over and interviewed me, took down the pertinent information, and were about to leave when I got a phone call from Carlo Vincente, whom I had never heard of before. He said he knew of Master Gilsen's disappearance (I believe that's how he put it) and that he would like to meet me to discuss the matter. He said that he would meet me the next day in the hospital cafeteria.

"Now, I don't have to tell you that this phone call just shook me to the core. And it perked up the ears of the two detectives. So, the next day they came back over and they had me wear a little broach that they said would send an emergency signal to them. And so we went to the hospital and we split up, but they stayed within sight of me. And, right where he said he'd be, I met this most kind, elegant, but unusual man named Carlo Vincente. I don't have to tell you, do I, just what kind of impression he makes on a person?"

"No, I'm afraid that you don't. But that's for a little later on."

"Well, we just sat down in a room off the main cafeteria where he told me his most amazing story. He told me that he came from Shepperton Island, apparently some island between

Scotland and Ireland where he had been recruited, along with his guild of painters and potters. He further intimated that his time was not our own. He spoke of some great and powerful person named Drachma who had been orchestrating some grand plot that involved both their time and ours. He talked as well of some youthful person, who I found out later was named Josh, and of Josh's own arrival in the ER, his later surgery, and how Bob came and went from that operation, which I later found actually happened. And he told me of a nurse named Judy, and who figured prominently in all this.

Marilyn continued. "Now, his story seemed somewhat fanciful, and yet the details checked out. The details of Bob's doings, as well as Judy's—virtually everything could be verified. And let me tell you that as he told his tale, there was no pretense, no hiding, no asking—nothing but what seemed to me to be the unvarnished truth.

"And I asked him if he knew what actually happened to Bob. But he didn't directly say; however, he said that he believed that Bob was now on Shepperton Island, back in his time. And he gave me this token, which he said told of Bob's health, and that I should keep it with me. Now I understand that it is a drachma— an ancient coin from Greece."

Marilyn reached into her purse, pulled out the little box, and opened it.

"If we can get a close up of this box," said Charlie Stephens. "Here, hold it up just a little bit—there. Now this is, in fact, a drachma from ancient Greece. And I would suggest that you put it back into your purse for safekeeping. And may this be the last time that it is on display. Thank you, Marilyn."

Charlie then continued, "You didn't know it at the time, but that little broach that you wore was actually a special microphone, and your conversation with Mr. Vincente was being recorded, isn't that right?"

"That's what I have been told, but to tell you the truth, I haven't listened to the recording—nor do I want to. It's just that the experience was a one-time thing, and it would probably be a bit too emotional for me."

"Well, let me tell you that I have read a transcript of that conversation, and for what it's worth, Marilyn, it was a very moving experience, even for me.

"Now, back to our story. What happened next?"

"If you think that what you've heard has been a bit hard to believe, just you wait, it gets even stranger. As you can well imagine, my nights were sleepless, with all the worry, but eventually I had finally gotten some exhausted sleep. Then I had a very vivid dream of Bob, as he was walking along at night with some young person in the courtyard of a great castle. And there was this absolutely beautiful harp music playing. And, then, as Bob and his companion were walking away, he turned to me and said, "Drachma," and then he just walked on.

"And when I got up the next morning, under the little box, which I kept at my bedside, was a note, which I have here."

Marilyn again reached into her purse and pulled out the folded paper, which she handed to Charlie. He then took the paper and displayed it so that it was visible on the monitors.

"For those of you that can't read the note," he went on, "it says:

> Janie Crabtree.
> If you but seek her,
> And take to her this coin,
> She shall tell you what you
> Wish to know.
> Know that I wish you peace.
> Drachma

"And so, with this most mysterious note now in your possession, what did you do?"

"Well, the next thing that happened was that you called me to set up the interview. And that sort of got this whole thing rolling. I called Edgar Bryant and told him of your phone call, and I was able to get hold of Janie Crabtree on the phone. Then I went over to the Crabtrees and had lunch."

Charlie turned and said, "And here, on my left, we have the Crabtrees—Janie and Earl. And now, let us hear your own story, if we may, Janie. And as with Marilyn, don't hold anything back, no matter how weird or unusual it may seem. Now, you're the mother of Josh Crabtree, isn't that right? A long-standing patient of Dr. Gilsen's?"

"Oh, yes, Mr. Stephens. We've been seeing Dr. Gilsen for close to ten years. You see, Josh had a congenital heart condition, which gradually got worse as he got older. Now Dr. Gilsen always acted as Josh's advocate, and he was pushing the surgeons to do the necessary repair, but they had been reluctant, understandably, because of Josh's other medical problems. In any event, Josh was finally operated on, and he did well for a period of weeks. Then unforeseen complications did develop, and we had to bring Josh back into the hospital in the middle of the night. Dr. Gilsen was obviously heartbroken, and he really pulled out all the stops to try to save Joshua's life. He got another surgeon to do a replacement valve surgery in conditions far from ideal. Anyway, Dr. Gilsen stayed in the hospital with Josh all this time.

Janie paused, as if some private memory intruded then went on, "There were some strange things happening this whole time. And it was about at this time that Judy Morrison seemed to get involved. She seemed to me to be the measure of sanity and compassion all rolled into one person that we needed. It seems that Judy herself had been getting some very peculiar messages, including a message written on this same sort of paper, also from this person named Drachma. And, also, she apparently ran into this Mr. Vincente, who told her to seek out a 'doctor of hearts, named Gilsen,' and who gave her this same little box with the silver

coin in it to give to Dr. Gilsen. How it has ended up in Marilyn's possession is both a wonder and yet somehow appropriate.

"Let me tell you that it was Judy Morrison who had made it possible for me to keep my sanity. She was with me when Josh died and was there at his funeral—both of which meant so much to us. And it was after his funeral that she was last seen."

Charlie next turned his attention to Earl. "Okay, now, as I understand it, Earl, it was then that you became involved in all this, albeit reluctantly."

"I guess you could say that." Earl looked uncomfortable, sitting there on the couch with the cameras rolling. "I was something of an unwilling witness at first, preferring to act as a social support system in all of this, but I guess you could also say that I became sort of instrumental in Judy's disappearance."

"Oh, and could you explain yourself?"

"Well, this is going to sound kind of odd, but I had a couple of dreams before Josh died, in which this fellow, this Drachma person, told me that I would know that this "lady healer" was going to be helping him, but I never got the connection to Judy until we got the mail that day, while Judy was still at our house after Joshua's funeral."

"And could you explain what you mean?" Charlie pressed.

"It's kind of difficult, but in this dream, there was this old guy who called himself Drachma the Elder of the Forest, who spoke to me and told me that Josh's death was not in vain, and that I would find out about it on my own deathbed. But he said that I had a more immediate task, which was to identify this "lady healer," and when we both recognized his picture, to tell her that she would be joining in Master Gilsen's tasks and that her way would be made clear.

"Now, I just put this off as a strange, recurring dream until the mail arrived with Judy there, and out of the mail, there pops this letter on this strange stationery. Now, I've got the envelope right here."

He reached into his coat and pulled out the envelope in its plastic sandwich bag with the red wax seal and the name written on the other side: Master Earl, esq.

"And where is this letter that was in the envelope?"

"We gave it to Judy because it was obviously intended for her. But it was the most amazing letter. It had this engraving of the old man on it. The message was something about a wise old man on a horse, and that they were expecting her. But the fact that Judy and I both recognized him at the same time, and my realization that it was Judy who was this "lady healer" did it for me. I told her that she had been chosen. Oh, man, I'm really starting to sound like a looney, I'm so sorry..."

"No, you are not Earl"—it was Marilyn. She reached into her purse again and fetched a note, which she turned over to Charlie. "Now, just look at that engraving and see if you recognize the face."

Charlie showed Earl the note. Earl looked at the note, rubbed his eyes, and looked again. He made a low whistling sound and sank back on the couch.

"Yeah, that's definitely the same face. There couldn't be two of them. And it's the same handwriting on the top of the note. And, let me guess, that's Dr. Gilsen's writing at the bottom of the note..."

"You got that right," said Marilyn.

"Well, folks, it's time for a commercial break, but don't you go anywhere. There's a lot more to come."

When they started up again, Charlie had laid out the notes and the envelope, and he had the cameraman pan them close up.

"As you can see, we've got quite a story here. We've started with a cardiologist—well loved, and doing the things he knows best to do, namely taking care of very ill patients at Memorial Hospital, who just up and disappears. And along with this, we

have the disappearance of a nurse, who is compassion and caring incarnate, and who also disappears mysteriously. Now we have people here who know something of their disappearance, but who did not witness any of it.

"And we have this intrepid reporter, who was quite convinced that this involved some sort of hank-panky. I did interview Marilyn Gilsen and got nothing substantial from the interview, which just seemed to get under her skin. I thought about pushing harder, but something held me back at that point. Then, as I was leaving after the interview, I found that this old man was riding in the back seat of my car, who introduced himself as Carlo Vincente. And I'll tell you that this was only the beginning.

"Normally, investigative reporters do not tell of their own involvement in cases that they bring to the public eye, but let me tell you that I was spooked by this old man just sitting in the back seat of my car. He went on about Master Gilsen and Lady Judy as if he had some first-hand knowledge of their doings. Now I tried to listen, sort of half-heartedly, as he went on. Then, while I was stopped at a traffic light, the old guy just got out of my car and told me that he would be seeing me again, soon.

"I tried to put this whole thing out of my mind, but it just kept nagging at me, robbing me of sleep. Then, one night, I got up to find that this Mr. Vincente was sitting down in my kitchen, and he told me that he had been to see Mrs. Gilsen, and she told him that if I wanted the story of my career, that I'd better listen to what he had to say. So, I'll turn it back over to you, Marilyn, and have you tell us just what went on that evening."

"Why one evening, while I was at home, Mr. Vincente just showed up...I mean, he just simply was there in my own kitchen— he didn't knock, or ring the doorbell, or even, as far as I could tell, open the door. He was just there. And he had in his hand that note that you saw with Drachma's picture on it with the handwriting at the top. But below this was Bob's own handwriting and, believe me, I know his handwriting. Apparently, this note accompanied

a patient, admitted to the ICU with respiratory failure, who had been intubated and had machines do his breathing and was unable to provide any history. Now this note, in Drachma's handwriting, indicates that whoever bears this note does so with his blessing and approval and is under his protection, and it is signed by Drachma, the Elder of the Forest. And below that is where we have a note, written in Bob's handwriting, in another ink, and, here, I'll let you read it."

Charlie then read, with some difficulty, stumbling on the medical terms:

> "To whoever is taking care of this man, let it be known that he is the Earl of Shepperton, who is gravely ill with pneumonia, which may be from water-borne bacteria, I would strongly recommend initial therapy be started with ceftriaxone and erythromycin. And please call in the best pulmonologist you can to take care of my friend.
>
> R. Gilsen MD
>
> P.S. Please tell Marilyn that I love her."

Marilyn dabbed her eyes as he read that last line.

"In any event, Marilyn, you got this somewhat startling note handed to you by Mr. Vincente. And then what happened?"

"I really didn't know what to say at this point. I was flabbergasted that someone from his time was here, and in our hospital, and that Bob somehow was involved with sending him—and then, why couldn't he just send himself back? I just don't know. Anyway, Mr. Vincente just told me what he knew and said that this was his liege lord, and that he was desperately ill, but still clung to life, and that this had been deemed the right thing to do.

"I also found out a lot about the politics and the people of Shepperton—of how there was this struggle with the earl and the ruling council, and someone named Reordan, and how he

figured that Reordan had somehow poisoned Mr. Vincente's own adopted daughter, and now he had done the same to their earl. And he told of his own guild of painters and potters and how it seems that a number of them had taken sides against him, and against the earl, who had provided them protection through the years. He told me more about this Drachma person and his background. All in all, I found out a lot more than I could ever understand about people from some bygone era, who had now made a connection with us.

"And so I told him to seek you out. That's when I found out that he already knew you, that you were a reporter and were probably quite interested in all of this. And further, in a moment of weakness, I told him that if he wanted, I would 'adopt' this earl, if it could be arranged, for it seems that he was here now and without anyone to claim him. And I did so, as much for my own husband as anything. So, he left, with the intention, I believe, of visiting you."

"Ah, yes, he did that," answered Charlie. "He came into my house and was sitting in my kitchen, having gotten in by the same method that he used with you—that is, he just walked in, with the door locked. And when I asked him about it, he just gave me some evasive answer. Anyway, here I was at two or three in the morning, with Carlo Vincente in my kitchen, and he tells me that you've got the story of my career, and that you had a note to show me.

"Well, first thing we do is to go visit this John Doe in the hospital. On the way to the hospital, he tells me of how they brought him in, how he was having extreme trouble breathing, and how they hooked him up to a machine to do his breathing for him. He said that before he succumbed, though, that he said the word *Drachma* to him. And when he tried to intervene, some *girl* held him back, saying that the earl was yet alive and was being cared for. And then this girl told him to find this note that had been in the hands of the earl, but which they now had in some drawer somewhere in the ER, and to take it to Madame Gilsen—I presume that was how you ended up with the note. When I asked him about the girl, he said that he had never before met her, but that she lived where he was going.

"When we got to the hospital, it was dark and deserted, and he took me in some back way. It was evident that he knew where he was going. He took me up to the fifth floor where we entered the ICU, and there in one of the beds lay this earl. Now I have no way of verifying his name, but everything was consistent. And everything about the man said power, wealth, and influence. And he got down close to the earl and spoke quietly to him, telling him that he was there and that you, Marilyn, were aware of his presence. He told him that you and I would be taking care of him. And then he disappeared into the hallway where the little girl was waiting for him—and I haven't seen or heard from him since."

"Now this has got to be the first time where a reporter, on an interview program, has ever talked so much," Marilyn chided gently.

"Or gotten this involved.

"Well, I think that it's time for another commercial break. Now, don't you go away. We'll be back with the conclusion of our story."

When they returned, Charlie had two more guests. Along with Marilyn and the Crabtrees, he had Chris Lewinsky on the couch with them, as well as a dark-suited man none of them recognized.

"Welcome back, folks. Now, we've gotten kind of complicated with our story, haven't we? As you can see, instead of just the missing cardiologist and nurse, we now have a John Doe in our Intensive Care Unit at Memorial Hospital, who might just be this earl from another time and place.

"We are very fortunate to have with us Mr. Chad Breidling of Memorial Hospital's Administrative Staff. Now, Mr. Breidling, I understand that you are the community liaison. Is that right?"

"Yes, that's correct."

"And just what would your role be in all this?"

"Well, you can think of me as a spokesman for the hospital."

"A sort of mouthpiece, if you will?"

"I guess…"

"Well, then let me ask you this—how does the hospital view this recent disappearance of one of its premier cardiologists, as well as their night ER nursing supervisor?"

"We are very upset with the disappearance of both Dr. Gilsen and Ms. Morrison. And we are doing everything in our power to get to the bottom of this business."

"And tell me, realistically, what does that mean? What are you doing?"

"Well, we're cooperating with the police in their investigation."

"Hmm. Cooperating. And just what does that involve?"

"We have searched the whole hospital and done everything that we have been asked to by the police."

"Does that include turning over Dr. Gilsen's car to the police?"

"Oh, yes, definitely."

"Anything else?"

"Well, we've been very cooperative…"

"Yes, I got that. Thank you. And I imagine that you cannot give out any information about this John Doe in your ICU?"

"John Doe?" Mr. Breidling seemed genuinely confused.

"Oh, yes, this man of mystery up in the Medical Intensive Care Unit."

"Oh, no, I'm not at liberty to tell anything about any patients we currently have in the hospital."

"Well, thank you very much, Mr. Breidling.

Charlie next turned toward a petite woman at his left. "And now, we have Detective Chris Lewinsky of our police department

here on my right. And let me ask you, Detective Lewinsky, you're here because of something that has happened to one of your colleagues, am I right?"

"Yes, you could say that. You see, originally, it was Detective Edgar Bryant who was assigned to this case, and I was his assistant. And now, Detective Bryant is also in Memorial Hospital, recovering from major surgery. Actually, he is lucky to be alive. He had a rupturing abdominal aneurysm and was taken to the hospital the other day, taken to surgery, and is now, thank God, recovering, and, amazingly, will probably be going home in a couple of days. He wishes to extend his special good wishes to Mrs. Gilsen. And let me tell you that he gave his permission for me to talk about all of this, and I presume that he's watching this show right now."

"We extend our best wishes to Detective Bryant at this time and thank him for letting you on our show. I understand that Detective Bryant has received some visitors this week."

"Yes, he did," Detective Lewinsky answered. "Just yesterday, Mrs. Gilsen, Mrs. Crabtree, and I went and visited him in the hospital. He seems to be recovering well."

"And did you talk of anything in particular?"

"Of course. We talked about Dr. Gilsen's disappearance and Judy's disappearance. And we talked of how this all came about and what we're going to do about it, which, at this point, is—nothing at all. For without any evidence of foul play, and nothing more to go on than stories, there really is nothing more we can do. And if Dr. Bob and Judy can one day be found, well, we'll have some stories to tell our grandkids.

"And next, we talked of this new fellow that had arrived, evidently with nothing in the way of identification, and, so far, not able to talk. We don't even know what language he speaks. Now, because his presence seems to be related to the disappearance of the other two, they assigned it to me, so I'm in charge of investigating this whole thing. And I've agreed to help Marilyn

with the legal matters, though nothing substantial has turned up yet. We've run a set of fingerprints on the earl (for that's what we're calling him now), and there are, of course, no matches. I think it should be interesting to see what happens if he can come off the respirator. I'd really love to hear his story. And you know what? I'd be willing to wager that his story will jive very precisely with Mr. Vincente's."

"That's interesting, Ms. Lewinsky, very interesting, for you don't hear police talk as you have…"

"Oh, I know. We like our cases cut and dried. But to tell you the truth, ever since we stepped into the Gilsen's home, I got this feeling that things were not going to be that staightforward. And this meandering trail is not one that we, as the police, are likely to be making any clearer."

"If you don't mind, then, Detective Lewinsky, and I really don't mean to put you on the spot. Could you tell us what you really believe happened to Dr. Gilsen with Judy Morrison, and now this fellow we've come to regard as the Earl?"

"Do you mean what I'm going to put in the official record, or what I really believe?"

"How about both?"

"All right, and remember, you asked for it. What I'm going to put in the official record is that, due to lack of evidence, this missing persons case is closed, without presumption of innocence or guilt, and may be revisited should any evidence turn up in the future. And as to the case of the earl, however, it is still ongoing, and what I've already told you is what I know of this matter.

"But what I really believe happened is that Dr. Gilsen and Judy Morrison have been called to another place and another time. And I hope, as I've never hoped before, that their own stories are ones that I can hear and tell my own grandchildren around the fireplace on dark and rainy nights."

"Thank you so much, Detective Lewinsky."

Charlie next turned his gaze toward the camera. And his voice was not the raspy, irritating voice that his audience had gotten to know. There was an emotional depth to what he said and a weight and conviction to his words.

"Now, to you viewers out there, I had asked you to suspend your judgment and your belief until the end, and we're almost there. Consider the stories—we have a cardiologist who gets called out in the night in a blizzard, who has no affiliations except those obvious ones to his patients, to his marriage, and to his hospital, who, now, while doing that which he is trained to do, simply disappears. And we have a nurse, who by accounts from those who knew her, was also doing what she does best—namely, providing exceptional comfort to those in need—who also disappears. But there the stories diverge. For Judy was getting messages that she found hard to ignore, and they were messages that were confirmed by Earl Crabtree, who appears to be as sane and skeptical as you or I. And she drives off in an oncoming blizzard and is never heard from again, nor has her car been found, nor are there any traces of her at her apartment, no mysterious notes, no unusual bank deposits; nothing.

"Now, the police records indicate that there were no notes or letters sent, nor any received by the participants in this drama. But you have seen that there were, in fact, notes—just not the ones that we would think appropriate to mention to the very sane members of the police. And these were sent in one direction only—from "there" to "here".

"And there is the very troubling presence of a Mr. Carlo Vincente, who could be the byproduct of fevered imaginations, except for three things. One, is that Mr. Vincente has been seen by multiple witnesses, including Marilyn Gilsen, two members of the police, and me. The second is that there is a recording of his voice, which was made by the police and is in their custody. And then there is the even more disturbing thing to note—that all of what he has told us of his time here is verifiable.

"And you know, there is one more thing about this Carlo Vincente, and that is the medical record. He was apparently in the ER twice as a patient, the first time he was treated for a dog bite on the leg and the next time he was seen for acute congestive heart failure and cardiac arrest, unable to be resuscitated. His body was taken to the morgue and the medical examiner was called, but when the medical examiner came to get the body, it was no longer there. And of further note, Judy Morrison was in the ER as his nurse on the first occasion, and on his last visit, Dr. Robert Gilsen was called and presided over his attempted resuscitation.

"And lastly, there is the unfinished business of the earl, now gravely ill in the ICU of Memorial Hospital, who arrived in respiratory distress, who is now on a respirator, and whose secrets remain to be told, but whose care, it seems, should he recover, will be in the hands of this very devoted, this very brave and honest woman, Mrs. Marilyn Gilsen."

There was a pause, during which all the persons on that couch caught their breath. Marilyn looked at Janie with tears in her eyes. Janie was wiping the tears from her own. The only person who seemed composed was Mr. Breidling.

"So, you've heard it here. Now, what you make of this tale I cannot direct, but what I can tell you is that whatever you decide to believe, make certain that you do so with all the facts. Be careful of what you believe, and the truth will eventually win out; of that, I am certain.

"This has been a presentation of WIOX, Channel Five News, and I'm Charlie Stephens. Good night."

Chapter Twenty-Three

"Master Robert, Master Robert, come quickly, we have need of you." The page caught him at the entrance to the keep. "It's Master Reordan…I was sent to summon you."

"What is it? Is he ill or hurt?"

"I only know he has been injured and is bleeding, and they are carrying him to Sick Bay."

"Well, then, Hermes, if you can get my satchel and meet me at Sick Bay, and hurry. This sounds bad. Come on, Judy, this could really turn out to be something ugly."

Bob and Judy hurried across the courtyard and over to Sick Bay. By the time they got there, a small crowd had gathered about the doorway. They could see the trail of blood that led into the rooms, and they followed it to the place where they had him lying down.

"What happened—did anyone see?" he asked the few that were attending to the councilor.

The largest of the men answered, "Only that when Sigmund came by, he found him lying in a pool of blood on the walkway not far from the council chambers. He summoned help, and we brought him hence. The councilor asked for you by name."

Bob took in the measure of what was before him. He saw the councilor with bloodstained garments lying on a cot. He saw the man was pale, but he noted he was still breathing. Noticing

one of the attendants that he recognized, he asked him to get some clean cloths and some scissors. Then he went over to the councilor and examined him. Judy was at his side, and between the two of them, they quickly and quietly assessed the situation. It did not look good at all.

When the attendant came with the scissors, Judy deftly cut off his clothing, exposing multiple stab wounds to his upper abdomen. From one wound, blood was still gushing, and she quickly took one of the cloths and compressed his abdomen, and so doing, she was able to staunch the flow of blood.

Meanwhile, Bob was checking his carotid pulse, which he noticed was weak and rapid. He bent over and asked the councilor, "Do you know who did this to you?"

Though barely conscious, Reordan smiled up at Bob and said, "Thank you for coming. I know that I am dying…but I did… wish to say to you…before I died…that you are one…great… physician… It was LeGace…who did this…thing. He is…after my…my…"

Then the councilor gasped, turned suddenly rigid, then limp. And then rapidly, he was gone. No pulse. No respirations. Just like that—he was here, and then gone. Bob felt suddenly helpless again, but realized this time that there really was nothing that he could have done.

Hermes came running in with Bob's satchel.

"I'm so sorry, Hermes, but this time it was just too late.

"Now, does he have any family, anyone that we should notify?"

No one seemed to know.

"All right, then, let's call on Father Henri. And I guess we should notify someone in his household. In the meantime, let's get this place cleaned up."

As messengers were dispatched, the electricity in the air began to dissipate.

Bob and Judy then began the tedious process of cleaning up the body. When they were done, they covered him with a clean

sheet, while the attendants cleaned up the floor. Reordan's clothes were placed in a burlap sack and placed at his feet. No one spoke a word. Finally, within Sick Bay, the intensity of released turmoil could be sensed and felt like a general exhalation.

In the silence that followed, as they were washing their own hands, Judy turned to Bob and said, quietly, "You know, Bob, this is why I love you."

"How's that?" He stopped drying his hands. He was stunned by her confession. "What do you mean?"

"It's that, wherever you are, whatever you're doing, you remain so real, so approachable, so human, and so in touch with the needs of those around you. And others feel it, too. They can sense it. It's like your own aura."

"My aura? I wasn't aware that I had one, other than I think I need another bath."

Judy then wrapped her arms around him, hugging him tightly. "Just you wait until we're alone," she whispered to him.

Hermes and the others in the room looked at the two of them and smiled their secret smiles.

Craycroft and Rust were together, following the council meeting, sitting down in what was now rightly regarded as Craycroft's meeting room. They were both quietly sipping on brandy when Judy and Bob appeared at the door.

"My good Master Robert and Lady Judy. I was just sitting down here with my friend, the councilor. Would you care to join us? There are two more chairs, and I'll see if we have some more glasses for brandy."

"I'm sorry, Mr. Craycroft," Bob interrupted. "But Judy and I just came back from Sick Bay. I'm afraid that Councilor Reordan has been killed."

There was stunned silence in the room.

"Killed, you say? How, and at whose hands?" Rust managed to ask, at last.

"He was stabbed four times in the upper abdomen. He had lost considerable blood by the time we were called to see him. I'm afraid there was nothing we could do. He said that it was LeGace who did this. And then he said that LeGace was after something of his, but he died before saying what it was."

Again there was silence.

"We must notify Kerlin at once, and Drachma. For if ever there were anyone capable of doing this, and much more besides, it would be Master LeGace."

Craycroft quickly dispatched two of his pages with the message that Kerlin and Drachma were needed at once.

"Well, now, Master Robert," Rust continued. "It would appear that you are now truly one of us, for better or worse. You have witnessed our own council at work, and now this. As much as I disliked the councilor, this is woeful news, indeed."

He got up and pulled over a chair for Judy, as Bob brought another over and sat down. When Craycroft rejoined them, he looked intense and quiet. He brought down two more glasses and filled them with brandy before sitting back down. He was obviously deep in thought.

Craycroft looked directly at Judy and asked, seemingly out of the blue, "And so, now, m'lady Judy, I ask you, as one who has no right to know but who does remain curious, what think you of all this? What are your plans? And would you consider it presumptuous of me to ask, whereas Master Robert has chosen to stay, shall you also stay with us?"

"Oh, my. I wasn't aware that I had any choice in all of this."

"Ah, but I believe you still do, my good lady. For it would seem that Drachma does, indeed, have but one more opportunity for you to return whence you came."

"Well, then, what I'll tell you is that I am staying. And you can tell Mr. Drachma that he chose me for some purpose, which I do

not feel that I've fulfilled yet, and that my future belongs with Bob, here, as he has made his decision to stay among you."

"What? Oh, Judy, I made my own decision when I sent the earl to our time in my place. That was my decision, and your decision has got to be your own as well, not dependent on mine."

"Then, Master Robert," Judy said, deliberately using the terminology of the time. "Would you accept, as a gift, the life of this woman, who knows that love can conquer, and who has already been conquered by it? And further that I hold nothing back from you or your own choice. This is simply a gift."

"My God, Judy, I really don't know what to say. And, your gift, it is too much, too valuable."

"Oh, come on, Bob. It's only me. And it looks like you could use some companionship, or would you rather do this alone?"

"Alone? Oh, no, Judy, it's not that…it's just that I don't feel as though I deserve what you offer."

"Well, then let me put it another way. What do you want? Do you want me or not?"

Craycroft was smiling, for he knew that Master Robert's fate had now been sealed, and upon his answer lay the future of his own world.

"You know, Judy, don't you, that my own answer can only be a small part of a much bigger puzzle. But to answer your question, yes, I not only want you for today, but for life. And it is my hope that I won't disappoint you, or anyone else. And yes, I love you. I love you with all that I have to offer and all that I am or will be."

That was all it took for Judy's emotions to spill over with her tears. It was all she had been hoping for, seemingly all her life. As she clung to Bob, Craycroft could do little but smile at Rust, who nodded, as he too understood what this meant to them all.

Drachma then walked in, along with Falma. And they, too, smiled. For what they saw was that Judy had made her choice, along with Robert. None spoke, as there was nothing to say for the moment, but gratitude, which could not be expressed but was evident on Drachma's countenance.

Kerlin was next shown in, along with Proust. And after he had recovered his equilibrium, Bob told them all of the events that had unfolded since the council meeting. There was an intense silence that pervaded the room at this news. Kerlin then informed them of the fate of Carruthers, whose body had been found with his own stab wound in the abdomen, surely by the same man who had apparently vanished along with the deepening evening hours. Kerlin then gave Proust the task of protecting the castle's inhabitants against any more attacks, and to look out for Antoine LeGace.

Drachma bemused that it would be most unlikely that LeGace would strike again so soon, as it was apparent that he had gotten what he was after and was probably off the island by now. Nevertheless, he agreed that the safety of all was paramount. And he did wonder when they would be hearing from Master LeGace again.

The clock tower bells rang seven times.

"Well, my friends," said Craycroft. "It appears that the hour is here for our dinner, and you are all most welcome to come."

Proust thanked him profusely but said that his new tasks must be attended to anon. Craycroft nodded and wished him much success. Rust told him that this day had taken every bit of reserve that he had, and that there were many things that he needed to do before retiring, but he thanked him for his kind offer.

"Well, my good friend, I understand," Craycroft said, as he placed his hand on the councilor's back. "But mind that you shall have a glass raised to you in thoughtful appreciation by those in attendance. And that your efforts on behalf of all of us here shall be forever remembered. Now, go with the best wishes of all of us here, and me, in particular."

"There is a man for us all," said Drachma after Rust had gone. "One whose principles do lead him in his works, and one to whom I am forever grateful."

Dinner that evening was at the earl's dining hall. Craycroft sat at the head with everyone else seated around the great table.

The mood in the dining room couldn't adequately be described, but it could definitely be felt—it was jubilant, yet tempered by the unexpected death of their conquered foe. It was intense, and yet there was a feeling of anticipation, as if it marked both the end of a fierce struggle and the beginning of something new and challenging. It was marked by the invigorating newness of relationships unfolding and of relationships that had recently ended, with time insufficient for mourning. Overall, there was the sensation of simultaneous excitement and serenity.

For Diane, this was the first time that she had felt love so intense that it made other relationships seem commonplace. She felt the giddiness of a childish crush, along with the security of sharing everything with the object of her affection. Even the arrival of her old love could not shake her. She was honored to know that Derrymoor did care for her and that his love for his own son did endure, despite bonds that never really had time to form. It was when Derrymoor had seen Eustace's broach and this had made him weep with remembrance that she truly felt fulfillment for Eustace, who could now proudly bear the burden of its responsibility. And yet at the same time she knew that Cayman's love for her was one of solidity and that they, together, would protect Eustace as none had been able to do thus far. She had even visited with Father Henri, and he knew that it was right and had agreed to perform their wedding after all the funerals were over. Meanwhile, Cayman just beamed at her side. While looking over toward Derrymoor, she found his presence now to be a comfort, not a threat. She reached over and took Cayman's hand as he closed his eyes in grateful appreciation.

Jeanne felt her time of trial and intensity had now come to a close. Her relationship with Felicia had been one of such

involvement, such magic, and such sorrow, that few, besides Craycroft, understood. It appeared that her new position with Craycroft allowed her fulfillment and a certain calmness, which her life to that time had lacked. She felt that she could even search out what her grandfather, Charlie McFerris, had done without feeling guilty or suspicious. She knew that her old life would not have to haunt her again.

And as for Falma, he was now feeling the fulfillment that only a few in this life can feel. He had been instrumental in bringing the Lady Judy to safety, through the unimaginable terror of being taken prisoner in a world that made no sense to her, and yet threatened her. And still he learned from her what it was to be a healer, to have that touch, that connection to the soul of others. And to think that she discounted that as nothing. Now, he watched Melchior—his own apprentice—really just getting started with the most remarkable teacher that he had ever seen. The look upon his apprentice's face, the eagerness of his stride, the amazement in his voice; he could not help but feel that this was his own journey, which he was now fulfilling through his apprentice.

To Kerlin, it had been an awakening, having been a forest guard, serving dutifully out in the wild, and now the chief of security for the whole of Shepperton. With new confidence in his own abilities and the certainty to deal with threats to those under his care. And which would never have happened without the interventions of Drachma. Thinking back to that meeting with Craycroft, which felt like years ago, after losing both Tom and Falma and coming back to the castle, disheartened, in chaos, how he was not punished, but rather promoted had to have been something inspired by Drachma. And what now of Reordan and LeGace? What was it that Robert told him—that LeGace was after something that Reordan owned? Could it be his wealth? His property? He would have to investigate that.

No one, it seems, had been changed as much as Tom, coming as he did from being a humble page who had been pushed into that fateful spiral, which actually began with his accompanying Rust, to the amusement of his fellows. But then, he found himself entangled in that web with Lady Felicia, Craycroft, and Falma, and he could gradually feel his own adventure beginning. And now he had found that he was the grandson of Drachma and Felicia and was about to become the adopted son of the island's liege lord. The changes did not stop there, because there were changes on the inside as well. He was now the one to have recently read that fateful book from which all that Drachma had done had come about. He had also been instrumental in Master Robert's discoveries, which not only led to finding the cause of the illness of Felicia and the earl, but also promised more—so much more. But what had truly changed Tom the most was discovering his mother, Maggie. The fact that others had seen her he still found vexing, and he so longed to see her, to hear her voice, and to talk over books with her. But for now, at least, her own room, with its vast library, would have to do.

So the thoughts and feelings ran, as they all ate and drank of the magnificent meal prepared for them. As they were now nearly done with eating and drinking, and the servants began clearing away the dishes, Craycroft addressed his guests.

"Well, my friends, I again thank you for dining with me. And what a day this has been! And let me say that we have collectively won the hearts of Shepperton, and I feel certain that we are now headed toward a time of renewed peace, but one with an intensity that I am certain is borne of our troubled times. And I would like to recognize the author of much of our hard-won peace, and that, as all of you know, is Drachma, the Elder. And, in particular, I should like to have Drachma address us with his own peculiar vision of what it is that we are doing here, and why. But before he does that, I wish to recognize one who is not here this evening, but was instrumental in our battle today—Councilor Rust. To his

courage in the face of perils he alone understood, let us raise our glasses. To Rust!"

"To Rust. Here, here!"

"I shall be speaking with him and shall extend to him your warm thanks and well wishes. And now, Drachma, if you would be so kind as to tell us all of how we got here and why."

"Well, I should be brief, but as some of you know, that, for me, is difficult when given an opportunity like this one. Let me say first how grateful I am to Master Rust and Lady Diane for their finding of this ancient text." He pulled out of his cloak the gray volume and passed it around the table. "Now there is with this book, as with most ancient texts, a history—and this one is not an exception.

"Upon the Isle of Patmos, in the year of our lord, four hundred and seventy-three, there arose a tiny uprising, which came about as a result of some followers of Saint John the Divine, who happened upon some wise men from Persia. These were wise men who had been studying the ways of time and who happened to discover holes in the fabric of time, which could connect our time with other times—both times that had existed and times yet to occur. And what these followers of John discovered was there existed a connection to these holes, and how human need seemed to be the key—that human minds, when all were thinking of their perceived need, could set things in motion, and that these holes could be used to help them in their need. But this did not come without a significant price, namely that persons could travel one way or the other, but not both. This whole concept was seen as heresy, as far as doctrinal thought was concerned, and the reason that we know of this is a brief notation in their book of order. It states simply that a certain man, named Tashkent, was found guilty of this heresy and would do "severe penance" for the offence.

"These scholars had written down their findings in a book, which they called *The Book of Drachma*, named after their own

leader. But their search for answers caused considerable turmoil, and this small group disappeared into the hills and was not heard from again. At least that was the stated thesis. However, within the lands around Greece there existed a small, secret clan that kept the story alive. There were two things that did inspire me, at a much later time, to perform my own search. The first was my mentor, after whom I am named, who told me that there was this book written by men of his own lineage, which contained truisms for later generations. And while he kept the book, I was able to read through it while still quite young. He said that there were but a very few translations of this book in the world, and he thought that the original was somewhere in Spain. And the second was having heard the tale of Brother Philip, which he told me—the tale of Brother Philip and his journey. "I did happen to find the small priory where Brother Philip and Leonardo had worked. There, within the priory's library, was this work. Though a copy, it proved to be everything that had been foretold of it. The original was not for the public, but it kept within the reliquary of the priory. I stayed at this priory for a month and made notes, which I later incorporated into my own book, which is now back within the library that it came from."

He glanced at Tom, who looked back at his grandfather, a knowing smile on his face.

"I am now going to tell all of you within this room what really happened, as to why Master Robert and Lady Judy are here and what transpired with Lord Vincente. I know that none here have heard this entire tale told. And it should be repeated only with care, for there are still powers out there that seek the destruction of what we have come to hold dear."

Drachma took a long drink from his ale, set his tumbler down, and, with all eyes upon him, began his story.

"To begin with, I would refer you to a small passage in this other book of prophecy, which does belong to our Lady Diane,

who had graciously agreed to loan it to me this evening. Within this book, we find the following passage:

> For years the tales told would lie quietly within the books of wonder. And he would rise yet again, in time still to be. But not as one who would be noticed as a warrior. Rather, he would be a scholar and a healer, a doctor of hearts, named Gilsen. He would be the one to turn the tides of ignorance and usher in the new age of learning. These, then, are the words of Drachma of the Highlands.

"Now I would ask you to consider, that these words were written some three hundred years ago and found their way to our time. And I also ask you to consider whence they came. They speak of a time when this Drachma of the Highlands was being driven out of his homeland and forced to locate within the hills of Greece. He had with him a very small group of faithful followers who did keep to themselves and did keep his teaching alive by word of mouth. Nothing much was written down except in a few of these texts. But we, who are of that lineage, did know that name, Gilsen, and knew that he would become one of us.

"Think back now to years past, when Carlo Vincente was younger and brought with him his guilds. He did not seek out this position, but it was thrust upon him, as the one who could lead by example. And so he did. His curiosity was as lively as his talent with pottery. And so he read, and he read everything he could. One day, as he was visiting with me, he noticed a book within my library that he had seen before, years ago. It was a book of prophecy, and it included the passage that I have just read to you. There was no context given, and that particular passage had always challenged him. And so he asked me about this puzzling text. I explained that it would be foolish for us to decide just when and where it was to be fulfilled, and whether we would even be involved, but I could tell that it would not let him rest.

"Meanwhile, I had discovered that there was a way that could enable one to actually travel both ways through these windows of time, but that it would carry some risk to those that sought to travel. It would require an object that symbolized everything to the one seeking travel, everything that one would be willing to give up, and could release any control that one might have over the circumstances that one would encounter. And, if that object itself were to be given up, that the object would then take on powers of its own, for as long as the window of time remained open, perhaps even longer.

"As I explained this to Lord Vincente, he became obsessed with one incredible notion. He determined that I did have an ancient coin, a drachma from Greece, of which I was particularly fond, as it came to me handed down from my namesake, who, in turn, had it handed down to him from generations, back to the Isle of Patmos. In any event, this was more a matter for discussions with Falma, Carlo, and me, over drinks and in front of a comfortable fire on long nights in winter, than anything that we truly considered acting upon. And this object was being kept for me by Falma, within his own place in the castle.

"But then everything changed. Carlo came to me, very worried, after one of his travels abroad. He said that he had heard that there were, among his own guildsmen, those who were telling of our amazing pots to those back home, and that here, upon this isle, our own craftsmen were selling some of the pottery on the sly to a councilor for some very high price and with some unknown stipulations. And now, to make matters more alarming, word of our pottery was getting back to a Count Gregorio in Italy who was the count from whom the guild had originally escaped. This count was not at all above committing murder or treason for his own sake, and he would use whatever influence he had with the king to allow him to steal back the guild.

"And then, Carlo took me aside and explained that he himself had become ill, and that he did not think that he would last much

longer. His fatigue was becoming more significant, and he was getting more breathless as each day passed."

Then Drachma took a drink from his glass, as he let this all sink in. To Bob and Judy, it was beginning to make some sense, especially the part about that incredible coin, and it also explained something of Carlo Vincente's demeanor, as well as his death within their time.

"Let me ask you," said Judy, "what of the painters and potters who became ill? That was the thing you told me that made this decision for you. Was that merely a ruse, or did that have something to do with all of this?"

"As ever, m'lady, your eyes see directly to the heart of the matter. Before I answer your query directly, I would like, once more, to hear from Master Robert, and what he found out in his investigation of our painters and potters."

"Bob? What have you not been telling us?"

"Well, Judy, my investigation of the mysterious deaths of these painters and potters is still preliminary, so I have not made it public. And also, it has been hampered by not having standard textbooks of toxicology at my disposal. But I'll tell you what I have uncovered so far, thanks, in great part, to the writings of one medical genius named Cartho.

"In searching through what he had written, I stumbled upon a most interesting bit of writing. It seems that there is a particular small mushroom that grows high up in these woods, somewhere up by a place called Lough Langor, way up in the hills somewhere, and apparently only there. This mushroom gives off an incredibly bright, yellow pigment, apparently from its spores. It would be a very useful pigment in paints, except that it is highly toxic and causes severe illness, which, from the description provided by Master Cartho, sounds like it causes liver and kidney failure, from which persons so afflicted almost universally die—generally within three weeks.

"I've had a chance to review what Mr. Craycroft had written about the illness of these potters and painters, and it sounded to me just like what Mr. Cartho described years before. Anyway, I am convinced, now more than ever, that what was killing off our artists was a toxic exposure, resulting from their own contact with this mushroom.

"So, I set about to prove this in some way. And this included talking to one of the survivors of this plague—a certain painter named Fabbiano. And you know what I discovered? Well, it seems as though, before they became ill, that these potters and painters were using a rare yellow pigment in their designs, and that there was one source for this yellow pigment, a certain employee of Carlo Vincente named Guarneri who is now, unfortunately, off the island.

"Further, we note that this material, or something remarkably like it, became available to our painters and potters at the very time that they became ill. Not only that, but we have it that this was made available to our painters and potters by none other than our own Carlo Vincente. And lastly, we have a note, sent to one of the unfortunate victims of this plague, which has been identified as being written by none other than our Mr. Vincente, indicating that this poor soul would be the next victim. This hardly seems like coincidence to me."

"Nay, Master Robert, it is not," said Drachma, in a calm, somewhat subdued voice. "And I thank you for your most erudite exposition, Master Robert. Which brings us back around to your question earlier, Lady Judy. And nay, it was no ruse, but rather it was the culmination of all these events that persuaded me to let loose these forces, which led to your coming among us. As to Carlo's own motivations, I would have to surmise that he did target those among his guild that he thought were threatening to it, and to Shepperton as a whole, and I got the feeling that things spun out of Lord Vincente's control and ended up teaching no

lesson. I say this with the knowledge of what he wrought, for he did tell me of this before he left.

"And as to his last days among us, remember that he spoke of the drachma, which was to me that which I was most reluctant to let go. And so, with some hesitation, I did procure it from Falma. And taking that same coin, we did try to connect with the future times with some success. And what I am about to tell you is that Carlo did go, briefly to your world, and within that time was able to determine that there did exist a physician, or doctor of hearts, named Gilsen—now this news was enough for Carlo Vincente, and it did confirm what I had already found. So he did decide to go, as an ambassador, if you will, to your world, and to seek out this doctor of hearts named Gilsen, and he took with him my own coin, the drachma, and did release it upon your world. And, it did, as you have indicated, seem to develop its own purposes and power.

"As I understand it, while that coin did serve a purpose all its own, it is still within your world, Robert, within the possession of your wife, Marilyn, which she does keep as a token of your health. And as to Carlo Vincente, I can only say that he is now with the angels, having done what he could to perhaps undo or to mitigate for that which he had wrought upon his own world."

"Let me ask you, Drachma," said Tom, "of that coin. For I did have it, if oh so briefly."

"I was aware of that, Tom, indeed."

"Now, Tom," said Falma, unexpectedly. "If you recall, I did give you that coin, shortly before our Lady Felicia did die. What I did not tell you was how that coin did appear within its little box with the blue velvet. You recall that Drachma said that he did give the coin to Carlo Vincente, as he was released to go to Master Robert's and Lady Judy's world. When I returned to my own place, I returned as one from whom all life had been taken, and I did sleep the sleep of death. But I did dream, and within that dream, I did see you come to me, carrying a certain book

within your cloak. And within that dream I heard the voice of your mother, Maggie, who instructed me that I should give you the coin and that you would become as great as your grandfather. And when I finally did waken, there, upon my own bed, was that coin. And so, I took your mother's advice and gave to you the coin."

"Which is no longer in my possession," said Tom. "And that makes me wonder as to what the significance was of the coin."

Then Derrymoor spoke up for the first time.

"Let me just say, first of all, that I am most honored to share this table and this opportunity with all of you. I came to your island with the most mistaken idea of conquest, and also for the possible purpose of meeting with my first love and my child, who had been but a rumor to me. And you have turned my world on its side. I could not conquer a people so proud, and who represent what is so good about humanity. You have now given me, and my son, an opportunity to blossom into the promise of new life as never before. And further, Eustace is now under the caring wing of your own liege lord, as well as his mother, and her true love—and for that I am grateful.

"But let me tell you of that which I consider symbolic, and perhaps this is what young Tom needs to hear. My own son has with him, around his neck, a symbol of the House of Derrymoor. And that symbol does carry with it certain powers and opportunities. This is especially true, as I have no other sons to carry on my own legacy, and shall, for his lifetime, be that which identifies his place in our hearts. Now you, Tom, as I understand, carry on this great and noble tradition that has been established by one also named Drachma, and you shall be the heir of all that tradition. Your worldly goods and your worldly powers shall be evident, as the son of our liege lord, Craycroft. But that is only part of your legacy. It would seem fitting to me that you have seen and have held the symbol of your true power—the drachma of ancient Greece. For this is whence you obtain your true nature,

your true power, and your own true purpose. So, for Falma to have given you that symbol, and for you to have beheld it, speaks for the ages. And for Falma to have recognized that it was your own mother who told him, and to have noted that you shall also be great, as your grandfather is great, speaks to the ages as well."

"Well said, my good earl," responded Drachma. "And to have heard it from one who is not of this island makes the whole message all that much more significant. In anticipation of your returning to the mainland, my earl, you shall need to meet with Craycroft, Kerlin, and me before too long."

"Oh, aye, my good sir, and might I request that young Tom and Eustace join in our meeting."

"Ah, but of course. It would only seem right that they now are part of this island's future."

Judy sat in the chair opposite Bob. They were now alone in Bob's own suite. A couple of flagons of Carlisle's Brew sat on the table between them. Bob looked at Judy, who appeared surprisingly at ease. He couldn't help but be comforted as well by her aura, which she exuded in that carefree manner that he had come to know and to love.

"All right, then, Miss Morrison. Now that you've got me, what are you going to do next?"

Judy smiled and said, "Well, in this time and place, I think it only proper that this lady should wait upon her man to make the next move."

Bob got up and came around to the back of her chair. He leaned over her, clasped her around the middle, and hugged her gently. His newly grown beard tickled the back of her neck, sending chills down her back. This was more than she was able to resist, so she got up, turned toward Bob, clasped his face in her hands, and gave him a deep and satisfying kiss. Bob grabbed her

firmly and held onto her as though this was the first time he had ever held a woman and meant it.

The struggles of the past month melted away, the coldness of the winter outside dissolved, and the acceptance of their newness enveloped them. There came a soft breeze, which carried with it the promise of springtime, the smell of the pines and hardwoods, the feel of the warm earth, with fragrant grass below their feet, and the smell of newly turned earth.

Epilogue

They sat outside, in the garden prepared and cultivated by Angelica, in one of the real treasures of Glen Oak Forest. It was a perfect day, late in springtime, with a gentle, warm breeze blowing through the trees, carrying with it the smells of the awakening forest. They sat and drank of Angelica's concoction, with its own deep notes of earth and forest. Falma, Bob, and Craycroft sat and talked of amazing things that were being done back at the institute. Drachma, along with Hermes, Eustace, Tom, and the women, were discussing Judy's and Jeanne's latest proposal, to build the first of its kind, an actual clinic in Shepperton, where persons could obtain the benefit of their ever-expanding knowledge of human illness and injury.

Meanwhile, Angelica herself watched from her kitchen window and smiled contentedly as the breeze wafted in from outside, carrying the scent of lavender.

"Ah, Maggie," she said quietly, so as not to let on, "so this is what ye were doing all the while. Tending these wayward sheep. If I could but see thee, rather than simply feel yer presence every now and again. Oh what I wouldn't give for that. Just look at yer son, out there among the people of my heart. Oh, dear one, it does my heart such good. Now, if I could but simply cast this spell upon them all."

With a sudden shift in the breeze, she was gone again, but not before imprinting the words on the heart of the old woman that she should be back, to claim her as her own, and Falma as well. A solitary tear escaped the old woman's eye. After taking a moment to compose herself, she went out of the kitchen, down the hallway, and through the small door to the garden. Outside, she was touched by the wonder of it all; the warmth in the air, the feel of the earth's renewal, and the conviviality of her guests. She then went up to Drachma and whispered to him that it would be but an hour before dinner would be ready and that Willie himself would be joining them that evening.

So Drachma stood and announced that dinner would be served in about an hour and that they could expect be joined by a very special guest. Next, he went up to Judy and to Bob and asked that they accompany him, as he had something very special to show them.

The threesome headed down a path, out of the garden, into the deep woods, into the silence of the primeval forest. All around them were towering pines and hardwoods. The sun filtered in through the leaves, dappling the forest path. They heard the sound of running water and headed toward the sound.

It dawned on them gradually that they were, in fact, walking the path of their dreams. It was here, now, in this place and this time, where they had committed to come, seemingly so long ago. Judy was crying, silently, as she stepped down to the water's edge. She took off her shoes and walked into the cold stream, bent over and gathered the water into her cupped hands, and suddenly splashed a spray of water in the direction of Bob and Drachma. Drachma smiled as Bob joined Judy in the stream.

They stayed in that place for the better part of an hour, as contented as children. Hardly a word was spoken, but still they communicated. And as the shadows deepened and the coolness of the evening enveloped them, they silently put on their shoes and headed back. Bob held Judy close as they walked.

Then Drachma stopped, and they too stopped and listened. There was no question—it was Willie playing! They just stood there, outside, listening, as the music filled the evening with magic. It wasn't until he finished his piece that they went on the rest of the way inside.

"My, Willie, was that indeed music or was that magic I heard?" asked Drachma as they entered. "And fitting, as my friends here can attest."

"Oh, Willie. That was truly inspired," added Judy. "Never have I heard such playing. Please, do go on."

"M'lady, it was but for you that I was playing. Now, do come in, get you some of this wonderful food and drink, and be at peace."

It was not until Bob, Drachma, and Judy had eaten of the food and wine and Willie had consumed his flagon of ale that he began again. This time he began with a simple melody, which he embellished at each return until the melody itself was lost within his amazing fingers and what they produced from his incomparable instrument. It was truly music as if the very heavens were listening. But then, as he was finishing that piece, he turned toward Judy, winked, changed keys, and began another tune, which Judy recognized with sudden astonishment as the one she knew from childhood. Encouraged, she sang along; sang of the hills, and the birds, and the legends which lived on, which lived here upon this isle, among the hearts of these people.

And when they were done, the silence itself sang and filled that deep place within themselves for which they ached.

It was much later that night, when everyone was in bed, sleeping the deep sleep of the content, when she returned. She went quietly, first to Falma, and then to Angelica.

"Come, my friends, it is time now. See, there before you, the path. They will all be coming, but not now. Know that what you

have done and what you have said shall be forever upon their hearts. But come. He is but waiting to greet you."

Angelica hesitated then said, "Before I go, my dear Maggie, might I but take ye by yer own son, that he might but know of your love for him?"

"Oh, aye," said Falma. "'Twould be but fitting, for I have often heard him ask after thee."

So the three of them went by the bed where Tom lay fast asleep. While there, Maggie bent over and touched her own son's cheek, letting a tear fall upon it. Tom did not fully awaken, but he did recognize his own mother in his dreamlike state and smiled. Maggie touched his chest, and felt his heart beating. She then pulled a flower from the air and laid it gently on his form as he fell back into that sleep, as profound as an abyss.

And so they left. Those who stayed had much more to accomplish. With the new day about to break, new and even greater things were on their individual horizons.

Characters in
The Book of Drachma

Aaron: Page of the castle
Allen of Burridge: An old carpenter
Alonza Chavez: ER nurse
Ambrose: Page of the castle
Angelica: Long term companion/caretaker of Drachma
Anil Ramchandran: Pulmonologist at Memorial Hospital
Antoine LeGace: Generally evil individual
Armaugh: Guard of Drachma
Barbara Greshin: Cardiovascular surgeon
Barncuddy: Proprietor of Barncuddy's Ale House
Bedford: The earl of Derrymoor's first mate
Bernard: One of the Forest Guard
Bev: Waitress at 42nd Street Diner
Blackfist: One of the Forest Guard
Blodwen: One of the Castle Guard
Brother Philip: The monk who found (and translated) The Book
 of Drachma
Cairn: One of the Forest Guard
Carol: ICU nurse
Carruthers: Servant to Reordan

Cayman: One of the Castle Guard

Cartho: The original Healer of Shepperton

Carlo Vincente: Felicia's adoptive father, and master of the guild

Chad Breidling: Community Liaison for Memorial Hospital

Charlie McFerris: Musician, and recluse

Charlie Stephens: Investigative TV reporter

Chris Lewinsky: Police detective

Clarice: Maid of the Castle

Constance: Cook at the castle

Councilor Rust: Member of the Council of Lords

Count Greorio: Power-hungry Italian count

Craycroft: Fifteenth century healer, locally trained by Cartho

Diane: Waitress/cook at Barncuddy's

Donovan: One of the councilors

Dowdell: One of the Castle Guard

Drachma the Elder: Enigmatic character–part intellectual, part teacher, part wizard

Dunstan: Castle groom

Earl Crabtree: Josh's adoptive father

Earl of Derrymoor: Earl with previous ties to Shepperton

Earl of Shepperton: The reigning earl, and liege lord of Shepperton

Edgar Bryant: Police detective

Emile: Diane's adoptive father

Erich: Potter and Hermes' father

Erik: Leader of the Druids

Ervin: One of the Forest Guard

Eustace: Son to Diane

Falma: Alchemist, Loremaster, but much more

Father Henri: Prior of the Shepperton Church

Felicia Vincente: Grand lady of Shepperton, and grandmother to Tom

Felicity: Cook of the castle

Felix: Page of the castle

Finch: Mercenary, hired by Reordan

Fitzgibbon: One of the councilors
Frankie: Butcher
Frieda: Housekeeper to Felicia
Genet: One of the councilors
Gilbert: Reordan's Chief of Security
Hermes: Page of the castle
Herschel: Caretaker of the castle pigeons
Jeremy: Street urchin
Jerry Beasley: ER doctor
Janie Crabtree: Josh's adoptive mother
Jeanne: Lady-in-waiting, and confidante of Felicia
Jimmy: Page of the castle
Johnny: One of the Forest Guard
Josh Crabtree: Longstanding patient of Robert's
Judy Morrison: Nurse, and friend to Robert
Kerlin: One of the Forest Guard, who becomes Craycroft's Chief
    of Security
Kevin: One of the Forest Guard
Leonardo: Urchin, who became Philip's apprentice
Maggie o' Killiburn: Tom's mother (and more)
Malcolm: One of the Forest Guard
Marcus: Page of the castle
Maria: Cook of the castle
Marilyn Gilsen: Robert's wife
Martha: Jeremy's aunt
Mark Hurwitz: Cardiovascular surgery fellow
Martin: One of the Forest Guard
Maxim: Jeremy's uncle
McGill: One of the Castle Guard
Melchior: Apprentice of Falma
Melinda: Chief cook of the castle
Michel: Forest Guard
Nigel: One of Derrymoor's mates
Old Leroy: Old beggar, and more

Proust: Leader of the Castle Guard
Raymond: Man of Champour
Reordan: Leader of the Councl of Lords
Robert Gilsen: Overworked late twentieth-century Cardiologist
Ron: Cameraman to Charlie Stephens
Rowan: Street urchin
Russ: Page of the castle
Sean: Forest Guard
Silvo: One of the councilors
Sondra: Diane's adoptive mother
Stoneheft: One of the Forest Guard
Tierney: Blacksmith of the castle village
Tom (Drachma the younger): Page in the castle (to begin with),
    yet much more
Torpin: Prisoner of the king
Wheezer: Street urchin
Willie Minstrel: Musician

www.ingramcontent.com/pod-product-compliance
Lightning Source LLC
Chambersburg PA
CBHW061925170626
46813CB00006B/2303